Reaper was pushed back into the seat by the acceleration of the Checker. The engine roared out a solid wall of sound though the muffler cutouts. The speedometer climbed as Reaper hung onto the wheel. He no longer needed the handgun laying on the seat next to him. He was at the wheel of a huge projectile, a guided missile, one he was able to aim very precisely.

As the sound of the nitrous-boosted engine boomed out, Reaper watched as Arzee went onto the gravel shoulder and lost control of his car. As the distance between the two vehicles closed, he saw the Vette spin out and stop sideways across the road. Reaper could now see Arzee sitting at the wheel struggling to draw a weapon. That wasn't something Reaper was going to allow to happen.

Indecision was not something a SEAL could tolerate. Neither could he afford to be reckless. Reaper knew that Arzee was his best lead to finding his family. But if Arzee killed him, he couldn't do his family much good. He would just have to be very careful and precise.

Avon Books by
Dennis Chalker & Kevin Dockery

THE HOME TEAM: UNDECLARED WAR
ONE PERFECT OP
HELL WEEK

Avon Books by
Kevin Dockery

FREE FIRE ZONES
THE TEAMS
POINT MAN
SEALS IN ACTION

THE HOME TEAM

UNDECLARED WAR

Command Master Chief
DENNIS CHALKER, USN (Ret.)
with **KEVIN DOCKERY**

AVON BOOKS
An Imprint of HarperCollins*Publishers*

This is a work of fiction. Names, characters, places, and incidents are products of the author's imagination or are used fictitiously and are not to be construed as real. Any resemblance to actual events, locales, organizations, or persons, living or dead, is entirely coincidental.

AVON BOOKS
An Imprint of HarperCollins*Publishers*
10 East 53rd Street
New York, New York 10022-5299

ISBN: 0-06-051726-3
www.avonbooks.com

First Avon Books paperback printing: October 2004

Printed in the U.S.A.

10 9 8 7 6 5 4 3 2 1

I dedicate this book to a legend in the Teams, Timmy "Ho Ho" Prusak. He has brought so much value, knowledge, and camaraderie to the Teams, especially to the men that worked under him. I know, because I was one. I also dedicate this to his lovely, supportive wife Ingra and the rest of his family. Some day we will meet again at the Pearly Gates. He will be waiting with a hot dog or two, a six-pack, and of course his small telephone pad. He is one of the best. To you, Ho Ho!!

THE HOME TEAM

UNDECLARED WAR

Chapter One

"It was a dark and stormy night; the rain fell in torrents—except at occasional intervals. . . ."

"Just what in the hell are you talking about?" Edward Ward said from his place in the driver's seat of the M998 series High Mobility Multipurpose Wheeled Vehicle (HMMWV), commonly called a Humvee. The heavy military vehicle was moving slowly through the rain, hardly an unexpected weather situation in northeast Bosnia-Herzegovina. The wide military vehicle bumped and jostled the passengers as it passed over a rough and rutted road that was little more than a cart path.

There were some better roads on the northeastern slopes of the Majevica mountain range, but these men were intentionally avoiding them. The vehicle rolled along quietly, hidden in the dark on a path few other people would choose to travel even in full daylight.

The passengers in the wide, boxy vehicle stood out as much as their ride did. The men had an unearthly, alien look about them as most of them wore AN/PVS-14 night-vision devices on their faces. The single large extended eye tube of the PVS-14, along with the frame that strapped to their faces, gave them a bulging cyclops look.

The only one inside the vehicle who was wearing a different style of night-vision device was Ed Ward, the driver. He had a set of AN/TVS-7 night-vision goggles on his face—the goggles giving him excellent depth perception. Ward had no trouble driving the Humvee in almost complete darkness, even with the vehicle's headlights turned off.

"Just thinking about the beginning of a book I heard about," Chief Ted "Grim" Reaper said from the front passenger seat. From the backseat of the vehicle, Titus "Bear" Parnell spoke up.

"You know, when I first got to Team Two, Mike Boynton was the master chief," Bear said. "He always said that back in Vietnam, rainy nights like this one were great to operate in."

"That's because no one in their right mind would be going out in this shit," Mike Martell, the fourth SEAL of the group, said from where he sat in the back, listening carefully to the radio over the headset he had clamped over his left ear.

"So, that must be why we're out here," Ward said.

"Ho, ho, ho," Bear chuckled. His teammates were used to the fact that the big SEAL actually laughed like Santa Claus. That laugh usually drew a second look from anyone else who happened to be around when his deep voice boomed out. One look at Bear would tell you where his nickname came from, and evaporate any thoughts of Saint Nick. None of the

SEALs were small, but Bear looked like a beer keg with legs and arms—thick, muscular legs and arms.

At his place in front, Chief Ted Reaper continued to look out of the window of the Humvee at the driving rain of Bosnia-Herzegovina in the early spring. The snows were gone, but that just made the poorly kept, muddy country roads a quagmire. He and his fellow SEALs made up the Navy contingent of their detachment from the Joint Special Strike Force (JSSF). They had been attached to the U.N.-mandated Stabilization Force, the SFOR, that was trying to maintain stability in the war-torn area of the Balkans. The JSSF was put in place to react quickly to any situation. They could rapidly evaluate a problem and either decide to deal with it themselves or call in a greater strength force from the SFOR assets scattered around the country.

The men of JSSF also conducted classic special operations missions: special reconnaissance operations to locate potential rogue groups or war criminals, direct actions in the form of strikes against designated sites or personnel, and civil affairs, where they tried to develop good relations among the civilian population of an area.

To secure maximum flexibility in conducting these operations, the Joint Special Strike Force had been put together from the Navy, Army, and Air Force special operations forces. The Air Force contingent of this JSSF detachment were two combat controllers, who were the best field air controllers in any of the services. The Army contingent of six Special Forces troopers made up the bulk of the JSSF detachment. In overall command were two professional Intelligence officers who had a great deal of experience running covert paramilitary operations for the CIA.

Chief Reaper was the senior noncommissioned officer (NCO) of the detachment, which didn't always sit well with the Army guys but didn't cause any real friction. The SEALs bumped heads and cracked jokes with the Army troopers on occasion, and both groups of men made fun of the Air Force contingent. The jokes came from years of traditional rivalry between the services.

Underlying the gags was an unspoken respect the men had for each other. The operators were all professional warriors and knew the skills and capabilities each man brought from his branch of the service. The only real unknown factor was their commanding officer.

There were two officers in the detachment, Lieutenant Mark Franklin, who was the executive officer and Captain Cary Paxtun the commanding officer. Both men had been in the Army Special Forces before changing their career paths and going into intelligence work. Franklin had remained in Army Intelligence while Paxtun had gone on to operate directly with the CIA.

Both men had spent years working in Afghanistan and other parts of the world, Paxtun as part of the paramilitary forces of the CIA and Franklin with the Army. Between them, they spoke seven languages including Arabic, Serbo-Croat, Pushtun, Afghan, Persian, and Russian. They had both come back to Special Operations because that was where the action was now, and Reaper was of the opinion they should have stayed where they were.

Neither man's skills were in question as far as Reaper was concerned, but their attitude very much was. In the SEAL chief's opinion, both of the officers had forgotten what it meant to work as part of a team, something that the SEALs take very seriously. Paxtun acted as if he just considered the men under his command to be tools for his own advancement. Franklin wasn't much better but at least tended to stay with the Army members of the unit and left the SEALs alone.

Besides directing the JSSF detachment, the two officers had been working hard at setting up an intelligence network among the many different groups in the area. They were often away from the headquarters the group had established in a house in the small town of Argulak. As far as Reaper was concerned, both officers could be out chasing goats in the mountains, that would be fine with him. All he wanted was for the officers to do their jobs and allow him the leeway he wanted to make sure his men were protected and that the mission was accomplished.

Neither Paxtun or Franklin told the men of the JSSF who they had talked to, what had been discussed, or even why they would be talking to a particular person in the first place. The specifics of who the agents were and how the intelligence was developed wasn't a question that Reaper or the rest of the men felt that they had to know. The information that the two men did learn, they held very close to their chests. That was something Reaper was concerned about. If there was information regarding a target, a location, or forces in an area that could affect his men or his mission, Reaper wanted to know about it.

Information—good, reliable intelligence on an

area or enemy—could be more important than ammunition on an op. Since he felt that his leaders couldn't be completely trusted to tell him everything they knew, Reaper fell back on an old SEAL tradition. As the Teams had done in Vietnam, Reaper and the SEALs developed their own intelligence sources among the locals.

The SEALs' mission that night was intended to help increase the good relations that had been developing with some of the displaced locals—at least that's what Lieutenant Franklin had said. When Yugoslavia had broken up years earlier a whole bunch of old tensions and hatreds, nursed for years among parts of the population, had lifted up like a bunch of serpents tasting the air.

Ethnic cleansing was a new term for an old idea, hate people for their religion/race/background/whatever. One of the missions of the JSSF was to prevent any further atrocities from being committed against anyone. Presently, they were helping a group of Muslim refugees who had moved into an abandoned village in a resettlement area at North Sapna.

The people had been badly mauled by the Serb forces over the last several years but were finally coming to trust the men of the SFOR, and especially the SEALs of the JSSF detachment, and listening to what they had to say. The lives of the Muslim refugees had been as hard as could be imagined. Almost no families were left intact by the ravages of ethnic cleansing. Few husbands were around, and the haunted eyes of many of the younger women answered questions that the SEALs never asked.

There was a meeting that night in the local village schoolhouse, the biggest building in the area that still had walls and a roof. That was where the remaining elders of the refugees would make their final decision about staying. Paxtun wanted the SEALs to be in attendance to observe the meeting and give a show of support.

"Things have been pretty calm among the Serbs for the last couple of months," Bear said from the back of the Humvee.

"Yeah," Reaper agreed, "but something is in the wind over this relocation of the Muslims. There haven't been any reports of recent Serb movement in the area, but some of the locals are nervous as hell. Can't blame them given the way they've all been treated in the past.

"Those fundamentalist Muslims who claim to be in from Pakistan have been preaching around, trying to stir things up. Personally, I think they all are ex-mujahideen fighters from Afghanistan, not just the few Paxtun says are part of the group. At any rate, none of the villagers want to have anything to do with them. They've all had enough war to last them the rest of their lives.

"But it's going to be a few years yet before there's any kind of really stable government over here. Even with the fighting having at least died down, things are more political than ever. Everybody wants to be in charge. And those Muslim fundamentalists are the worst of the bunch. They're offering protection to the villagers from the Serbs claiming we can't do our jobs. It looks like just another old-fashioned shakedown racket.

"The last thing we need around here is a Serb attack in a protected area. With all the different factions in the area, this whole region is like a pot just barely simmering. It could boil over at any time. We've worked too hard to take care of these people to let them down now. I want to keep a close eye on things."

"I still think Paxtun's going to be mightily pissed when he sees you took his Humvee," Bear said.

"Well," Reaper said, "his idea to conduct a lightly armed, low-provocation, high-presence recon is a bunch of crap. Just because things have been quiet does not mean they're going to stay that way, no matter how much we'd like them to. If anything happens, I want the firepower to say—go the fuck away—loud and clear."

The firepower Reaper was referring to was in the form of the Mark 19 40mm grenade launcher attached to a ring mount on the roof of the Humvee. The big weapon was the size of a box that would hold a large pair of cowboy boots. On the back of the this "box" were two vertical handles for aiming, and a piece of wrist-thick pipe sticking out of the front.

The barrel of the grenade launcher could spit out half-pound 40mm high-explosive grenades at a rate of around 350 a minute to a distance of over 2,000 meters. The Mark 19 was a formidable piece of hardware by anyone's measure.

"Paxtun wanted us to stick to the main roads," Ward said as he guided the heavy vehicle through another deep set of muddy ruts in the roads. "If he isn't pissed about our taking his vehicle, he will be if we bring it back with a busted axle."

"Then you just pay attention to your driving,"

Reaper said. "If we're going to do a recon, we'll stick to the same roads that any Serb forces would use. It's not like you guys don't know the rule. . . ."

"Never take the easy way in," Ward, Bear, and Martell said in rough unison.

"I don't think even the Serbs would try this goat path in the dark," Ward said. "There aren't even any goats on it. It is a hell of a lot shorter than that paved road around the mountain, though. We're going to get to the village a couple of hours earlier than planned by the looks of things."

"The goats heard Bear was in the area and made a run for it," Martell said from the back.

"Speaking of making some odd friends," Ward said, "Captain Paxtun has been pretty friendly with the Russians up in Uglyville. Maybe he knows nothing is going to happen."

"Or he knows something is coming down and just doesn't feel like telling us," Bear said.

"Belay that talk," Reaper growled, "Paxtun's our CO and knows our mission. He talks to a hell of a lot more people than the Russian SFOR contingent up in Ugljevik. I don't like those Afghan mujahideen he meets with, but he built a rapport with them while they were fighting the Russians in their own country. And they hate the Russians. If the Serbs were planning something in the Russian sector, we'd know."

"Oh, yeah, he's buddies with the mujahideen all right. He's about the only source of human intelligence we have on those people, it's not like Lieutenant Franklin knows a bunch of those mujahideen by their first names. But the only information we really have on Paxtun is based on rumor. And rumint has it that he became a hardcore Muslim himself in Afghanistan," Bear said. "He may have been hot shit against the Russians over there, but I still don't like him."

"Rumor intelligence is worth what you pay for it," Reaper said. "It's nothing more than military gossip. You don't have to like him. You only have to follow his orders. Basing your opinion on nothing better than rumint doesn't make you look any better. I don't care what he has to do, or did, as long as he can keep a lid on those Afghans."

"Besides," Martell said. "Isn't he from your home state, Bear? You guys should be asshole buddies by now."

"Shit," Bear said. "He's from Dearborn. That city has the largest Arab population outside of the Middle East. I didn't exactly spend a whole lot of my life there. You even told me that he made you itch, Reaper when . . ."

Bear stopped in midsentence as Reaper put up his left hand in a fist to signal that he had spotted something. No one spoke as each SEAL instantly snapped into sharp attention. The rain had stopped and the early evening air was clear. "I have lights moving to the east of the village," Reaper said.

Just past the crest of a rise, the Humvee eased quietly to a stop, facing partly downslope. All of the occupants of the vehicle could see the few moving lights to the east of the village a few hundred meters away.

The third-generation light-amplifying tubes of the night-vision devices the SEALs were wearing showed everything in shades of green. The lights

Reaper had seen were invisible to the naked eye, but were plain to see through the electronic tubes. The dimness of the lights suggested that they were probably screened in some way, like the red lens used on a military flashlight. That was not something a group of refugees would be using.

The outskirts of the small village weren't more than a few hundred meters away, starting at the foot of the hill the SEALs were stopped on. The schoolhouse was just a few meters farther on down the single village street. It was in the woods beyond the village, approaching the schoolhouse, that the scattered lights moved in closer.

The kerosene lamps lit in the schoolhouse gave a soft golden glow to the light pouring out the few windows of the building. That light was magnified to a brilliant level in the night-vision devices. The drawback the devices had was that they robbed the users of natural night vision when they were taken off. The very new AN/PVS-14 NVDs eliminated that problem by being a monocular design. Only a single tube was placed in front of one of the operator's eyes. The other eye just looked out into darkness. The effect was a little strange before you got used to it, but the extensive training the SEALs did to prepare for any of their missions made these men well practiced in using their equipment.

"Bear, with me," Reaper said, "Ward, get on the Mark 19, Martell, contact Paxtun and give him a sitrep."

Not another word was spoken, it didn't have to be. Mike Martell turned to his radio to send the situation report that the unit was investigating a possible contact. Ed Ward secured the Humvee and reached up to unlock the hatch cover above and between the two front seats.

As Ward was opening the half-moon-shaped hatch cover, Reaper and Bear pulled up the black balaclava hoods they had been wearing around their necks. Their faces and heads were now completely covered except for their eyes and the gleaming monocle of the AN/PVS-14s. Without a further word, the two SEALs opened their doors quietly and slipped into the moonless night.

The hillside was wet and slick, but the two SEALs moved smoothly and quietly over the rocks and mud. Behind them, Ward stood up in the weapon platform mount on top of the Humvee. There, he pulled the cover off the Mark 19 40mm grenade launcher and removed the travel retaining pin to release the mount.

The sixty-two-pound box of ammunition on the feed bracket of the weapon only held a single forty-eight-round belt of grenades. Even a big SEAL would be hard put to quickly manhandle a fresh box of ammunition that size into reload position. An accurate gunner wouldn't waste ammunition—and Ward was a very accurate gunner. With two careful and quiet pulls on the charger handle, Ward prepared the big weapon to fire in support of his Teammates out in the darkness.

Moving carefully from cover to cover, neither SEAL had a need to speak as they approached the village. Constant training had almost removed the need for words between them. The two men had worked together so long that each knew what the other would do in any situation. They were a shooter pair, and they had done this kind of target approach a hundred times in all kinds of terrain. Holding their M4 carbines out at the ready, the SEALs stealthily moved and froze in concealment to assess the situation.

As they came closer to the village, the two SEALs could make out more and more detail through their night-vision devices. The village was made up of a number of cottagelike homes of white walls and tile roofs, the same as could be seen in thousands of European countrysides. The houses faced a central street, which the SEALs' Humvee would have reached if it had continued on its way. At the far end of the village was the larger schoolhouse. The rubble of a small mosque was near the school, the house of worship having been destroyed by the Serbs and not yet rebuilt.

Beyond the school were open fields interspersed with woods, and it was in those woods that the SEALs had seen the moving lights. But it was more than just their eyes that gave the two SEALs information about their surroundings.

The rain had stopped, but the night was still wet. The musty, earthy smell of the rain covered a lot of the night's odors, but Reaper could still pick up the sharp tang of wood smoke from some of the village's chimneys. And there was the slightly sweetish stink of the decomposing grass and leaves that had been uncovered by the spring thaw. The bite of the still-cold night air dulled some of the SEALs' sense of smell, but they could still notice odors well enough to file away the information.

The one smell that was not consciously noticed by each SEAL, but would have been of immediate concern by its absence, was the smell of his partner. They knew each other's smell in the dark. They had worked and trained that intensely together.

Both SEALs had sharp hearing. The men heard the burring sound of the light wind as it pushed away the storm clouds. There was a slight rustle of cloth as each SEAL moved through the night, a slight rubbing of their Gore-Tex jackets or trousers against the hard nylon of their assault vests and body armor. In spite of this being planned as just an observation mission with no action expected, each of the SEALs was wearing a full loadout of weapons, equipment, and ammunition. The gear included an assault vest filled with ten loaded thirty-round magazines for their M4 carbines, a SIG P-226 pistol in a low-slung assault holster secured to the right thigh, three spare fifteen-round magazines to their pistols, and a knife. This was in addition to a first aid kit, signaling flare, Motorola MX-300R radio, throat mike and earpiece, and tactical Level IV B/C hard body armor that could stop a standard bullet from an AK-47 or M16.

In spite of all of their equipment, the most valuable thing the SEALs had with them was their training and experience. There was no noise from their gear. Each piece of equipment had been examined, taped, and padded as necessary until nothing made any unintentional noise. The rustle of their clothing was so faint it couldn't have been heard more than a few feet away. The loudest thing that the two SEALs could hear was their own breathing, but they knew that couldn't be heard by anyone else around them—if there was anyone there.

Both men quickly slipped past the schoolhouse and into the woods beyond. The question of who might be out there was partially answered by the sounds of metallic clicks and bangs as loose pieces of equipment and rifle slings tapped against each other in the darkness. There were probably armed men in the woods, not more than a few hundred meters away. Almost that same distance behind the SEALs were their Teammates at the Humvee.

Suddenly from the dark came a sound that confirmed the SEALs suspicions, the sharp metallic clack of an AK-47's safety being clicked into the firing position. A unique sound that was instantly recognizable to anyone who had heard it in serious circumstances. And both SEALs knew that the villagers were not armed.

Taking cover behind a tree, Chief Reaper partially covered his mouth with his hand. Keying the throat mike to his MX-300R radio, Reaper whispered, "Smokestack Four this is Smokestack One. Contact, I say again, contact. We have an unknown number of hostiles in the woods to the east of the schoolhouse."

The response from Martell back at the Humvee astonished both Reaper and Bear who heard the answer over his own radio.

"Smokestack One this is Smokestack Four, return to the ride. I repeat, return to the ride."

There was no question but that Reaper and Bear would get back to the Humvee as quickly as they could, while still maintaining a silent movement. They slipped through the woods and village area like two shadows. Martell wouldn't have called them back unless the need was serious. It was only a matter of minutes before the two SEALs were back inside the vehicle.

"What's the problem?" Reaper said not seeing anything out of the ordinary.

"Chief," Martell said, "it's Engine One. Captain Paxtun said we are to immediately cease operations and return to base."

"What?" questioned Reaper. "Get me Paxtun on the box right now."

As Martell started calling out on the radio, Bear just looked at his chief and shrugged his shoulders. As Reaper was going to say something, Martell reached forward and handled him the microphone from the radio and clicked on the speaker.

"Engine One, this is Smokestack One," Reaper said as he pressed in the bar at the side of the microphone.

"Smokestack One, this is Engine One," Reaper and the rest of the SEALs in the Humvee heard. "Have you started back to the train?"

"That's a negative, Engine One," Reaper said. "I don't think you understand the situation here. We have hostiles closing in on friendlies. I suggest a full tactical response."

"Negative on that request Smokestack One," the speaker replied. "I have put out a cease-action order on all operations in our area of responsibility effective 2000 hours today. You are to immediately proceed to the train. Restricted rules of engagement are in effect and you may not fire unless fired upon and in imminent danger."

"Sir," Chief Reaper said as he began to lose his temper. "We have friendlies in danger from a hostile group of eight to ten . . ."

"Stand down, Chief," came out of the speaker. "You have a direct order to return to base and cease all actions immediately. There are no hostile forces known to be in the area."

"Sir," Chief Reaper spoke angrily, "I'm looking at the hostiles! I wish to immediately refer this up the chain of command to headquarters in Tuzla on an Emergency Flash Priority."

"That is a negative, Reaper," Captain Paxtun's voice came over the speaker. Anger could now be heard in the officer's voice. He must have been shaking with anger as Paxtun had just committed a serious breach of communications protocol by using the chief's real name over the air. "There is an electrical storm over the Majevica mountain ridge that is breaking communications with higher command. You will immediately return to base or face charges under the . . ."

Martell, observing Chief Reaper's knuckles grow white as his hand clenched the microphone, suddenly reached over and twisted a dial on the faceplate of the radio, then he flipped a switch.

"Sorry, Chief," Martell said with a grin, "it must be all of that electrical interference. When those electrical storms hit the mountains, radio reception just goes to shit and . . ."

Gunfire suddenly erupted to the east of the

Humvee's position. Immediately Martell stopped talking and everyone looked toward the schoolhouse. The sound of gunfire was slightly muffled, but there was no mistaking the deep stuttering boom of an AK-47 fired on full automatic. Between the shots could be heard the screams of the refugees. Whoever those troops were, they were attacking the schoolhouse and slaughtering the unarmed refugees inside.

"Bear, with me," Reaper said. "Martell, try to get command at Tuzla on the horn."

Before actions could be put to the chief's words, there was the sound of glass breaking in the distance and a wail cried out as a small body was thrown from the schoolhouse. The cry of the little boy was cut short as the child struck the stony ground near the schoolhouse.

The limp form of the child lay still. In the green glow of the night-vision devices, the pitiful body looked like little more than a discarded bundle of rags. Even at a distance, the child was so small he could not have been much older than Reaper's own six-year-old son back in the States.

A cold fury settled in on the occupants of the Humvee. Without a word being spoken, Reaper and Bear exited the vehicle and headed for the schoolhouse in a low, crouching run. In spite of their haste, the two SEALs would alternately stop as one covered the other's advance. As the leading SEAL knelt in a crouch and covered with his weapon, the trailing SEAL would move forward and pass the other.

The practiced leapfrogging movement was quick and efficient—eating up the meters between the

Humvee and the far edge of the village where the schoolhouse was. The gunfire increased as the SEALs grew close, then suddenly tapered off. As they came close to the side of the schoolhouse, the SEALs passed the small, still form of the child who had been tossed out onto the rocks.

There was no time to feel anything for the child, or even to stop and see if he was still alive. There were others in immediate danger inside the schoolhouse—if it wasn't already too late to save them.

Reaper did not feel rage. Even the anger he felt against the astonishing orders of his commanding officer had melted away with the need for sudden, precise and controlled action. Only a cool head would prevail in such a situation, and Reaper could be as cool and hard as old bone if the situation warranted. It was one of the reasons he had long ago received the nickname "Grim" Reaper.

Other figures were slipping away into the woods as Reaper and Bear moved up to where they could see the door of the building. As a figure came out the door, Reaper could see that the man was wearing the same mottled, gray-and-brown camouflage uniform that so many of the mixed regular and irregular forces in the war-torn country used.

On the man's head was an odd thing, a flat round cloth hat with a rolled brim. It was a Pakol, the traditional Afghan hat. But it was the objects in the man's hands that seized Reaper's eye. In his right hand was an AK-47, held away to shield the man from the smoking-hot barrel. In his left hand was a child's rag doll. The man was laughing and saying something in what sounded like Arabic to Reaper. Coming out of the well-lit schoolhouse, the man probably never even saw Reaper standing nearby.

The gap-toothed smile on the raider's face was enough to heat the SEAL's cool resolve. And the weapon in his hand registered as a threat. Reaper didn't even consciously think of his action as the muzzle of his shouldered M4 carbine settled on the center of the man's chest. The short stutter of a three-round burst was quick justice for a single individual's action of ethnic cleansing.

Just to the right side of Reaper's field of vision, he saw the orange-white flower of an AK-47's muzzle blast bloom in the night. Before Reaper's mind could do more than register the light, there was a smashing pain against his chest. A thundering blow knocked the big SEAL down to the ground. Multicolored lights danced in front of Reaper's eyes as he tried to just draw in a breath. As he fell back, the rest of the rounds fired from the AK-47 passed over him.

His hands tingled oddly as Reaper pulled up his M4 and fired back. Or at least he tried to fire back. When he squeezed the trigger, the M4 refused to fire. Without conscious thought, Reaper let go of the M4, which dropped to his chest, and he reached for his SIG P-226. In a smooth movement, his right hand grasped the pistol, his thumb releasing the restraining strap of the holster as his fingers closed around the rough, checkered finish of the plastic grips.

As the bearded face of the man who shot him came up from the darkness, Reaper was already pulling his pistol up and thrusting it out. As he pulled the trigger and double-actioned the SIG, time seemed to change in its natural flow. As if in slow motion, Reaper could see his pistol come up even as the hammer was going back for the shot. The bearded man appeared to be moving very slowly as he started to point his rifle. There wasn't much of a question that there wouldn't be a second place finisher in this race. The winner would be the only one who lived.

Reaper noted the thick, bushy black beard of the man who was trying to kill him. There were broad black eyebrows above eyes that were widely open. As the man opened his mouth, Reaper could see teeth stained from years of neglect and tobacco use. Then the face dissolved in a mask of red as Reaper won the race and the SIG in his hand bucked and roared.

With the immediate threat neutralized, the passage of time went back to its normal rate of flow. There was the sharp report of another M4 being fired as Bear took down one of the other armed men who had come to wreak havoc among the unarmed villagers. Then Reaper heard the slow knocking, spaced-out, thunk . . . thunk . . . thunk . . . of a Mark 19 being fired. It took a moment for the fist-sized 40mm grenades to travel from the muzzle of the weapon to the target. Just a second or two after the sound of firing rang out, the spaces between the trees bloomed with the flowers of high-explosive grenade detonations.

Back at the Humvee, Ward fired the Mark 19 grenade launcher in a long burst, tracking the grenades so that they would explode in the woods beyond where his Teammates were fighting. The blasts would convince the raiders that rapidly going someplace else would be a very good idea.

Thousands of ripping steel fragments from the exploding grenades slashed through the trees and brush of the woods. As the razor-sharp steel cleared the area, Reaper quickly picked himself up from the ground and shook off the effects of the blow to his chest. His M4 carbine, dangling across his chest on its sling, was not going to be of much help to him. Even without the night-vision device strapped to his head, Reaper would have seen the large dent and hole in the receiver where the weapon had stopped the first round from that AK-47.

"Well, fuck me," he said quietly to himself.

His SIG pistol had served him well enough and would have to continue to do so. As Bear ran up to his chief, neither SEAL could see any sign of more activity on the part of the raiders. Whoever they had been, they had cut and run, leaving their dead behind. They didn't have the stomach for a protracted fight when what they had thought would be a soft target had suddenly turned very hard.

The open door of the schoolhouse was behind the two SEALs. As Bear maintained watch, Reaper went up to the door and looked inside. Light was pouring out of the door, bathing the two SEALs in a golden glow, as fires started from the broken lamps in the building spread their flames.

Reaper pushed his AN/PVS-14 NVD up on his forehead. The light from the fire was more than enough for him to see the scattered bodies of nearly twenty villagers—men, women, and children—scattered around the room. The torn and limp bodies told Reaper all that he needed to know. There would be no refugees accepting the offer of a safe haven by the SEALs, the JSSF, or anyone else.

Chapter Two

A subdued Humvee full of SEALs returned to the "train," the radio code name for their headquarters established in a house near the city of Rastosnica. The large house was isolated enough from other buildings for security's sake, and large enough to comfortably hold all of the JSSF detachment.

The unit's two officers, Captain Paxtun and Lieutenant Franklin, had their quarters on the upper floor of the house, but only Paxtun was waiting when Reaper returned with his men. Two of the unit's other Humvees were missing when the men pulled up to the house. Their vehicle was still parked where they had left it.

The results of the night's actions weighed heavily on the SEALs. They had gone out with the intention of simply supporting a "hearts and minds" campaign to help win over some of the locals who had suffered so much. A show of strength and solidarity to show the refugees that they were finally safe in an area they could call home.

The SEALs' mission had been a complete failure. It wasn't because of any lack of action on their part. But the people they had been trying to help were dead, and there wasn't anything that could be said to make that result easier to accept.

One of the things that had been bothering Reaper during the entire drive back to their headquarters was just who the hell the village attackers had been. The bodies that the SEALs had searched revealed very little—but what they did find looked important.

The Afghan Pakol hat the one raider had been wearing was odd, but the really significant find had been the pocket copy of the Koran that had been on the body, the small book neatly wrapped in waterproof cloth. There was no way that a Serb raider would have been carrying a copy of the Koran. A Serb might have considered the Muslim holy book to be a source of paper at most. He certainly wouldn't have been carrying it carefully wrapped and protected as its owner had been. No, the raiders had been Muslims—and they had killed their own people.

As the SEALs entered the house, Captain Paxtun was waiting in the front room. It was immediately obvious to Paxtun that his orders had not been obeyed—the tear in the front of Reaper's vest and the damage to the weapon hanging across his chest were plain to see. It wasn't the kind of thing that could happen to a man who was in a vehicle accident. Reaper had been in combat, against direct orders.

"Chief Reaper," Paxtun said, "are any of your men casualties?"

The tone in Paxtun's voice gave Reaper the impression the captain would have preferred that all of the SEALs were casualties. There probably would have been less paperwork for them than for the kind of attack that he and his men had witnessed.

"No, sir," Reaper said. "My troops and I are fine. I would like to dismiss them to stow their gear and grab some chow."

"Fine, Chief," Paxtun said, "dismiss them. You and I have to have some words about the incident this evening."

"Yes, sir," Reaper said.

Turning to Bear, Reaper continued, "Clean yourselves and your gear, get something to eat and grab some sack time."

"Chief . . ." Bear started to say.

"Belay that," Reaper said, "you have your instructions."

Reluctantly, the SEALs left the front room, leaving the two officers and their chief behind them.

"Where is Lieutenant Franklin and the rest of the men?" Reaper asked.

"They're out on another scouting mission," Paxtun said. "I don't expect them back for some time."

"I hope their operation goes a lot better than ours did," Reaper said.

"Chief," Captain Paxtun began, "there are cause-and-effect situations here that you have no knowledge of. The political situation is at a critical stage and we cannot afford another Serb incident making the news for . . ."

"Serbs," Reaper exploded. The frustration and shock he felt since almost being killed that evening evaporated in a wave of anger and rage. "How the hell can you jump to that conclusion? Those weren't any Serbs who killed those people. Those raiders were Muslims themselves. No Serb would ever be caught with this in his pocket."

With that statement, Reaper threw the Koran that he had in his pocket down onto a chair next to where Paxtun was standing.

"And just where in the hell do you think a Serb would have gotten this?" Reaper said and he threw the Pakol hat into the captain's face.

Ducking to the side, Paxtun dodged the cloth hat and allowed it to fall to the floor behind him. The officer was almost shaking with rage at the SEAL chief standing in front of him.

"Chief," Paxtun snapped out. "You will get hold of yourself right now, soldier."

"Wrong, sir," Reaper growled, "I'm a sailor."

Being corrected by the SEAL chief enraged Paxtun even more. "You will stand at attention when addressing me . . . sailor," Paxtun snapped. "I don't care what service you're in, you can be brought up on charges of insubordination and assaulting an officer right now. This minor material you've brought in from somewhere could come from anywhere, and mean anything."

Taking a moment to get control of himself, Paxtun looked at the SEAL chief and the hat on the floor.

"Chief Reaper," Paxtun said in a much calmer voice, "there has been no Serb activity reported in this area for some time. It was just the villagers' bad luck that an incident took place while they were all in the same building. It's possible that the Serbs heard of the meeting and decided to stage a raid disguised as Muslims. Maybe we were simply due for some action breaking out in this area again. Any thought that there was a group of rogue Muslims attacking their own is just supposition on your part. The present political situation among the local Muslim groups is far too sensitive to allow such inflammatory suspicions to be voiced without solid proof."

Reaper just looked at Paxtun with astonishment. He was denying the evidence that was right there in the room. Just what in the hell was going on here? Reaper thought.

"Suspicions?" Reaper said. "Just what do you mean, suspicions? How the fuck can you deny what happened tonight? That wasn't a raid, it was a planned slaughter of those refugees and the villagers who were putting them up.

"Those raiders knew where everyone would be and surrounded most of the area. That wasn't a schoolhouse—it was a killing zone. If you hadn't called me back to the vehicle, my men and I might have been able to save a few of those poor people. As it is, they're dead and the bulk of the raiders got away. If we had taken the route you originally planned for my patrol, we wouldn't have gotten there until well after . . ."

Reaper paused at the realization that Paxtun's intent may have been just what he was about to say—he had wanted the SEALs to miss the incident. They were just supposed to have shown up and count the bodies.

"That's it, isn't it, sir?" Reaper said as he closed the distance between himself and Paxtun. "You made some kind of deal with those assholes. We were never supposed to have ever even seen them, were we? My men and I were just to be witnesses to the aftermath of another Serb slaughter."

"That'll be enough of that shit, Reaper," Paxtun almost shouted. Paxtun rarely swore and that told the big SEAL chief that his words were hitting home.

"Just what is it," Reaper said, "you have cooked up with the people who sent those raiders? Just what were you supposed to get out of the deal? Intelligence? Some kind of information that would make your career?"

Reaper looked deeply into Paxtun's eyes as he spoke. He didn't see enough of a reaction to tell him that he had guessed right yet. Paxtun was angry, but the captain remained cagey and in control.

"If not intelligence, what?" Reaper said. "Money? Guns? Drugs? Just what the hell could someone offer you that would be worth the lives of all those people?"

"Take control of yourself, Chief," Paxtun said sharply.

"Sir," Reaper said as he drew himself rigidly to attention, "I respectfully request permission to report to SFOR headquarters in Tuzla. I will personally deliver a full report on the incident this evening to the authorities there. The relocation project is their responsibility and they can make the final determination of the situation and which parties might be held accountable."

Paxtun looked shocked as he realized just how close he was coming to losing control of the situation. It was now obvious to anyone who may have seen them standing there that he didn't want Reaper reporting anything to anyone. There was suddenly near panic showing in the officer's face. Whatever the situation was, Reaper knew from looking at Paxtun that something was wrong and he was up to his asshole in it.

"Just a moment, Chief," Paxtun said in a reasonable tone. "Any reports coming from this unit will be made by myself or my executive officer. It is obvious that you are too upset by the action today to think clearly. The accusations you are making are outrageous. I'm sure you'll see just how wrong they are after a night's sleep. You make out your report tomorrow and I will see to it that it reaches the proper people."

"I will be making my own report to Warcom, my own Navy command, sir," Reaper said with a special emphasis on the last word. "And I will make it tonight. I do not require your permission to do so."

The anger that washed through Paxtun showed plainly on his face. As the big Navy SEAL turned to leave the room, the shorter officer said, "This is my command, Chief, not yours. And I am the intelligence professional. Any reports that come from this unit will come directly from my desk. I will inform command in Tuzla of the situation—and of your part in it."

"My part in it?" Reaper said.

"Obviously, Chief," Paxtun said, "the strain of working under these conditions was too much for you. Something at the refugee village must have simply set you off and you opened fire on them. I would of course expect your men to say whatever they had to in order to cover for their chief, but you have obviously lost control of yourself. That is what

I will tell both the Tuzla command, and your own people."

Relief swept across Paxtun's face as he thought that he had taken control of a situation that had threatened to get completely out of hand. The blame for the slaughter would be put on the head of what he could say was an undisciplined SEAL who had lost control. He had disobeyed specific orders as to how he was supposed to have approached the village and what path he was to have taken. What other standing orders may he have ignored? Their story would fit the facts well enough to confuse the issue badly. A small smile slowly spread across Paxtun's face.

For a moment as he stood there, Reaper no longer could see the smirking face of the officer in front of him. What he saw was a small bundle of rags being tossed through a schoolhouse window. And all he heard was a child's whimpering cry suddenly cut off. He had to get out of that room now, before he did something he would regret.

"The hell you will," Reaper said very softly. "I'll be making my own report, and it will be going through Navy channels."

Reaper turned to leave the room without another word. The soft tone of voice Reaper had used had a lot in common with a quiet wind blowing through a graveyard—they both were heard mostly by the dead. If the intelligence officer had learned more about the Navy SEAL chief, he would have known to be afraid of that voice. What Paxtun did realize was the seriousness of what Reaper was threatening to do.

The smirk that had been on Paxtun's face just a

moment before had been replaced with something that looked a lot like sudden fear. Paxtun wasn't a big man, just a little over five feet six. And he certainly didn't have the build of the six-foot-tall, 215-pound Reaper. But he still tried to physically stop Reaper from leaving the room.

"Don't you turn your back on me, mister," Paxtun said. "I am not done talking to you yet!" He grabbed at Reaper's left shoulder and tried to twist the big man around.

An iron-hard right fist, toughened by years of exercise, salt water, and rough use—the same hand that had rubbed the short hair of a six-year-old son back in the States months before—shot up from behind the SEAL's right hip and smashed squarely into the officer's jaw. Paxtun flipped over backward and landed flat on the floor. The angle of his jaw was anything but natural as the nearly unconscious officer groaned from where he lay sprawled. The broken jaw would keep the man from eating solid food for some time—and it spelled the death knell for Reaper's military career.

Chapter Three

Months after the JSSF incident in Bosnia, a blue Pontiac Firebird sped along the northbound lanes of I-395, heading in to Washington, D.C. At the wheel of the car was Navy captain Alan Straker. For a high-ranking officer, Captain Straker's deeply tanned skin and heavy muscular build made him stand out as someone who hadn't spent his career behind a desk.

The brilliantly shining gold Trident, the Naval Special Warfare breast insignia, in plain view on the upper right side of Straker's uniform, was a big giveaway as to just how he developed that tan and those muscles. The Trident could be worn officially only by men who had passed through training and been accepted as active SEALs by their peers in the Teams. That symbol on his chest proclaimed him to be a Navy SEAL operator—no matter what his rank or assignment.

Not all of his muscles came from having been in the SEAL Teams. Straker's bright blue eyes had looked out from under a sweating mass of thick black hair at a number of opponents during his days on the wrestling team at the U.S. Naval Academy. He had always accepted a challenge, and reveled in overcoming them. The challenge he was facing right now was simply the irritation of having to maneuver through D.C. traffic.

Straker decided on parking at the Pentagon and grabbing a ride in on the subway. He could make his appointment at the huge Department of State building between Twenty-first and Twenty-third Streets by just getting aboard the Metro at the Pentagon and getting off at the Foggy Bottom stop south of Washington Circle. The walk was only about half a mile down Twenty-third Street, and the late September weather in D.C. wasn't so bad that he would arrive in a sweat-soaked uniform. Besides, finding a parking spot at the Pentagon was going to be one hell of a lot easier than conducting a parking search in downtown Northwest D.C.

While standing at the subway stop at the bottom of the very long escalators at the Pentagon, and during the ride itself, Captain Straker maintained a pensive look. At only slightly over five ten, but carrying 245 pounds on his broad-shouldered frame, Straker wasn't jostled a lot by the other passengers on the subway. Certainly no one poked at the big SEAL to see if there was a soft spot indicating flab instead of muscle. Only his six-year-old niece would ever think of doing such a thing anyway. A small smile slipped onto the face of the SEAL as he thought of his sister's youngest, the smile evaporating as his mind went back to his mission at hand.

At present, Captain Straker's assignment in the Teams was a general one. He was working TAD (temporary assigned duty) at Special Warfare Group Two at Little Creek, Virginia. His present position was only to last until the confirmation of his promotion to rear admiral (lower half). Once at flag rank, he would go on to the Special Operations Command in Tampa for a tour of duty there.

With the temporary duties at Group Two, also came a job that no SEAL ever wanted—investigating the possible wrongdoing of a fellow operator. Straker had been ordered to investigate the incident of a SEAL chief petty officer being accused of willfully disobeying orders, assaulting a superior officer, and the murder of foreign nationals. The charges were seriously inflated in Straker's opinion, and the situation a foul one.

Only the classified seal the State Department had thrown over the whole affair had so far kept it out of the hands of the Judge Advocate General's office. Somebody at State wanted a SEAL's ass as a sacrifice over this one—and they wanted all of their ducks in a row before final charges were brought. Straker intended bringing the situation to a close before the JAG's office became inextricably involved. State wanted a straightforward guilty plea, and Straker was going to play that desire for all it was worth.

As he walked south to the State Department Building Straker reflected how, at his rank, politics had become another battleground. In this fight, words did more damage than any bullets ever could. If the present situation burst in his face, that admiral's star was going to go back into the box. But no SEAL had ever been left behind, living or dead. Even if all you could do was go back and bring out a body, if that's what it took that's what you did. It had been a mantra in the Teams since well before Lieutenant (j.g.) Straker had gone through training. He certainly was not going to be the first one to break that tradition by abandoning a Teammate to the military-hating cookie-pushers at the State Department.

It took some time to travel through the huge building to locate the conference room that Straker had been told to report to. Already in the room and busily shuffling papers was Martin Rosacrantz, the midlevel State Department bureaucrat who was pushing ahead with the case against Ted Reaper. Rosacrantz was a tall, thin individual with a receding hairline and a superior attitude. Straker wasn't surprised. He had yet to meet any people from State who didn't feel they were superior to the military. Even though it was the military who had to keep cleaning up the messes or carry through the ideas of the moment for the present administration.

"Thank you for being prompt, Captain Straker," Rosacrantz said. "Please have a seat and we'll get right to business."

Without waiting for Straker to sit, Rosacrantz began talking.

"This meeting should be little more than a formality before formal charges are brought against Chief Petty Officer Reaper," Rosacrantz said.

"I hardly think that the decision to bring capital charges against anyone should be considered simply a formality," Straker said.

Rosacrantz looked at Captain Straker with surprise showing on his face.

"But you can hardly argue against the evidence

and the gravity of the situation. You have a highly trained operator who had a serious failure of judgment that resulted in the murder of two native Muslim defenders of a refugee group. It's quite possible that his slaying of the militia members directly resulted in the slaughter of the villagers.

"The situation in Bosnia-Herzegovina is very unstable right now. The peace accords have been kept in place by very careful diplomatic maneuvering by State with both the local governments and NATO. The U.N. has a direct interest in just how well we handle the situation. This incident must be handled properly."

"If by properly, you mean railroad an enlisted man who has given fifteen years of exemplary service to his country," Straker said more than a little heatedly, "then you will not have the cooperation of the Navy or of Naval Special Warfare."

Straker continued before Rosacrantz could get over his shock at the SEAL's blunt manner of speaking and hard tone of voice.

"I have personally examined the reports of the incident and interviewed the bulk of the personnel involved. Additionally, I have gone over the service records of everyone involved in some detail. More than that, I put Chief Reaper's history under a microscope. Nothing, and I mean absolutely nothing, in his record indicates anything but exemplary behavior on his part along with the utmost professionalism in the execution of his duties."

"The situation in Bosnia-Herzegovina was a combat environment," Rosacrantz said, "with severe stress on everyone stationed in the area. It would have certainly affected the judgment of a man not used to the intricacies of operating with foreign nationals with their own set of morals and ideals."

Straker swallowed the expletive he almost burst out with. "The level of stress you seem to think so extreme is exceeded on a regular basis during our normal training in the SEAL Teams," Straker said. "And Reaper had been in combat before. His conduct under fire with a detachment from SEAL Team Four during Operation Just Cause in Panama demonstrated coolness under fire. He was able to absorb severe hardship without complaint and without wavering from the objective at hand.

"After his combat experience, he went on to be a First Phase instructor at the Special Warfare Training Center in Coronado. Again, he showed proficiency and competence in his job while also looking out for the welfare of the students placed in his care. He is a completely professional military man.

"The same can't quite be said in regards to Captain Paxtun. I find his military records interesting for their brevity. In fact, he doesn't seem to have existed except perhaps in a vacuum before more than a few years ago. It's been a few years but I've seen this kind of military record before, back when I was a young officer in Vietnam. This is the record of an intelligence operative seconded to the military and given a protocol rank. This man isn't a commissioned officer or even really a soldier, he's a spook!

"I don't know just how deeply you've looked into the backgrounds of this officer—and I use that term with reservations. Maybe you're just working from a limited briefing. But with one of my SEALs' career on the line, you can be sure that I've looked deeply into all the backgrounds of everyone involved.

"Did you even know that Paxtun had been captured by the Soviets while under deep cover in Afghanistan? After being disavowed by our own government, he was finally rescued by members of a local mujahideen faction. For months, he stayed at the Amir Muawia camp in the Khost province of Afghanistan. That place was originally set up by the CIA and the ISI, the Pakistani military intelligence service. Now, it's nothing more than an Islamic fundamentalist base—a training camp for terrorists. On top of that, the ISI is corrupt as hell and ass-deep in the opium trade and gun running.

"That man should never have been allowed back into a combat zone. Certainly not put in charge of a special operations unit. And most emphatically not put into an area where Islamic fundamentalists were trying to gain a political foothold among the Muslim refugee population.

"We've traced at least one of the Islamic fundamentalist factions operating in that part of Bosnia directly back to the Khost region of Afghanistan. If I can find that out just from my contacts in the intelligence community, how in the hell did you guys here at State miss it completely?

"Those Islamic fundamentalists could give lessons in enthusiasm to Baptist missionaries. Don't you think the men who rescued Paxtun from the hands of the Soviets just might not have a bit of influence over him?"

Having visibly wilted under Straker's verbal onslaught, Rosacrantz quickly recovered his composure and spoke back to the big SEAL.

"Captain Paxtun was fully debriefed after his unfortunate problems in Afghanistan," Rosacrantz said. "It was to his credit that the man never broke under the enthusiastic interrogations of his Soviet captors. At that time, the Soviet military would have liked nothing better than to have had a U.S. intelligence officer taken prisoner from that particular part of the world. It is to Paxtun's credit that he was able to immerse himself deeply in the local Muslim culture and prevent his cover from being blown.

"Paxtun was considered more than able to command the special operations people of that JSSF contingent. His special knowledge of the customs and culture of the Muslim people was expected to be a great asset to the mission. It is unfortunate that the men from your command did not seem to be able to take their direction from a capable and well-trained officer."

"Are we reading the same reports?" Straker said. "Do you really have any idea just what the true situation is over there?"

"You are hardly qualified to judge the . . ." Rosacrantz began to say.

"Oh, but I am qualified to judge this situation," Straker interrupted in a menacing tone. "I have been put in very bad situations in the past by self-serving intelligence operatives who overreached themselves and wanted someone else to blame when things went bad. And I will not stand by and allow it to happen to the men I serve with.

"The idea that the Serbs conducted the slaughter at the relocation village has nothing to support it. There were no Serb forces operating in the area that

SFOR knew of. There were no Serb forces that the Russians knew to be operating in the area. And the Serbs themselves say they had no units within miles of that village during the time of the attack."

"You could hardly expect the Serb forces," Rosacrantz said, "who are themselves suspect in a number of criminal atrocities, to admit that they were the ones who conducted this action."

"No, I would hardly take their word for it," Straker said. "But it is significant that their information correlates with everything we can get from other sources. And there is the evidence that was recovered by Chief Reaper after the incident that points the finger at Islamic extremists doing the killing."

"You cannot accept as evidence the described finding of a minor piece of clothing and some religious tracts," Rosacrantz said. "The materials simply don't exist."

"That in itself is interesting to me," said Straker. "The only evidence described by Chief Reaper never made it up to higher headquarters. But the funny thing was, all of his men who were questioned separately about the incident described exactly the same things. And Captain Paxtun had been conducting extensive contact ops on his own accord without informing his men, or anyone else that I can locate right now."

"If Paxtun is the experienced intelligence operative that you describe," Rosacrantz said, "you could hardly expect him to give out sensitive information when there wasn't a need-to-know."

"I saw a number of Intel people try to hide behind the sensitive information shield before," Straker said. "That may have worked on a naive young officer twenty-five years ago, but it won't work now. You try and push these swollen charges forward and I will make it my responsibility to uncover everything that was going on in that particular piece of the world.

"Chief Reaper is not going to plead guilty to anything at this point. He will not roll over and play dead no matter how badly the State Department wants him to. Reaper has told me his suspicions regarding the situation over there and Paxtun's involvement in it. It does not make a very pretty picture.

"Paxtun could have been just trying to gather intelligence on the situation in that area of Bosnia-Herzegovina. He could easily have been cooperating with an Islamic group he felt he owed something to. Or he could have been going behind everyone's back to just line his own pockets. Smuggling guns, drugs, whatever, has been going on in that part of the world for decades. Some of the Islamic organizations are raising their operating funds by selling opium out of Afghanistan. It wouldn't be the first time an intelligence officer took advantage of being in the middle of the situation to add to a personal retirement fund.

"Accusations are easy. There is no hard evidence as yet to support these suppositions—only the words of several SEALs who I trust. But if JAG was to become involved in an official investigation, I'm sure corroborating witnesses and evidence could turn up.

"And before you tell me that security classifications will keep me from learning what I want to know, I should tell you that the Special Warfare community is a very tight one. We have been in the business of gathering intelligence for this country for a very long time.

"The Teams were working for the intelligence community since before the CIA even existed. There are a lot of ex-Team guys in the Intel world right now. This thing stinks and I will find out just what is rotten. I think that some very bad judgments were made in regards to our allies in that part of the world. And there are some extremist groups around there who have their own agendas. Agendas they have every intention of following no matter what they have to do or who they have to kill.

"I don't know who, or to what extent, Captain Paxtun was involved with over there—and I don't particularly want to find out unless I have to. And if I do, you can rest assured that it will become part of the official record."

Martin Rosacrantz was stunned by the tone of the big SEAL's words as much as their content. As the bureaucrat sat back in his chair and stared at the SEAL, Straker considered it time to take a new tack. Now it was his turn to play diplomat and push a cookie across the table. Chief Reaper couldn't get out of this situation unscathed. The bit about exposing some kind of possibly unsanctioned ops or corrupt activity had hit the bureaucrat harder than Straker expected. Offering an alternative punishment for Reaper, and making it sound worse than it was, could give the State Department, or just Rosacrantz, a means to save face.

"There is the fact that Chief Reaper struck a superior officer," Straker said. "Even one who may not have been a true commissioned officer. That is a serious breach of military discipline. There are no witnesses to the incident, but Paxtun's jaw being broken in two places speaks for itself.

"Making Reaper face charges under the Uniform Code of Military Justice would bring a great deal out during a court-martial—some of which the State Department may not like shown even to a secure court.

"I think I could convince Chief Reaper to accept one option. He could leave the Teams and return to the fleet, maintaining his rank as a Navy chief petty officer. That would keep him under military control and he could retire as soon as his twenty years were completed."

Straker had no real expectation of Rosacrantz accepting his first suggestion of punishment for Reaper. The people at the State Department had the reputation of being bargainers and Rosacrantz was no exception. What he wasn't saying to Rosacrantz was that Reaper had already admitted to having struck Paxtun. That the SEAL chief was ready to stand up for what he had done and accept whatever punishment would be due him for his actions was one of the factors that put Straker solidly on Reaper's side.

"No," Rosacrantz said emphatically, "Chief Reaper will leave the service entirely. Paxtun has been stripped of all rank and relinquished all claims for any benefits he may have accrued. He has been expelled both from the military and the intelligence community. Your chief will not receive any more lenient treatment for his involvement in this affair."

"Chief Reaper is up for reenlistment within a few weeks," Straker said. "As a career military man, he has to put in his twenty years before he becomes eligible for any retirement. If he was not allowed to reenlist, he would have to just leave the service. Any actions taken by him after he left the Navy could jeopardize any benefits that would come to him down the road. His discharge is already in the works." Straker neglected to mention that the discharge would be an honorable one. "I'm certain Chief Reaper can be shown the benefits of ending his career."

Captain Straker had a bad taste in his mouth even as he said the words. They could keep Chief Reaper from facing any kind of trumped-up charges. The fact was that a number of Balkan-area Islamic groups that had been supported by the State Department had turned out to be terrorist organizations. That was something that State didn't want talked about. The situation in the Balkans was a mess, and the present administration didn't seem to be able to do anything about it as things got worse. Getting Reaper the hell out of the line of fire would be the best Captain Straker could do. He would just have to get by in the civilian world.

Chapter Four

In the years following the massacre of Muslim civilians at the village, the story never left the immediate area of Bosnia or the halls of the U.S. State Department, Intelligence agencies, or military. Coming from a land that had seen the worst of war for years, the story of a handful of villagers being slaughtered didn't make even a footnote in the international news.

The loss of a few personnel to the Intelligence community and the Navy, even the small ranks of Naval Special Warfare, were absorbed without notice. Lives were changed in major ways, without directly affecting the U.S. government in the least. In other parts of the world, the policies of the U.S. administration of the 1990s, especially those of the State Department and Intelligence community, were going to affect the government, and the world.

A large part of the operating funds that al Qaeda and other organizations depend on came from their involvement in the illegal drug trade. Growing opium poppies had always been part of the Afghan farming scene. When Iranian drug merchants came into Afghanistan, fleeing revolutionary justice in Iran, they helped set up drug processing labs inside the country to convert opium first into morphine-base and then into heroin. The high-quality heroin produced was quickly slipped into the drug pipeline.

The Balkans had been developed by al Qaeda and others into a southeastern approach into Europe. The drug pipeline stretched from Afghanistan and central Asia, through the Middle East, north to Bosnia, and on to Italy and beyond.

Heroin flowed by the metric ton from al Qaeda labs in the mountains to addicts in Germany, Norway, and England. These were productive markets and money poured into the coffers of al Qaeda as Afghan heroin saturated Europe. That money helped to finance a number of extensive operations by Islamic extremist groups.

In spite of the success of their narcotics trade, what was desired above all by al Qaeda and their brother organizations was a secure connection into North America and the United States markets. Having returned to the States while still maintaining his contacts in Afghanistan and elsewhere, Cary Paxtun was happy to supply that connection.

Paxtun had come from the large Arab and Muslim community in southeastern Michigan. His ethnic Middle Eastern background had served him well when he had been working as an intelligence agent among the mujahideen in Afghanistan. But he had been out of the United States and away from his home area for a long time.

What Paxtun needed was a local contact to help him set up a major drug distribution network. He found that business partner in Steven Arzee, a younger Muslim who had been running a small nightclub in Detroit. Out of his club, Arzee had also been conducting some drug deals and other illegal business with the assistance of a number of his extended family members.

The fastidious Arzee was not a soldier, in spite of the airs he gave himself. But he was a dedicated Wahhabi Muslim with a good deal of street smarts and some very loyal and trusted men with him. With Paxtun's knowledge and connections and Arzee's manpower, their illegal and legal businesses quickly grew.

Creating private secured bank accounts, money laundering techniques, surreptitious transport of materials across international borders, and other such skills had been part of the trade craft that Paxtun had learned during his time in the intelligence community. This knowledge base, combined with the contacts Paxtun had in the mujahideen brotherhood, helped both Paxtun and Arzee to become very successful.

North of the center of Detroit exist a number of smaller factories surrounded by tract houses and old neighborhoods. A loss of jobs had caused most of the factories to close down years earlier. Both the local neighborhoods and many of the factory buildings fell into a bad state of decay.

One old manufacturing center had undergone a

resurrection of sorts, though not to make cars as it had years before. The Factory, as it was known, was now a nightclub for the adventurous in Detroit. Built on the first floor of the old auto plant, just off the intersection of two major highways, the Factory was a modern playground for the clubbing youth of both the city and the surrounding suburbs. Young Canadians from across the Detroit River in Windsor also came to taste the night life at the Factory.

The Factory had been organized along the lines of a permanently located rave. It had proven itself popular as a rave in spite of the protests of the hard-core rave devotees who insisted that such an event had to remain portable and underground to be a true rave.

With its grittiness and progressive electronic music, the Factory won over even the hard-core ravers. A rave was a place to go to release tensions and burn off excess energies. The subculture who flocked to raves preferred a place that offered them their distinctive style of techno music, dress, dance, and visual effects. It also would allow them to combine the atmosphere with open sexual behavior and consumables that included alcohol and psychedelic chemicals.

What neither the suburban upscale clubbers or the ravers knew was that the Factory was just another means of feeding their decadent habits and taking their money in the process. Many things went on in the six-story old building, besides the frenzied dancing and sexual antics of the clubbers. Those who wanted to could find that there was more than alcoholic drinks and exotic cocktails available to them. Various top-quality drugs were available on the floor of the Factory.

Sales of such things remained inside of the building and a very hard force of security goons saw to it that any entrepreneurs who sought to sell their own wares on Factory grounds quickly chose another line of work, once they had healed. Those who continued to sell never had the chance to heal after dealing with security a second time. The bulk of the security force had been recruited from the Arab community in Dearborn and surrounding areas.

Speaking among themselves mostly in Arabic, the security people distanced themselves from the customers even as they watched them. All the security force were deeply committed believers in Wahhabi Islam, as such they considered themselves immune to the entreaties of even the prettiest of the clubbers.

Local drug gangs let the Factory alone as long as it kept its retail share to itself and didn't extend into their turf. If any of the dealers thought that their wholesalers might be supplied from the Factory, they kept that theory to themselves.

Police and drug enforcement agencies never had any proof to substantiate a search warrant for the Factory. Informants knew better than to even consider dealing any information on the Factory to the authorities. The few who had tried had never been found, except as some unidentified parts left as private examples to others.

The most modern scanning techniques and shielding kept listening devices from ever transmitting from inside the building, and wiretaps turned up nothing useful. The police and DEA never connected more than rumors to the Factory, and that wasn't enough to get a warrant. Not that any authorities expected to get past the first floor of the place with any real chance of finding anything. The huge plant was small only by automotive manufacturer's standards. The block-long edifice was a nightmare to a police agency.

On the first floor, there were still remnants of the conveyor system and frames that had assembled cars decades before. The place could be a whirling flux of gyrating bodies during peak hours, and just a huge area to cover during slack times. All attempts to infiltrate undercover agents into the club had failed. Without having hard intelligence on what was going on inside the building on the upper floors, the police could do nothing. The only thing that was known was that the public owner had his offices on the sixth floor at the east end of the building.

The owners of the Factory according to official documents was a consortium of investors. The listing of investors consisted of other businesses, holding companies, even mutual funds. Following the line of ownership would only result in running up against a blank wall as the paper trail disappeared into foreign finance laws. Liquor licenses and such were all in line with the necessary requirements, no legal details had been missed.

A very stylish Steven Arzee showed himself on the club floor on occasion. He was listed as the executive manager of the club, but he reported to the real manager regularly.

Cary Paxtun had opened the club several years earlier with funds from his overseas investors. He did not maintain quarters or offices in the Factory. The money from the legal aspects of the club were quite lucrative though they were small change in comparison to the profits from the drugs, money laundering, and other activities.

Part of that money had gone through more fronts and businesses to pay for several very major land purchases. Two whole islands in Lake Michigan had been purchased almost outright by Paxtun through cutouts. He now maintained his quarters between a luxury high rise in downtown Detroit and the mansion of a private hunting club on South Wolverine Island in Lake Michigan. Paxtun's privacy was very important to him, and so was the maintaining of cutouts between himself and his trusted lieutenant Steven Arzee.

But in spite of his security and distance between the illegal activities of the Factory and himself, Paxtun was anything but a relaxed man. He had his own bosses that he had to satisfy. The overseas investors who not only had supplied him with funds, but were also his source of high-grade narcotics, had made demands on Paxtun. These demands were ones that he could not refuse, and must not fail to satisfy, and he was in the process of failing them now.

". . . officials said that the quantity of arms seized was the largest ever taken in Canada. Elsewhere in the news . . ."

A thumb punched down hard on the remote control. The TV screen across the room immediately faded to black with a dull "snap" as the sound clicked off. Cary Paxtun looked up from the desk and snarled at Steven Arzee standing nearby.

"How the fuck could this have happened?" Paxtun said. "That route was supposed to be solid. The weapons had been built into the bottom of the shipping container itself and shouldn't have even been detectable through the insulation. There was no reason for anyone to have even been looking at that shipment—we spent a bucketful of money to make everything seem as legitimate as possible."

The fact that Paxtun was cursing indicated just how angry he was—a fact not lost on Arzee. He knew that the situation was a serious one. The seized weapons were intended for people who expected them. They wouldn't have accepted the shipment even being delayed. The fact that the authorities had found them was a disaster.

"It was just blind, stupid, bad luck they were ever discovered," Arzee said. "The Toronto port authorities had asked for a demonstration of a new mobile scanning system. They were trying to meet the demands of the Homeland Security Border and Transportation people. The damned system uses some kind of new X-ray technology called Z(R) Backscatter. It was set up at the exit gate and it checked every container that was going out of the port. The truck driver couldn't have turned around even if he had known about the system.

"I checked with our people in Toronto. None of them knew the system was going to be demonstrated that day. The setup that was being demonstrated was packed in a van that just parked next to the exit. It was just bad luck, there was no way to have foreseen it."

"Bad luck, huh," Paxtun said. "Everything's fucking gone. The guns, the grenades, the missile launchers, the ammo, explosives, everything. A few hundred thousand dollars worth of ordnance just gone with no decent explanation for its being missing, at least not one that Ishmael will be willing to hear. Or do you want to tell him that he won't get his shipment because of bad luck?"

Arzee's face blanched at the idea of telling the terrorist leader any bad news at all. Paxtun could see in his lieutenant's face that he wanted nothing at all to do with Ishmael, that he was terrified of him. And Paxtun couldn't blame Arzee for his fear.

Ishmael was not the man's real name. It was a kunyah, an Arabic pseudonym adopted from the names of the Companions of the Prophet and other heroes of Islam. A kunyah was used to disguise the name of a faithful while he was on a mission.

No matter what this man's real name was, he was dangerous to anyone who blocked his path. As the leader of a major terrorist cell infiltrating into the United States, Ishmael would kill anyone he saw as a threat to his mission. And he would kill them quickly and without hesitation. Paxtun knew the man well because it was Paxtun's organization that was bringing the cell members into the United States and Ishmael had been one of the first men brought in.

The demand to bring in the terrorists had been made of Paxtun by people that he could not refuse. It wasn't a matter of money, or even of stopping the very lucrative flow of drugs he was receiving. You refused al Qaeda only once, and that was when you felt tired of living. Failing them was a quick ticket to Paradise.

After the events of 9/11, the Afghan drug traders there expected U.S. reprisals against targets in their country. That fear caused them to dump their stockpiles of heroin and opium before they could be destroyed by U.S. military action. Accepting a low profit margin was considered better by the traders than a complete loss of their stocks.

A large amount of these drugs found their way into Paxtun's hands. And he took advantage of the situation to build up his distribution network, and profits. The heroin out of Afghanistan was an 80 percent pure narcotic. It was known as Heroin No. 4, or White Heroin, by the addicts who craved it.

Al Qaeda didn't mind the increase in business by Paxtun, they also benefited from the profits of his drug sales. The drugs were simply considered another sign of the decadence of the infidels, another means of attacking them. Osama bin Laden liked destroying the West through its own sins and indulgences. He had specifically financed the development of a new liquid heroin, the "Tears of Allah," to help corrupt the population of the West even faster.

Paxtun, Arzee, and their people had accepted al Qaeda's help, and their money. Paxtun had proven himself trustworthy by his deeds in Afghanistan and his later actions in Bosnia and finally the United States. He had proven himself so trustworthy that his organization was considered a hawala, part of an ancient form of money exchange. A hawala used trusted people around the world as a way to transfer millions of dollars in cash without documents. Money was left in a hawala and the responsible person was simply told who to give it to.

At the moment, Paxtun was holding over several million dollars in cash in an al Qaeda hawala. But that would mean little if he failed to supply Ishmael with what he needed. And Ishmael wouldn't speak to an underling, even one as highly placed as Paxtun's second in command. Arzee was a fellow Muslim, but he hadn't proven himself in the jihad. That meant Arzee was off the hook in telling Ishmael the bad news. It was going to be Paxtun's task, and that had him thinking quickly.

"There were just too many things that could go wrong with the shipment," Paxtun said, "and a number of them did. Delays due to plain bad weather made the ship late. But we planned for that possibility. Now, we've just run out of time. Ishmael has told me to expect the time schedule to change again. He won't tell me the operation, but he's probably going to move the timetable ahead again."

"He's probably never told you his real schedule anyway," Arzee said. "The man is more than paranoid about security. If anything, he's gotten worse about holding back vital information until damned near past the last minute. He even kept the arrival schedule of his men to himself until they were practically waiting at the border. Ever since Khalid Shaikh Mohammed was captured in Pakistan back in March, Ishmael and his bunch have become even tighter about keeping things to themselves."

"We have to accept the situation for the time being," Paxtun said. "We're in way too deep for there to be any way out for us now. There's nothing we can do but carry on supporting Ishmael and his people. Besides, we owe them our lives and they have no problem in reminding us of that fact."

"Well," Arzee said, "at least the money has been good the last couple of years."

"Yes," Paxtun agreed, "there's no question of that. But that's not going to help us. He wants firepower, a lot of it. And he's going to want it right now."

"Supplying something like that's going to be next to impossible," Arzee said. "It's not like anyone advertises heavy firepower and we can't just buy the weapons he wants. Maybe if we had enough time to go out into the underground market. . . ."

"What did you say?" Paxtun asked.

"Go into the underground market?" Arzee said. "I mean the contacts are there. But Ishmael didn't want to trust any kind of black market to supply his needs. And to get what he wants would take time we don't have."

"No, no," Paxtun said with excitement rising in his voice. "What you said before that."

"What?" Arzee said. "Just buy the stuff? There's no way to really do that. It's not like you can just walk into a gunshop and they'll have the kind of hardware we need. Nobody carries that kind of military weapon, no matter what the movies say. And Ishmael is going to want the real deal. Full automatic fire and lots of it."

"So what if we had a source of the guns and someone who could build what we wanted?" Paxtun said.

"Around here?" Arzee said. "Where?"

"Something Nicholas was talking about a while back," Paxtun said.

Raising his voice, Paxtun called out, "Nicholas, get in here."

Nicholas Murat was a cousin of Arzee's. As such, he and his brother Amman, held positions of high trust in the organization. This wasn't a matter of simple nepotism. It was very common in the Arab community for a business to use many members of an extended family. Blood counted for a lot, and loyalties inside of a family were strong.

At first glance, Nicholas and Amman Murat didn't look like brothers at all. Amman was taller than his bother as well as being a bodybuilder. Heavy muscles covered Amman's frame, and he liked to use his strength to solve problems. His mean streak was satisfied when he helped enforce his cousin's directives. And he knew that Paxtun was in charge.

Nicholas Murat was the physical opposite of his brother, but no less mean. His smaller size was balanced out by being much faster than most people. Nicholas hadn't put his speed to use learning a martial art. Instead, he had developed a taste for and skill in the use of firearms. Taste would be something of an understatement. Nicholas was fascinated by guns, all kinds of guns. He made up for his slight stature by using large and powerful weapons. And he kept up on the latest developments in the firearm market.

Moving into the office from his usual position near the outside door, Nicholas came to see what

Paxtun wanted. Not being one to speak a lot, the gunman waited quietly for his boss to speak to him.

"Nicholas," Paxtun asked, "what's the hottest piece of firepower on the market at this moment?"

"That would depend on what you mean, boss," Nicholas said, "hand-held, vehicle mounted, what?"

"Something an individual could use for an assault."

"Well, there's an outfit down in North Carolina that's making a pump-action 40mm grenade launcher. They're reproducing one from the Vietnam War."

"A grenade launcher?" Paxtun said. "No, that would have too many ammunition supply problems for what I'm thinking of. Besides, North Carolina is too far away to consider. Anything made closer to here?"

"There's just been an article published in *Small Arms Review* about a full-automatic shotgun going on the market," Nicholas said as he warmed to his subject. "It was demonstrated earlier this year down in Florida at the SHOT show. It's called the Jackhammer. Ten-round magazine and a really short overall package. Hottest piece of hand-held firepower there is right now, and the company making it isn't more than an hour's drive from here, somewhere up near Port Huron."

"Do you have that magazine available?"

"Yes," Nicholas said, "I was just reading it a while ago."

"Could you get it for me please?" Paxtun said.

As Nicholas left the room, Paxtun sat with a pensive smile on his face. "A machine shotgun," he said. "That would be just the weapon for a fast raiding party. Its effective range would be pretty short compared to a rifle, but close-in, it would rip a target apart."

Quickly returning with an issue of *Small Arms Review* in his hands, Nicholas laid the magazine down on the desk in front of Paxtun. Pointing to the cover, he said, "They must have thought a lot about this weapon themselves, they mentioned the article right on the cover. I marked the page for you there."

Flipping the magazine open to the indicated page, Paxtun just looked at the picture that led off the article. It showed a large man holding a very futuristic-looking weapon. Nicholas took Paxtun's intent look at the article as showing interest in the weapon.

"This was written by Matt Smith," Nicholas said, "he says he was at the demonstration firing. That's it, the Jackhammer Mark 3-A3 shotgun. It's only thirty-one inches overall length. That's barely more than an inch longer than a military M4 carbine with the stock collapsed. And the bullpup design puts the firing mechanism behind the trigger group, that lets the weapon have nearly a twenty-one-inch-long barrel and still be very compact. It's short enough to hide under a coat.

"That big drum at the rear holds ten rounds of twelve-gauge ammo. With magnum 00 buckshot, that's twelve pellets downrange for each shot. It fires on full automatic at four rounds a second—that's sixty-four pellets downrange in one second. That swarm of buckshot can rip a house down. And you reload just by dumping out the drum and slapping a new one in place."

Looking up from the magazine, Paxtun had a strange look on his face.

"You don't have to sell me on this, Nicholas," Paxtun said. "I acknowledge your greater expertise."

Nicholas positively beamed with pride at the unaccustomed praise.

"Where can we find this weapon?" Paxtun asked.

"The address of the shop is at the end of the article," Nicholas said as he pointed back to the magazine. "It's near Marine City north of Lake Saint Clair. The article does say that the Jackhammer is only made as prototypes right now. But it's been months since the SHOT show and they may have gone into production by now."

"Thank you, Nicholas," Paxtun said, "would you excuse us for now?"

As Nicholas left the office, Paxtun looked down at the magazine open in front of him and the smile grew across his face.

"Oh," Paxtun said, "this is too good."

"What?" Arzee said. "The weapon?"

"No," Paxtun said as he turned the magazine around on the desk. Pointing to the picture of the man holding the Jackhammer he said, "This man is Ted Reaper, late of the U.S. Navy. I now believe that this is indeed a very small world."

"Reaper?" Arzee said puzzled. "Reaper? You man that guy who screwed up your deal in Bosnia five years ago?"

"The very same," Paxtun said with a smile. "Allah works in interesting ways. He's not only set the tools we need into our hands, he delivered an old enemy to me. This man crossed me badly once, he will now learn just how foolish that was."

"But you can't imagine he'll sell us what we want?" Arzee said. "And what the hell is he doing in Michigan?"

"Making guns, by the looks of things," Paxtun said. "And no, I certainly wouldn't expect this man to sell us anything no matter what we offered. He's as upright as a Boy Scout. But he will have a weakness, everyone does.

"I want you to find that weakness. Find out everything you can about this man and his business as quickly as you can. And you have to keep it quiet. I don't care what it takes, costs, or what favors you have to call in—you find a handle that we can use to control this man.

"It would be very sweet to force this particular individual to break the law in order to help us. But it will take something very solid to make him hand us over the weapons. If there aren't enough of them available, he can just make more of them. This article lists a shop address and phone numbers. You find out if he has a family, parent, kid, girlfriend, whatever it is that brought him to Michigan or that he has around here. The records are out there, you just have to find them.

"This man tried to take me down once," Paxtun said with hatred in his voice. "Which makes using him all the better."

Chapter Five

A loud buzzing roar filled the small room as the big man in the dark blue shop apron held the long steel bar against the wheel, the flexible cloth buffing wheel spinning at more than 1,700 rpm. With his feet spread out for stability, the big man leaned close to the buffer and ran the long steel bar across the face of the wheel. The buzz increased in volume as the rapidly moving cloth stripped dark, cloudy layers of buffing compound off the surface of the steel—leaving a bright shining surface in its wake.

His face hidden behind the rubber and cloth of a respirator mask and his eyes behind safety goggles, the man leaned into his work, concentrating on the path the steel took as he guided it across the surface of the buffer. His hands were covered in Kevlar gloves, the fingers of which were wrapped in layers of worn tape to insure a good grip. A solid grip was important not only to make sure that the steel was guided properly across the rapidly moving cloth wheel, but also necessary for safety as any observer could quickly see that the object being so carefully buffed and polished by the man was the long blade of a broadsword.

In his dark blue shirt, jeans, and black boots, the man was almost completely still except for his hands guiding the steady passing of the blade back and forth across the wheel. His concentration was on keeping the shape of the blade distinct, smooth, and even—while not allowing the sharp edge to dig into the cloth wheel. The power of the spinning wheel would tear the blade from his hands and drive it into the floor, wall, or possibly something that could bleed quite a bit.

Watching silently from the doorway, the stocky, gray-haired man sitting in a wheelchair knew not to interrupt the man standing at the buffer. He waited quietly until the man at the machine stopped and straightened up. After looking along the edges and body of the blade to be certain he hadn't missed polishing a spot or blurred the lines of the blade's edges and corners, the man switched off the buffer and the wheel whined down to a stop.

Pulling down his respirator, the man turned to the doorway and noticed the individual sitting there. "Oh, didn't know you were there," Ted Reaper said as he pushed the safety goggles up to his forehead.

"Somehow, it didn't seem to me to be a really great idea to bother a man either while he was buffing, or holding a yard of sharp steel," Keith Deckert said with a big grin spreading out under his bushy white mustache, his teeth splitting the features of his face. "But you did want me to remind you when it was coming up to lunchtime."

"Thanks," Ted said as he looked at the watch on

his left wrist. "I've got just enough time to clean and box this thing and get back to the house before Ricky gets home."

"You might want to take a moment to wash up as well," Keith said with a chuckle. "You look like a reversed raccoon."

Catching a glimpse of himself in the glass front of a cabinet, Ted could see that the goggles and respirator had protected his eyes and lungs, but the greasy residue from the buffing wheel had spattered the exposed parts of his face with gray muck. The only parts that were clean were his mouth, mustache, nose, and eyes.

"Here, give me that pigsticker," Keith said. "I'll get the tape off the grip and pack it while you clean up."

"Thanks," Reaper said as he handed over the blade, hilt first.

Deckert turned his powered wheelchair and ran it over to a tall workbench on top of a large parts cabinet where he laid the sword down on a carpeted surface. Turning the armrests inward across his chest, he moved a control and his LifeStand Compact Model LSC wheelchair began to unfold and extend the back and seat upward. In a moment, Deckert was in a standing position, secured to the chair by the armrests, which had formed a padded brace against his chest. In an almost straight up-and-down standing position, the muscular arms of the man could reach the top of the workbench and manipulate the materials there easily and skillfully.

"And a mighty big pig you could stick with it, too," said Keith as he started stripping off the dirty masking tape that had been protecting the finish of the blued-steel cross-guard and wire-wrapped grip.

Reaper stepped away from the grinding room and walked to a small workbench where he kept his own toolbox and materials. He unclipped the small Uncle Mike's pocket holster he had in his right front pants pocket and placed it and the stainless steel Taurus Model 445 five-shot .44 Special concealed-hammer revolver it held into a large central drawer in the toolbox.

Since he had been in the civilian world and not in the military, Reaper had to have a need to go armed. Security was always something you had to think about in a gunshop, even one frequented by customers who were in law enforcement. The shop hadn't always been a gathering place for cops, and civilian customers still came in. It would take a fairly stupid crook to rob a gunshop, but dumber things had happened.

Moving across the workshop, Reaper went over to the opposite wall where a large utility sink stood next to a long, shallow, steel tank with a tight-fitting cover.

There was a smell of solvents coming up from the covered cleaning tank, but the smell would have been a lot worse if the shop had been hot. The tall, barnlike shop building was well insulated against the winter cold or summer heat, both of which could get pretty extreme in southeastern Michigan. But even if it wasn't as heavily insulated as it was, there would be little enough to hear in the way of noise this far out in the country.

The steel building was attached to the back of a

two-story brick farmhouse and sat on twenty-five acres of land less than five miles from the Saint Clair River and the border between the U.S. and Canada. The location was closer to Port Huron than Detroit, both cities being less than an hour's drive away. The area was open countryside with stands of trees separating fields. The house and barn were set back from the main road, a quarter-mile of black-topped driveway leading to a semicircular drive at the front of the house, with an extension leading out to the back shop building.

It was an out-of-the-way location for a business, but that's what the farmhouse and steel barn had been converted into. The front part of the first floor of the house was a gunshop, the barn a well-equipped machine shop with facilities for polishing and finishing metal and wood.

D & R POLICE SUPPLIES AND GUNSMITHS was all it said on a small sign on the white siding at the front of the house. The sign was a fairly new one, the paint on it being much fresher than that of the tan-painted twin doors leading into the house. The doors were at the top of a long ramp, allowing the owner's wheelchair easy access to the building.

There would be plenty of room for additional workers once business picked up. The gunsmithing and small gun shop had been at the farm for a number of years, but the police supply business was new. So for now, there were just the two men living and working in the building.

The farm and buildings were both owned by Keith Deckert, a big, gray-haired ex-Army sergeant who had lost the use of his legs several years earlier in a racing accident. Outside of the limitations on his mobility, the only thing remarkable about Deckert's body was that his arms, shoulders, and chest were even more muscular than when he had been an Army Ranger.

As Reaper was scrubbing his face and arms, Deckert was polishing the grip and hilt of the sword with a soft cloth.

"Damned big for a knife," Deckert said with a chuckle. "This from some movie or something? One of those Harry Potter books? Conan?"

"Sort of," Reaper said from across the room. "Ricky saw one like it in that Hobbit movie, *Lord of the Rings: The Two Towers.* Apparently, there's a sword like it in some role-playing game he's into with his friends."

As he was drying his face and hands on a wad of paper towels, Reaper walked over to where his friend was placing the sword in a long, wooden box. The shining blade, diamond-shaped and double edged, was thirty-six inches long with a simple blued-steel cross guard. The round disc pommel was also blue steel and secured an eight-inch grip that was covered with twisted steel wire. The pattern of the wire seemed to almost flow in an optical illusion as you kept looking at it.

"Hopefully, he'll like it," Reaper said as he tossed the wad of towels in a trash can. He looked with a critical eye at the blade lying on a bed of red velvet in the long, polished wood case, but could see no flaws in it. "I made it real, not a toy. It'll be something that can stay with him forever if he wants, maybe better than his old man did."

"Things haven't improved between you and Mary?" Deckert asked quietly.

"No," Reaper said with a note of sadness in his voice. "And I'm not sure they ever will. But I have to make certain that Ricky knows it isn't his fault and that I still love him. So I made this for him, something from my own hands."

"Well, it's a little big for him now," Deckert said. "But I'm pretty sure he'll grow into it. You'll have to get him fencing lessons so he knows how to swing one."

"You don't learn how to wave one of these around in classical fencing," Reaper said. "He's getting into something called the Society for Creative Anachronism, SCA they call it. Bunch of kids, some adults, too, get together and re-create the knights of old. They stage sword fights with padded fake blades and other weapons."

"Uh-huh," Deckert said, "sounds weird as hell. But at least it doesn't seem like something that would keep him sitting in front of a computer all day."

Reaper closed the lid on the long wooden case and secured it in place with two brass latches. Picking it up by the leather handle, he turned to the nearby door that led into the house.

"Nope," Reaper said, "the boy does like his activities. Gets out and moves around, better than a lot of kids today. He's smart enough to like getting on his computer and playing games with his friends. But he doesn't spend all day sitting in front of a computer or game console."

"Sitting down all the time isn't necessarily all bad," Deckert said as he pushed a control and his wheelchair started to slowly collapse back into a sitting configuration. Chuckling at his friend's mild embarrassment at what he had said, Deckert turned to the doorway and started to roll toward it.

"So, you hear that news out of Canada?" Deckert said, to let his friend off the hook and change the subject.

"What news?" Reaper said. "I've mostly been in the grinding room the last few days and the noise level isn't the best for listening to the radio."

"There's these great new inventions called headsets," Deckert said as he rolled through the door Reaper was holding open. "You should look into them. At any rate, seems that Canadian customs up in Toronto found some container ship with a bunch of guns and ammunition on it. At least they found one container with a load of hardware hidden in the walls—you know how the news exaggerates these kinds of things."

"Yeah," said Reaper following Deckert out of the shop and into the house. "They find a couple of boxes of shells and two weapons in a takedown and the guy had an arsenal of guns and ammunition. So what did they find really? Did you hear?"

"Seems it really was a bunch of small arms," Deckert said. "Real bad-guy stuff. Military AK-47s, RPG-7s, ammunition, even grenades and explosives."

"Shit," Reaper said surprised. "Sounds like they

busted a supply run for some terrorist cell. Did they get any leads on where the stuff was going?"

"Not that I heard," Deckert said. "According to the news, they didn't know if the stuff had arrived for some Canadian group or was headed somewhere else. It was close enough that it could have been heading here to Michigan, Chicago, or maybe that big ship terminal down in Toledo. The Canadians made a great big deal of finding the stuff, not a hell of a lot of guns in the Great White North."

"They would have made a big deal of finding that kind of stash even here in Detroit," Reaper said. "Good to see that the security is starting to work."

"Yeah, well you better change into something a little cleaner than those clothes before you head to see Mary and Ricky," Deckert said as he rolled past the kitchen of the house and into the office that had originally been the dining room.

"There's an idea," Reaper agreed as he laid the sword case on the kitchen counter and headed to the stairs leading to the second floor. He had been living in the shop/house for some months now—ever since he had separated from Mary, his wife of fifteen years. Times had been hard since he was forced to leave the service, and he knew that he hadn't treated his family the best way that he could in the intervening years.

Losing his career and being forced to leave without any retirement or benefits had been hard—both financially and emotionally. He had gone out with his buddies from the Teams a few too many times while the family lived down in Imperial Beach in Southern California. It was when his old friend and

Teammate Bear, who had now retired from the Navy, had looked him up that things had seemed as though they would improve.

Bear had said that there was a friend of his back in Michigan who could use some help. Being that Reaper had spent more than a little time working in the armory, and had learned metalworking in high school, Bear thought he would be a great addition to his friend's gun shop. It was the chance for a good job doing something Reaper would like.

Going out to Michigan, Reaper met Keith Deckert for the first time and the two men hit it off well. Mary and Ricky were tired of moving across the country as they had so many times when Reaper was in the Navy. But he had sworn that this would be the last time. The bulk of the family's savings had been spent in making the move.

Things had improved a bit in Michigan for the Reaper household, at least the cost of living was a hell of a lot better than it was in Southern California. Mary had been able to do part-time teaching, which she had always loved. Ricky was making friends in school now. He even was starting to like winter sports, not exactly the sort of thing he could have done in the San Diego area.

In spite of the good things, there was still a lot of hardships. Reaper wasn't making much money at the gun shop. It was grating against Reaper that his family was living more on what his wife made as a substitute teacher than on his earnings. The lack of his retirement pay was keenly felt at least once a month. But he was working hard to change that.

Months earlier, Reaper had put forward the idea

of making his friend's small custom gunsmithing shop into a larger business. The production rights were available for the Jackhammer assault shotgun and Reaper felt he had the contacts to make it a successful seller. The big growth in Homeland security, customs, and police response units looked to be a good source of revenue. Deckert agreed and had put in his savings to expand the business. They secured the rights to the Jackhammer shotgun and had built a number of prototypes. These had been displayed and demonstrated by Reaper at a number of police, military, and trade shows.

The new shop had missed out on the market that had boomed just a few months before with the outbreak of the Iraq war. The Jackhammer had not been picked up by any of the services yet. Losing that business had put Ted Reaper back in the dumps, especially since his friend Keith Deckert had risked his farm and home as collateral to expand the shop.

That depression had resulted in more than one argument in the Reaper household. Finally, he had separated from Mary, moving into one of the mostly unused upstairs bedrooms at the farmhouse. Deckert had told him that the rooms weren't a lot of use for him right now, he had already converted the downstairs family room into a bedroom to keep from having to use a lift to get up and down the stairs.

So Ted had moved out of his home, leaving his wife and twelve-year-old son living in the small house they had bought with what they got out of the place they had sold in Imperial Beach. The house was in a nice, old neighborhood south of Mount

Clemens—and only a relatively short ride from the farm on Ted's Harley. His 1983 Electra-glide was a holdover from his Team days.

Deckert had a hell of a nice garage, fitting for an old Detroit-area gearhead. He still had the hot rod that was built up from an old Checker cab, and his customized 2001 Chevy Venture van. The van had a power lift installed on the driver's side rear door that Keith could strap his wheelchair into. Once in the van, he locked his chair in place and could drive the van with its modified controls. There was still room in the garage for Reaper's bike. Even some space left over for a good collection of weights and work-out gear.

After changing into a clean pair of Levi's and a thick black sweater—it could still get cold in Michigan on a bike, even in mid-May, just the month before there had been a winter snowstorm—Reaper placed the sword case in a green canvas barracks bag to protect it and strapped it to the back of his bike. Slipping on his leather jacket and helmet, he climbed onto the bike and started up the engine. Hitting the remote secured to his handle bars, the overhead door opened up behind him. He pushed the bike back out of the garage and roared off on his way.

Chapter Six

The ride wasn't a long one, and the spring air made it a pleasant run. There were long stretches of open country roads between the shop and where Reaper's home had been. The earthy, wet smell of the marshes that lay along some of the roads helped clear away the gloomy thoughts that Reaper had about coming from where he lived now rather than going home.

The trees lining the street that his old home was on were growing leaves fast, and the bud husks all around the ground crunched under his wheels as he turned up the driveway of a modest single-floor, ranch-style house in a working-class family neighborhood. In spite of the bright promise of new life on the sunny day, pulling up to the house just didn't feel like coming home anymore.

Ricky hadn't come barging out of the house as the bike pulled in, so he probably wasn't home from school yet. Mary was standing in the doorway, an unreadable expression in her brown eyes as she watched Reaper set the kickstand on the bike and climb off the seat. The sight of the slender, blond woman still stirred feelings in Reaper, but the lack of greeting in her face told him that the feelings probably were not mutual.

"Hello, Mary," Reaper said as he walked up to the door. "Is Ricky home from school yet?"

"No, not yet," Mary said as she stood to the side and opened the door. "He wanted to stop by a friend's house on the way home to see some new game or other. He should be home any moment now. You know you're late, don't you?"

As Reaper stepped into the house, his shoulders slumped a little at Mary's accusatory tone. A feeling of fatigue crossed through him was he walked into the living room, carrying the barracks bag that he had taken from the bike. The home was small, but it was clean and tastefully furnished. He knew that was all Mary's doing. His tastes were what she considered "military spartan" when she was being polite. And it did make for a good place to raise a boy, in spite of the chill Reaper felt in the air.

"And what's that?" Mary said as Reaper drew the long wooden case from the barracks bag and laid it down on a low cabinet along the wall of the living room.

"Something I've been making for Ricky," Reaper said as he unlatched the case. "It's a sword from that movie he liked so much, *The Two Towers.* There's some reproductions of the movie blades on the market, but this is a lot more like the real thing."

"A sword?" Mary said with exasperation in her voice. "That's what you consider a present for him?

Just what is he supposed to do with it? He's a twelve-year-old boy and you made him a weapon an adult would have a hard time handling."

Suddenly, Mary stopped talking and just looked at the floor. When she lifted her head, she looked as if she hadn't slept in a day.

"You said things would change," Mary continued in a tired voice, "I waited after you had to leave the Navy, and things didn't change. You went through job after job and things didn't change. No job was good enough, or exciting enough if you really want to be honest about the situation. You spent your time training and staying in shape in case something came through that would let you strap a holster on again—and it never did.

"You never spent enough time with Richard. You still call him Ricky. He prefers the more mature name Richard now. Instead of learning what your own son liked, you were always trying to make things better for us, and just succeeded in making them worse. You weren't there for us when you were in the Teams, and you aren't there for us now. Instead, you try to buy your way back into a boy's heart with gifts—long, sharp, deadly gifts."

"It's not all that sharp," Reaper said.

"And that means what coming from a SEAL?" Mary said sharply. "That you can't shave with it?

"Oh, Ted," she continued in a sad tone of voice, "don't you see that nothing has changed really? I know that your heart's in the right place, but your judgment is still flawed. This is just an example of that. He's just a twelve-year-old boy, and not even that until his birthday next month.

"Now you go and make him this extravagant gift. It's not a toy, or something he can safely play with. It's not even something that he can show his friends outside of the house. It's a weapon. One made for a man, not a young boy. If he was to take this to school to show the class what his father had made him, do you know what they would do? They would expel him for bringing a weapon onto school grounds!"

Reaper made a strong effort not to raise his voice or get angry. He was not going to let his boy come into the house just to hear his parents having another argument, a habit that they had been seeming to fall into every time they got together over the last months. But he was getting heated up, Mary knew instinctively which of his hot buttons to push, even when she didn't seem to intentionally want to. This lecturing-schoolteacher mode of hers was one that had always grated on him.

This was what their marriage had become, one long set of arguments. Sometimes the fights had been about money, a lot of the time it had been about work, or his drinking, or his going out with friends until all hours of the night. Sometimes, the reason for the arguments just seemed to be to have a fight. It wasn't how two people were supposed to live with each other, certainly not while trying to raise a young son. It was the constant fighting that had finally driven Reaper out of the house, officially separating the marriage, months before.

He knew that a lot of what was wrong came from his frustrations at trying to start up a new career. He had been exercising hard, working out with weights and running, to try and burn out some of the stresses he had been feeling. But here he was with his wife again, and she had made him feel inadequate and stupid within minutes of his entering the house. And what she had to say next made him feel worse.

"I just can't keep going on like this, Ted," Mary said, "and I won't. It's not healthy for either of us or for Richard. I've contacted the lawyer and told him to go ahead with the paperwork for the divorce."

"You didn't have to go through with that," Reaper said. "We said we would give it some time and try to get things back together. This," he pointed at the sword, "this was just what I could do right now. I'm not trying to make up for anything by giving him this. I thought he could put it up on his wall and think of his old man. I'm trying to make it better, the shop, the work, it all has a chance of getting better. It will just take some time. . . ."

"I did give it time, Ted," Mary said cutting him off. "And things haven't gotten any better. You know it scares me when you come home sometimes now. I never know if you've gone out and tied one on again. And Richard is afraid, too. The lawyer told me that if I had a restraining order put out on you, it would cost you your job. That the new gun laws would make it illegal for you to have firearms if there was a restraining order in force against you. So please, just listen to what I want and leave. You can see Richard some other time."

Reaper just stood there for a moment frustrated at the situation and the fact that he couldn't do anything about it. He wouldn't take it out on this woman, whom he had loved deeply and was the mother of his son. This wasn't a fight he had been trained for—though the situation was common enough among the men of the Teams. Right now, it would be better if he left rather than say something to make the situation even worse.

"Please let Ricky, I mean Richard, have the sword when he gets home," Reaper said tightly as he kept a grip on himself. "You can always just put it away until he's older. Tell him that I love him and I'll see him later."

"All right," Mary said, "I will. But please call first before you come over. I'll let you know what the plans are for his birthday next month."

"Thank you for that much," Reaper said as he turned to the door. Seething with anger but keeping it tightly under control, he went to his bike and kick-started it hard. He backed out of the driveway and roared down the street. His anger at the situation was clouding what would otherwise be a constant alertness to his surroundings. He never noticed the Ford van parked down the street with its engine running, with two men sitting in the front seats of the van and watching his house. As he turned the corner a block away and sped on, he never saw the van start moving forward toward his house.

During the ride back to the shop, Reaper considered just keeping going for a while. The words of Bob Seger and the Silver Bullet Band's song "Roll Me Away" ran though his head. He was more than "tired of his own voice" in the words of the song. But he wasn't going to be feeling free for a while, he had responsibilities to others and headed back to the shop. But the thought of heading to the mountaintops sure sounded good at the moment.

Once back at the shop, Reaper put his bike back on the kickstand and went into the house. Without looking for Deckert, who had already heard the garage door slam behind the big SEAL, Reaper headed back to his workbench in the shop. He slipped his Taurus back into his pocket, securing the spring clip that held the holster in place more from habit than from really thinking about it.

Pulling a stock Springfield Armory M1911A1 .45 automatic from the work rack next to his bench, he began to strip the weapon down in preparation to doing some custom work on it as ordered by a customer.

As he manipulated the parts of the pistol with an ease from long practice, Reaper found that he just couldn't concentrate on his work. After a few minutes of doing basically nothing with the gun, Reaper put the box he had placed the parts in back into a rack next to his bench and went up into the house to find Deckert.

"Keith," Reaper said as he entered the front showroom of the shop, "I'm going out for a run around the block."

Looking up from where he was bent over a log book on the front counter, Deckert just said, "okay," and went back to what he was reading. Deckert knew that Reaper was angry about whatever had happened back at his old home. Probably had another argument with Mary, was Deckert's thought.

The situation was too bad, he had hoped the couple would be able to get their problems behind them.

But Reaper was going out for a run, so things hadn't gone well.

An old habit from the Teams: when you felt bad, go for a run, when you felt good, go for a run. Hell, when it was raining, sunny, hot, or cold—you went for a run. And considering that the "blocks" in their part of the country tended to be one mile on a side, at least if you only counted the paved roads, Reaper was probably going to be gone for a while.

Reaper hadn't done anything more to prep for the run other than take his shop apron off and leave it by his bench. Trotting off down the road, the SEAL set out at an easy pace. Passing up the first side road, Reaper continued on with his feet steadily eating up the distance. The warm sun, clean air, and sounds of the spring peeper frogs in the ditches helped clear his mind. As he turned onto a one-mile run to the next major road, he was starting to feel better.

There wasn't anyone talking, there weren't any life decisions to make. There was just the steady effort of putting one foot in front of the other, the sound of his own easy breathing in his ears, and the country road stretching out in front of him. Keith Deckert referred to Reaper's penchant for working out as "getting his endorphin fix." The ex-Army sergeant was probably right, though Reaper would always say that he had to stay in shape for the training contracts they hoped to get for their new business.

Reaper had spent a tour of duty in the Teams as a First Phase instructor at BUD/S, the basic Underwater Demolition/SEAL course, teaching land warfare among other skills. Combined with his other experiences in the Teams, he could be a real asset to a police or security organization, training their people to face the new threats in the post-9/11, Operation Iraqi Freedom and Operation Enduring Freedom, United States. That was what he had convinced his friend Keith was a real business opportunity.

So they had extended themselves in the shop. They now had their Type 07 federal firearms license and had paid for their special occupational tax stamp.

All that expensive paper meant that they could deal in any kind of firearm, including National Firearms Act (NFA) weapons such as automatic weapons, suppressors, short shotguns, and the like. That was how they had legally obtained the license to produce the Jackhammer. Now they could stock additional NFA weapons, such as they could afford, in order to demonstrate them for possible sales to police departments. Along with the guns, they were carrying a select line of police and security equipment.

Even with the possible divorce, maybe Reaper could still make things work out between himself and Mary—for the sake of their son if not for themselves. He had stopped drinking almost altogether—the exercise had helped with that. Besides, he didn't have his Teammates around at all hours as they had been in San Diego. Which was actually something that he missed from time to time.

As he started approaching the shop, Reaper's mind was calmer than it had been when he set out for his run forty-two minutes earlier and six miles ago. As he approached the shop, he could see two cars in the driveway in front of the house. One of the cars was a black 2000 Pontiac Grand Am GT. A nice enough car and not the usual thing that was parked in front of the shop.

The other car in the drive was a real classic, a 1972 silver Corvette Stingray hardtop, complete with the chrome bumpers, the last year they had produced the car in that style. The fiberglass-bodied sports car looked like a low, flat shark with a bright silver grin. As Reaper trotted up to the front door of the shop, he figured maybe he was spending too much time talking about cars with an old-school Detroit gear-head like Deckert.

The overall good feeling Reaper had from his run evaporated instantly as he stepped through the doors of the farmhouse and turned into the retail showroom of the shop. He quietly took in the stunning scene without showing any surprise or emotion. Deckert was sitting in his chair at the far right corner of the customers area of the showroom. He was on the public side of the counters, but that was the least of what was wrong in the room. Reaper immediately accessed the situation as a combat equation—and the factors of that equation were three other men in the room.

In the center of the room was a slender man of medium height and slightly swarthy complexion. In his light brown camel's hair blazer, gray woolen trousers, light blue silk shirt with a silver silk tie, and black leather kidskin gloves, Arzee looked like a country gentleman who might be trying out top-grade double shotguns prior to going out on a grouse hunt. The Jackhammer shotgun in his hands looked like anything but a graceful hunting weapon. Still, the open breech of the weapon told Reaper that it was empty and the man wasn't an immediate threat.

The tailored suit and styled haircut did not disguise the oily nature of the man underneath it all. His highly polished black oxford shoes looked as if they were replaced immediately if they were ever scuffed. From all of the man's carefully crafted style, Reaper figured he knew who drove the Corvette, the man he was identifying as Suit.

The glass display case on the wall behind the Suit was empty. That was where the four prototype Jackhammers had been racked up. The long boxes of ammunition cassettes that had been on the bottom of the case were missing along with the other three guns. These three thugs did not appear to be running a simple gun robbery, otherwise they would have probably just shot Reaper as he came in the door. No, they had been waiting for him to return from his run. There was something more they wanted.

Reaper's training and experience had him immediately identifying the levels of threat in the room, assessing the situation, and quantifying his response. For all of its complexity, his reactions spanned barely seconds before he had completed his judgments. He didn't know the threat's names, and didn't care. Reaper quickly put his own identifiers, as good as a name to him, on the strangers in the room.

Immediately to his right, barely a step away, was a thug who Reaper categorized as little more than a musclehead. Maybe five feet ten, 235 pounds, with swarthy skin and buzz-cut black hair, the thug was heavily muscled with almost no neck showing. The tan sports jacket and black turtleneck sweater were probably intended by the man to maximize the visual impact of his size.

The muscles looked to have come from hours of pumping iron, but their appearance told Reaper that this was a vain man. Although his workouts were the kind that increased the size of his chest and arms, the musclehead didn't look like he spent as much time on his legs, building up his size in a more symmetrical manner.

The man also moved stiffly, musclebound from all of his exercise. In spite of a more limited range of motion in his arms and legs, the big man was fast enough. Stepping up behind Reaper, the musclehead grabbed the SEAL from behind, securing a solid grip on both of his upper arms. The thug held no weapon and probably thought with his muscles and little else. But at that moment, he didn't need a weapon.

To the left, standing behind the Suit so that he could clearly cover both Reaper and Deckert, was a gunman who was pointing a massive Desert Eagle semiautomatic pistol at Reaper. The gunman had covered the SEAL from the moment he had entered the room. The muzzle of the big pistol looked to be about a .44-magnum caliber.

The gunman was only about five four in height, slight in build with tan skin, black hair, and a bushy mustache, wearing a loose brown sports jacket, unbuttoned over a black shirt and black pants. Reaper classified him as a gun weasel—he had the look of a little man who had something to prove with a big gun. That big gun made him the most immediate visible threat in the room.

He may have been slight in stature, but the gun weasel held the Desert Eagle in a steady hand. The hammer was back on the big pistol. That fact cut back on the possible openings for Reaper to secure the gun.

But who in his right mind would carry such a massive piece of hardware? The gun was impractical to carry concealed for someone even Reaper's size, and it was heavy to drag around as well. For all of its weight, the power of the Desert Eagle made it a real handful to control. But that same power was probably why this gun weasel carried such a piece—compensation for his stature and build.

The little man had the only two threatening weapons visible in anyone's hands in the showroom. The Desert Eagle remained steady in the man's right hand while his left kept covering Deckert with an M1911A1 .45 automatic. By the look of the smoldering hate combined with frustration in Deckert's face, the gun weasel was probably adding insult to injury by threatening him with his own weapon.

Reaper noted the location of everyone in the room and cataloged their probable threat level. He just watched as the man snapped the thumb safety on to the M1911A1 and slipped the pistol into the waistband of his trousers. As the gun weasel approached Reaper, he pulled the big Desert Eagle back against his right hip, keeping it out of the way of a chance grab. Reaper didn't move at all as the other man used his free left hand to snatch the Taurus revolver from Reaper's right front pocket.

After slipping the Taurus into his own pocket, the gun weasel conducted a cursory pat-down. With a curt "he's clean," the gun weasel stepped back away from Reaper. The little man didn't realize just how serious a mistake he had made in his poorly done search. He had taken the obvious weapon, but hardly the only one the SEAL had.

In Reaper's right front pocket, clipped behind the holster and along the rear seam of the Levi's, was a green G10-handled Emerson CQC-7BW folding knife. The 3.3-inch-long chisel-ground Tanto-style blade was razor-sharp. Not exactly a sword, but better than nothing in the hands of a trained man. And Reaper was a very well-trained man.

Chapter Seven

Turning to the counter to his right, Arzee casually set the Jackhammer shotgun down before turning back to Reaper.

"Mister Reaper, I presume," Arzee said with a small smile, "so good to meet you. I've read excellent things about your work here."

"You'll have to excuse me if I don't shake hands," Reaper said. "And you are?"

"Yes," Arzee said, "well, I thought it would be necessary for my friend there behind you to restrain your enthusiasm lest it get the better of you. And I think we can forgo the formality of names for now."

Reaper could see the reflection of the man he now thought of as Musclehead, in the glass of a display case. The big thug smiled broadly at Arzee's words and squeezed down hard on both of Reaper's upper arms. Reaper showed no reaction to the crushing of his arms. His hands started turning dark red and then Musclehead lightened up his grip after a sharp word from Arzee. Gun Weasel, the SEAL's name for the little man, just kept watch on Reaper and Deckert, no smile, no reaction, and no wavering of the big Desert Eagle in his hand.

Sure of his own strength, Musclehead was holding Reaper in what he considered a firm, unbreakable grip. But Reaper knew half a dozen ways he could disable Musclehead and break free in a moment. Gun Weasel was another matter entirely. After he had put away Reaper's and Deckert's guns, he had moved to a spot on the other side of the room where he would watch both men without having to turn his head. He knew the weapons he was holding gave him range, and he was using that distance as a safety measure.

Gun Weasel was more than six feet from Reaper. If the range had been four feet, Reaper may have had a chance. But more than six feet was too far away. One thing Reaper had was patience. The Suit wanted to talk about something. If this had been a robbery or some kind of straightforward murder, Reaper and Deckert would already be dead. So the SEAL stayed very alert, watching for his opportunity to show itself. It would come, and he could wait for it while listening to what Arzee had to say.

The thugs did not know how hopelessly they were outclassed. But Arzee knew, or at least suspected. The specter of sudden death was fluttering its leathery wings around the room, and that was making Arzee nervous. In the final analysis, Arzee was nothing more than a street thug who had made good. Now, he was looking at someone who was truly dangerous—a cleaned-up junkyard dog was looking at a timber wolf.

"I wouldn't want anything to happen to you until we concluded our business," Arzee said to Reaper.

"This is not the way people normally conduct a business meeting," Reaper said. "Besides, what possible business could I have with you?"

"Why, the gun business, of course," Arzee said. "It seems I'm in need of someone with the proper materials. This weapon of yours is just the thing to aid some associates of mine. We already have the others packed away outside, I was just admiring this specimen as you came in."

"You have got to be out of your fucking mind," Reaper said. "What kind of crack-brained raghead idea is that? You catch something that affected your mind while out there butt-fucking these girls you brought with you?"

Reaper was speaking with deliberate crudity. If he could get this character to lose his temper and get in the line of fire between himself and Gun Weasel, that could make the opportunity Reaper needed to begin his move. But Arzee wasn't taking the bait.

"Please, Mr. Reaper," Arzee said. "You are much more intelligent than that. I realize that you are not going to do business with me openly—you never would. I couldn't offer you enough money to do so. And these men aren't going to be what it takes to convince you to supply what I want. They could break you into pieces and you would try to spit in my eye with your last breath—and by the looks your partner there is giving me, he would do the same if not more."

Deckert just sat in his chair and looked at Arzee. He also had lots of patience and would wait as long as needed. Deckert knew the limitations his wheelchair gave him, but he also knew that if he could force an opening, Reaper would react to the chance. He didn't know these people from Adam, but it was obvious that at least the snappy dresser had history with Reaper. Suddenly, a cellular phone began to ring.

"Excuse me for a moment," Arzee said with exaggerated courtesy as he reached into his pocket. Pulling out a phone, he snapped it open and listened to it for a moment.

"Ah, as I expected," Arzee said. "It's for you, Mr. Reaper."

Reaching out, he set the phone down on the carpet-covered counter and slid it to within reach of Reaper. Musclehead turned Reaper toward the counter and released his right arm.

"Careful now," Arzee said to Reaper as Gun Weasel pointed the Desert Eagle and pulled up the M1911A1 with his left hand. "I'm certain that this call will be very important to you."

Reaper's face showed no expression as he reached for the phone. He was puzzled as to just what might be going on, but he was also still watching for his opportunity. The voice at the other end of the phone caused Reaper's blood to run cold for a moment. A buzzing seemed to fill his ears as he heard a quavering voice at the other end of the line. A very familiar voice.

"Hello?" said Mary, with stark terror obvious in her tone. "Ted? Is that you?"

"Mary," Reaper said with a catch in his voice, "are you all right?"

"They haven't hurt me," she said. "Two men

wearing masks barged in just after you left. They waited until Ricky came home and took us both from the house. They put blindfolds on us and made me make some phone calls after driving us somewhere.

"Oh, Ted," Mary said as her voice started to break down completely. "I'm so scared. Why is this happening to us? What do they want? Who are these peop . . ."

And the phone was cut off at the other end of the line.

"Before you make any unnecessary threats of retribution," Arzee said, relaxing now as he felt he fully had the upper hand, "let me tell you that nothing is going to happen to your family as long as you do what I want."

He reached forward and took the phone from the SEAL's unresisting hand. Folding it, Arzee slipped it into Reaper's shirt pocket.

"You will be contacted on that phone with further details," Arzee said. "It's completely untraceable so there's no use trying to track me down with it. Only I have the number to it, so only I will call you on it. Please do not feel beholden for the small gift, I have another I assure you," and he patted his inside jacket pocket.

"Do as I say and complete our business, and the last call will be directions for you to meet up with your family. Oh, and I really wouldn't bother calling in the police or FBI. It seems your wife called some people and told them that she was leaving the area with your son for a while. She didn't feel quite safe what with a pending divorce and all. So she took your son out of school, made herself unavailable for work, and, for all intents and purposes, has disappeared for a while. Seems having an ex-SEAL for a husband makes a woman being frightened for herself quite understandable to some people.

"So, even if you go to the police," Arzee said with a broad smile, "the chances are that they will blame you for her being missing.

"And the words of a fellow veteran," Arzee said as he turned to Deckert, "would at best be discounted. If not, well, I'm sure you can figure out that very little evidence will be found. And you can't be sure just where that evidence would point."

"It seems you have all the bases covered," Reaper said calmly. "What do you want me to do?"

If Arzee had known the big SEAL at all, he would have recognized that soft tone of voice as being the warning of a very dangerous situation. Paxtun hadn't known that in Bosnia, and Arzee didn't know it now. Reaper was fluid and smooth, and ready to explode into action, with nothing showing as a warning at all.

"I will be leaving first," Arzee said, "just so there are no misunderstandings. Neither of my two companions here know where your family will be staying, so they couldn't tell you anything if they wanted to.

"After I am safely away, you and your partner here will set to work making more of these nasty pieces of firepower. You have three days, seventy-two hours from now, to produce four more of these weapons along with a half-dozen of these ammunition cassettes for each of them. I have been told that is a reasonable number and shouldn't be any problem for you to make.

"And I assure you, if any problems do arise, you

had better solve them instantly or someone else very dear to you will pay the penalty. You simply deliver the weapons and we will have concluded our business. Your family will be returned to you and we will go on our way."

"How do I know I can trust you to return my family no matter what I give you?" Reaper said.

"You don't," Arzee said with a nasty smile. "But your options are very limited. I suggest you and your partner plan on some long work days. Make a big pot of coffee."

With that, Arzee headed toward the door. Even Gun Weasel was more relaxed as he let Arzee pass through the line of fire between him and Reaper, dropping down the Eagle's muzzle as the man went by. But he still had the .45 aimed at Deckert, so that was not the opportunity Reaper was looking for.

Musclehead was still holding Reaper by the arms, though his grip on the SEAL's right arm was very light. Arzee went out the door and the men all heard the sound of a 454 cubic inch Big Block V-8 fire up a few moments later. The rumble of the engine's 270 horsepower quickly faded as the Corvette moved up the driveway and turned west down the main road.

"So, little man," Deckert said as he looked at Gun Weasel. "Your boss left you holding the bag while he made sure of his getaway?"

Gun Weasel turned and looked coldly at the big man in the wheelchair.

"Feels neat doesn't it?" Deckert said. "You come along just so that you could look down at somebody shorter than you? That must be it. Little man, great big gun. You probably need such a stupid gun because you hit like a pussy. I wonder just what you're trying to compensate for? Short stature or short something else?"

With a sudden movement, Gun Weasel stepped forward and snapped out with his left hand, backhanding the steel slide of the .45 across the left side of Deckert's head. The blow rocked the big man in his wheelchair as blood spurted from a cut on his left ear. It was just by luck that the cushioning of the ear had kept the blow from breaking the squamous portion of the temporal bone of Deckert's skull.

As the big man slumped in the chair, Gun Weasel suddenly laid the .45 down on the counter to his right and grabbed the armrest of the chair. Twisting and lifting hard, Gun Weasel flipped up the chair and dumped Deckert to the ground. Deckert lay slumped and unmoving as Gun Weasel panted at the exertion. It had been a much heavier chair than he had expected. Turning, he faced Reaper—less than four feet away.

Without a single outward sign of preparation or tension, Reaper exploded, suddenly snap-kicking Gun Weasel square in the groin. The top of Reaper's foot drove Gun Weasel's scrotum up into his pubic arch, the testicles just missing being crushed against the juncture of the ossa innominata bones of the pelvis.

The intense pain of the blow drove a cloud of blackness through Gun Weasel's brain as green and yellow lights flashed in front of his eyes. The small man wasn't dead, but he was going to wish he was when the blessing of unconsciousness wore off. He slipped to the ground as the huge Desert Eagle pistol fell from his nerveless fingers.

As part of the same action with which he snap-kicked Gun Weasel, Reaper shoved back with his left leg, forcing himself back against Musclehead. The SEAL's powerful leg smashed Musclehead's back against the shelving units on the wall behind him. A steel reloading press extending out from a shelf smashed into the thug's back, bruising his right kidney and forcing him to throw up his right hand in shock.

Reaper smashed back with an open-fist backhand blow from his right arm, striking Musclehead above his right eye, splitting open his eyebrow. Reversing the motion of his hand and arm, Reaper snapped his right hand into his right front pants pocket.

A practiced grip secured the Emerson CQC-7BW between the thumb and first two fingers of Reaper's hand. Continuing the motion, Reaper smoothly drew the folding knife back, pulling it out and down while dragging the back of the blade against the rear seam of the pocket. The Wave, a small semicircular notch on the back of the blade—the *W* in the identifier of the knife—completed its intended purpose by snagging against the rear seam of the pocket and forcing the blade to open against the resistance. The blade pulled open and was secured by the liner-lock snapping into place.

Reaper pulled his hand forward and up, still holding the blade between his thumb and two fingers, allowing the weight of the open blade to pivot the knife into a point-down position. Grabbing hold of the handle in a hammer grip with his thumb over the pommel for additional leverage, Reaper pivoted on his left foot while pulling his left arm away from Musclehead's weakened grip.

Grabbing the injured man's arm, Reaper slammed it down on the carpeted top of the counter to his left. In a continuing motion, Reaper drove the knife down in an icepick stab—right through Musclehead's forearm.

The angular Tanto point and slicing chisel edge of the blade slipped through skin, fascia, and muscle—missing the major blood vessels and tendons though it nicked the posterior interosseous vein as it passed between the radius and ulna bones. The tip of the blade sliced through the carpet that padded the top of the counter and sank deeply into the wood beneath. The knife had penetrated so deeply that part of the grip was driven into the wound.

For such a large man, Musclehead made a very high-pitched scream as he sank to his knees, stopping short as his arm pulled against the embedded knife. The entire action, from the start of the snap kick to the blade sinking into the wood, had not lasted two seconds.

Musclehead was not going anywhere for a while, certainly not until someone removed the pinning knife. The pain of the wound, and the fact that the side of the blade was pressing against a branch of his median nerve, would keep Musclehead from even considering trying to pull the blade out himself.

Continuing with the circular motion of his body, Reaper turned to face where Gun Weasel lay on the floor. The Desert Eagle was to the man's side, where Reaper stepped over and picked up the huge weapon.

Gun Weasel was unconscious, though breathing raggedly. He was not an immediate concern.

Turning back to Musclehead, Reaper took a quick glance at his handiwork with a knife. He could see that there was no arterial spurting from the wound around the blade, the hilt of which was deep into the arm. It wasn't that he was at all concerned for Musclehead's welfare, but he might need information from him later. The thug probably wouldn't bleed to death, though falling into shock was a very real possibility. Reaper grabbed Musclehead's right hand and slapped it down against the thug's inside upper left arm.

"Hold it or die," Reaper said grimly. Then he turned to where Deckert lay on the floor.

His friend's eyes were open and he was aware of what Reaper had done—he had been only feigning unconsciousness to try and give Reaper his chance.

"You about done now?" Deckert said.

"Yeah," Reaper said as he pulled his friend up and righted the wheelchair. Helping Deckert back into the chair, Reaper grabbed the M1911A1 lying on the counter and put it in his partner's hand.

The situation was moving fast and Reaper didn't notice the mistake he had just made. His immediate concerns were for his friend and his family. And the only certain source of information about Reaper's family was getting farther away by the moment. Snatching up a rag from the counter, Reaper pressed it against the side of Deckert's head where he was still bleeding.

"Okay, enough," Deckert said, "I'll be all right.

You have to get after that asshole in the suit. Take the cab, I can hold these two."

Deckert waved to the key cabinet underneath the cash register behind him. "Get the keys and move you slow-ass squid," he growled. "Leave this mess to me."

His friend was hurt but functioning. And Reaper knew that his family was in real danger. Reaper accepted the situation and dashed around the counter, slowing only long enough to grab the indicated set of car keys as he headed back to the garage.

But just as Reaper was leaving, he heard Musclehead, still in his pained voice, futilely scream at the unconscious Gun Weasel, "Get up. We've got to stop that crazy Marine from going after Arzee!"

Now Reaper knew who he was chasing—this Arzee character could expect a lot of pain unless Reaper found his family, safe and alive, soon.

Chapter Eight

Closest to the house door of the garage was Keith Deckert's favorite vehicle. Even if he wasn't able to drive it as he had in the past, he meticulously maintained the stealth hotrod he had built, keeping it ready to go at a moment's notice. As Reaper dashed into the garage, hitting the garage door opener on the wall, he lowered the hammer on the Desert Eagle that he was still holding and stuck the big pistol into his pants pocket. Then he started pulling the protective tarp covering off the car as the door started to rise.

Removing the tarp revealed nothing more exciting-looking than a 1972 model Checker cab. The square, boxy front end of the cab, with its two pairs of headlights held in oval chrome metal frames at the upper corners, had the styling of a 1950s-era family sedan. The vehicle even had the white plastic roof light with the name CHECKER on it in block lettering. The whole body of the cab was bright yellow with a white-and-black checkerboard stripe running along either side of the body and doors. The outside of the vehicle was purely just a Checker cab, but a lot of the inner workings no longer were.

The car was a "sleeper." What you saw was not what you got. Keith Deckert had built the Checker cab over years as a pet project. The only time the Checker was really seen in public was during what was called the Woodward Dream Cruise in the summer where the sound of the vehicle was a popular favorite.

Under the hood of the Checker was a 454 Chevy Big Block V-8 engine bored out oversize to 505 cubic inches and fitted with forged extra-strength pistons. The engine had large diameter custom-formed headers and a big single 2x4 Holley four-barrel carburetor giving it a base horsepower of 550. A precharger kept the engine's oil up, lubricating the system and eliminating warm-up oil problems. The Checker could move out at top speed very soon after starting.

The power of the engine went through a rebuilt heavy-duty Turbo-Hydramatic 400 transmission with a Griner aluminum billet racing valve-body and a 3.73:1 differential gear on the rear axle. The suspension of the cab had been beefed up with extra control arms with solid bushings. A remote cutout in the exhaust system allowed the muffler to be bypassed by the driver at the flip of a switch.

With the muffler cutout operating, the roar of the engine could deafen people standing close by. More than just a noise producer, the cutout system added a few more horsepower to increase the speed of the cab. That wasn't the only trick under the deceptive body of the Checker. The vehicle and engine had been fitted with a Holley Cheater nitrous oxide system (NOS).

In the trunk was bolted down a twenty-pound bottle of nitrous oxide. The gas bottle had a Holley NOS remote bottle control so the driver didn't even have to open the trunk to turn on the main valve. Turning a switch on the dashboard would remotely open the gas bottle and charge up the system.

After Deckert had tuned the big Chevy engine and knew what he wanted, and what the V-8 would accept, he had fitted the carburetor with his choice of the metering jets that finally bled the nitrous oxide into the air/fuel flow. A remote key switch on the dashboard would arm the NOS system. Lifting the red safety cover and flipping the lighted blue toggle switch underneath it would open the electric solenoids that released the nitrous oxide into the engine.

With the nitrous going, the roar of the Chevy V-8 would sound like it belonged on the deck of an aircraft carrier as the exhaust cutouts would automatically open if they hadn't already been set that way.

It was a lot more than sound that resulted from dumping nitrous oxide into a carburetor and an engine system tuned for it. For a maximum of thirty seconds, the engine would suddenly have 250 extra horsepower. The top speed of the Checker was over 130 miles an hour with the tricked-out V-8. Pushed by 800 horsepower, the Checker would top out at over 160 miles an hour as it accelerated from the nitrous. The Checker became a huge, blunt steel missile.

The weakness of the system was that the vehicle

just couldn't maneuver well. At speed, the cab had a huge turning radius, and even then it risked flipping free of the road surface. In a straight line, the vehicle was in its element. The main limiting factor of the Checker was that it couldn't push the air out of its way any faster.

Opening the door and climbing into the cab, Reaper pulled out the Desert Eagle and tossed it down on the seat next to him. He pulled up the seat harness with its double shoulder straps and locked it in place around his waist. Sticking the key into the ignition, he fired up the big engine and it caught on the first crank.

The interior of the garage echoed with the sudden roar of something that was definitely not your average car engine. The sound quickly settled into a muted rumble as the muffler of the exhaust system suppressed the sound of the engine. Stopping for a moment, Reaper used both hands to disconnect the NOS safety key from the key ring. Sticking the key into its socket on the dashboard to the right of the ignition key, Reaper turned it and the light came on under the NOS switch. The red safety cover of the nitrous switch now glowed like a spot of blood on the dashboard, the lettering that said ARMED easily visible.

Reaper quickly backed out of the garage and started after the Corvette. The expression on his face was one of grim purposefulness, one you would not want to see if you were the reason for it in the first place.

Being way back in the country now worked very well in Reaper's favor. There was only one way back to the highway, the main road to Detroit. The chance that the Corvette had turned north was minimal. The only thing for miles in that direction was more open country and then Port Huron thirty miles away. To the east was the Huron River and Canada on the other side. But the Corvette had Michigan plates on it. Reaper followed his instinct and turned in the direction of the highway.

Having lived in the city for most of his life, Arzee did not spend much time in the country. Having grown up in the dirt and squalor of the industrial areas around Detroit, he hated the dirt fields and mud of the country. He did find the open rural areas had one advantage that appealed to him. While traveling over the country roads, Arzee had been speeding, but not by very much.

He barreled through a long S-curve in the road and felt the Vette stick to the ground like it was running on a track. Traffic seemed to be nonexistent on the well-maintained long country road. There was a huge stretch of marshland to his left and just the occasional farmhouse, barn, or outbuilding breaking up the trees and fields to his right.

Coming out of the turn, he was looking down a several-miles-long stretch of empty road that had no stops, turns, or traffic, very little even in the way of crossroads except for one every mile or so. It was a big temptation to let the classic Corvette stretch out a bit, a temptation that Arzee indulged himself in.

The 350 cubic inch V-8 under the long, low hood growled louder as Arzee fed more fuel into its four-barrel carburetor. Two-hundred horsepower pushed the streamlined sports car down the road as the speedometer swept past sixty miles an hour, on its way to seventy.

Arzee was a few miles from the gunshop and well satisfied with the way things had gone. Paxtun had told him that Reaper was an ex-Navy SEAL, as if that was supposed to frighten him. Reaper may have helped force Paxtun out of the service, but that hadn't meant anything to Arzee when he met Reaper. Sure, the guy looked like he could be a hardcase, but you didn't always judge things just by looks. This tough SEAL crap was just a bunch of Hollywood hype and TV bullshit. When it had come right down to it, Reaper had just stood there and done nothing while Arzee had told him exactly what was what and how things were going to be done. So much for tough looks.

As far as Arzee was concerned, it didn't take much in the way of brains to pull a trigger for the military, and Arzee had little respect for those men who had joined the Army, Navy, or whatever rather than try to make it on the outside as he had.

The plan Arzee had put together to secure the guns and maintain a tight leash on Reaper looked as if it would work fine. If Reaper went to the police and complained about his family's disappearance, he would have to convince the officers that his wife had been kidnapped, and that might take some doing.

It was far more likely that the authorities would think Reaper had done in his family himself—the idea of a rogue ex-SEAL committing such a crime wouldn't be hard to swallow. The phone call the wife had been forced to make to the local police saying she was in fear of her life would reinforce that idea.

When Reaper supplied the guns they wanted, their firepower should be enough to satisfy Ishmael that Paxtun's organization was doing all that it could to support their Islamic brothers in their struggle. If the guns were recovered down the line after Ishmael had used them, they could only be traced to Reaper—who would have already committed "suicide" in his remorse over killing his wife, and then his business partner. At least that would be the way any carefully planted evidence would point.

The problem about the lost weapons looked to be under control. Arzee was very glad he had found the information about Reaper's family and was able to put it to immediate use.

His men would be leaving the gunshop about now, if they weren't already gone. Arzee expected little trouble from that quarter. The hardware would be secured. He was certain that Reaper and his partner would work their asses off to turn out more of the exotic shotguns over the next three days—just as they had been told to.

From what Paxtun had said, Chief Reaper's weakness for children and families had been demonstrated in Bosnia. The kids there hadn't even been his brats. With his own wife and child being held hostage, he couldn't risk any harm coming to them.

Arzee was quite proud of the way his plan had unfolded. There would be loose ends, but those could be made to disappear. With Reaper as a cutout, any investigation leading to him would stop there. What specifically was to be done with him, his friend, and his family could be decided later after his usefulness was at an end.

The S-curve wasn't much more than a quarter mile behind Arzee when he noticed another vehicle coming up behind him in the rearview mirror. Whatever it was, it certainly wasn't a cop car unless he was passing by Mayberry out here in the sticks. His radar detector hadn't gone off and it didn't look like any cop car he had seen outside of an old movie or TV show. It was some kind of boxy, vintage design, with a front grill like an old Plymouth or something. Still, the old beast was catching up to him. He'd let it get closer and figure out what it was before bolting away in a real performance car.

When he looked in the mirror again, Arzee could see that the old car was noticeably closer. He could make out some details now and was astonished to see that it was a cab of all things that was catching up to him. His surprise caused him to let up on the gas, slowing slightly, allowing the cab to close up even more.

Just what was a cab doing way out here? Some farm clod needed a ride? That was going to be some fare. This was not the area where you could expect a cab to just be passing by. The driver must have had the gas pedal pushing through the floorboards to be catching up to the Vette the way it was.

Then the cab was close enough that Arzee could make out real details, and what he saw caused his blood to freeze. There was a sudden buzzing in his ears as his blood pressure skyrocketed and his skin itched from muscular reaction. Behind the wheel of that cab was Reaper! And his expression made him look like death itself was driving that horrible yellow car.

Arzee was suddenly so scared that he whimpered a little, though he couldn't hear himself do so. In fact, he would have found it almost impossible to make any coherent sound given the fact that his mouth and throat had suddenly gone as dry as a sun-pounded beach in August. He pressed down on the gas pedal, trusting in the power of his classic car to run away from the devil in a box that was right behind him. Slowly, he started to pull away.

Chapter Nine

Reaper watched the Vette start to accelerate. Whatever was under the hood, it was a sure thing that the Vette could outmaneuver the Checker. For the moment, the straight stretch of road they were on took away that advantage. Now they were in a race that the Checker could win—if he could stop the speeding sports car.

Reaper reached down to the seat next to him and put his hand on the Desert Eagle. For a moment he considered opening fire with the big pistol, which he had confirmed was a .44 magnum with a fresh round in the chamber. The Vette was low and fast, but Arzee wasn't moving around the road much at all. He was just trying to outrun the Checker. His mistake.

The fiberglass body of the Corvette Stingray wouldn't offer very much resistance to the 240-grain jacketed hollow points loaded in the Eagle. They would barely be slowed as they smashed through the body of the sports car. Of course, that was also the problem. If Reaper misaimed or one of the magnum slugs was deflected off a metal component, he could end up hitting Arzee. And that could cost him the only solid source of information that he could be sure knew where his family was.

No, the pistol wasn't going to be the answer, and Reaper lifted his hand away from it. Instead, he reached to the dashboard and flipped the switch that operated the muffler cutout solenoids. The exhaust pipes were now blowing straight out into the open air. The sound of the big V-8 roared out unabated. A flock of ducks in the marsh to the left jumped into the sky, flying away quacking and protesting the violent noise. The drop in back pressure inside the exhaust system gave the Checker more horsepower and increased its speed.

The reaction inside of the Vette was close to being the same as that of the ducks. There wasn't any quacking, but Arzee was starting to feel a little panic. He could hear the sound of the Checker's engine even over the roar of his own 350 V-8. That yellow beast was going to catch him. He would have to try to outmaneuver it.

Coming up in the distance, Arzee could see a road sign that showed he was approaching a T-intersection. According to the sign, another road would be going off to the right. If he could make the turn, the Checker couldn't at the speed it was going. It would either have to slow down to make it, or it would miss the turn entirely and have to come back to it. Either way, it would put a lot of space between the two cars and give Arzee a better chance of getting away, or maybe even ambushing the Checker himself. It was going to be a desperate gamble, but Arzee knew his driving was up to the challenge.

Arzee allowed the Vette to drift over to the left side of the road. The extra space would give him a better chance of making the upcoming turn. The gravel shoulders of the road would be a danger, but that was something he knew so he could watch out for it. Just as he was committing himself to the turn, a horrible blasting roar sounded out from behind him when the Checker cut out its muffler.

Startled by the sound, Arzee made the mistake of making the Corvette fishtail slightly as he jerked at the wheel. That was his undoing as he started to lose control of the car.

The rear of the Vette swung to the right, and Arzee twisted the steering wheel to compensate. The rear of the sports car then swung back to the left, going past the hard road surface and slipping out onto the gravel of the shoulder. The wheel on the gravel lost traction and spun, increasing the sideslip of the Vette. Overcompensating, Arzee pulled the wheel hard over to stop his skid—but it was far too late.

The back end of the Vette came back onto the roadway much harder than it should have. The car was now in a full spin and it was going to keep going until it lost speed or Arzee brought it under control. The side road Arzee wanted so desperately to take went past as the back end of the Vette skidded past it. The car was sideways across the road and still turning. It did a full turn and a half, finally coming to rest on the left side of the road, sideways across both lanes with the nose of the car pointed out to the marsh. Arzee was stunned, but he had the presence of mind to draw his weapon.

From underneath his jacket, Arzee fumbled trying to pull his SIG Pro automatic from his Galco Miami Classic shoulder holster. The handgun was hanging horizontally underneath his left arm and his hand finally grabbed the grip as his thumb popped free the safety strap. There was a reassuring feeling to the weapon and Arzee's hand started to pull it from the holster. The ten rounds of .40 Smith & Wesson ammo that were in the weapon would take care of Reaper. And there were two more full magazines under his right arm to help if he had to reload. Then Arzee looked out to the left of the car, toward the approaching sound, and his own scream was lost in the noise.

The two cars were almost evenly matched as far as top speed went. Reaper knew the area and turns were coming up where the Corvette would have the edge over the powerful but heavy Checker. This race had to end fast so Reaper decided to play his ace in the hole. Reaching over to the dashboard, he flipped up the red safety cover over the NOS switch. Bracing himself, Reaper flipped the switch.

Solenoids popped open and, from the rear of the Checker, nitrous oxide flowed forward into the carburetor and the combustion chambers of the engine. Suddenly, it was like the big V-8 was running on rocket fuel. Originally invented in order to give piston-engined fighters during World War II a source of emergency power, nitrous had been almost forgotten during the age of jet aircraft. Racers had rediscovered the advantages of the additive during the 1970s. Now, there were speed records held by cars that had been running with nitrous oxide boosts.

Reaper was pushed back into the seat by the acceleration of the Checker. The engine roared out a solid wall of sound through the muffler cutouts. The speedometer climbed as Reaper hung onto the wheel. He no longer needed the handgun lying on the seat next to him. He was at the wheel of a huge projectile, a guided missile, one he was able to aim very precisely.

As the sound of the nitrous-boosted engine boomed out, Reaper watched as Arzee went onto the gravel shoulder and lost control of his car. As the distance between the two vehicles closed, he saw the Vette spin out and stop sideways across the road. Reaper could now see Arzee sitting at the wheel struggling to draw a weapon. That wasn't something Reaper was going to allow to happen.

Indecision was not something a SEAL could tolerate. Neither could he afford to be reckless. Reaper knew that Arzee was his best lead to finding his family. But if Arzee killed him, he couldn't do his family much good. He would just have to be very careful and precise.

Moving his steering wheel only slightly, Reaper lined up with the rear of the Vette. He saw Arzee's mouth open in a scream just as the juggernaut that the Checker had become smashed into the Vette. Reaper had carefully aimed the cab to impact on the right side of the Vette's back end. The heavy truck frame of the Checker absorbed the energy of the crash with ease. The bodywork crumpled a bit at the left front fender, but that would be repairable. What happened to the Vette was not something that looked even salvageable.

The whole back end of the sports car had disappeared in a cloud of glass fragments and shattered fiberglass. The chrome back bumper flew off to land somewhere in the marsh, twisted and unrecognizable. From behind the front seat back, the Corvette Stingray ceased to exist. The front part of the car spun around completely before going off the road and partially sinking into the marsh. The huge noise of the impact terrified a large gaggle of Canadian geese who took off deeper into the marsh, the large birds honking in panic as their flapping wings and running feet took them across the top of the water.

The terrified flight of the big birds tore up the reeds and cattails in their way. The plants grew in huge patches all over the marsh. Now there were dozens of open paths ripped through the green plants radiating away from the crash site.

Chapter Ten

Arzee was spun about in the crash. Dizzy and disoriented, he realized that he had lost his weapon. That was the least of his worries for the moment. The recognizable portion of the Vette had slipped into the shallow water and he now was in real danger of drowning. What was left of the car was lying parallel to the road it had just left, the driver's door facing into the marsh and already half underwater. Clawing at his seat belt release, Arzee freed himself and pushed at the door. It wasn't latched, there wasn't anything left for the door to latch to—the rear door post was gone.

Scrambling out of the wrecked car, Arzee could hear the Checker screeching to a halt. He only had seconds before Reaper would come back for him. Now in a full-blown panic, Arzee half-crawled, half-swam, out into the marsh. Ducking under some plants and mulch, he clawed at the mud to pull himself forward. An almost primitive instinct to hide from the predator was all that directed his motions.

Covered in mud, slime, weeds, and dead brown cattails, Arzee pulled himself to the far side of a muskrat mound and stuck his face down into the stinking mud to hide.

Reaper flipped the safety cover down, shutting down the NOS system once the smashed Vette was well behind him. Pushing hard on the brakes, Reaper made the Checker's tires smoke as he brought the cab to a stop. Quickly shifting into reverse, Reaper again tore rubber off his tires as he backed the vehicle up to where the remains of the Vette lay sinking in the marsh.

Bits of the car's body were scattered all around. The rear axle was down the road from the impact site, mangled and barely recognizable as part of a power train. Only the single wheel still in place identified the axle for what it was. The other wheel was nowhere to be seen. It had probably been thrown a good distance and had sunk into the dark waters of the marsh.

On the shoulder and facing into oncoming traffic on the wrong side of the road, the Checker came to a stop. Reaper rolled down the driver's window and looked over the wreckage. The Desert Eagle was in his hand, the hammer back and safety off. Reaper carefully looked for any signs of a possibly armed and uninjured Arzee. There were no signs of the man and nothing but the slowly sinking front half of a smashed and smoking car to show he had even been there.

Opening his door and stepping out of the Checker, Reaper went down to where the wreckage of the Vette lay. Stepping into the water, the SEAL looked for the missing man. There was no sign of Arzee, or of any blood indicating an injured man had been in the driver's seat. Reaper's best source of information was gone.

In spite of possibly not being injured, Arzee had to have been badly shaken up by the crash. Normally, Reaper would be in his element tracking a man across a plant-filled marsh. But it seemed as if nature itself was going to take that ability away from him.

The dozens of paths torn through the marsh's weeds and plants from the panicked dashing of the geese extended far from the shore. The birds were gone but the damage they had done prevented Reaper from being able to identify any specific trail that Arzee may have made as he crawled through the marsh. There was nothing to be seen of the man anywhere in the water. His body could be sinking into the mud, or the man could be hundreds of feet away hidden in the luxuriant growth of the marsh.

Gritting his teeth in frustration, Reaper turned to the remains of the Vette. Reaching into the smashed car, Reaper pulled out a briefcase he spotted sticking out from under the passenger seat. The wet case had probably been thrown under the seat during the violent maneuvers of the crash. Arzee was too smart to have left anything incriminating in the case, but it might hold a clue of some kind about where he might go next. Pulling open the glove compartment with more than a little difficulty, Reaper grabbed up all of the papers inside and stuffed them into his shirt. That was all Reaper could get from the wreck that looked at all valuable from an intelligence standpoint.

Time was slipping away. Reaper realized that his only remaining sources of information about his kidnapped family were the two thugs back at the shop. He had to wring out anything they knew about the location of his wife and son before they might be taken farther away or worse. Whoever was working with Arzee was going to be expecting him. How long it would take for the man to be missed couldn't be known.

Anyone else involved might just decide to cut their losses and kill Mary and Ricky, an option Reaper refused to accept. He had to tell Deckert not to call the police or do anything until he had come back and talked to the two thugs.

He would have to move fast to get back to the shop before Deckert did anything. With a reluctant final look around the crash site, Reaper stepped back into the cab. Starting the car up, he spun it through a tire-smoking U-turn. As the roar of the engine blasted out, he flipped the cutoff switch and put the muffler back into the exhaust system. He needed some speed, but he did not want to attract any more attention than he would just by driving down a country road in a yellow Checker cab with a damaged left front end.

As he was driving, Reaper remembered the cell phone Arzee had slipped into his shirt pocket. Pulling it out, he flipped back the cover and held the phone up so that he could see the road as well as the face of the phone. It was just a cheap phone, one of those prepaid models that couldn't be traced to a specific owner.

Working the phone was easy enough. Punching up the shop's number one-handed, Reaper hit the send button and waited. The first three rings at the other end of the line seemed to take forever. Never before had Reaper noticed just how long it took a phone to ring. Finally, on the fourth ring, Deckert picked up.

Chances were, Deckert was using the phone on the wall behind the cash register. "Keith," Reaper said. "It's me, Reaper."

"Yeah, Ted," Deckert said. "I'm still here playing babysitter."

Deckert's voice sounded strained, probably an effect of getting slapped upside the head with a .45 automatic. He would have to be taken to an emergency room and get checked out for a possible concussion.

"I caught up to the Vette but lost Arzee," Reaper said, "I tried to track him through the marsh but couldn't find him. He could be dead or just hiding for all I know. So those two you have are the best . . ."

Reaper heard a rapid pair of loud shots roar out from the phone. Then there was a grunt and a thump and clatter as if the phone had been dropped to the floor.

"Keith," Reaper shouted into the phone. "Keith!"

There were a few more sounds over the phone that Reaper couldn't make sense of. Then the line went dead as the other phone was hung up. Reaper snapped the cell phone closed and slipped it back into his pocket. His full concentration was now on just getting back to the shop.

The trip took longer than Reaper thought he

could stand. First his family had been hurt, now his friend and partner was in trouble, probably shot, maybe dead. The nitrous wouldn't do him any good in this race, he would never have been able to negotiate the turns in the road if he were going too fast. Every driving trick he had learned as a SEAL stuck with him as he barrcled back to the shop. He cut through turns as if he were a professional race car driver.

Pulling up to the house, thc first thing Reaper noticed was that the black Grand Am was missing from the driveway. Somehow, Gun Weasel or Musclehead had managed to get hold of a loaded weapon and had overcome Deckert. Reaper jumped from the Checker and ran into the house, not certain of just what he would find.

Coming into the showroom with the Desert Eagle at the ready, Reaper could see no one standing or attempting to conceal themselves behind the glass cases of the counters. What Reaper could see was Deckert's body lying on the other side of the counter, next to where the phone hung on the wall. Gun Weasel and Musclehead were gone. There was also a big chunk of the carpet missing that had been covering the counter. A drying pool of blood where the carpet had been showed where Musclehead had been pinned.

But all of those details were unimportant compared to Deckert lying on the floor. Reaper could see two bullet holes in the back seat of the wheelchair. Somebody, Gun Weasel most likely, had punched two rounds into Deckert while he was speaking on the phone. Reaper had been right, his friend must have been a little dingie from the blow he had taken. If he hadn't been injured, the ex-Army Ranger would never have turned his back on the two thugs.

Kneeling down next to Deckert, Reaper immediately noticed that there wasn't any blood on the ground. As he touched his friend, he could feel him stir and then a low groan came from the prostrate figure.

"Take it easy, Keith," Reaper said. "You took two good ones in the back."

There wasn't much question of where Deckert had been shot. As close as he was, Reaper could now see the two dark holes in the back of his friend's shirt, holes that matched up pretty well with the two in the seat back of the wheelchair.

"Oh, Christ!" Deckert groaned out. "Lord save old men from their own stupidity. I am way too old for this shit."

Reaper helped his friend turn over and sit up a bit. Now, with his hands on him, Reaper could feel the body armor that Deckert was wearing under his work shirt. Under the two holes in the back of the shirt, Reaper could feel the lumps of the bullets that had been fired into, and stopped by, the vest Deckert had been wearing.

"Oh, damn," Deckert said. "I will never bitch about going to the bank again."

"Huh?" Reaper said, puzzled at the odd remark.

"I had been planning on going to the bank this afternoon," Deckert explained. "So I had my vest on since getting dressed this morning. A fat old man in a wheelchair makes a tempting target and body armor helps give you an edge. It sure proved its worth today. Now help me up into my chair."

Reaper knew his friend's self-depreciating humor was just how he dealt with life in general. As he lifted the big man up, he could feel little in the way of fat under the hard layers of muscle that made up Deckert's back, shoulders, and arms. His legs might not have been of much use to him, but there was nothing the matter with his strength.

"You all right?" Reaper asked as Deckert settled into his chair.

"Not particularly," Deckert said sarcastically, "I've been pistol whipped, shot, and dumped on the ground twice so far today. Right now, I feel like Nolan Ryan hit me in the back with two fastballs. I've had better days."

"You want me to get you to a hospital?" Reaper asked.

"No, I'll be fine," Deckert said. "Besides we have to get on to the trail of whoever those clowns were."

As he settled into his chair, Deckert gasped as his back hit the seat back.

"Oh, that wasn't fun," Deckert said as he leaned forward.

"Your back is probably a bruised mess and I'll bet the slugs are still in your vest," Reaper said as he stood over Deckert. "Get your shirt off and let's at least get those slugs out of there."

Deckert winced as his arms were pulled back to clear the shirtsleeves.

"Any idea what the hell happened?" Reaper asked as he helped his friend get out of his vest.

"Not much I can say," Deckert said. "I gave the

big one a rag to help him stop the bleeding after you had left. Tried to pull the knife out but he screamed as soon as I touched it. The little bastard was still laying curled up on the floor so I figured he wasn't worth bothering with—besides, my head hurt like a bitch.

"Then you called and I answered the phone. Not a lot to say after that, the room went boom and the next thing I knew, you were kneeling there."

While Deckert was talking, Reaper had been examining the back panel of the vest. He pulled a SwissTool from underneath the counter and unfolded it into its pliers configuration. With a little digging, Reaper pulled out a flattened lead slug.

"Motherfucker," Reaper said. "I'll bet that little bastard still had my Taurus on him when I left. This is a .44 Special semiwadcutter bullet, or at least what used to be one. The same thing I keep in my weapon. I forgot to search that sucker before I left. He must have pulled it out and nailed you when you answered the phone. God damn, Keith, I'm sorry. I screwed the pooch this time."

"How the hell do you figure that?" Deckert said. "I'm the stupid one who turned his back on the little fucker. It's not like you didn't have something else on your mind at the time. What the hell is my excuse? There's a whole rack of handcuffs over there and I didn't think to put a pair on him."

"Shit, mistakes all around, I guess," Reaper said. "I lost the Vette at Saint Joe's Marsh. The car was chopped in half so I know that overdressed asshole couldn't drive away, but I couldn't find him before I called you."

"Nothing to be done about it," Deckert said as he winced and held his head. "How's the cab?"

"Good enough to get you to a hospital," Reaper said.

"I'm fine," Deckert protested.

"You won't be any help to me if you pass out from a concussion or start spitting blood from a broken rib," Reaper said. "I'll report the accident to the sheriff's officer when we take you in."

"But your family," Deckert said. "Those ass-wipes were pretty sure of themselves. We have no proof that they were even here. Before you came in, the snappy dresser had sent the gun handler into the office. They pulled the tape from the surveillance cameras."

"Shit," said Reaper. "I'll think of something."

The two men put together a fast story of how Deckert had been hit by some falling steel stock in the shop. Falling out of his chair, he had struck his head on a workbench. The story was enough to satisfy the people at the hospital. The emergency room doctor said that there were no broken bones or a concussion, but that they wanted to hold Deckert overnight for observation. Deckert's protests overrode the doctor's suggestion and the two men headed back to the shop.

When Reaper called in the accident, he acted as a passerby who had just seen the Vette in the water. There was a surprising answer from the sheriff's deputy. There was some wreckage still near the intersection by the marsh, but no car was anywhere around. It looked to the deputy as if someone had just lost a load of junk and not bothered to pick it up. With no car and no one hurt or complaining, there wasn't anything to interest the department.

Calling around to the other local emergency rooms Reaper learned that no one had come in from a car accident that day—seriously injured or otherwise. Returning to the crash site, Reaper further searched the area. There was even less to examine now than there had been before. The front end of the Corvette had completely sunk into the muck bottom of the marsh. The only thing new that Reaper found was what looked like a trail where someone had staggered out of the marsh and up to the road. If the man who had taken his family had a cell phone, it appeared that he could have just called someone to come and pick him up.

Chapter Eleven

Physically, Arzee had not suffered anything more serious than some bruises and abrasions from his accident with the Checker cab. His pride and nerves had taken a severe beating. His favorite classic Corvette was nothing more than a scattered pile of parts in a marsh. The actions of the day before had put Arzee's nerves into little better shape than his vehicle was in.

He had been in firm control of the situation and it had still gotten away from him. How had that happened? It was unbelievable that Reaper would risk anything happening to his own wife and child. They were his own family. He had lost his career over children that weren't even his own in Bosnia. How could he put his own in jeopardy?

Everything that Arzee knew told him that Reaper should have done exactly what they wanted, let go of the weapons and delivered more, all to get his family back. The plan had even accounted for the police or other authorities, removing any support for

Reaper from that source. The situation should have completely subjugated Reaper to their control, and it hadn't.

That Reaper's family would be the control for the ex-SEAL was something that Arzee had been counting on. Paxtun had approved of his plan, indeed had been enthusiastic about it. It would not only replace the weapons they needed—there was a delicious irony about using the man that had cost Paxtun so much, and costing him even more.

Paxtun had been so certain of the plan that Reaper's family had been sent on to the facilities on South Wolverine Island. It was the most secure site they had available to them and was where Paxtun could keep a personal eye on the hostages. Paxtun was already on the island and Reaper's wife and kid had arrived there the night before.

Arzee had already contacted Paxtun that morning—calling him over a prepaid cellular phone that had been part of a bulk purchase made elsewhere in the country. Speaking in Arabic and in coded phrases added security to a point that seemed extreme. But nothing was too extreme for the group of operatives that had been sent over by the overseas investors that were backing Paxtun's and Arzee's enterprises.

Just the existence of the operatives, and especially their leader, had been kept a very closely guarded secret. Amman and Nicholas were Arzee's cousins and he trusted them for his most sensitive operations. Along with two more family members, his cousins Hadeed and Joseph, they were the only ones who had a direct hand in the kidnapping of Reaper's family and the extortion of the guns. But his cousins knew only that the operation had been done partly for revenge—something they could understand very well. But they hadn't been trusted enough to know the significance of Ishmael or his men.

The leader of the action group had taken the kunyah Ishmael for his name during the operation. Historically, Ishmael was the son of the biblical Abraham and Hagar. Hagar was the handmaiden of Sarah, Abraham's wife. According to Islamic heritage, Ishmael was considered the father of the Arab people. It was a fitting name for someone who felt that he was going to help lead the true believers of Islam into a new world free of the infidels and their influence.

This modern Ishmael considered his planned operation to be a sacrifice to Allah. He had a twelve-man crew of hand-picked men to help him complete his mission. For their kunyah names, the men of Ishmael's group had taken names of the sons of the legendary Ishmael. The whole group was known as the Sons of Ishmael and preferred to be addressed as such by Paxtun, Arzee, or anyone else in Paxtun's organization.

The Sons of Ishmael were an action cell of al Qaeda, and they had a significant operation coming up in the United States. Arzee knew none of the details of the mission, target, or timing of the operation, and he didn't want to know any. The eyes and faces of every member of Ishmael's cell that Arzee had met had shone with a dedication that bordered on the fanatical. It would not be safe to cause any difficulty at all to such people.

The only thing that Arzee was certain of was that Ishmael was terrifying. He considered his mission to be like the sacrifice of his namesake, the biblical son of Abraham. According to Islamic legend, it was Ishmael who Abraham had been going to sacrifice on God's order, not Isaac. Legend further stated that Ishmael had been spared through God's intervention, and that his sons and their descendants became the first true Arab people.

Ishmael had told Paxtun and Arzee that he felt he was going to help re-create the Arab people as a major power in the world. The United States would be forced to leave the Islamic world and the Middle East. Free of the influence of the infidels and the Great Satan, the Islamic world would soon grow to become the dominant culture of the entire planet.

That level of fanaticism was hard to face. If Ishmael considered someone a threat, or even a possible threat, to the cell or their mission, he would kill them without hesitation. Right now, Ishmael was up at the mansion on the island with Paxtun. The more than 250 miles that separated Detroit from that island in Lake Michigan still felt far too close for Arzee's mental comfort.

Both Paxtun and Arzee had converted to Muwahhidan, what the West and many Arabs called Wahhabism, in Afghanistan. The austere, conservative form of Islam was what their rescuers had believed and it had appealed to Paxtun over the months he had spent in the mountains of that desolate country. Paxtun had in his turn convinced Arzee that conservative Islam was the way, though Arzee may have also been swayed by the appeal of the huge amount of money offered by Paxtun and his proposals.

Arzee considered himself a true believer in Islam. He knew that the path to righteousness required adhering to the dogma of his chosen faith. But he was not a religious fanatic. His years on the streets of Dearborn and Detroit had influenced him greatly. His religious convictions were not as solid as he thought they were.

There was an unbelievable amount of money to be made in the various criminal activities of Paxtun's organization. The drug distribution network Paxtun and Arzee had developed was making huge profits with relatively little personal risk to either man. The money had proven worthwhile to everyone involved. Even the Taliban had been happy to take a cut of the profits from the product of the Afghan poppy fields.

Now the military actions of the United States had taken the Taliban out of the picture. But it had not eliminated al Qaeda as a functional organization. Paxtun and Arzee had been told that they would support Ishmael and his men—and the demand could not be refused.

So the organization had been hard at work bringing in Ishmael and his men to the United States. A training and staging area had been prepared and set up at the private island in Lake Michigan. The most recent group of cell members, Ishmael's "sons," had been sent up north to the island some days earlier. Not having them hiding out at the Factory, acting as janitorial and maintenance staff for any onlookers, was the only good thing that had happened to Arzee in the last few days.

The loss of the weapons shipment looked to have been a disaster for Arzee and Paxtun. Paxtun was going to have to explain to Ishmael how new security procedures were being put into place by the Office of Homeland Security. Those procedures and new technologies were intended specifically to find such shipments of weapons and ammunition as the one that had been seized. It was while Paxtun was explaining that to Ishmael that Arzee was supposed to be arranging for new firepower.

Right now, Arzee had their resident drug chemist hard at work making high-quality explosives to replace some of what had been lost. As far as the guns went, they already had the weapons from the gun shop. They still had Reaper's wife and son as prisoners and could force the SEAL to do what they wanted. So more of the new weapons should be available by Saturday afternoon.

Paxtun had suggested that Arzee call Reaper and tell him that the clock was still ticking on the deadline for more of the Jackhammer shotguns. Arzee wouldn't admit it to anyone, not even himself, but he was more than afraid of the SEAL who had chased him down. He wasn't going to call the cell phone he had left with Reaper. His reason was to make the big SEAL sweat over the fate of his family even more by not hearing anything. The truth was, Arzee didn't know how he would react if he heard the man's voice on the phone any time soon.

Arzee believed that once Reaper realized he could do nothing about the situation, he would do what was demanded of him. But the pain Arzee felt in his muscles and bones lessened his faith in the plan. And his most trusted men, his cousins, were in much worse condition than he was.

Nicholas wasn't too badly injured by his introduction to SEAL close-quarter combat. The private doctor had said that Nicholas should refrain from doing whatever it was that had caused his groin injury. He was lucky there was no permanent damage. But the small man was still walking very gingerly—and sitting very carefully.

Amman had been another matter. His left forearm had been severely damaged by the knife that Reaper had used to nail him to that counter top. It had taken both hands for Nicholas to pull that knife out of the table, and he had done more damage to his cousin's arm in the process. If Nicholas hadn't used that same knife to cut a chunk of carpet to wrap around the wound, Amman might have bled to death before he had gotten back to the Factory.

As it was, Amman had a large bandage wrapped around his left arm and was taking pills for the pain. The two cousins were only good for standing guard around the offices until they healed up. But at least they could be trusted to watch the new project that was moving along well. The project looked as if it would be yielding a profit soon.

The offices and quarters Arzee used were on the sixth floor of the old auto plant. The bulk of the sixth floor, at the top of the building, had been the paint shop. That was where a clandestine laboratory had been set up in one of the old paint booths. The ventilation and filtering system prevented any of the fumes from the lab escaping into the atmosphere in a detectable form.

Fazul Daoud, the graduate student in organic chemistry from a local university, had been cultivated by Arzee and Paxtun in order to manufacture designer drugs for the organization. Having the young chemist and the laboratory available had proven a possible lifesaver when it had been able to produce a large amount of sophisticated explosives for the Sons of Ishmael.

Ishmael had thought that the ability to manufacture the explosives he wanted had been a very professional backup put in place to fulfill his possible needs. Now that the immediate demand for explosives had been satisfied, the lab was already back to producing more financially lucrative items.

Leaving his offices, Arzee went out the door and across the hallway to the old paint shop. Stairs led up to the offices, the entrance to the stairway being heavy steel fire doors secured with chains and padlocks. The building's elevators could only be operated with a key—and all but one of them were kept shut down between floors for security.

The only other way to the top floor was to go up a ramp along the north wall of the building. A very heavy steel bar and lock sealed the ramp door. By the time a police raid unit could force access to the floor, any evidence would have been long destroyed. There were five such ramps, originally put in place to move racks of parts from floor to floor while constructing cars. At the top of each ramp were thick steel fire doors. Each door had to be penetrated before finally reaching the sixth floor.

Near the middle of the huge floor at the top of the building, surrounded by racks, conveyors, and the other refuse of heavy manufacturing, were several large steel rooms. The boxlike rooms had wall-sized doors at either end. The doors were kept as securely sealed as every other entrance to the floor. Whole car bodies had been moved in and out of the rooms on racks. Some of the rooms had been set up for painting, others serving as large ovens to bake the paint.

Amman sat outside of a standard door in the side of one of the steel enclosures. He was looking a bit the worse for wear from the expression on his face, and by the sling on his left arm. The big man stood a bit unsteadily as Arzee approached. Then he unlocked the door and opened it for his boss without speaking a word.

Arzee passed into the room, and listened to the sound of the air being sucked through the area by the ventilation system. Along one wall of the enclosure was a rack of bubbling laboratory glassware, tall assemblies of glass, rubber tubing, and metal clamps, all held to a framework of steel rods. There were a dozen of the same apparatus setups all running at once. The tall glass rigs were filled with liquids that bubbled and flowed. On top of each setup was a glass condenser, water flowing through the cooling jacket. The condenser was the only piece of apparatus that Arzee could name, the rest was a complete mystery to him.

But the bubbling mass was not a mystery to Fazul Daoud, the white lab-coated wizard who managed the illicit laboratory. He turned as Arzee came in and raised the protective plastic shield he had over his face.

"Nothing dangerous going on that I should be concerned with, is there?" asked Arzee seeing the shield.

"Not really, sir," Fazul answered. "It was much

more dangerous when I was turning out that pentaerythritol tetranitrate you wanted."

"The what?"

"I'm sorry sir," Fazul said. "The PETN high explosive you asked for. The worst part of that was working with the formaldehyde and acetaldehyde to form the precursor. I had to wear a respirator for that. The nitration and purification was straightforward enough."

"Speak English, Fazul," Arzee said, "talking like this does not impress me and I don't have time for it. Now is this procedure going ahead smoothly?"

"Yes, sir," Fazul said. "Right now, this is just a straightforward extraction. The hydride and ether being used could be very dangerous if mishandled. They are quite flammable, even explosive."

"You are trusted to prevent any mishandling from happening," Arzee said. "Now, how long is the process going to take, and how much are you estimating the yield to be?"

"The extraction takes about sixty hours," Fazul said as he warmed up to his subject. He was completely in his element talking about his laboratory work. "The balance of the process should be completed a day after that. Since this is being done in a laboratory and not on an industrial scale, these Soxhlet Extractors only hold a relatively small charge. I expect the yield to be about thirty-five grams per unit, so between 400 and 450 grams of pure Methylenedioxy-n-methylamphetamine."

"That is pure MDMA?" said Arzee. "Raw Ecstasy?"

"Yes, sir," Fazul said. "The process is much the same as that used by some of the biker gang cookers to crank out their crystal methamphetamine. But their process is crude at best. Our system is much more sophisticated and efficient. The product here is of much greater purity than any other brands available on the street. Once I have diluted the final product down with a buffer and pressed it into tablets, they will be ready for sale. The customers should be well satisfied."

"These clubbers will pay well for their Ecstasy tablets," Arzee said. "How long do you expect to take to manufacture the pills themselves?"

"Each thirty-five-gram batch should make about 580 tablets at the popular dosage," Fazul said. "Using the press and dies does take some time to actually form the final pills. I expect to have several thousand tablets available for you in four days. They'll be marked and shaped as double-stack white Mitz, a very popular underground brand."

"Excellent," Arzee said. He was happy something was working out according to plan for a change. "Do you need any relief or other support?"

"Nothing I can think of, sir," Fazul said. "The process is pretty straightforward for the extraction. As you can see, the extractors run themselves for the most part. I can get what rest I need well enough as they run."

Arzee looked at the rows of glassware bubbling away. The liquid would rise in the Soxhlet Extractors until it reached a certain level, then quickly be siphoned off into a large round flask nesting in an electric mantle heater. Each setup would make a quantity of Ecstasy, the popular club and rave drug, that would have a final street value of more than

$11,000. And there were twelve setups running at once. Over $130,000 profit would be a good return for a few thousand dollars investment in chemicals and glassware.

Even wholesaling the drug would be more than profitable while minimizing the risk. Maintaining a pure product is how they had cornered the heroin trade. This would be no different. And the process, chemical, and equipment, could even be sold to some of the biker gangs that they worked with on other projects. Arzee had a smile on his face for a change as he headed back down to his offices.

Chapter Twelve

In northern Lake Michigan, almost twenty miles from the closest point of the mainland, is South Wolverine Island. About five miles to the northeast is North Wolverine Island. Covering more than 3,300 acres of ground, South Wolverine Island is shaped like an inverted fat banana with the stem end pointing due south and the other end curved over to point northwest. The island is a little over five miles long and about a mile and a half wide. North Wolverine Island, shaped like a straightened comma mark, is two and a half miles long and barely over a mile across at its widest point.

Both islands are covered with trees, brush, and grasslands. There are wide sand beaches at several points along the shoreline of South Wolverine, while North Wolverine is almost completely surrounded by a thin border of sand beach. The grasslands and trees offer good cover and grazing to the herds of deer and other game on the two islands. The only industry that had ever come to the islands was logging, as it had on most of the islands of Lake Michigan during the late 1800s and early-to-mid 1900s.

The logging camps were long gone, but there were still traces of man on both islands. North Wolverine Island had a few cabins along its west shore. On the widest part of the northern end of the island was a 1,000-meter-long grass landing strip for aircraft. The island was covered mostly with grasslands, broken up by patches of scrub brush and low trees. Some small hills rise up from the relatively flat island at its southern end.

South Wolverine Island holds a large area of trees and brush in the rolling ridges that cover over two-thirds of the island. At the southernmost point, separated from the main part of the island by 400 meters of sand, stands a single automated lighthouse. Near the metal-framed light are the remains of an old brick lighthouse along with a single-story structure that had been the living quarters of the lighthouse keeper almost a century earlier.

The decaying structures at the southernmost point of South Wolverine Island are not the only buildings on the island. A mile almost due north of the old lighthouse is a huge two-story mansion built decades earlier. Seeing the island as a summer refuge, a lumber baron had established a large estate on South Wolverine.

Years after the lumber baron was gone, the estate was bought up and improved by an automobile magnate from Detroit. He had a two-story summerhouse built on the island. The mansion-sized house held six bedrooms, each with their own bathrooms, a maid's room with bath, and a rambling first floor. This floor included a billiard room, music room with a separate chamber for the pipe organ, a library, and a twenty-by-forty-foot indoor swimming pool.

Built on a hillside, the summerhouse had a walk-out basement foundation with over a dozen rooms and chambers including a photographic dark room, several walk-in refrigerators, a coal cellar, four huge cisterns holding thousands of gallons of water, and even a single-lane regulation-sized bowling alley that runs along the east side of the pool structure. At the opposite side of the pool is a collection of utility pipes that lead to a six-foot-wide tunnel connecting to a powerhouse two hundred meters away.

The powerhouse holds large diesel-electric generators that supply power to the house and other structures and facilities on the island. The powerhouse is part of the hangar facilities and garage that stand at the southern end of a 1,200-meter landing strip. At the west shore of the island, directly across from the large rise that the mansion stands on, are the boat docks and landing facilities.

The offshore waters teem with fish at different times of the year. Shallow water shoals extend for more than three miles to the north of the main island. The South Wolverine Island Shoals, a long expanse of treacherous shallow waters, extend for more than nine miles to the south of the island. Thirty-foot-deep channels separate the different parts of the southern shoals. The three most dangerous areas of shallow water are marked with lighted buoys. It was to warn boats from this stretch of water and the hidden dangers there that the lighthouse was designed to do.

The geography and location of the South and North Wolverine Islands made them excellent places for sportsmen. But, except for the small spit of land above the sand that holds the inactive lighthouse, the islands are private property. Even the lighthouse was not open to the public, so very few people landed on the posted property of the islands.

The islands were a huge, private playground for the rich of several cities, lying roughly 250 miles equidistant from either Detroit or Chicago. The auto magnate and his family had long since left the area. The properties had gone through a number of hands, each trying to make something more of what was available at the remote location. The previous owner had established a hunting lodge on South Wolverine Island, surrounded by thousands of acres to support exotic imported game.

The owner of the hunting lodge had failed to see his private club become a successful concern. He had fallen on difficult times, both personal and professional, something Paxtun had been able to take advantage of. Obtaining both North and South Wolverine Islands for under market value, Paxtun now had a very large, very isolated facility available to him. That was something his investors had ordered him to obtain for their use.

Now, the hunting preserve and lodge were listed as being closed to the public for renovation and upgrading of the facilities. That explained a large number of workers going to and from the islands whenever the weather permitted. One thing that had not been announced publicly was when the hunting club would reopen, if ever.

Having finished leading the morning prayers with his men, the man called Ishmael sent them out of his suite of rooms. The main room of his sumptuous quarters at the mansion was easily large enough to hold all of his men. Ishmael was a tall, medium-built, intense man. His close-cropped, thick black hair, beard, and mustache framed an oval face with a very high forehead. Shaded by thick eyebrows were bright, intense, dark brown eyes.

Ishmael had been with al Qaeda since its beginnings and had spent his share of time sleeping on little more than rocks. His quarters now were what had been called the "Owner's Chamber." The suite had an almost thirty-foot-square room with an attached semicircular enclosed sleeping porch and two separate large combination dressing rooms and baths. Ishmael thought it shameful that just the cupboard space and closets of one of the baths were larger than what many families called a home back in his adopted Afghanistan.

Not that he hadn't been used to luxury at one time in his life. Ishmael had been born into a privileged family in 'Ajman, in the United Arab Emirates. He had been educated and raised a devout Muslim, and remained so even when studying abroad in Europe and England. He spoke a number of languages, including English, German, French, and Arabic.

When the Soviet Union had invaded Afghanistan in 1979, the young man who would become Ishmael went to fight the infidel invaders. He joined the mujahideen and took part in the jihad.

The fighting hadn't stopped with the Soviets abandoning their actions in Afghanistan. The occupation of holy Muslim soil by the infidels from the United States had incensed Ishmael as it had many other fundamentalist Islamic Muslims. It had been obvious to any devout true believer that the U.S. had been bent on driving Iraq from Kuwait solely for its own benefit.

The defeat of Iraq had only been the United States' opening gambit into the Arabian peninsula as far as Ishmael and his contemporaries were concerned. The justice that had been brought against the United States by the Prince, bin Laden, had been used by the infidels as an excuse to destroy what had become Ishmael's new home in Afghanistan.

Planning had been going forward for several years for a new strike against the Great Satan, deep in his own homeland. That planning had been modified by the horrendous invasion of Iraq by the U.S. forces as they went forward with their intent of occupying the Middle East. But Ishmael and his men were now in the United States itself, deep in the heart of their enemy. And they would very soon be striking fear in that heart—fear that would reverberate throughout the world and let their Muslim brethren know that the fight was not over.

Paxtun retained his office down the second-floor main hallway from what had been his personal quarters now used by Ishmael. For his own sleeping quarters, he had moved into what was called Chamber 4, part of an extended suite of rooms. From

Chamber 4, he could pass through a dressing room and vestibule and be in his outer office.

Made from one of the major sleeping chambers of the original mansion, Paxtun's office had a large central chamber, sixteen-by-twenty-five-feet in size, as well as an attached bath and separate dressing room. The main chamber was his outer office, that Paxtun used for meetings and such. The enclosed semicircular sleeping porch just off the main chamber was where he kept his private inner office.

Sleeping arrangments were not of major concern to Paxtun at the moment. Since Ishmael's arrival weeks earlier, he had done little in the way of sleeping. And what sleep he did get was restless and unsatisfying. Ishmael was a demanding taskmaster. Nothing short of perfection was acceptable to him in support of what he considered his holy duty.

Paxtun had yet to be fully informed of the details of the operation. The only thing that he knew was the code name of the attack, Operation Shaitan's Blessing. That could mean anything and take place anywhere. It made for a situation that he had a hard time accepting. It wasn't that his conscience bothered him about being responsible for a possible major terrorist attack in his home country. It was the fact that he didn't know enough of the details to insure that he was protected from possible discovery.

Inside his inner office, Paxtun still felt safe and relatively in control. His extensive knife and sword collection was in cases and racks both on the walls and several glass-topped tables. On the table between the two doors that connected the inner and outer offices was his most recent acquisition. The long, flat wooden case that Hadeed, one of Arzee's cousins, had brought to him didn't hold an antique or foreign blade. It did hold the sword made by Reaper's own hands. Arzee's relatives had known of Paxtun's passion for blades, and they had brought him the sword as well as a real prize—Reaper's family.

The wife and son of the man who had forced him to relinquish his military and intelligence career were in his complete control. For the time being, he had them secured in a storage room in the basement. It amused Paxtun to have the woman and child secured in the windowless, concrete-walled room. Twice a day, they were taken out to make use of the toilet facilities. All the rest of their time was spent in their prison room. Even their meals were brought to them there.

Paxtun hadn't quite decided what to finally do with the two hostages yet, but he had time. They had to be kept alive to insure Reaper's cooperation—for the time being.

As Paxtun was contemplating the good parts of his situation in his inner office, Ishmael strode in from his room down the hall. His arrival instantly brought Paxtun out of his reverie. The news had come in from Arzee that he had secured four of the Jackhammer shotguns. Any additional weapons would be available in two days. The exotic weapons would help replace part of the firepower confiscated by Canadian customs. Additional weapons would take longer to obtain—there just weren't any more immediately available.

This was not the news Paxtun wanted to give Ishmael. That the man was a fanatic went without question. Causing him difficulties could set off what Paxtun had quickly learned was a violent hair-trigger temper. Ishmael and his superiors had proved a very profitable group of partners for Paxtun's enterprises. Now that the time had come to pay back some of those investments with interest, Paxtun was having some second thoughts about the arrangement. It was one thing to very profitably distribute narcotics and build an infrastructure to support activities in the United States. It was quite another to actively take part in a terrorist action within the continental United States itself.

Paxtun had little choice in how events moved forward now. The last group of Ishmael's men were coming into the country that night. They would be at the island base the next day if everything went according to plan. That was another bit of good news that Paxtun could pass on to Ishmael. But even that news had a bad taste to it for Paxtun.

Once all twelve members of the Sons of Ishmael had joined with their leader, the group would greatly outnumber Paxtun and his handful of men on the island. Ishmael had insisted that there be as few support people as possible on the island to insure security for himself and his men, an insistence that Paxtun had to go along with.

Even the cook and caretaker staff had been removed from the island more than a month earlier. Paxtun had one of his junior men doing the cooking, something that was wearing thin over the weeks. Coming to the island was a strain now, especially after the fare they had been used to from their usual expert cook. He was tired of food that was microwaved or had come from cans. There was no wine at the meals either. Drinking alcohol would be a sin in the eyes of Allah. More importantly, it would piss off Ishmael and his men.

Ishmael entered Paxtun's office unannounced and without knocking. The arrogance of the man was just another bitter pill that Paxtun had to swallow.

"Good news, Ishmael," Paxtun said, "the final group of your men have arrived in Windsor. They'll be brought across the border tonight."

"You are certain that your procedures will work?" Ishmael said in flawless English. "And that their papers will stand up to the closest scrutiny?"

"No problem whatsoever," Paxtun said. "The crossing procedure is the same as we used for yourself and the other four groups of men. The papers are the very best available. Each man will have an authentic U.S. government passport with his picture in it as well as a Michigan driver's license.

"We used the photographs of your men you forwarded to us. The driver's licenses are as authentic as anything issued by the State of Michigan. No police officer or customs agent would be able to tell them from the real thing. The passports are of the same quality.

"Before they cross the border, each man is given pocket litter to go along with his papers—money, random documents, receipts, and ticket stubs. Those items would mark him as just another tourist out of the thousands that cross the border every day."

"I will not accept any errors at this stage of the

game, Paxtun," Ishmael said. "There is far too much at stake and the timing is becoming critical."

"It might help if you let me know what part of the mission timing is tight," Paxtun said.

"That is of no concern of yours," Ishmael said firmly. "You are simply to make sure that there are no flaws in the support that is asked of you."

"No flaws at all," Paxtun said, trying to steer the conversation away from the delicate matter of Ishmael's mission. "We have men of the one faith in a number of different areas who have been brought into the plan but have no knowledge of their specific part in it."

There were more details on how Paxtun had obtained the identification papers that he had told Ishmael. But he did not feel it necessary to tell the terrorist leader all of his secrets.

"The actual border crossings," Paxtun explained, "were planned to take place at the times of the highest traffic volume. The vehicles used all had multiple passengers and were known to frequently visit the gambling casinos on both sides of the border. Once in Canada, your men were issued the passports with their photos and descriptions inside and their original documents were taken away. For all intents and purposes, they were U.S. citizens from that point on.

"They would cross back into the States by another route than the one the vehicle had originally crossed over by. As far as the customs people were concerned, they were looking at U.S. citizens coming back from a good time across the river. The passports were just a backup, the driver's licenses alone have proved enough for each crossing so far. The driver knew what to say and coached each person in the van as to just what answers to give at the border.

"Your people came into the country without ever even raising a blip on the radar of customs. The Immigration and Naturalization Service wouldn't even think to look for them. By the next day, they are on their way here to the island."

In spite of the detailed and methodic nature of Paxtun's techniques, and the fact that they had worked flawlessly so far, Ishmael still felt it necessary to prevent his subordinate from feeling too full of himself.

"The loyalty of your people is something I question," Ishmael said. "You simply buy it, which is not the same thing as true loyalty at all. My men have loyalty unto death for our cause. Your people are less than mercenaries. They betray their own country for mere monetary gain."

The rebuke was directed at Paxtun and the line about money was intended to sting him. The mild insult didn't mean anything to him. He had been listening to such for weeks now anyway. But what he had to tell Ishmael next did worry him.

Finally, Paxtun told Ishmael the news about his missing hardware behind the closed doors of his office, quickly adding the news about the new firepower that had been acquired. The reaction of the big terrorist leader was everything Paxtun had expected and feared.

The fact that his mission might have been put in jeopardy by another's incompetence filled Ishmael with rage. The tall, slender man stalked back and forth across the room like a caged tiger. He paused for a moment and gazed quietly at Paxtun who stood next to his large wooden desk that faced away from the four large windows in the curved outer wall. Then Ishmael crossed his arms and lowered his head as if in deep thought, walking past the desk and near where Paxtun was standing.

As Paxtun took a step closer to Ishmael, the bigger man suddenly turned and viciously backhanded Paxtun across the face. As Paxtun staggered and almost fell, Ishmael lashed out with another stunning backhand with his opposite hand. The smaller man reeled and fell against the heavy desk. Only his hands gripping the edges of the desk kept Paxtun from collapsing to the floor in a heap.

"You think some new toys would cover up your incompetence?" Ishmael snarled. "There is no tolerance for failure. We cannot afford to let mistakes hinder our cause. The only reason you are not dead now is that you may still be able to serve the cause—an arrangement that has paid you very well.

"You have served us well in the past," Ishmael continued in a deceptively softer tone. "That is why you reap the benefit of our compassion. You brought us weapons when we needed them to drive the Soviet invaders from our country. Perhaps it was too much for me to expect you to be able to do so again on such short notice.

"Others who I respect told me that you were once a warrior. You have been living here in this decadent country for too long since leaving Afghanistan. You were once hard, but these surroundings have softened you and made you easy. Your own country proved itself false to you and your faith when it abandoned you once. Then it so unjustly turned you out after your service in Bosnia. We are the only ones who have accepted you fully and made you a trusted brother of ours.

"It was arrogant and stupid of you to assume that I did not know of the lost shipment of arms the instant that it happened. Do you consider me so slovenly that I would leave a detail as important as the delivery of such a thing solely up to you? I know that you had to put together a plan for obtaining replacement weapons in a very short time. And that woman and her child that you brought to the island last evening are part of that plan.

"Let me assure you," Ishmael said in a soft, dangerous tone as he leaned in close to where Paxtun still held himself up at the desk. "That woman and child had better not turn into a threat against us. If anything you do risks me, my men, or our mission, you will be the first one to die. I agree they make good hostages no matter what your original plan may have been. The Americans are soft that way about their own women and children.

"Not that they extend that compassion to anyone else in the world," Ishmael said as he started pacing the room. "They have bombed our women and children, attacked us out of the sky, and out of our reach. When the much-vaunted U.S. military finally came down to the ground, they did so in their heavy tanks and armored vehicles—smashing everything in their way."

Paxtun now realized with certainty just how great

a fanatic Ishmael was. His fate was inextricably intertwined with this madman who walked about the room, ranting as if he were giving a speech to his men. It was as if the man wanted to keep convincing himself.

"In their arrogance," Ishmael said, "they overthrew our governments and killed our leaders. They defiled our holy places of worship, robbed us of our antiquities, our heritage, our past. They claimed we had weapons of mass destruction. That was the reason they used to justify their actions in the eyes of the world.

"But we are here now," Ishmael said as he came close to Paxtun again and stood facing him. "Here in the very heart of the United States. We had not yet obtained such weapons as we had been accused of. But we can take such things from the infidels themselves. We will turn the poisons of their own making back on them."

Realizing that he was saying more than might be prudent, Ishmael had a very serious look come over his face as he stood straight and faced Paxtun.

"The importance of our mission was not allowed to rest on a single shipment of arms and materiel," Ishmael said. "There have been other arms shipments sent to various action cells throughout the United States. Those cells have already been made aware of our needs and are sending materials to us as we speak. They should begin arriving tomorrow. Whatever additional plans you have to replace the lost shipment may go forward as necessary. Those arms will have to replace those sent to us from the other cells.

"It is a pity that we lost the U.S.-made Stinger

missiles that were in that last shipment. Obviously the existence of such weapons frighten the authorities. They neglected to tell the public of their seizure when they took the shipment. No matter. We have other Soviet weapons that will be available to us. But there would have been a certain irony in using the U.S. weapons against their own people.

"My experts have been examining the guns that came in last night. They say the firepower they represent may replace some of what was lost through your incompetence. At least they are devastating in a close assault. They have helped buy your life back—for now."

Switching to a very commanding tone, Ishmael said, "I have been told to expect the first arrivals of equipment tomorrow. You will have your people pick them up and transport them here when you bring in the last group of my men. The explosives your chemist made have been judged as adequate by my technicians. They will be of use in replacing some of the more specialized pieces that were in the shipment that was lost. Their delivery was another saving grace for you. It would be best if there were no other errors or delays on your part."

"There shouldn't be any difficulties," Paxtun said as he finally found his voice. "Everything is ready. You tell us where to pick up what and we'll do it. Another truckload coming in here will not be a problem."

"It had best not be a problem," Ishmael said, and he strode out of the room.

Ishmael's violent manner almost made Paxtun angry enough to have the man killed immediately. He had the sudden urge to grab a blade and chase the terrorist leader down in the hall before he even reached his own room. But Paxtun knew that Ishmael's men would kill him long before he could leave the island. If he did get away, al Qaeda had a long memory, and an even longer reach. Paxtun wouldn't live out the year. That thought stayed his hand as it inched toward a weapon, Paxtun knowing that it would be suicide to take on the man physically.

On top of the ingratitude of the terrorist leader for everything Paxtun had done to replace the lost weapons with some of the best hardware available was the shock that the whole thing had been unnecessary. Ishmael had put his own backups in place, showing just how important he considered his mission to be. By not telling Paxtun about more weapons being available, he had forced the man to use extreme measures to obtain guns. The satisfaction Paxtun had felt in holding Reaper's family hostage had evaporated—it had never been necessary.

The ex-Army officer and drug lord just accepted Ishmael's insults and orders. Paxtun had no choice in the matter. Ishmael would eliminate him just as soon as he stopped being useful. It was good that he had been paid a lot of money and lived well at the old resort—he was going to be earning every penny of it. He only hoped he would have time later to enjoy his gains.

Chapter Thirteen

The situation for Reaper was quickly becoming the worst he had ever endured. His career in the SEALs and Special Warfare had exposed him to levels of stress that could bring the average man quickly to his knees. But none of his training or experience had prepared him for a direct threat to his wife and child.

His family was missing and no one was able to tell him where they had gone. It was only the morning after they had been taken, but the hours that had passed were the longest that Reaper had ever lived through. There was so little that he could do, and a feeling of helplessness was not something he was used to. He couldn't go to the police; the only ones he could turn to were his friends. But the kind of people that Reaper could call his friends were a very competent group of individuals.

Reaper and Deckert were in the office of the house, converted from what had been the dining room. They were working from the one slim lead they had. The name "Steven Arzee" had been on the car registration papers Reaper had taken from the Corvette's glove compartment. Deckert had been conducting a search for information on Arzee over the Internet. Like everything else that had been tried by the two men so far, the search had proven fruitless. Reaper leaned back from his seat at the side of the desk and stared into space thoughtfully as he drank from the cup of coffee in his hand.

"Ted," Deckert said as he pushed himself back from the computer desk, "I've called in every favor I know. Every cop or detective who's ever come through that door and left his number has gotten a call from me. No one knows anything. In fact, no one even suspects anything. When the kidnappers had your wife call her school and say she was going away, they believed her.

"The two of you have had trouble in the past. If she felt threatened and told a bunch of people that you were the cause, they believed her. Being a SEAL has worked against you here. Hell, man, even her sounding nervous over the phone was considered understandable by people who think you guys should be kept under glass and only taken out in time of war.

"That Arzee asshole covered all the bases. We're not even sure that's the name of the guy who was here. Whoever he is, he's probably still alive, maybe not even hurt very badly. No hospital or emergency room in the area had an accident victim brought in. And if he is still alive, he's got you by the short hairs."

"Damn," Reaper said, "I know you're right, but what the hell am I going to do about this? Even if we wanted to give them what they want, he hasn't called on this damned cell phone to demand anything more. I have never felt so fucking helpless in my life."

Deckert didn't know what to say to his friend. He, too, felt helpless to do anything to affect the situation. Reaper had been working with Deckert for some time now, and the two men had become close friends. In the military, you learned how to judge and who you could trust. It was a skill you needed when your life could be on the line at any time.

As the two men sat thinking about the situation, they heard the sound of a motorcycle coming up the driveway. Without saying a word, Reaper and Deckert separated to be able to cover the maximum area inside the house.

Reaper headed into the kitchen where he could see down the hallway leading to the front doors of the house. Deckert moved into the retail area, and took up a position behind a counter. He extended his chair so that he was able to look out over the display case. Underneath the counter top, he held an eight-shot 12-gauge Remington 870 police shotgun with a folding stock. The shotgun was loaded with Tactical-brand #4 buckshot and had been fitted with a DuckBill choke on the muzzle.

The shot spread through the special DuckBill choke would completely cover the front door from Deckert's position. The twenty-seven copper-plated .24-inch hardened lead pellets in a single Tactical round could easily deal with most targets. The stock was folded up over the top of the receiver and barrel for compactness and ease of movement in a confined space. With his hands and arms powerful from work and rolling his wheelchair for years, Deckert could handle the big weapon as if it was a pistol.

In spite of his favorite Taurus revolver having been taken, Reaper was far from unarmed. In his hands he held a SIG P-220 semiautomatic pistol. The blued steel, double-action weapon was chambered for .45 ACP, the same round that Deckert preferred for his M1911A1.

There were eight Federal 230-grain Hydra-Shok hollowpoints loaded in the SIG's magazine, with one chambered and ready to fire. The special Hydra-Shok ammunition would expand as it struck a target, penetrating deeply and leaving a rat tunnel-sized hole behind it. Even if the man was wearing body armor, he would feel as if he was hit with a thrown cinder block. Neither Reaper nor Deckert intended being caught as they had the day before.

The sound of the approaching motorcycle stopped as the bike reached the house and the rider shut off the engine. A few moments later, the front door opened and a burly biker in dusty black leathers and heavy boots stepped into the house. He wore a helmet that completely covered his face and head. Pulling off his gloves, the man turned to the right and entered the retail shop.

Pulling his gloves off occupied the man's hands for the moment. But Reaper wasn't going to take any chances. For the moment he was going to stay at his more centralized location. There was no window behind Reaper's back and he could see the front door while still covering the other two entrances to the house from the garage and the shop. He knew that Deckert would be more than ready to deal with their new customer.

In the retail store, Deckert watched the big man move easily and confidently into the room. He didn't recognize the man in his biker outfit and the shop was pretty out of the way for walk-in traffic. If they hadn't been waiting for something to happen, like somebody just walking in the door, he would have solidly locked up the front.

"Can I help you?" Deckert asked from his place behind the counter.

"Yeah," the stranger said in a gruff voice still muffled by the helmet, "I'm looking for Ted Reaper. I was told I could find him here."

"He's not available right now," Deckert said. "What's your business with him, maybe I can help?"

"I don't think so, I'd just like to see him. It's kind of personal."

"I'm sure he wouldn't mind if you told me," Deckert said.

"No, I'd like to speak to him first," the stranger said. As he spoke, he reached up to his jacket pockets with both hands.

As soon as the stranger's hands went up, Deckert raised his shotgun above the counter. He didn't have to turn the barrel, the weapon had been leveled at the biker from the moment he had come through the door.

"Stand real still," Deckert said. There was a sharp twinge of pain across his back as he raised the Remington—a reminder of the two big bruises from the bullets of the day before. The muzzle of the shotgun looked even larger than it normally did with the big DuckBill choke on it. The inch-wide V-slot of the choke added even more to the intimidation factor of the weapon.

But the big biker didn't seem intimidated to Deckert. He just froze in his movement.

"I wondered just what kind of cannon you had under that counter," the big biker said. "I should have known an Army guy would need a big gun to make up for something."

As Deckert stared at the man, the biker started to chuckle quietly. The sound quickly grew to a loud laugh, a very distinctive loud laugh.

"Ho, ho, ho," the man roared. "You should see your face Deckert. Having that mean old squid working for you making you a little bit jumpy now?"

The sound of that laugh snapped Reaper's head toward the front of the shop. The voice had sounded a little familiar but muffled by the helmet, he hadn't been able to place it. But that laugh was something he would never forget.

Reaper strode down the hall and into the retail shop. He looked at the back of the biker, who had not moved since Deckert had raised the shotgun.

"Can I take my helmet off now?" the man asked.

"Go ahead," Deckert said, not lowering the shotgun an inch.

As the black helmet came off the man's head, Reaper stepped to the side and looked into the face of an old Teammate and friend.

"Damn," Reaper almost shouted, "Bear! What the hell are you doing here? God damn, but it's good to see you."

"Damn, I should have known it was you," Deckert

said as he lowered the weapon. "Sorry about that."

He laid the shotgun on the counter top, the muzzle pointing away from Bear, but with the weapon still within reach.

"Hey, no problem, man," Bear said with a big grin on his face. "I figured if you were just going to shoot me, you would have done it when I came through the door."

Bear turned to Reaper while still holding his gloves and helmet in his hands. The two men wrapped their arms around each other in a powerful embrace, slapping each other's back as they did so. Standing back, Reaper took a look at his old partner.

"It is good to see you, Teammate," Reaper said. "But you really picked a time to finally come around. I invited you out here last summer."

"Well, I couldn't make it then," Bear said. "I've been traveling around a lot since I retired from the Teams. But when Keith here gave me a call yesterday, I rode all night to get here."

"So, Keith called you did he?" Reaper said looking at Deckert. "Did he tell you what was going on?"

"Just that there was trouble and you could use some help, was all," Bear said. "It was not the most detailed phone call I've ever gotten, but it didn't have to be. He said you needed help and here I am. Things must be interesting. Or do you two greet all of your customers with guns in your hands? If you do, this place isn't going to be staying open long."

With that, Bear stepped over to the counter and laid his helmet and gloves down. Sticking his hand out to Deckert, the two men shook hands with a strong grip.

"Real good to see you, man," Bear said. "I hope having this old Navy chief here is working out for you."

"He keeps life interesting, that's for sure," Deckert said. "And just what in the hell were you reaching for a minute ago anyway?"

"Reaching for?" Bear said puzzled. "Oh, you mean when I was going to put my gloves in my pockets?"

"Yeah, with a gun pointed at you," Deckert said.

"Just what in the hell is that thing on the end of that barrel anyway?" Bear said as he looked down at the shotgun on the counter. "It looks like something the Teams carried back in the Vietnam days."

"It is, sort of," Deckert said as he laid his hand on the weapon. "A reproduction, anyway. It's a Duck-Bill choke. Some friends of mine make them now, they're copies of the ones the SEALs carried in Vietnam. Change the pattern from a circle to an oval four times as wide as it is high."

Deckert picked up the Remington and hung it by its sling from the back of his wheelchair. "Kind of turns the gun into a big chain saw. Makes it hard for us old guys to miss."

"Not bad, even for an old guy," Bear said.

Turning to Reaper, Bear continued. "Shoot man, if we're done handling guns, you got a beer around here someplace? I've got enough road dust in my throat to cover a highway."

Reaper went over and locked the front door and Bear followed him to the rear of the house. Bear and Reaper sat down at the table in the dining nook next to the kitchen. Deckert had passed through the office and into the kitchen, stopping at the refrigerator to pull out three long-necked bottles of Corona Extra beer. Wheeling himself over to the kitchen table, Deckert paused to take a bottle opener off a peg next to the refrigerator. He set the bottles and opener down onto the table.

"Hey," Bear said as he reached for a bottle and the opener, "classy. All the modern conveniences. Bet you've even got indoor plumbing."

"Well, it is a bit better than some of the places we've stayed at," Reaper said as he opened a bottle. "Warmer at least. Dryer, too."

"Okay," Bear said. "We've said all the nice things and you showed me the wrong end of a great big gun. You officially have my interest. Now just what in the hell is going on here?"

"What did Keith here tell you?" Reaper asked.

"Nothing much," Bear said. "Only that you were in trouble and needed some help. That was enough to bring me in. As far as details go, I don't know a damned thing."

"And you didn't think to ask?" Reaper said.

"You would have?" said Bear.

"Okay, I can't argue much with that, brother," Reaper said. "Well, the short version is that a guy showed up yesterday along with a pair of goons. They tried to strong-arm me into giving them a bunch of new guns that we've been developing here. Keith got caught up in the fallout."

"Some butthead came in here to strong-arm you?" Bear said a little incredulously. "How the hell did he expect to get away with that?"

"He had some of his boys grab up Mary and

Ricky," Reaper said quietly. "When he came out here, he already had them secured someplace. I went after him to try and get him to tell me where they were. I took out his wheels but he got away."

"He's got Mary and Ricky?" Bear said with surprise evident in his voice. "So why don't you get the cops or the FBI on his ass? This place should be crawling with detectives right now."

"The son of a bitch had Mary contact her boss and tell him that she was taking Ricky and getting out of town for a while. Seems everyone was able to believe that she would be afraid of an ex-SEAL husband."

"Sorry, brother," Bear said. "I had heard that you were having some family trouble—not that that's too unusual with Team guys. But why don't you go find this guy and beat the intel you want out of him?"

"Because when Reaper here tore the ass off that guy's Vette," Deckert said, "he ducked into a marsh and disappeared. We're not even sure he's alive. The last thing he said to us was that we had seventy-two hours to build him some more guns. Since then, there haven't been any more demands made, no calls, nothing. When Reaper here thought I had been shot, he quit looking for the guy and came screaming-ass back here."

"You got shot?" Bear asked. "You look pretty good for a dead guy."

"I was wearing a vest," Deckert said disgustedly. "But while Reaper was heading back here, the two guys who had come in with this guy got away. I really owe something to the small one who got the drop on me."

"Don't beat yourself up," Reaper said. "I'm the

one who didn't do a good shakedown on the guy."

"I seem to remember being the one to tell you to get out after that guy," Deckert said. "And now all we have to show for it is a damaged hot rod, a single name, and a beat-up briefcase."

"Damaged hot rod?" Bear asked.

"You should see what a souped-up Checker cab can do to the fiberglass back end of a Corvette," Reaper said. "Like hitting dry wood with a splitting ax."

"Okay," Bear said. "I'm sure there's more to that part of the story. But what about the briefcase?"

"It was just a briefcase I found in the front end of the Vette," Reaper said. "There wasn't anything else in the car but the case and what I grabbed up from the glove compartment. None of it was anything incriminating—not a damned thing we could go to the police with. The only name we've got is Steven Arzee, and we're not sure that's his name.

"What we found in the case was mostly business correspondence and paperwork about some kind of bar in Detroit called the Factory. All of it looked legitimate, invoices for booze, food, things like that. The most interesting thing was a bunch of business cards for the place with Arzee's name on them. The cards have the title Executive Manager on them."

"I've been looking on the Internet and found some interesting stuff on this Factory club," Deckert said. "It seems to be a pretty popular place with the young crowd, at least its Web site shows a bunch of bands rotating through the place."

"You don't know about that place?" Bear said. "I've never been there myself but a bunch of the local bikers know about it. It's built in an old auto plant, that's why they call it the Factory. From what I know about it, it's a great place to pick up chicks. Some of the guys have said you can score just about anything you want there, too."

"It looks like our only solid lead on this Arzee guy, or whoever he may be working with," Reaper said. "Those cards say manager, not owner. So there must be somebody up the line from him. Maybe we can learn something from them."

Bear looked over at his friend. "You wanna go for a visit?" he said as a big smile split his face.

Chapter Fourteen

The situation had changed for Reaper. Now he had something tangible to direct his energies against. Reaper's family probably wasn't being held at the Factory club. It wouldn't do to assume that Arzee was stupid. He wouldn't keep kidnap victims at his own place. He would have them stashed somewhere else, or at least that was the way to plan. The Factory looked to be the best chance of getting a lead on Arzee's location. If Arzee was the guy they wanted, once he had his hands on him Reaper was sure he could convince the man to talk to him.

There was an unknown factor to the equation—who might Arzee be working for? Did he have a boss? If he did, they had yet to show themselves.

To act on the situation, they needed intelligence: they had to gather information on Arzee and the best lead they had for now was this Factory club. A reconnaissance of the club would have to be conducted, a straightforward urban sneak-and-peek.

Conducting covert recons of an area and then setting up a concealed observation post was something Reaper was very experienced at. His friends Bear and Deckert were not going to allow him to go that mission alone. One very good thing about the situation: if Reaper had to go into a bad area with minimal support, Bear was the Teammate he wanted at his side.

The location of the Factory club was easy enough to find. The street and Web-site addresses had both been on Arzee's business cards. Specific information on the place wasn't any harder than looking it up on the Internet. They even showed a map to the club's location.

The Web site told about how the Factory was a modern techno music club with all of the amenities. What wasn't mentioned on the site or anywhere else, was Steven Arzee by name or as the executive manager. More hours of research on the Internet, combined with a number of phone calls, uncovered nothing more useful than a bewildering morass of company names, limited liability corporations, and a lot of dead ends.

Deckert's police connections in Detroit knew about the club, but that was about all. The place had its share of trouble in the past but nothing unusual, nothing that made it stand out as more than a bar or dance club. The Factory just didn't raise any particular red flags on the police radar.

While Deckert and Reaper were doing their research, Bear made some calls of his own and then left on his Harley. About an hour later, Bear returned driving a nondescript Chevy van with his bike in the back. He just said that he had borrowed the vehicle from an old friend, figuring they would need something low-key to operate from. Reaper could only marvel at how Bear seemed to know somebody everyplace he went. The man had more contacts than a politician.

Transportation was laid on and the target had been located. It was time to gear up and head out. When Bear came into the house, Reaper was back at the kitchen table packing a bag with gear. Reaper was using a Camelback HAWG backpack. The green backpack had a number of attachment points for gear on its outside surfaces. There was also room for 1,100 cubic inches of gear inside it.

All the space in the backpack would be needed for the camera gear Reaper was laying out on the kitchen table. There was the camera itself, and a single telephoto lens that was almost half a foot long. A huge black-and-white cylinder with a number of bars and posts attached to it sat on the table. The big cylinder was over a foot long and half that dimension thick. A compact folding tripod, a small pair of Carl Zeiss 8x30 binoculars, and several other small bags and packages made up the balance of the gear going in the backpack.

Reaper had already filled the 100-ounce flexible liquid reservoir that fit in a special pocket in the backpack. The water that filled the reservoir was available simply by biting on a mouthpiece and sipping at the end of a tube that went over the shoulder strap and into the pack. You could wear the pack and never need to pull out a canteen.

"Damn," Bear said. "You got enough to take a few snapshots there?"

"Just the essentials for a long surveillance," Reaper said. "I've got another one here for you."

He reached down to the floor and picked up a second backpack from a different manufacturer that their shop had started carrying. The pack was a Hydrastorm Tsunami and also had a 100-ounce water reservoir inside a special pocket. A delivery tube went over the shoulder and had a bite valve on the end.

"I gotta carry all that shit as well?" Bear asked.

"No, just what you think you'll need for a twenty-four-hour observation post," Reaper answered. "We may not have the OP set up that long, but that's the way I want to plan. I recommend you fill that reservoir with water and toss in something solid to eat. There's some oatmeal bars in the drawer over there."

"Oatmeal bars?" Bear said, now recognizing several of the brown-wrapped rectangular chunks lying on the table. "You mean MRE oatmeal bars?"

"Yeah," Reaper said as he continued to check through his gear, "Keith likes them and bought a couple of cases from a supplier a while back."

"Never trust an Army guy to have good taste in food," Bear said as he dug through the drawer. He pulled out several of the oatmeal bars, as well as a handful of chocolate bars. Going back over to the table, he dropped his pile and picked up the Hydrastorm Tsunami. As he held the pack, he took a closer look at the sophisticated camera gear on the table. The huge black-and-white cylinder with the protrusions all over it turned out to be a short, fat telescope.

"Just what is that rig anyway?" Bear asked.

"This?" Reaper said pointing to the telescope.

"This is a Celestron C5 Schmidt-Cassegrain telescope set up with a T-ring adapter so that it can act as a 1,250 millimeter f/10 telephoto lens. Basically, it's a five-inch diameter reflecting scope with lenses. You get really fine details with it so you can blow up the shots as big as you want."

"Uh-huh," Bear said, "and this is?"

"This is a Nikon D100 six-megapixel D-SLR digital camera body along with a 75- to 300-millimeter telephoto lens spare battery pack and a one gigabite Lexar compact flashcard—digital film. There's a spare charged ENL3 battery-pack battery and another Lexar flashcard in the boxes."

"Right," Bear said. "Do you really have any idea of what you just said?"

"Not really," Reaper said with a grin. "Mostly I just read all that stuff from the box."

"This kind of thing is just laying around a gun shop?" Bear asked.

"No," Reaper said. "This rig belongs to Keith. He uses it to take pictures of birds. Puts them up on his computer."

"He watches birds?" Bear said a little incredulously.

"Yeah, birds," Reaper said. "Said he had a pair of peregrine falcons nesting near here a few years back. When you shoot on the range next to the shop, hawks start circling downrange watching for any game you scare up."

"Bird-watching," Bear said. "Chief, I'm worried about the two of you. You guys have got to start getting out more."

Reaper grinned at his friend, then looked back

down at the gear. He remembered the reason he was packing it and the grin quickly faded.

"With this kind of camera rig," Reaper said, "we won't have to develop any film before we can see the pictures. Keith has all the computer programs and stuff he needs to make us any kind of enlargements or hard copies *we* might need. This rig eliminates a possible security leak because we don't have to go out and get film developed. Pack whatever you want to take, we're leaving soon."

Bear knew that the joking was over and set to work. Besides the packs, there were two bundles of cloth rolled up and secured with line. In addition to the camera gear and other materials, Reaper was stuffing a towel into the HAWG pack to pad out the camera and lenses. Since Reaper had a concealed carry license for Michigan, he was taking his SIG-220 secured in a Galco leather PLE paddle holster set behind his right hip. Over his left hip he wore a Galco double magazine case with two spare magazines to the SIG.

In the right front pocket of his Levi's, Reaper carried his older Emerson Commander-BTS folding knife. The five-inch black G-10 epoxy handle held a 3.75-inch-long black-T coated blade. The knife was larger than the CQC-7BW that Reaper had been carrying, but that blade had disappeared along with Musclehead and Gun Weasel—the names Reaper was now using for the two goons from the day before. The value of a good Emerson pocket knife was well proven. Reaper wasn't about to go out without one.

As far as Bear was concerned, all he needed for the recon was a folding knife. They weren't planning to do an assault on the Factory, not even penetrate it for a sneak-and-peek. With nothing in particular on him, Bear could possibly slip into the club with the crowd. No one had seen him with Reaper so there was no reason to connect the two men.

The two SEALs were going to conduct a drive-by to check out the area. If things looked good, they would then set up for a longer observation post. It was a mission they had done dozens of times, both during training and on real-world ops in the field.

The only thing that Reaper was certain about as they headed down to the Factory was that the place was popular. The Web site had listed a number of upcoming events, both raves and several concerts. That could put innocents into the line of fire, another reason to keep that portion of the operation low-profile—a soft probe.

The Factory may have been popular and doing well as a club, but it sure wasn't doing anything for the immediate area around it as far as Reaper and Bear could tell. Their first impression of the neighborhood around the Factory was that of urban decay. In a several square block area, the Factory was the only place that looked as though it wasn't about to fall down or rot away.

Located near the crossroads of the Chrysler and Ford Freeways, two of the major highway arteries in Detroit, access to the Factory wasn't a problem. Moving around the area freely might be. The east end of the block-long building was the only part of the structure that had a good coat of paint on it. That, and the big sign that said THE FACTORY in huge block letters, pretty much showed which end of the building was the main entrance. The other three sides of the six-story structure had been tagged frequently, gang and just plain street graffiti covering every accessible surface.

In their beat-up van, Reaper and Bear drew no particular attention as they drove around on the surface streets near the Factory. Bear needed little in the way of disguise to blend in with the locals, his biker jacket, heavy boots, and faded Levi's did not stand out any more than did his beard and sunglasses. Reaper also wore Levi's over work boots, and had a long black nylon jacket zipped up over a gray sweatshirt. Dark glasses and a knit cap completed his street outfit.

The men did not want to stand out in the neighborhood around the club. Red and gray brick houses that had seen their heyday more than forty years earlier made up the neighborhood that surrounded the Factory to the south and west. To the north and east were smaller factory buildings, most of them vacant and empty. Just as empty were the boarded-up houses that used to hold the workers who manned those factories.

Both SEALs felt as if they were traveling through a war zone. The occasional pair of suspicious eyes that looked out a window just reinforced those feelings.

"Damn," said Bear, "we saw better areas in Bosnia."

Reaper just grunted in agreement as he watched the Factory building looming up in front of the next street corner. They were going to do a drive-by on several sides of the Factory. Then they would head up one of the surface roads and cross a bridge over the highway. There was an industrial storage building directly across from the plant.

The south face of the Factory building had been the loading docks and storage area when it had been an active auto plant. There were still stacks of steel frames and piles of industrial debris along the fence line—too open to make good cover during a penetration. The fence wasn't in the best of repair, but it was all standing with no holes or gaps in the fifteen-foot-tall wire mesh. Three strands of barbed wire on top of the fence extended into the yard on angled supports. The wire was tight and clean with no breaks or missing strands. There were a number of large rollaway gates in the fence, all but one secured with heavy chains and padlocks.

The only gate that looked used was at the far southeastern corner of the property. As the van passed the gate, Reaper took a number of pictures of the gate, fence, and yard area behind it. A draped towel covered and hid most of the camera from prying eyes during his pass—Reaper aiming and shooting the camera by feel. Lots of pictures would help make up for any misaimed shots. The telephoto lens showed a good view of the power system for pulling the gate open and closed with a chain drive.

At the center and southwestern corner of the main building were rectangular concrete extensions that looked as if they held stairways and big freight elevators. The elevators would have moved the cars up and down through the floors.

"Bear," Reaper said, "look at those two big elevator stacks. See the square chimneys between them?"

"Those bolted-together ones?" Bear asked.

"Yeah," said Reaper. "See any problem in climbing up them?"

Several of the stacks were very close together—only a few feet apart at most. Reinforcing bars and flanges stuck out from all sides of the stacks. To experienced climbers like Reaper and Bear, those stacks were as good as a stairway or ladder—only a lot better for concealment.

"Nope," Bear said agreeing with Reaper. "All of that stuff sticking out from those stacks will give us as many foot and handholds as we could need. It has to be strong enough to support us or those chimneys would have collapsed of their own weight long ago."

The two men drove on past the Factory and the side street along the west side of the building. Half of the block to the west of the Factory was a huge parking lot. The lot had a few standing double streetlights, and scattered weeds growing through the blacktop. A fifteen-foot-tall chain-link fence stretched around the lot, the fence brown with rust.

The west wall of the Factory had four rows of green glass windows on the upper floors. The windows along the bottom two floors had been bricked over. The few windows that remained were glazed with thick, wire-reinforced glass in steel frames. There were no doors on this end of the building and no cover in the open parking lot.

Brown brick industrial buildings extended for several blocks north across the street from the Factory building. There were no cameras mounted on telephone poles or any surveillance gear that either SEAL could see anywhere around. No one seemed to care about the area, and no one was on the streets at all. Even the fire hydrant next to the Factory had a yellow circular sign hanging off one of the pipe caps reading OUT OF SERVICE.

Rather than pass the factory again, Bear turned the van left onto a side street as Reaper lifted his camera and took a rapid series of pictures of the north face of the Factory building. Just the same as they had seen on the western wall of the building, the north side of the Factory had four rows of windows along the upper floors. But there were no windows at all along the bottom two floors. Those areas were filled in with what looked like steel paneling.

There were three sets of steel fire doors spaced out along the first floor of the building. In addition to the door openings, there were two sets of fire escapes extending up from the second floor to the sixth floor. These were the obvious ways into the upper floors and would probably be alarmed.

There was no graffiti on the north face of the Factory above the sidewalk level, the upper wall was clean. If none of the local artists felt like going up those inviting fire escapes, then Reaper and Bear weren't going to climb them either. Going in the easy way to a target had never proved to be the safe way.

Going north along a side street away from the Factory, Bear turned right and then drove the van across a bridge to the eastern side of the highway. At this point, the Chrysler Freeway was eight lanes of divided highway at the bottom of a man-made valley.

Facing the east end of the Factory building from across the highway was a five-story storage warehouse. Half-filled dumpsters and scattered construction vehicles were the only signs that the place was still active. The dumpsters had a lot of cardboard boxes in them that were unweathered. Since it had rained just the week before, the condition of the boxes told Reaper and Bear that somebody had been working around these dumpsters recently.

Trash had to be generated by somebody, and that meant there was probably activity in the building, something neither of the two SEALs were particularly pleased to note. The storage building had a clear view of the east side of the Factory on the other side of the highway. It was from the roof of this building that Reaper wanted to set up their observation post.

Chapter Fifteen

Reaper and Bear were conducting their mission as if they were well behind enemy lines with no support. They had no backup on call, no emergency extraction, no fire support. Everyone in the area of the Factory or the chosen observation post (OP) location would be assumed to be the enemy, with no exceptions. The rules of engagement were simple, there would be no engagements. Contact would be avoided—period.

The two SEALs had worked on operations like this before, but never where the stakes had been so high. It wasn't their own lives the two men had to be concerned with, it was the lives of Reaper's wife and son. If discovered, they could expect no mercy from the kidnappers. And if they were caught by the police, the only thing they could reasonably expect would be for the kidnappers to cut their losses, and eliminate any witnesses.

There was no question that Bear would support his Teammate in any way that he was capable of. But the real cost of their success or failure would be held by Reaper alone. The only way he could operate under this much pressure was to cut it off, shut out personal feelings, and deal with the task at hand. This was something they learned in the Teams, you could either compartmentalize your life and concentrate on your job, or not remain an operator.

The ability to ignore the pain, the distractions, and keep going, was something Reaper needed very badly right now. For the time being, those aspects of his personality that made him a father, a husband, a lover, were closed off. The compartments in his psyche that were left open were the ones that made him an experienced, efficient, Navy SEAL chief.

But he was not alone on this operation. His Teammate being with him meant a very great deal to Reaper. SEALs didn't operate alone, they were always part of a Team, even a team as small as two men. Bear and Reaper had trained together, frozen, sweated, and ached as one unit. In the field, one would know what the other was thinking automatically. In any situation, they knew what the other man would do, how he would react.

So Reaper was not completely alone; he had Bear and Deckert to work with. Deckert had proven himself a very valuable resource. From his desktop computer, Deckert had come up with hard intelligence that was proving very valuable right now.

Besides detailed maps of the area they were traveling in, Deckert had located aerial and satellite photos on the Internet. These shots gave a lot of information about the Factory and the area surrounding it. The drive-by that the two SEALs had completed confirmed the intel Deckert had developed.

The east end of the Factory faced another fenced-in parking lot. Then there were the lanes and ramps of the highway intersection. There was nothing close-in that the two SEALs could use for cover, no place where they could park a vehicle overnight without drawing attention. It was the building complex across the highway from the Factory that looked good. Behind the storage building were a number of areas where vehicles were parked and construction equipment stored. They would launch their mission from that area.

Up close against the side of the warehouse was a large billboard mounted on tall posts. The billboard would supply cover for the two men as they climbed up to the roof of the main building. On top of the roof were two huge elevated billboards, plainly visible from the highway and the area across the street. It was there, at the base of those huge signs, that the SEALs would set up their hide, their camouflaged hidden position, and establish their observation post.

Bear's bike was secured in the back of the van along with the rest of their gear. Some of the equipment was very high tech. Other pieces were from the much lower end of the technology scale. Two sets of generic dark coveralls would cover the two SEALs and help them to blend in with any workmen in the area. In the pockets of each of the coveralls were a pair of FOGs (Fast-rope Operator Gloves) and a Hatch balaclava hood made of lightweight black Nomex. Two five-gallon plastic buckets with lids, some rolled-up dark cloths, a couple of sections of carpeting not much bigger than medium-sized throw rugs, and a few coils of parachute cord made up the bulk of their equipment.

Two additional pieces of gear would look odd to anyone but a SEAL: a pair of extendable aluminum painter's poles. The top of each pole had a two-pronged steel hook attached to it, the prongs of the hooks well padded with heavy tape. With a line that was fixed to it, the hook slipped down into the hollow pole. Catching the tines of the hook on an object would pull it from the pole, securely attaching a climbing line to the target.

The modifications had converted the painter's poles into climber's extension poles, the same kind of tool that the SEALs used to board ships with. Normally, a coiled caving ladder was used with the hooks. Instead of the ladders, Reaper was using lengths of 9/16-inch tubular nylon webbing. The flat nylon webbing took up little space and was very strong. Using it to scale a building wall took a lot of upper-body and grip strength, something Bear and Reaper had plenty of.

Bear pulled the van around and parked it among some trucks and other vehicles. The van was beat up enough that it didn't stand out in the lot. A little maneuvering parked the van so that the back end was clear and Bear's bike could be rolled out. The area in front of the van was clear so that it could be driven forward and onto the road quickly.

The two SEALs were now in their element. They were operational on a hot op. It didn't matter that they were in civilian territory. Working together as they were was like putting on an old coat. They were comfortable and at ease while also working at a heightened state of awareness.

The two men changed into their coveralls, gathered up their gear, and left the van. Both men had a set of keys to the van and to Bear's Harley. The devil was in the details. Little things like spare keys was something that couldn't be missed. Eventually, your luck would run out. Mr. Murphy was always prepared to screw over you and your mission.

Anyone who noticed the two men leaving the parking lot would only see another pair of workers. An observer would have had to look fast to see the two workers disappear next to an old and faded billboard.

While Bear kept watch, Reaper scrambled up the side of a ladder attached to the billboard. The bottom of the ladder was slightly out of reach overhead, but Reaper just jumped and started up the ladder using the strength of his arms. A platform surrounded the billboard and that was where Reaper stopped. The gear buckets came up next on the ends of the nylon lines. Bear clambered up the ladder not as gracefully as Reaper had, but with just as much obvious strength.

The five-story storage building that Reaper wanted to reach was at the northwest corner of a block of four structures. They were now within reach of the top of the two-story building at the southeast corner of the block. This place seemed a little newer than the others in the area. It did have more security than the others. Someone had secured concertina coils of shiny, sharp new razor wire along the edge of the roof coaming to block possible burglars.

Razor wire was sharp, it was nasty, and it was

something that Reaper and Bear had seen a number of times during their training and while out on missions. They had faced much more sophisticated barriers during some of their training when they penetrated classified Navy installations to test security.

This was the only avenue of approach the SEALs could use to get on the roof in broad daylight. The upper part of the billboard stuck up past the edge of the roof, protecting it from view.

The billboard was not going to be enough to protect the two SEALs from the observation of anyone who was on the roof of any of the buildings in the block. The aerial photos that Deckert had located showed plain, flat tar roofs on two of the structures they would have to cross. The two men would have to get on the roof and cross it quickly to avoid being seen.

Both men quickly set to work without a word being spoken between them. They broke out and secured the gear, then left the buckets on the platform. As Bear extended a climbing pole and attached a webbing coil to the hook, Reaper undid one of the cloth bundles. Wrapped around the outside of the bundle was one of the sections of carpeting.

Using the extended climbing pole, Bear set the hook on the edge of the roof. Reaper secured the carpet section to his belt with a piece of nylon webbing. Then he grabbed the webbing leading to the hook, stepped out, and walked up the side of the building, ignoring the three-story drop below him. Grabbing hold of the edge of the roof, Reaper pulled himself up enough to peer out across the flat tar.

No one was there. It was just a flat expanse of roof with about sixteen inches of wall surrounding it. The only movement was the fluttering of some plastic shreds where discarded bags had stuck to the razor wire coils. A quick glance across the other roofs didn't uncover any possible observers to Reaper.

Pulling the carpet section up, Reaper tossed it across the razor wire. Pulling himself up and over the carpet, Reaper made climbing onto the roof look easy.

Now that one of them was exposed on the roof, speed became essential. Bear quickly got onto the roof and pulled up the climbing pole. Crouching low, the two men crossed over to the next building they had to climb. This roof only went up a single story above the one they were on and part of the structure blocked anyone's view of the two SEALs.

No fancy climbing technique was used to get to the next roof. Reaper secured one end of the nylon webbing to his belt. Then Bear cupped his hands and Reaper stepped into them. Bear lifted Reaper up to where he could look out over the next roof. No razor wire or observers could be seen, only the dark, dirty windows of another wall.

Pulling himself up to the roof, Reaper pulled the web line off his belt. Bracing his feet against the wall, Reaper leaned back with the webbing tight in his hands. A quick yank on the line and Bear climbed up to the roof.

Crossing to the last wall, the two SEALs repeated their technique and within a minute, both men were on top of the building where Reaper wanted to set up the observation post. It was a good location and both men could see the Factory plainly on the far side of the highway.

There were two huge billboards on top of the

storage building. Reaper wanted to set up their OP at the base of one of those billboards. A small shacklike building up against the western side of the roof topped a stairwell to the inside of the building. The doorway of that shack was where any guard or observer could be expected.

A worn fiberglass and metal tubing chair next to the stairwell door was a bad sign. The chair was flipped over and leaning against the stairwell top, just as it would be if someone used it regularly and didn't want rain to be caught in the seat. For the moment, the roof was empty of people except for the two SEALs.

Chapter Sixteen

Now that both men were finally on the target roof itself, they moved fast to get into a concealed position—what they called their hide. The huge billboards were set on top of steel columns that were secured to the roof by a heavy girder and mesh frame. There was almost two feet of space between the steel mesh on the frame and the tar and gravel surface of the roof itself. Reaper intended to set up their observation post in the space under the frame.

The billboard structure stood right next to the stairwell. With Bear next to him, Reaper crouched low and ran to the platform. Ignoring the sharp edges of the gravel, both Reaper and Bear lay down and scrambled underneath the edge of the frame. Crawling up to where they could look out over the roof coaming, they began to set up their observation post.

Their first move was to secure the observation post from the view of anyone looking from the Factory. To do that, they unrolled a length of Hessian screen and hung it up in front of what was now their hide. Hessian screen was nothing more than plain, rough-woven jute cloth—simple burlap. The weave of the dark brown cloth was open enough to easily see through it if you were on the shaded side and looked out toward the light. Looking in from the lighted side, you couldn't see past the cloth.

The billboard platform was a heavy steel grid welded onto a framework of I-beams. The whole platform was raised above the surface of the roof on a bunch of short steel legs. The legs ran around the edge of the platform as well as down the middle the long way. To hang up the cloth screen, Reaper and Bear clipped it to the bottom flange of one of the I-beams with wooden spring clothespins. Once the screen was up, the rest of the observation post, now a camouflaged hide, could be completed.

The two collapsed painter's poles were used to support a dark drop-cloth cover over the hide. With the cloth in place, it would be very hard to see the two men in the shadows even if someone were standing on the grid. The poles leaned in against the front I-beam with their back ends on the gravel roof. The open end of the tentlike hide was covered with the Hessian screen.

The carpet sections now proved additionally useful as Reaper and Bear pulled them up and rolled the strips out across the gravel. They would protect the men from some of the coarse chunks of rock as well as cut down on any noise they might make. A quick look around the outside edges of the hide didn't show any light, so if the two SEALs couldn't see out, no one could see in. The hide was secure and they were in place.

Both men started to assemble their cameras and

observation equipment. The Celestron C5 scope that Reaper was using was so big it sat on its own small folding tripod. There was a T-ring adapter on the back of the scope that connected it to the Nikon D100 digital camera.

Bear had brought Deckert's spare camera, a Minolta Dynax 7000i 35mm film camera. The film camera was a backup in case something went wrong with the digital system. The dozen rolls of film Bear had in his pack shouldn't even need to be used on the mission.

There was an old adage in the Teams regarding mission-critical gear. "Two is one, one is none." If one piece of important gear was all you had brought with you and it failed, then so did the mission. And this mission was far too important for any details to have been overlooked.

Picking up his binoculars, Reaper looked out across the highway to the Factory building about 275 meters away. He cupped his hands across the top and sides of the binoculars. With the sun still high in the midafternoon sky, Reaper's hands protected the lenses from flashing in the light. The simple precaution was second nature to the man. To his right, Reaper could feel Bear setting out the spare camera and telephoto lens as well as his own binoculars.

Not a word had been spoken between the two men since they had left the van. Now they settled in for a long vigil. From any side of the roof and even through the steel grid of the platform, all that could be seen was a dark pile of loose cloth, as if a tarp had been shoved up underneath the platform, or blown there by an errant wind.

With their black balaclavas pulled over their heads, the two men disappeared into the shadows of their hide. There was no way that anyone from ground level could see up into the area five stories above where the SEALs lay. From the Factory, even a person using a powerful telescope and who knew where to look would have seen nothing more than shadow.

The basic infiltration of the target area had been completed. Now the two SEALs would take careful note of all activity around the Factory. This would be a long, painstaking operation. They were on the military equivalent of a police stakeout, only Reaper and Bear didn't have anyone to come and relieve them. They could only lie still and watch.

Through his binoculars, Reaper could see the entire east wall of the Factory building, the parking lot that lay between the building and the highway, and the fields to the north and south of the empty lot. Running along both the south and east sides of the fields were major multilane interstate highways.

The Ford Freeway passed over the Chrysler only a few hundred meters south of where Reaper and Bear lay. The intersecting highways made for a mass of bridges and curved ramps crossing over one another. The ramps, lanes, shoulders, fences, and excavated area put a no-man's-land more than a hundred meters wide between the hide and the beginning of the parking area to the east of the Factory.

The east parking area of the Factory was a huge, square, fenced-in area of concrete—one hundred meters on a side. It appeared to have regular activity as the concrete surface was in fairly good repair. There were no signs of the weeds and grasses that broke through the surface of the parking area to the west of the Factory.

Light poles stood in the parking lot and it was surrounded by a fifteen-foot-high chain-link fence topped with barbed wire. At each corner of the lot were closed-circuit TV cameras on top of tall poles.

South of the parking area, across a two-lane road, was a weed-choked vacant lot. The most prominent feature of the lot was another massive billboard raised up on a steel framework. The advertising sign was huge, more than eighty feet wide and almost a third of that tall. The bottom of the billboard was raised up nearly a hundred feet into the air so that it could be clearly seen from both the northbound Chrysler and westbound Ford Freeways.

There was a much smaller billboard next to the massive one, the smaller facing to the southwest and connected to the larger at its southern corner. The larger billboard had a wide platform around its base with a ladder leading up to it along one of the support pillars. These billboards could be seen a long distance away along either highway. They also had a direct view into the front windows of the Factory.

Reaper and Bear examined all of these details through their binoculars. In spite of the cameras available to them, both men each carefully sketched out a map, a panoramic view, of what they saw. They would compare the two sketches later to see if either man noticed something the other had missed.

His area sketch finished, Reaper turned his attention to the Factory building itself. It was the east-facing wall of the factory that Reaper studied through his binoculars. Then he attached the Nikon to the back of the Celestron scope and carefully photographed every feature of the wall.

Almost the entire eastern face of the building was made up of windows. It consisted of six floors of windows, each floor having seven panels of glass separated by white columns. The window panels were made up of dozens of glass panes held in a steel frame.

The huge front of the building was half a block wide and twenty-five-meters tall. Thick blinds were on the inside of the hundreds of windows to block the blinding morning sun. Now, with the sun past noon and lowering to the west, the windows remained covered on the inside—not a good situation for outside observation.

It was only midafternoon and there was still a full day to go.

Chapter Seventeen

By 3 P.M., 1500 hours in Reaper's log, the traffic on the highways increased considerably as the local rush hour began. By 1530 hours, the traffic on the highway ramps below the SEALs was bumper-to-bumper. Traffic was heavy, but nothing was going on at the Factory that Reaper or Bear could see.

At 1613 hours, Reaper was watching as a brown UPS truck pulled up to the front of the Factory. The driver stopped on the street and walked up to the two sets of double doors underneath the big Factory sign. With his clipboard in hand, the delivery driver knocked at the doors and waited.

Reaper was watching the driver through the Nikon camera attached to the big Celestron scope. As Reaper continued to watch, the delivery became more interesting as the man just kept standing at the doors. Even after repeated heavy knocks, it was a few minutes before someone finally came to see who was there. Either the cameras in the parking lot couldn't see the front doors or the person on watch didn't care that anyone was there. Sloppy security was something that particularly interested Reaper. He continued to take pictures and watch the scene.

Whoever had come to the door wasn't the man the driver wanted to see. The doors closed in his face and again, the driver just stood there. The little show in front of the Factory was at least something to watch and helped keep Reaper's attention up. Then there was some action at the door that grabbed Reaper like a hand at his throat.

The front door of the Factory had opened and Steven Arzee was standing there in what looked like a fancy bathrobe.

"Son of a bitch," Reaper said quietly.

Bear had been watching the delivery through a pair of binoculars. The limited magnification of the glasses did not give him as clear a view of the man standing in the door as Reaper had through the big Celestron.

"What?" Bear said softly.

"That's him," Reaper said. "That's Arzee signing the clipboard."

"That's him?" Bear said. "Sure doesn't look like much, does he?"

Reaper continued to concentrate on the action and ignored Bear's comment. Bear looked over at his friend and could see Reaper taking pictures. The concentration in the SEAL's face was obvious as he watched Arzee walk back into the building. As the front doors closed, Reaper snapped a last picture of the scene, his finger steady and firm as he applied pressure to the shutter, the same firm pressure he would have used to pull the trigger of a rifle.

"We found him, Bear," Reaper said. "We've got him."

"What do you want to do now?" Bear asked. "Go after him or what?"

"We maintain surveillance," Reaper said. "Let's see what else shows up."

Bear could tell that his friend was hoping for a sign of his family. It was going to be a long night.

Bear took over the watch at the bottom of the hour. The UPS truck was long gone and there hadn't been any more action at the target. Then, at 1645 hours, a white passenger van pulled out of the single-story structure at the southeast corner of the Factory.

Swinging the big Celestron scope over on its tripod mount, Bear aimed it toward the corner of the Factory fence that had the powered gate. Twisting the deeply knurled silver focusing knob on the back of the scope brought the scene into sharp clarity. Centered in the middle of the scene was the van that had pulled out of the garage and stopped.

Lying to Bear's left, Reaper could also see what showed on the bright LCD screen in the back of the digital camera. Every little detail of the van was in clear view as it stopped at the electric gate. Bear snapped a number of pictures of the van, paying particular attention to the vehicle's license plate, the driver—who couldn't be seen through the darkened window except as a slight silhouette—and a magnetic sign stuck to the side of the van's door. It didn't look as if anyone else was in the van except the driver.

"Check this out," Bear said in a quiet whisper. "They're running some kind of bus service."

Reaper had his binoculars pulled up and focused on the van.

"What does the sign say?" Reaper whispered.

"Golden Casino Tours," Bear said. "What the hell does that have to do with a nightclub for the young crowd? They don't go to casinos for the most part."

"Sounds like something they might be running on the side," Reaper said as the van passed through the now open gate and turned to the west. "Did you see anyone get out or use a hidden touch pad outside the van to open that gate?"

"Nope," Bear said.

"So they must either use a remote control opener or someone inside the garage used a switch," Reaper said.

"Can't see into the garage door from this angle," Bear said. "But it could be a pressure plate or hose on the ground."

"Don't think so," Reaper said. "That van had to sit there for a while, as if someone had to try to find a remote. A pressure switch would have opened the door much faster and started as soon as the van approached."

While the two SEALs whispered their conversation, the powered gate began rolling shut. As the gate closed, other cars started arriving and pulling into the fenced-in parking area to the east of the Factory building.

"Looks like someone is starting to show up," Bear said quietly.

Most of the half-dozen vehicles that arrived over the next fifteen minutes only had a single person in them. Several older sedans had a pair of women stepping out of the doors, one had three ladies leave it. Both Reaper and Bear figured that they were looking at the wait staff arriving for work. The fact that most of the people who got out of the cars were young women reinforced that thought.

"Maybe just a bartender and a bunch of waitresses," Bear said.

"Probably," Reaper replied. "But that guy who drove the Mustang looks a little big to be a bartender. I figure either a front door screener/greeter or maybe a bouncer."

A quiet grunt was all that came back from Bear in the way of an answer.

Time in the hide went by, as did the local traffic on the highways. A few more vehicles had pulled into the Factory parking lot. Arzee may have left in the van, but Reaper didn't think so. Deckert's research and contacts had not been able to come up with a home address for Arzee. Even the address on his Corvette's registration was given as the Factory. Arzee probably had his living quarters someplace in the old auto plant and didn't leave them. It didn't make a difference now, Reaper knew that he was going to have to raid the place they were watching.

To stage a covert raid, they had to continue the surveillance. How things worked at the Factory, who went where and what went on when the place closed, would be vital information. So Bear and Reaper kept their position and watched. Rotating on a thirty-minute schedule kept alert eyes on the target—one of the men watching while the other rested.

They drank sparingly from the backpack containers. Staying hydrated was something both SEALs had learned a long time ago. The oatmeal and chocolate bars would be enough to keep the hunger pangs at bay. Movement had to be kept to a minimum. So they had no chance to get up to take a leak, and no place to do it anyway. Peeing on the side of the building might not seem like much, but the smell could easily catch the attention of a curious guard. The only option remained to simply gut the situation out.

Watching the action at the target helped Reaper and Bear ignore their discomfort. Customers had started to show up, at least cars came in and mixed couples of young people got out and headed into the Factory. Each car was noted and photographed. The same procedure applied to each couple. Then, at 1845 hours, a vehicle showed up that hadn't been expected.

"Hey, Reaper," Bear whispered, "check this out. That casino van is back."

Reaper was already looking at the big white passenger van as it pulled up to the gate. The van rolled into the driveway, a clear view blocked by the closed gate. It sat there for a few moments without either the gate moving or the van doing anything.

"Look, the sign is gone," Bear whispered.

Reaper had noticed it, too. The sign about "Golden Casino Tours" wasn't on the side of the van. When the vehicle had left only a few hours earlier, there had been signs on both front doors—the side away from the SEALs visible for a short time as the van drove west. Now, the sides of the vehicle were clean.

As both SEALs watched, the driver's side door of the van opened and a man got out. He walked up to the gate and yanked at it. The gate jerked and started to roll open.

"Somebody needs to do their preventative maintenance," Bear said.

"Be sure to get shots of the side windows of that van," Reaper said.

"Already on it, Chief," Bear said.

When the driver opened the door and got out of the van, the interior dome lights came on. The van was in the shade of the building and the inside light made it possible to see through the screened windows. Inside the van, people filled every seat. Checking the screen of the digital camera after the van passed into the garage and the gate closed, Reaper and Bear were able to count four silhouettes for certain, with a possibility of one or two more.

"Now why would they try to slip people into the club though the side door?" Bear asked.

"And why take the signs off the van to do it?" Reaper said.

"Curiouser and curiouser," Bear replied.

The two SEALs returned to their vigil over the front of the Factory building. As the sun set, it became possible to see lights on through the windows on the east side of the building. Only a few lights shone through the upper floor windows, but the shades kept any details from being seen.

The only other activity after the arrival of the white van was an increase in the number of customers. By 2045 hours, it was dusk and the sun had just set. An hour later little had changed, although now some couples were leaving as more arrived.

"You know, Reaper," Bear said as he stood his

watch on the Factory, "there's only one way to really get more information on that place."

"And what is that?" Reaper said in a soft voice.

"One of us is going to have to go in there," Bear said.

"I know, but it isn't going to be the safest thing in the world to do," Reaper said. "Neither of us look like the average customer."

"No," Bear agreed, "but there have been a few bikers in the crowds going in. I could blend in pretty well with them."

"You're volunteering?" Reaper asked.

"You already said that Arzee knows you," Bear said. "So you sure as hell can't be the one going in, and I'm the only other one up here from what I can tell."

Reaper knew that Bear was right. One of them had to go in to gather information from inside the place and Bear was the logical choice. Even though Reaper didn't like the thought of letting his friend face possible danger without immediate backup at hand, he had to agree with Bear's logic.

"Okay, you go," Reaper said finally. "But you get back out and up here by 2300. If you don't, I'll come in and get you in spite of them recognizing me."

"Don't worry, Sweetie," Bear said with a grin. "I'll be back before the streetlights go on."

"Just get the fuck out of here," Reaper said with a smile.

Bear slipped out from under the tarp and went back off the roof by the same route they had used to climb up. Inside of fifteen minutes from Bear's leaving, Reaper heard a Harley's powerful engine being started and driven away. As the engine noise disappeared, Reaper was left alone in the darkness with his thoughts.

After about ten minutes, Reaper noted the arrival of a big motorcycle at the Factory. The bike slowed at a corner, then roared up to the entrance to the parking lot, turned in and stopped. As Bear climbed off his bike, he signaled Reaper that he was all right in his own personal style—he scratched his ass and then waved his hand in the air.

"Clown," Reaper said quietly to himself, smiling as he did so.

No new customers showed up after Bear went into the Factory. Two couples left the club, one at 2150 hours, the other at 2207 hours. Neither couple appeared rushed in any way, so Bear probably hadn't raised a ruckus inside the place.

The last couple to leave appeared in anything but a hurry. They openly showed their feelings toward each other while in the parking lot. When they finally got to their car and climbed inside, the vehicle sat there for a while.

Reaper resisted the urge to swing the big scope around and see exactly why the windows of the car began to fog up so heavily. He didn't think that Bear would have done the same thing on his watch.

The silence of the night was broken by the crunching, grating sound of a steel door being opened—the steel fire door at the head of the stairway leading down into the warehouse underneath him. Someone was coming out of the warehouse and onto the roof.

Reaper could do nothing as he listened to footsteps crunch in the gravel. Then the footsteps clanged as they moved onto a steel grate. The sound was coming from hard-soled shoes on iron steps, and the only iron steps on the whole roof led up to the billboard platform, the platform that Reaper lay hidden beneath.

The steps grew louder as they clanged across the steel grid, then stopped. The tarp over the hide muffled the sound somewhat, but whoever paused up there had to be only a few feet away. Reaper heard the click of a lighter being flicked to life, then the sound of someone taking a drag and exhaling loudly. Somebody was taking a smoke break while looking out over the highway. And they were standing directly over Reaper's hide.

Reaper forced himself to relax and settle down and resumed his watch on the Factory. Now it became urgent that he spot Bear before he tried to return. Reaper's watch read only 2220 hours. Bear still had forty minutes to go before he was supposed to be back at the OP.

The minutes dragged by slowly. There was a "tink" sound and then a tap on the tarp almost on top of Reaper's head. Reaper thought the smoker must have finished his break and tossed away his cigarette. The sound of the shoes once more clanging across the grate and down the steps proved he was right. The door once more crunched shut and it left Reaper alone on the roof.

Ten minutes later Reaper saw Bear leaving the Factory. The only odd thing Reaper could see was that another big guy was escorting Bear to the parking lot. The man just stood at the gate while Bear got on his motorcycle and roared off.

Half an hour later, Bear was back in the hide.

"A guard came out on a cigarette break right on top of here not forty minutes ago," Reaper whispered.

"Yeah, that must be the guy I had to drop downstairs," Bear said.

"What!" Reaper questioned.

"Relax, I'm just fucking with you," Bear whispered. "I stayed below the edge of the roof and listened, then looked, before I came up. There's no one around."

"So why did that guy follow you to the parking lot?"

"You mean Ashel?" Bear whispered as innocently as he was able under the circumstances.

"You know his name?" Reaper whispered.

"Yeah," Bear said. "I've got an appointment with his boss tomorrow night to see about a job as a bouncer."

Reaper shook his head in admiration. "You've got the watch," he said.

Most of the vehicles had been long gone by 0230 when the last of the staff left. The door guard, Ashel, had escorted a number of the ladies to their cars as the club closed for the night. Then the last of the lights on the first floor were turned off and even Ashel left.

Lights were still glowing on the sixth floor of the Factory building, but only in a few windows. By 0245, those lights were off. It seemed odd that not even a single police cruiser had passed by during closing time. That had always been a prime time to bust drivers who had too much to drink before they were able to get out on the major surface streets. But no cops had showed, not one at all.

The morning rush hour picked up around 0500 hours. Both Reaper and Bear had become wet and cold from the morning dew by this time, a condition they had grown used to over the years. What you couldn't change or control, you endured, a basic truth of SEAL operations.

Movement at the garage end of the Factory caused both Reaper and Bear to forget about their uncomfortable surroundings. The white van had made another appearance. This time, the gate opened smoothly and the van exited, turning north. The casino signs still weren't on the van. The dark windows prevented any view of the inside or any occupants.

Normal traffic, both vehicular and on foot, took up the rest of the morning. People came to work and suffered through a Friday morning rush hour. By noon, Reaper announced himself ready to abandon the OP. The two men carefully policed the area. Outside of some scuffed gravel, not a sign showed that the SEALs had even been there. Reaper even tossed the cigarette butt that he found on top of the tarp back underneath the billboard support grid.

Climbing down the walls, the two men headed back to their van. Bear had already secured his bike in the back and they were ready to go. After almost a full day in a camouflaged hide, Reaper had something urgent to attend to. Standing in the cover of the van, Reaper relieved himself into the weeds.

Chapter Eighteen

The ride back to the shop was a somber one for Reaper and Bear. Outside of locating Arzee, they hadn't seen a single positive sign of Reaper's wife or son. Now reaction was setting in from their long mission. A numb, dead tiredness hung over them from being up for more than a day manning their observation post.

During the trip back to Deckert's, Bear had dozed off while Reaper drove. He only woke up as they pulled into the driveway leading to the farm. Bear leaned forward in his seat and stretched out with a wide jaw-cracking yawn and deep growling groan. Reaper thought Bear suddenly resembled his nickname even more than usual.

"You need a tree to scratch your back against before you crap in the woods?" Reaper asked as they pulled up to the house.

A loud fart was Bear's first response.

"Arrgh, me mouth tastes like a she-cat littered in it," he said.

"What?" Reaper said as he pulled the van back around to the rear of the house and parked out of sight of the main road.

"My favorite line from an old Viking movie," Bear said. "It was a Richard Widmark flick called *The Long Ships*. It had lots of great tits in it, too."

As Bear turned to look at his staring friend, he explained. "Hey, I just had the music going through my head okay? I used to think about it during those long swims back in the Teams."

"Whatever works for you," Reaper said with a grin and a shake of his head.

Inside the house, the two SEALs carried their packs with the camera gear into the office where Deckert was waiting.

"Here you go," Reaper said as he handed Deckert the memory card from the Nikon camera.

Without a word, Deckert started downloading the digital photos into his desktop computer. He had software that would let him easily manipulate the pictures the two SEALs had taken during their observations of the Factory. Important shots could be printed off as hard copies for further study.

While Reaper hovered over his friend's shoulder as he worked, Bear sat down at a desk and went over his notes and logbook. He added details and scribbled notes on the margins as he looked at the sketches he had made of the interior of the Factory club floor. There was little talk and no joking as they began to analyze the raw intelligence data gathered during their long vigil.

Looming over Deckert's shoulder got old fast for Reaper. He gathered up the logs, printouts, and other materials, and went out to the kitchen table where they had room to spread out a little. All types of information lay across the table top; satellite and aerial photographs, hard copy photos from the computer, maps, logbooks, sketches, even street maps, newspapers, and Detroit magazines. None of it told Reaper the location of his family. But it did show him the size of their target in graphic detail.

Bear stepped into the kitchen and poured himself a cup of coffee. Carrying his steaming mug, he walked around the counter to the table where Reaper sat. As Bear approached, Reaper put down the pair of dividers he had been measuring a map with. Pushing himself from the table, Reaper leaned far back in his chair and stretched, rubbing his face with both hands as he did so.

"So," Bear said as he sat down at the table, "figured out anything yet?"

"Yeah," Reaper said as he ran his fingers back through his hair, "it's big, really fucking big. That damned factory building is more than 480 feet long, 130 feet wide, and over ninety feet tall. That's more than 62,000 square feet per floor—and there are six floors. That's a whole lot of area for just two guys to cover."

Bear picked up a picture from the pile on the table as Reaper sat back straight in his chair. The picture Bear looked at showed the full east face of the Factory building.

"The first floor is pretty much a wash for anyone being there," Bear said. "It's mostly a big open space broken down into dance pits and band stages. There are a couple of bars and some areas with tables, but no place there could be much in the way of an office. The whole front area near the doors was the kitchen—at least that was where the food came from. There's a coat check on one side of the doors and that's about it. On the southeast end is a stairway going up. It's behind a set of steel fire doors and the guy working at the front door keeps a close eye on it."

"That stairway must also open up on the garage," Reaper said. "It's at that corner of the building."

"Makes sense," Bear said. "The only other way up to the other floors was by a ramp on the north side of the building, and that was closed off behind the main bar. There are three different freight elevators on the south side of the building, but the gates to those are chained and locked. Except for the smallest one up near the front, none of them even looked used. The two main elevators had their platforms up on the second floor, blocking them off."

"During the night," Reaper said, "the only floor that showed any activity besides the first floor was the top floor, the sixth. That one had lights on. Everything I've seen indicates that there's offices only on the eastern end of the building."

"That matches up with some of the stories Deckert came up with about when that was an active auto plant," Bear said. "All of the admin offices and white-collar work went on at that end of the building. The plant manager had his office somewhere on the top floor. Everything else was assembly lines. They even left some of the line machinery as decorations around the main floor—it separated some of the dance pits and stages."

"That makes the east end of the top floor the priority target," Reaper said. "By 0235 hours, all of the cars in the parking lot were gone. Even the working staff had left by then. But that enclosed garage at the southeast corner is an unknown factor."

"So," Bear said, "I'll watch the hallway and stairs while you search the office."

"I wasn't asking you to go in with me on this one, Bear," Reaper said. "This isn't any kind of sanctioned op. I'm going after my family and I can't ask someone to break the law and go in with me."

"Don't remember you asking," Bear said as he tossed the picture he had been examining back onto the table. "You figure you can keep me out of this, brother?"

Reaper looked at the man for a moment, unable to think of anything to say.

"You've been up what, thirty, thirty-six hours straight?" Bear said. "Small wonder you can't see what's right in front of your face. Get a couple of hours of sleep and we'll hit it again."

"Can't afford the time," Reaper said. "They are going to call for more weapons by tomorrow afternoon. We have less than twenty-four hours to find my family and stop this."

"What you can't afford is to make a mistake, Chief," Bear said. "Deckert is going to take some time to finish up processing the pictures anyway."

Reaper had to admit the logic of what his friend had said.

"Okay, you're right," Reaper said. "I'm going to grab a couple of hours of sleep, then look at all of this again."

"Sounds good to me," Bear said.

—

The insistent buzz of the alarm awakened Reaper after what felt like only a few minutes of sleep instead of a few hours. Years of iron-hard discipline had him turn off the alarm clock and swing his feet off the bed while the rest of his body still wanted to sleep. He was a little rested now, though not much. His eyes felt thick and gritty. If his breath smelled half as bad as his mouth tasted, he'd better be careful about where he breathed or he'd blister the paint on the walls.

A quick, scalding hot shower did a great deal toward clearing out the rest of the cobwebs in his brain. Reaper again was able to concentrate on the tactical problem of just him and Bear hitting the Factory. He knew that Deckert would want to help, but the practical questions regarding his mobility would keep him from an active role. Not really polite, but it was the truth.

A raid on the Factory had to be done quickly. The longer he waited, the greater the risk grew for Mary and Ricky. There was a good chance that they had not been kept at the Factory. If that were true, he had to eliminate that possibility quickly. The Factory was their best practical source for more intelligence and a way of developing further leads. Getting their hands on Arzee was a top priority. Reaper was more than willing to wring the man dry and toss him away like a paper towel.

Hitting the Factory and not finding his family, successfully snatching up Arzee, or even getting any new leads . . . that wasn't something Reaper found acceptable to think about.

Going back into his room, Reaper pulled on fresh jeans and a sweatshirt. Feeling a damned sight more human, he turned and opened the door to go downstairs. Voices could be heard speaking from what sounded like the kitchen area. And there were more people talking than just Deckert and Bear. A quick look out his bedroom window showed Reaper no police cars, but two new vehicles sat out in the driveway. There was a silver 4x4 pickup truck with the paint on the hood peeling and an older model Buick Century sedan. These certainly didn't look like the kind of vehicle Arzee's people drove.

Stepping back to his bedside table, Reaper picked up the SIG-P220 he had lying there and checked the load. Fresh brass shone back up at him as he drew the slide partway back. Lowering the hammer with the decocking lever, Reaper slipped the SIG under his belt at the small of his back, then pulled his sweatshirt over the weapon. Now armed, he went downstairs to check out the voices.

Pausing for a moment on the stairs, Reaper could now better make out the voices in the kitchen and what was being said. The conversation astonished him and he knew that he wouldn't need his SIG.

"So he came charging in from the sea with some maniac at the wheel of a PBR and pulled us out," one voice clearly said. "When I finally asked him how he found us, he said that he got a position fix on our last radio transmission before our commo went down. It was a good thing he did too because he showed up just as the ragheads were closing in on Kafji. If he hadn't shown up, my spotter and I would have been the first ground losses of Desert Storm.

That would be a hell of a way to make the history books."

Reaper came down to the kitchen to see a sight he never would have allowed himself to hope for. Deckert sat in the kitchen making something while around the table were Bear and another man Reaper immediately recognized.

"Well," Reaper said. "If you hadn't been a normal hardheaded Marine, you would have abandoned that hide before the Iraqis had gotten too close. Goddamn, Max, it's good to see you."

The slender younger man Reaper was speaking to stood up and embraced the SEAL chief in a fierce bear hug. As they broke the embrace, Reaper stood back and looked at the shorter man

"You're looking good, Warrick," Reaper said, "but the grunge look has been out of style for years, or have they stopped letting you have anything sharp since you left the Corps?"

Max Warrick let a wide grin spread over his face as he rubbed at the week-old stubble across his chin. Chuckling, he ran his left hand back through his unkempt, stark white hair.

"Naw," he said, "I was just coming back from transporting a bail jumper to Kansas City when I got a call last night from Bear here. He said that you needed help and it was important—so I just kept rolling past Chicago and headed on here. I've been on the road over a week chasing that jumper down. So I just figured I'd show up and see what the party was. Maybe I'll have time to make a run across the river to Canada and get some Cuban cigars while I'm here."

"It's damned good to see you here," Reaper said, "but I don't think there's going to be much time to make any smoke runs across the border."

"Just like a jarhead to become a bounty hunter to keep the blood moving," a second new arrival said from off to the left. "Must be the jazz, just like that A-Team character you look so much like."

"That's Bail Enforcement Agent to you Air Force pukes," Warrick said.

Reaper turned to face the new person coming into the room.

"Damn," Reaper said, "if they aren't coming out of the woodwork. Good to see you Ben."

He reached out and grabbed the smaller man's outstretched hand, pulling the slightly built speaker in close for a strong hug. The new individual on the scene was noticeably short, only a few inches over five feet tall, and very slight of build. To look at his craggy face, glasses, and thin brown hair, one would have first thought of either a drowned rat or a really skinny lawn gnome. But Ben MacKenzie, the ex-Air Force pararescue jumper—PJ for short—had fooled many people who had made the mistake of judging him by his outward appearance. The smaller man was engulfed by Reaper's embrace, but he hugged back just as fiercely.

Stepping back for a moment, Reaper stood to the side as Ben walked over to the table and sat down.

"It's not that I'm disappointed to see the two of you," Reaper said, "but what the hell are you doing here? I haven't seen you, Ben, since we left Bosnia, and that was what, five—six years ago? And it's probably been even longer than that since I've seen you, Max."

"I've been working as a paramedic in Indianapolis off and on at least up to last night," Ben said. "That's when I got the call from Bear that you needed help."

"And what's your story, Max?" Reaper said. "Ben operated with Bear and me over in Bosnia, but you never did. How the hell did he know he should call you?"

"I met him at a shooting competition and gun show down in Kentucky a year ago last fall," Max said. "He was wearing those motorcycle leathers of his with a Trident on them. One thing led to another and we spent a long night swapping lies at some redneck bar south of Louisville. My memory is a little hazy about the general details of that night."

"And you just took it upon yourself to call these guys in?" Reaper said as he shot a glance at Bear, who sat at the table and tried to look innocent.

"Well, yeah," Bear said. "I phoned them last night after I had left the club and headed back to the hide. Both of them demanded to know where and when after I told them you needed help, and why."

"Your family is involved," Ben said bluntly. "You don't go after a man's family, no matter what. So why don't you sit the fuck down and tell us what you need?"

Reaper stood for a moment looking at the table and the men surrounding it. He understood the brotherhood of warriors, how those who had shed blood together shared a bond that outsiders would find almost impossible to understand. But Reaper had never been someone who liked asking for help. He hadn't even thought of contacting men like these, his friends, to share danger with him. It took another member of that brotherhood to recognize the situation and put the call out. That would be something he would owe Bear for a long time to come, one of those debts that are shared between close friends but are never really spoken about.

Coming to a decision, Reaper sat down and started to brief his friends on the situation.

"Short version," Reaper said, "we have an unknown number of hostiles who have taken two hostages and are holding them at an unknown place. Our only suspected location of the hostages is at a nightclub in a converted six-story factory building near downtown Detroit.

"The building is in a poor neighborhood with a limited civilian population nearby. My intention is for Bear and me to conduct a penetration of the target building to either locate the hostages and bring them out, or develop further intelligence as to their location."

"How do you expect to develop that intelligence?" Warrick asked.

"I intend making a prisoner of the man in charge of the organization who took the hostages in the first place," Reaper said with a cold stare at Warrick.

"Do we have identification on this individual?" Ben asked.

"Yes," Reaper said, "he was positively identified at the target last night. His name is Steven Arzee. If he's not the top man in charge, he can tell us who is."

"I think he may still be pissed about Reaper ripping the ass off his favorite car," Bear said

"Always thought a Vette was a pussy-ass car," Ben said. "Count me in."

"Took your family, huh?" Max said. "Sounds like a good guy to mess with. I'm in. When did you want to take him down?"

Reaper looked at the men around the table. Bear leaned back in his chair with a soft smile across his face. Max and Ben both looked committed to action and intent on Reaper's every word. He felt a sudden surge of pride in the trust these men put in him.

"Time is something we don't have much of," Reaper said. "We go tonight."

Chapter Nineteen

Having made the decision to go ahead with the operation, Reaper lost no time in bringing Deckert, Max, and Ben up to speed on what he and Bear had observed the day before. All of the men around the table were experienced professionals. They knew the risks in conducting an operation—especially a clandestine one with no official support.

In fact, there was far less than official support for their proposed actions. What they were planning to do sitting around that kitchen table was just plain illegal. Even just talking about what they had in mind would be considered conspiracy to commit a criminal act. In spite of that, they committed themselves to the action without reservations. They knew Reaper and trusted his judgment.

And Reaper trusted the men he was briefing. Each of them would be able to recognize specific strengths and weaknesses in the tactical situation or in his plan according to their own experiences. The specific plan of assault on the Factory was something Reaper still had to work out in his mind. A bull session with his friends would greatly help him finalize that plan.

"Here's the target," Reaper said as he laid a large sheet of paper on the table. Thc sheet was an aerial view of the Factory and the area surrounding it. It had been made up by Deckert, taping together sheets of printouts from an Internet Web service to make a single large picture. The warped-diamond shape of the highway intersection stood out as the main feature at the bottom of the shot. Near the middle of the sheet was the roof of the Factory building. The angle of the shot showed some of the south side of the building but the detail was limited by the one-meter resolution of the original picture.

Pointing to the Factory building, Reaper continued. "The basic structure was originally a small-scale auto plant. On the east end of the building were the administrative and engineering offices. They were separated from the construction floor by cinder-block walls. On the construction floor there are concrete support pillars every twenty feet the length and breadth of the building.

"This is a great big son of a bitch and the location of the building is an interesting one. It borders two major highways, so there are very limited avenues of approach from the south and east. It's right on the border of three different police districts but lies inside the Thirteenth District. It isn't known if the owner has paid off the local police or has some kind of arrangement with them, but during our time in the observation post, we didn't see a single police cruiser anywhere near the building.

"We can't have any contact with the local police or fire personnel. If they come into the area, we either have to withdraw or lay up until they leave. They're friendlies, whether they know it or not, so this isn't a permissive environment. We can't open fire on our own.

"So we'll have to keep it very tight, people. No firing whatsoever unless it is absolutely necessary and you are sure of your target. We are going to operate as if it's a hostile environment—but the rules of engagement are solid and there isn't any room for mistakes."

Reaper went on describing the building and what he and Bear had seen during their long vigil. Bear pointed out details of the exterior of the building where he had seen them, and he carefully described the interior of the first floor and the layout of the club facilities there.

A single huge band and dance area dominated the western end of the building, the stage stretching half the width of the building. Four additional smaller band stages and dance areas stretched along the rest of the floor. Scattered about were sections of tables being served from the bar that ran along the northeast wall, and the kitchen area in the first floor of what had been the admin offices.

Bear had seen no sign of Arzee or the two goons that Reaper had carefully described. The briefing/planning session continued with more and more details being brought forward and described. The photographs that Reaper and Bear had taken had been cleaned, cropped, and printed by Deckert. Reaper brought these out and handed them around. In addition, Deckert had been doing research on the Internet about the plant and its history. Through that source, he had come up with a number of photos of what the inside of the plant used to look like.

An unusual feature of the cinder-block and steel construction building was that the floors were covered with thick blocks of wood. These blocks helped dampen vibration from the various machines when they had been running. Bear said that it made a very interesting walking surface.

But the biggest question couldn't be answered from the information they had in front of them—where was Reaper's family? Nowhere could they find a specific area where hostages would probably be taken. The only real clues they had came from the observations taken by Reaper and Bear.

"The only floors that were lit at all," Reaper said, "were the first and sixth floors. The first floor was lit up because of the club. The sixth floor had some of the offices on the eastern end of the building lit up during the evening, even past the 2 A.M. closing time of the club. That's a pretty good indicator that nothing much happens on the four middle floors of the building."

"Unless they just shield the lights," Ben said. "That's a pretty big floor area to try and search."

"No arguing that," Reaper said. "But we did see some lights being used in the middle area of the sixth floor. According to the information Keith came up with, there are no rooms or walls to speak of on almost any of the construction floors. So any rooms that we do see had to be added after the place was turned into a club—and we search them. But the main target I see is the sixth floor."

"There were ramps, a big stairway near the front door, and several elevators going up to the rest of the floors," Bear said. "But they are all either locked up or closed off. There's only one set of stairs near the front door that aren't secured with a lock and chain—and they have a guard, or at least a big goon acting like a bouncer, stationed right in front of them."

"Looks like the upper floor is it then," Ben said.

"Yes, I think it is," Reaper agreed, "besides, we have no other real choice."

"You know," Max said, "if I could climb up on this billboard to the southeast of the building, I could control the entire eastern face of the place with a good rifle. The trick will be getting up there with something like that without being spotted for what I am."

"Oh, I think we can find you something suitable for the job," Deckert said with smile. "There's some stuff in the vault downstairs that just might fit the bill perfectly. You leave that stubble on your chin in place, dirty up a bit, and wear some old clothes, and you could pass for a street person just wandering around. No one would even look at you twice."

"That's a hell of an idea," Reaper said. "We scrounge up an old shopping cart and fill it with crap and make up our own street person. We could hide a rifle easily enough with a little work."

"What I have in mind won't take a little work," Deckert said. "I'll be back in a minute."

With that, he rolled away from the table and went over to the door to the basement.

"Bear," Deckert said, "could you give me a hand bringing some gear up?"

"Not a problem," Bear said as he got up and walked over to the stairs.

A lift device had been bolted to the wall that combined with tracks on the stairs to let Deckert travel to and from the basement of the building. As soon as Deckert had cleared the stairway, Bear followed him down and the two men disappeared under the house leaving Reaper, Ben, and Max still sitting around the table planning.

While Bear and Deckert scrounged around down in the basement, Reaper and the others continued to detail out their assault on the factory. Max would provide fire support from his billboard sniper hide while Reaper and Bear went into the building itself. Ben would have the hardest job on the site. He would provide transport and maintain security around the outside of the building while Bear and Reaper conducted the assault. Deckert would remain at the shop where he could coordinate communications over cell phones.

By the time Deckert and Bear had come back up from the basement, Reaper and the others had worked out a basic plan. When Reaper saw the packages, cases, and boxes that Bear and Deckert had brought up from the security vault in the basement, he couldn't hide his surprise. He recognized what the men were carrying. This was more than he could have honestly expected.

"Keith," Reaper said, "you can't do this. These are the most expensive parts of our inventory. I can't let . . ."

"Shut up, squid, and give us a hand," Deckert said as he cut Reaper off. "It's not up to you to say what I can and cannot do with the inventory. I may not be able to go out and operate with you guys because of these wheels of mine, but I can damned well still be a supply sergeant if I choose to!"

Deckert and Bear quickly laid out the materials they'd brought on the kitchen counter. Deckert started opening up some of the boxes while Bear went back down to the basement for another load.

"I think you may find this to your liking, Max," Deckert said as he set out on the countertop what looked to be a soft-sided laptop computer case. D-ring attachment points were sewn into the back side of the black Cordura nylon case, making it able to be secured a number of ways for carrying. As Deckert unzipped the sides of the case, he folded back the top to display the contents.

Inside the case lay the components of a tactical sniper rifle—broken down so that no single part was more than sixteen inches long.

"Holy shit," said Max, impressed by what he saw, "just what the hell is it?"

"It's an Arms Tech Limited Model TTR-700 rifle," said Deckert. "That's their Tactical Takedown Rifle. It looks like something out of Hollywood, doesn't it?"

"I should say so," Max said.

"Well, this ain't from the movies," Deckert said. "This is the real thing. That's a modified Remington 700 bolt-action fitted and bedded to a custom Choate folding stock. The Schneider match-grade stainless steel fluted barrel is sixteen inches long with a recessed muzzle crown. It's also threaded for an MD-30 muzzle suppressor which is in the bottom of the case. There's a Leupold VARI-X IIc three to nine power, 40mm variable tactical scope on quick release mounts guaranteed to hold their accuracy. And there's room for two twenty-round boxes of ammunition. The whole weapon goes together in thirty to sixty seconds from the time that you open the case. It's chambered for 7.62 NATO and is black oxide-finished for protection and cutting down reflection."

"Is it accurate?" questioned Max.

"Fires to half an inch, a half-minute of angle, with the proper ammunition," Deckert said. "And we have the proper ammunition. There's Federal 308 Winchester Match, 168-grain boat-tail hollow-point ammo in these white boxes. In this blue box may be something you're not used to. It's Engel Ballistic Research Incorporated's 7.62mm Thumper ammo. That's match-grade 220-grain subsonic ammo. With the suppressor in place and using EBR's Thumper ammo, that gun isn't much louder than a mouse fart."

Max looked like a kid in a candy store as he professionally examined the weapon in the case, and started to assemble it. Bear had brought up the rest of the boxes from the basement and Deckert was displaying more materials and weapons. The next weapon Deckert laid out proved to be just as impressive as the take-down rifle in its case, only this weapon was much smaller still.

"That is the smallest shotgun I have ever seen,"

Ben said as he looked at what appeared to be a giant pistol.

"That's a Serbu Super-Shorty 12-gauge shotgun. That front operating handle folds down and locks into place so that you have something to hold onto when you fire it. And you need something to grab, this gun does not play nice. It's a modified Mossberg pump-action shotgun, fitted with a pistol grip and a folding front grip. The whole gun is only 16.5 inches long with a 6.5-inch barrel and weighs 4.5 pounds empty. It holds three rounds, two in the magazine and one in the chamber, but those are full-sized 12-gauge rounds.

"Right here," Deckert said as he opened up a cardboard box, "is from SKI Industries. It's the first holster made for the Serbu Super-Shorty. It's a black nylon CQB-style drop-down leg holster with a partial break-front that holds the shotgun with its forward grip folded. It has straps to hold it to your thigh, and an elastic restraining strap for the gun. The loops on the outside of the holster hold an extra three rounds and the whole rig is ambidextrous. You could fast-draw this thing if you wanted to. Makes it just about the biggest handgun you could ask for."

"Pretty much answers the question about whose gun is bigger, doesn't it?" Ben said.

"A manly gun for manly men," Bear said with a grin.

"Yeah, and a pretty special one with the ammunition I have for it," Deckert said, picking up a smaller ammunition box from a larger case. "This is Mark II Aerodynamic, drag-stabilized, expandable-baton shotgun ammunition. And it will feed and fire in that Serbu Super-Shorty."

"You sure you don't have a job with the company making this stuff?" Bear asked. "You sound like an ordnance salesman."

"Yeah, well it's not like I expect you to pay for it," Deckert said.

"Bear," Reaper said, "will you shut up? I think I know what he's leaning towards with this one."

"You got it," Deckert said. "These are really good bean-bag rounds. You load up the Super-Shorty with these and it'll give you a less-than-lethal option. These shells throw a forty gram nylon bag with a stabilizing tail at about three hundred feet per second from a standard riot gun. That stubby barrel on the Super-Shorty will cut way back on that velocity, but they still should be effective to at least twenty yards. It'll be like hitting the guy with a Sunday punch—while wearing brass knuckles."

"What else did you have me drag up from down there anyway?" asked Bear.

"An H&K MP5K-PDW," Deckert said picking up the small submachine gun. The folding stock that helped identify the weapon as the personal defense weapon model lay to the side of the almost pistol-sized 9mm sub gun. "And a Gemtech Raptor muzzle suppressor for it. This model uses the tri-lock system that Gemtech patented to lock the suppressor on the HK 3-lug barrel. Reduces the sound of each shot by thirty decibels.

"That other box there has a Beretta Model 92-F pistol in it. The barrel of the pistol is threaded for the Whispertech 9mm can in that long skinny box. The can's seven inches long and one and one-eighth inches in diameter. It's covered with a black moly-coat to kill reflections and it won't change the zero of the pistol or interfere with its operation.

"To really cut back on sound," Deckert said, "there are a couple of hundred rounds of EBR 9mm Hush Puppy ammunition in that last box over there. That ammo has a 147-grain bullet that fires at about 980 feet per second, even out of a submachine gun barrel. It will help make the sound of any shots from either the Beretta or the MP5K as quiet as possible by eliminating the sonic crack.

"Just as an added bonus, I put in some work in the shop last night while you guys were partying it up downtown," Deckert said as he pulled a black nylon case up from the floor. "This is the last one of these we're going to have for a while."

Opening up the case, Deckert drew out what looked like a futuristic rifle.

"Damn," Reaper said, "you finished one."

"Yeah," Deckert said, "and I used the last of the prototype parts to do it. This, gentlemen, is the Jack-hammer Mark 3-A3 assault shotgun. It is a bullpup-style, selective fire 12-gauge shotgun loading from a ten-round cassette magazine. The bullpup design puts the firing mechanism behind the pistol grip. That makes the weapon thirty inches long with more than a twenty-inch barrel length. It can be fired one-handed on full automatic. That long handle on the top of the weapon holds the sights. You can rip down a house with this gun—and those bastards who have

Reaper's family took the only other four guns in existence. I want them back."

"Keith," Reaper said after Deckert was done describing all of the gear and the Jackhammer, "I can't let you do this. What we're doing is illegal as hell. You'll lose your federal license at the least if anything happens to this gear."

"So, don't let anything happen to the gear," Deckert said simply. "Now go and get your family."

Reaper didn't have anything more he could say. Deckert's mind had been made up and, if he wanted to be completely honest with himself, Reaper had to admit he was damned glad to have the help.

Chapter Twenty

There was a hard time limit on how long Reaper and his men had to conduct their operation. Arzee had said that the additional weapons had to be ready by Friday afternoon—that was seventy-two hours after his raid at the shop. That time was only twenty-two hours away. The cell phone he had left had never rung.

Reaper had no way of knowing that Arzee was simply too scared to call before the time had run out. If he and Bear hadn't seen the man at the front door of the Factory, they would have thought he had been killed in the car wreck. Why he hadn't called wasn't important right now. The fact that he still held Reaper's family was.

While Max, Bear, and Ben caught a little sleep, Reaper sat down and worked out the details of a plan of assault for the Factory. When he had the operation sketched out to his satisfaction, he called everyone down to the kitchen and laid it out for them. The basic plan was simple, as all good ones should be. It called for Deckert and Bear to penetrate the building while Ben and Max acted as support. With all the men around the kitchen table, he described what he wanted to do.

"Max," Deckert said, "you'll be going in first to scout out the area and report to us. We'll stay in the area with the insertion vehicle. If you run into anything that you can't just walk away from, we can come in and get you out fast. After that, you'll establish your sniper hide in the southeast quadrant on the upper deck of this billboard."

Reaper pointed out the indicated billboard with his pen on the large aerial photo they had used earlier.

"Now, you're sure you don't see any problems in getting up to that deck?" Reaper said.

"No," Max replied, "none at all. Your pictures show two different ladders to get up there. The bottom rung is only about ten feet off the ground. I shouldn't have any trouble climbing up to it with a short length of rope and a grappling hook."

"We may be able to do you one better on that," Reaper said with a smile. "Dressing you up as a homeless person and giving you a shopping cart full of crap will blend you in so that no one will notice you at all. We'll just stick a hard-sided box or milk crate in your cart. Since you're going to have the cart with you anyway, you might as well make use of it. Climbing up on that will put you within reach of the lower rung. That'll be a lot easier that tossing up a line, less obvious, too."

"Sounds good to me," Max said, "but I'll take the hook and line anyway."

"We'll drop you in the area of this railroad bridge underpass a half-hour before sundown," Reaper said indicating the bridge on the print. "Under the bridge is dark as hell, no one will be able to see us from the target. Sundown is at about 2045 hours tonight. That should give you a good hour of light to make your way past the Factory to this field where the billboard is. You can scout out the target from as close as you feel comfortable, but remember, the bouncers are right there at the front door. They'll put the bum's rush on you if you try and go by the eastern side of the building."

"No problem," Max said, "I'll work my way over to the field and set up my nest for the night at the bottom of the billboard or at whatever cover looks best. The only problem I might run into is if another homeless guy is already there. If the bouncers see me, I'll only be another guy looking for a place to sleep. By the looks of these bridge overpasses here on the highway," Max pointed to the highway intersection and ramps just to the south and east of the Factory, "there's probably already a fair-sized homeless population up under them."

"We didn't see any during our OP," Reaper said, "but that doesn't mean they aren't there. So you set up as you see fit. But I want you up in the billboard by 2200 hours. That's well enough after dark for you not to be seen and you can relax in place a bit.

"We'll use your truck for the insertion vehicle. Keith's got a camper top behind the shop that we can mount up and use for moving you and your shopping cart into position without being seen. Bear and I can remain in the camper until we insert at 0230 hours. The raid itself is going to go down at 0300 hours.

"Bear and I will leave the camper here in the neighborhood just to the southwest of the target. There's almost no traffic to speak of in that area during the day, and in the middle of the night we'll probably be the only ones walking around at all."

"So you think," Ben spoke up. "What about gang-bangers or just street punks?"

"If we run into any," Reaper said, "it'll be a bad thing—for them. Both Bear and I will have suppressed weapons if anyone wants to push the question of our being on their turf."

The men around the table went silent for a moment. The situation was an extremely serious one. Reaper's comment did more to drive that point home than anything that had been said all day. Somberly, they continued listening to Reaper's plan.

"There are a number of large chimneys and ventilation stacks on the south side of the building. Several of them near the southwestern corner have reinforcing rods bolted to the outside of the stacks; some of them run right up along the corners. For Bear and me, those will be like a stairway to the roof."

"Yeah," Bear said, "a stairway with no landings—no place to stop and rest or look around. How high did you say that roof was?"

"About 120 feet," Reaper said. "We'll have two loops of line with each of us. If we need to rest or stay secured, we'll just wrap them around the pipe or rods with a prussic knot and stick a foot in the loop."

"Okay," Bear said. "I only wanted to see if you had accounted for my frail old bones."

"Right," Reaper said with a grin. "You'll outlast me."

Turning back to the photo printout, Reaper didn't notice the lopsided smile that Bear had on his face. He also missed the sharp look that passed between Bear and Ben MacKenzie. Whatever it was that the two men shared, they weren't willing to talk about it just then.

"So we go in from the roof and make the hit on the admin offices," Reaper said. "It should take us about a half-hour to forty-five minutes to make the climb and get onto the roof. That puts us on the target at 0330–0345 hours. We penetrate the building and search the offices. Anyone there, we secure them and continue the search. If we recover the hostages or Arzee is one of the prisoners, we leave by the stairs. If not, we extract the same way we came in with all the intelligence material we can find. Any questions?"

"I'm going to remain with the extraction vehicle?" Ben asked.

"Yes," Reaper said, "that will give you the fastest means of pulling us out of the area if the shit hits the fan.

"If we do have to abandon the target," Reaper continued, "our emergency rally point is here," he pointed to the print, "just north of the railroad bridge where we dropped off Max. There is no contact with the police, and as little contact as possible with anyone around the target. Guns are tight on this op, the rules of engagement have no slop in them."

All the men nodded their assent with what Reaper had just said. There could not be any danger to innocent bystanders on this operation. It was going to be as surgical a strike as anything they had ever done in the military. And the personal costs could be higher than any of them were willing to pay.

Speaking up, Bear broke the uncomfortable silence that followed Reaper's pronouncement. "You know, if we throw some mud on the camper and pickup, dab a little rust-red or primer-colored paint on it, it'll look just like a jarhead's paradise. No one will even want to look at it with that peeling paint it already has."

"Hey," Max said, "don't dis my truck, man. And don't get that damned silver paint GM puts on their trucks. I've seen it peel a bunch of times—so that's not my fault. She may look a bit worn, but my baby's mechanically as sound as anything on the road."

"Just as long as it's dependable," Ben said.

"As anything on the road," Max replied, "I'd stake my life on it."

"I think you are," Ben said.

The warriors had no further questions about the basic plan Reaper had laid out. Everyone now had his own preparations to go through to get ready for the operation. Only the fact that they had all gone though extensive training and had a wide pool of experience between them even allowed for the possibility of a raid on the Factory being staged at such a short notice.

Reaper continued to go over everything they had in the way of intelligence to see if he had missed anything. Deckert left in his van to shop for some communications gear. Ben MacKenzie had brought a variety of medical gear in the trunk of his car, the tools of his everyday trade as an emergency medical technician, and was checking over his trauma bag.

Bullet wounds were not something anyone liked to think about at any time, and especially right then, but Ben made certain to be prepared to deal with anything that he could. His skills as a combat medic were considerable and he felt that he could prevent anyone on the team from having to answer the uncomfortable questions a hospital would ask regarding the treatment of gunshot and other wounds.

For Bear, he dealt with the tools that made gunshot wounds. Behind the house and along the side of the shop, a measured range had been laid out for test firing and sighting in guns. Carrying all of the weapons both he and Reaper would be using, Bear headed to the range. Before they left for the op, Reaper would check out his own hardware himself, firing the weapons to refresh their characteristics to him.

Bear had it in mind to check out all of the guns at once to make sure that there weren't any mechanical problems at all. If any glitches arose in the guns, he still had time to fix the problems before they left for the op.

For his own primary weapon, Bear had picked the Jackhammer shotgun. The short, nasty piece of firepower appealed to him. And using the gun on the people who had gone to such lengths to get them just seemed fair. The ten-round capacity of the shotgun combined with its cyclic firing rate of 240 rounds per minute made it a very powerful and compact chunk of firepower.

For a secondary weapon, Bear would carry the Beretta 92-F with the Whispertech suppressor. Reaper would be using the H&K MP5K-PDW as his primary weapon That was a chunk of hardware that had always been a favorite of his back during his active Team days. Instead of a sidearm, Reaper would pack the Serbu Super-Shorty in the SKT thigh holster. The compact little pump-gun would be loaded with the Mark II beanbag rounds in case Reaper had to deal with someone he'd rather not kill.

There were only three ammunition cassettes ready for the Jackhammer that Bear could take with him on the op. If he had to get into a firefight, the thirty rounds of 12-gauge ammo would have to be enough for him. Switching cassettes in the Jackhammer was easy and fast. But removing the fired casings and then reloading the cassettes themselves was a slow process. All of the cassettes would be loaded with magnum Winchester OO buckshot, a heavy combat load Bear knew well.

This model of the Jackhammer would fire three-inch magnum 12-gauge ammunition. Deckert had told him that the other guns, the ones that had been taken, would only fire the standard 12-gauge shells. The fifteen .32-caliber pellets in these three-inch, 12-gauge loads could deal with people, as well as the locks or hinges of any secured doors they had to pass through. Reaper had a set of lock picks, and the skills to use them. But there could easily come a time during the operation where speed would be a lot more important than silence—such as if they had to blast their way out of the place with Reaper's wife and son in tow.

In the event that they ran into something really resistant, Deckert had some other Law Enforcement ammo from the same MK Ballistic Systems people who made the beanbag rounds he was using. The ammo was QB-slugs, antivehicle/antimaterial tactical ammo. As near as Bear could tell, the rounds were loaded with plastic-coated gray steel slugs. Deckert said they would tear through nearly anything, especially a steel fire door inside a factory. Firing those rounds through the Serbu Super-Shorty would not be fun, their recoil would be terrific.

Neat stuff all in all. They didn't have a lot of material to work with, yet no one could have found fault with Deckert's selflessness. He generously offered up everything he had available, despite the fact that the shop didn't quite have the same size budget as the U.S. Navy.

As Bear approached the shooting bench, he almost stepped on Max Warrick, who lay prone on the ground. Either the ex-Marine scout-sniper hadn't been shooting, or the ammunition and suppressor on his rifle constituted the best combination Bear had ever "not" heard.

Max had the TTR-700 rifle assembled and laid out across the rolled-up carrying case as a rest. As Bear stood directly behind Max, the TTR-700 quietly put out a round of EBR subsonic Thumper ammunition downrange. The bullet "clanged" into the steel gong target Max had set up behind the paper target holder. The shot had been incredibly quiet, almost undetectable as a suppressed gunshot.

The ringing of the target was much louder than the shot had been. After leaning over and looking through a sixty-power spotting scope he had set up on a small tripod next to him, Max carefully jotted down a note in the data book he had lying out open on the ground. After he had finished writing, Max turned and looked at Bear standing behind him.

"You need the range?" Max asked.

"Not if you still do," Bear said. "How much longer will you be?"

"I'm just about done here," Max replied. "I'm only confirming the final zero of the scope with this subsonic ammunition. A few rounds of 168-grain match ammunition to confirm where it hits and I'll be done."

"Why are you going to use the louder match ammo if that quiet-ass subsonic is so good?" Bear asked as he set his burden of weapons down on the range table.

"Might need the range of the 168-grain on the op," Max said. "This EBR Thumper stuff is tits, it fires to about one minute of angle, only half an inch bigger than the best groups from that Federal Gold Medal match ammo. But it has the trajectory of a thrown brick—all subsonic ammo does. With a one hundred-meter zero, the bullet is hitting the exact point of aim each shot with the Thumper ammo. With that zero, I have a drop of fifteen and a half inches low at 150 meters. The drop is forty-two inches low at 200 meters."

Settling back behind his weapon, Max snugged it into his shoulder. "According to the scale on that aerial photo you guys came up with," Max said, "the shortest range I'll have to deal with from the billboard to the southeast corner of the building will be 122 meters. The longest range will be 165 meters to the far northeast corner. Since I'll be so high up in the air on the billboard, my aim into the sixth floor will be a flat shot."

Raising his head, Max slipped several 168-grain supersonic match rounds from a ten-round red plastic holder into the magazine of the opened bolt action of the rifle. He closed the bolt and chambered a round in the rifle. He fired a shot that had a much louder, sharper "crack" to its report than the soft thuds of the EBR subsonic. The "clang" from the target sounded much louder when the bullet impacted an instant later.

"Why the steel target?" Bear asked.

"In case I have to put a round into somebody," Max said as he looked up with a blank expression on his face. "Deckert said that he could make a new barrel for this rifle within a couple of hours, and destroy the old one completely. As long as I police up my fired brass either here or at the target, there won't be anything to use as forensic evidence to connect this gun to this shop. That steel gong makes sure that there's not going to be any fired bullets laying around that could be matched up to something the police find."

"It's a weird mission having to look out for the legal end," Bear said thoughtfully.

"Yeah, it is," Max said as he settled back down behind his weapon. With a smooth, practiced motion, he eased back the bolt of the rifle and caught the ejected empty brass from his last shot before it sprang from the receiver.

"From what I can tell, Reaper's between a rock and a hard place," Max said as he looked at the brass cartridge case he held between his fingers.

"I figure that I wouldn't be around if it wasn't for him and what he did for me back in Storm," Max continued. "He has whatever help I can give him. If it takes a big chunk of my time afterwards because of some legal bullshit—so be it."

The ex-sniper punctuated his comment with another shot. The muffled crack of the bullet, immediately followed by another loud clang from the steel gong, took less than a second. The deformed slug fell to the ground among the others that had been fired that day.

"I think I'll just wait until you're done," Bear said thoughtfully. "Maybe I should use that same steel target."

"Maybe," Max agreed.

As Max finished up with his weapons, Bear drew out the Jackhammer from its case. The gun looked like something from a science fiction movie but was reasonably light and easy to handle. He had one cassette locked in place in the weapon and was ready to fire. Deckert had told Bear that the new Jackhammer had been test-fired and operated properly. But Bear wanted to familiarize himself with the firing characteristics of the very odd gun.

"Okay, Bear," Max said as he got up from his firing position, "the range is all yours."

"Great," Bear said and he stood a little to the side of where Max had been. The Jackhammer didn't eject fired cases. The ammunition stayed in the chambers of the cassette through the firing cycle. With no ballistic marks being left on shotgun pellets when they were fired, he didn't have to worry about leaving traceable projectiles lying about. So Bear just tossed an empty can downrange as a target. Before thc can hit the ground and bounced, Bear snapped the Jackhammer up to his shoulder and pulled the trigger.

Boom . . . Boom . . . Boom roared out as Bear fired a three-round burst in under one second. Gouts of dirt erupted into the air as the shot loads smashed into the backstop. The empty can was nowhere to be seen—it had almost disappeared when the first swarm of buckshot smashed into it. Even Bear was startled by the power and sound of the Jackhammer. Max just stood there for a second, stunned.

"I think you got it, Bear," Max said.

"Yeah, it does look that way," Bear said with a big, wide grin across his face. "You know, I think I may like this gun."

Chapter Twenty-one

Preparations for the operation moved forward rapidly and smoothly—a reflection on the level of professionalism of everyone involved. Reaper wanted the team ready to launch at 1900 hours. That would give them time to transport to the area, including a cushion in case something went wrong, something as simple as bad traffic. Reaper wanted to put Max and his gear on the street by 2015 hours at the latest.

It had been an incredible rush to get everything together. When the preparations were done and they stood ready to go, there was plenty of time to do one final briefing and a brief-back. For now Reaper declared them good to go, with only the final details to be worked out.

Deckert had proven himself more than capable, even without the use of his legs. He had almost literally stripped the shelves of their fledgling company to make certain that they all had what they needed for the mission. When the gear he wanted turned out to be something they didn't have, he simply went out and bought the stuff. Reaper knew he owed a deep debt to these men. Not only did they risk a lot, including their freedom, to help him get his family back, some of them had emptied their wallets out to pay for it.

Some of the setup for equipment had just been funny. For the op they would employ the weirdest insertion platform any of them had ever even heard of before. Max's pickup truck had been fitted up with a well-used camper shell that Deckert had behind the shop building. Keith had said that someone years back had given him the camper as a deposit on a high-level gun that the guy never came back for. After a few years had passed, he considered the camper abandoned and thus his property.

The only trouble with the camper was the fact that it had been up on cinder blocks and the lifting jacks had been torn off years ago when the camper fell over during a windstorm. Watching two SEALs, a Marine, and an Air Force PJ trying to lift the camper onto the pickup truck would have been a good video for one of those "funniest moments" shows.

Eventually, with much grunting and a liberal amount of cursing—Bear could swear in five languages besides English—they finally mated the camper with the truck. They adopted Ben's suggestion and applied copious amounts of dirt, mud, and a little rust-red spray paint, effectively matching the splotches of bird shit and peeling paint that already streaked the silver truck.

Removing the screws allowed the window between the camper and the truck to be fully removed, so that now any of the guys could crawl through from the cab of the truck to the camper and vice-versa. Ben and Max made bets as to just how long it would take Bear to crawl through the window—Bear declining to take up that particular challenge, arguing it was beneath him.

Pulling out the central convertible table/bed combination inside the camper made room for Max's shopping cart disguise prop. Deckert had spotted a reasonably rusted shopping cart sitting in a ditch behind a shopping mall while out buying commo gear for the team. He and Bear had driven back out and grabbed up the cart, as well as an assortment of milk crates, boxes, and general junk.

Max draped himself with some of the worst clothes that could be found, along with rubber boots that had seen better days. He had a pair of rubber-soled boat shoes with him that he slipped into the pockets of the very ratty overcoat Ben had pulled from his car trunk. The shoes were for climbing up the ladder to the billboard, the coat had been the one MacKenzie put on when changing a tire in bad weather.

With his cleaned, tested, and zeroed TTR-700 rifle in its case underneath his filthy fisherman's sweater, Max was now one of the best equipped and most dangerous street people soon to haunt the corridors of downtown Detroit. Max didn't carry a sidearm, but he did have a razor-sharp Gerber Command II combat knife in its scabbard hanging pommel-down underneath the left side of his sweater. A strategic hole in the sweater made the knife quickly available.

When slid silently from the black nylon of the scabbard, the nearly seven-inch-long blade with a serrated back edge at the tip made for an intimidating tool. Its appearance alone would make anyone Max might run into on the street pause before accosting him further.

To take care of communications, Deckert located several sets of Motorola "Talkabout" T5420 radios. The little transceivers, not much bigger than the average cellular phone, were about as secure as the Motorolas Reaper and Bear had used back in the SEAL Teams. The little hand-held radios had fourteen available channels and thirty-eight quiet codes to cut back on interference. Those same codes would help add to the communications security of the team. A two-way boom mike and earphone setup helped complete the communications rig. The voice-activated transmitter made it possible to use the radios hands-free.

A little discreet tinkering with the radios by Deckert deactivated the call tone that announced an incoming signal. It wouldn't do to have a radio beep, no matter what the tone, while Reaper and Bear tried to silently infiltrate what could be considered an enemy stronghold. Rechargeable batteries were abandoned since they just didn't have the time to charge up enough sets to use before Reaper wanted the operation underway.

Fresh batteries were installed in all of the radios and carefully tested. The little sets had a two-mile range over flat terrain; they would do extremely well over the limited distances of the mission site. Deckert taped a set of tested spare batteries to the back of each radio—just in case.

"It's amazing what one can buy at RadioShack," Deckert quipped lightly.

Ben MacKenzie wore his normal clothes, a long-sleeved denim shirt and dark Levi's. He would maintain the watch on the operation from inside the cab of the pickup truck. Deckert reprogrammed the police scanner that Max had installed long ago to make certain that they were matched to the local Detroit police and emergency frequencies. He set up a second scanner for State and Federal frequencies. For weapons, Ben had his own pump-action Remington shotgun, one with a standard five-shot magazine and an eighteen-inch barrel. A pistol grip replaced the stock of the Remington to make it more manageable in the close confines of the truck cab. The shotgun was Ben's primary vehicle weapon and he had clips installed under the front seat of the truck that held the shotgun securely and concealed.

Underneath the dash of the truck, Max had a second weapon secured, a blued-steel Smith & Wesson six-and-a-half-inch barreled Model 29 .44 magnum, the Dirty Harry gun itself. The big revolver showed signs of long, but careful, use. And the cylinder, filled with Federal Gold Medal 250-grain metal-cased slugs, gave it a deadly look. After showing it to Ben and Bear, Max slipped the magnum revolver back underneath the dash into a hidden holster accessible by the driver.

"Why drag such a huge thing around, even if you do carry it in a truck?" Bear asked.

"Full metal-jacketed loads," Max said with a smile, "high velocity. They kill cars dead."

"Uh-huh," was Bear's only comment.

For his personal weapon, Ben used what he had brought with him, turning down Deckert's offer of anything in the shop. Ben slipped a 9mm Glock 19 into a concealed holster in the Bianchi K.O. 200 fanny pack secured around his waist. Two spare magazines rested in the pouch of the fanny pack. The magazines and weapon were loaded with Winchester 125-grain silvertip hollow points, a load Ben said had served him well for years.

As a backup weapon, Ben wore a Brauer lightweight ankle holster holding a simple five-shot Smith & Wesson Chief's Special revolver. The compact little snub-nosed revolver had been modified by having the spur of the hammer removed. Other than that it remained a stock gun. Loaded with Federal 125-grain .38 Special jacketed hollowpoint Hydra-Shok ammo, the little gun could still be a potent stopper.

When Bear asked Ben why he carried such a small weapon in such an outdated holster, the smaller man answered simply, "You can draw it easily when sitting in a car, or an ambulance."

Giving the statement a little thought, Bear realized the logic of the man's choice. Sitting in a car, you could reach an ankle easily. When sitting, it would actually be faster to draw from than a belt or shoulder holster—something that made a lot of sense given Ben's job as an emergency medical technician, riding around in ambulances all day long.

The time had come for Reaper and Bear to gear up and make ready for the operation. Bear had tested all of the weapons, and Reaper had made time to check-fire them himself. Everything was mechanically fine and operating properly. Bear winced a bit as they finished up on the range. When Reaper asked him about it, Bear said that it was nothing, only a headache. After going back in the house to get ready for the op, Bear reappeared his old smiling self again after taking what he said was a handful of aspirin.

The gear both men would wear on the operation had been spread out across their beds. Everything they had was new, unworn, and unexposed to their everyday environment. There would be no isolated hairs, fibers, or anything else to give forensic people something to track. One couldn't seal off everything, but Bear and Reaper were determined to make sure they left as little as possible behind.

Black Royal Robbins 5.11 range pants, the choice of the FBI and other agencies, had also been the choice of Reaper and Bear on the op. A set of PACA Thunder concealable body armor went over their brown T-shirts. The Level IIIA vests, made of a hybrid Zylon fabric over 0.200-inch thick, had proven capable of stopping a 9mm full-jacketed slug moving at 1,639 feet per second.

Wrapping the waist straps around the flexible black vests snugged them in tight to their sides. Neither SEAL would be wearing the hard trauma plate that would have given them additional armor protection. The plates would have reduced their range of movement and they had a hard climb ahead of them to get on top of the Factory building. Armor couldn't protect everything, no matter how much of it you wore, so you simply had to decide when enough was enough and go with what worked for you.

Generic long-sleeve black cotton shirts went on over the vests. The shirts could be bought all over the country at department stores, but still they removed the labels from them. Slipping on the black Bates Spyder Sidewinder leather/nylon boots, both SEALs pulled the laces tight. The soft-sided flexible boots had a deeply formed rubber outsole that gripped well and made climbing a little easier.

A BlackHawk CQB/Emergency rescue rigger belt went on over the pants. The heavy belts were made of 7,000-pound tensile strength black-nylon webbing and had a 5,000-pound test black-anodized aluminum nonlocking snap carabiner snapped through the parachute-grade adapter that was part of the belt's construction. If they had to, both SEALs knew that they could hang by the belts and trust them to support their weight.

Pouches and holsters went on the belts. Reaper had the special thigh holster on his right side to hold the Serbu Super-Shorty shotgun. On his left side, he secured an Omega TalonFlex MP5/Flash Bang thigh rig pouch. The pouch held two spare thirty-round curved stick magazines for Reaper's MP5K-PDW. Each magazine was filled with a full thirty rounds of EBR 9mm Hush Puppy ammunition. With the magazine in his weapon, Reaper would have ninety rounds for the entire op—and he planned to come back with most or all of them.

What Reaper wouldn't be carrying on this operation was any flash bang distraction grenades. He had chosen his specific ammo pouch so that he could carry a half-dozen spare Mark II bean bag 12-gauge rounds, three in each flash-bang pocket. The Serbu Super-Short was a handy little shotgun, but it had a very limited magazine capacity.

In his right front pants pocket, Reaper slipped in his Emerson Commander-BTS knife—clipping it to the pocket so that its Wave feature could snap open the blade if needed. Reaper made a mental note to himself to keep an eye out for his Emerson CQC-7BW. That knife had disappeared along with Musclehead and his injured arm. He would have to try and get it back, while maybe discussing philosophy with Musclehead along the way.

Over his shirt, Reaper secured a Chalker sling, designed and patented by a fellow SEAL some years before. The Chalker allowed almost any shoulder weapon to be carried by a single attachment point. The weapon could then be shouldered without breaking the seal on a gas mask—something that wasn't a consideration for Reaper on this mission.

The sling also allowed a weapon to be dropped immediately so that a secondary weapon could be drawn—the dropped weapon hanging down from the center of the wearer's chest. Lastly, it was just a very good sling to climb with, and there was going to be a lot of climbing on this operation.

A Chalker Hi-port weapons catch was secured to the upper left shoulder strap of Reaper's Chalker sling. He clipped the standoff adapter at the back of the MP5K-PDW's receiver to the brass snap shackle on the center front of his chest. The snap shackle was rated at five hundred pounds breaking strength, so Reaper felt it could securely hold his submachine gun.

The Gemtech Raptor suppressor was attached to the barrel of the MP5K-PDW, the suppressor secured to the three lugs on the H&K weapon's barrel. The Hi-port adapter had a quick-release Velcro strap to it that wrapped around the suppressor on the weapon and secured it to the upper part of Reaper's left shoulder. The MP5K-PDW was so short that even with the nine-inch-long black Raptor suppressor installed, it still didn't stick up past Reaper's left shoulder. It would be well out of the way while climbing.

A pair of inner shells from a set of FOG—Fast-rope Operator Gloves—went on Reaper's hands. He didn't need the protection of the normal heavy leather padded outer FOG shells for this operation. But the glove liners would protect his hands, and help keep him from leaving any fingerprints around. Under the front of his belt, Reaper tucked a black Hatch Nomex balaclava hood.

The Nomex hood would protect his face from the flash and heat of a fire or explosion, not something Reaper expected to need. But it also covered his face with a nonreflective black cloth, all but his eyes. The hood prevented either SEAL from requiring black face paint. Black camouflage makeup was something that would be hard to get off quickly if they had to shed their gear and blend into a group of civilians.

In each of his back pockets, Reaper slipped a four-foot length of 7mm black Kernmantle nylon climbing rope. The two ends of the line were tied together with a fisherman's knot—making the rope a single big loop. The two loops would be used to make prussic knots if they needed them.

Prussic knots were a climbing aid that could slip along a rope or pipe. When pressure was put on the loop of rope hanging from a prussic knot, the knot tightened up and wouldn't slip down. Taking the pressure off loosened the knot and it could again be slipped upward. Using the knots, a climber could hold position easily and free his hands for other work.

Reaper strapped a black Casio G-Shock watch to his left wrist. Finally, he slipped the black Motorola Talkabout radio into his upper-left shirt pocket. The wire for the two-way boom headset went underneath Reaper's Chalker sling strap and was secured to his shirt with a simple safety pin. The EarGel earpiece had been fitted to Reaper's ear only a hour earlier, and it now slipped in snugly. After checking out his rig, jumping, twisting, and turning in it to see if anything shook loose, rattled, or snagged, Reaper signaled the others that he was ready to go. He pulled the earpiece out and let the light headset dangle from its wire.

Bear rigged up essentially the same as Reaper. He wore the same clothes, boots, belt, rig, and sling as his partner did with changes to fit his weapons. For a thigh holster, Bear wore a BlackHawk Omega VI assault holster with the bottom opened up to allow the passage of the Whispertech suppressor attached to the barrel of the Beretta M92-F pistol he carried. Bear carrying the Beretta gave both men a suppressed weapon for quiet shooting. Two straps secured the holster to Bear's thigh and a spare magazine went in the pouch on the front of the holster body.

On his left thigh Bear secured an Omega shot shell pouch. Each of the two pouches on the thigh rig held ten rounds of 12-gauge ammunition secured in place under inch and a half-wide elastic strapping loops. The Chalker sling and standoff adapter did fine for holding Bear's Jackhammer Mark 3-A3. With the adapter mounted just behind the pistol grip of the Jackhammer, the weapon balanced easily and hung freely in the muzzle-down position.

The same style of Hi-port adapter that Reaper had used held Bear's Jackhammer muzzle-up with the flash hider of the gun secured to his left shoulder. The two spare ammunition cassettes Bear had available fit into Blackhawk shotgun shell pouches. The pouches were intended to hold twenty-five rounds of 12-gauge ammunition, secured under an elastic strap, but each would secure only one of the thick, round ammunition cassettes. Bear secured the pouches to the front of his belt, one on either side of the buckle.

In spite of his different load of ammunition and equipment, Bear could move as well as Reaper in his rig. Now both men stood armed and ready to operate.

Putting on long, black overcoats covered up their gear with only a few bulges suggesting that the two men might not be all they seemed. The ammo pouches and thick action of the Jackhammer made Bear look almost potbellied under his coat. Anyone mistaking the SEAL for a jolly fat guy would have been in for a serious surprise. As Bear looked at Reaper, he broke out with a laugh.

"Ho, ho, ho," Bear laughed. "All you need are a pair of dark glasses and you would look like a Neo-wannabe from *The Matrix*."

"The what?" Reaper asked.

"A movie. You don't get out much, do you?"

"Not enough to go see a movie," Reaper said. "Now let's go down for the brief-back."

"And more," Bear said as he grabbed up a paper bag.

Reaper shook his head for a moment about his

friend's antics. Over the last day, Bear could be up or down depending on the moment. Yet he couldn't fault his friend for loyalty, and he felt incredibly grateful for his assistance.

Everyone else was already sitting around the kitchen table when Reaper and Bear came down the stairs, except for Max, who had been relegated to the kitchen counter, as close to downrange as he could be placed in the room. Part of Max's disguise as a street person included the wafty aroma of his dirty and somewhat moldy clothes. Basically, he smelled like a wine-soaked compost heap that someone had slipped something into that shouldn't be there. Simply put—he stank.

"Wow, nice disguise," Bear said as he exaggerated a swallow and twisted his head around.

Max refused to be goaded by the SEAL and simply sat and waited for Reaper to begin.

"Okay, brief-back time," Reaper said. "Each man tell his part of the plan. You go first Max."

"I get dropped off with my cart underneath this railroad bridge here," Max pointed at the map Reaper had spread out over the table, "at 2015 hours. Sunset is at 2045 hours. I have about an hour of light to get to the bottom of the billboard and nest-up. I'm to be in position on the billboard platform and good to go by 2200 hours. I have freedom to fire in support of the op but only with positive target identification. My time for drive-by extraction is 0445 hours. And I should bring my cart along if I have the opportunity."

"Okay, Ben," Reaper continued, "your turn."

"I drive the truck and maintain radio watch on the

scanners and our own commo throughout the op," Ben said. "If there's anything coming across the police or emergency net, I notify everyone and head for the emergency rally point. When possible, I maintain communications with Deckert here over a cell phone, keeping the net secure. After off-loading Max and his cart under the bridge, I park over in the industrial area across the highway where you and Bear did for your OP.

"Driving back into the target area, I drop you and Bear here in this neighborhood at 0230 hours. This is as close as I can approach to the target without chancing being seen. It only gives you and Bear a few blocks to walk to get to the target, most of that distance can be covered through the alleys. After dropping you off, sorry, inserting you . . ."

"You make it sound so kinky," Bear said.

"Knock it off, Bear," Reaper said, wondering what had gotten into his friend. Bear had never before wisecracked during the final prep for an op.

"Okay, after I drop you off, I park here." Ben pointed to a spot on the photo printout they had used during their planning. "If there's any foot traffic or I feel compromised, I move over to here and park." Ben pointed to another spot. "If I really don't like the area, I head back across the highway to the original lay-up point.

"If the shit hits the fan and we can't make the rolling exfiltrations, I drive around, passing through the emergency rally point at 0500, 0530, and 0600 hours. Extraction at 0600 hours puts us to within twenty minutes of sunrise so things are going to get noticeable after that. If no pickups at 0600, I head back to the shop."

"That's right," Reaper said, "and I don't want you hanging around trying to pick us up later. If we get in trouble and miss the last extraction at 0600, each man is to cache his gear and make his way back here as best he can. Everyone will have a hundred bucks cash on him and a calling card Keith bought this afternoon. If you can't make your way back here, call in. Okay, Bear, now you."

"You and I insert in the neighborhood to the southwest of the target at 0230 hours. We walk into the southwest corner of the structure, avoiding all possible contact. We then go over the fence at the corner of the building and climb up to the roof of this single-story structure." Bear pointed to what looked like a material-handling dock for taking away finished cars at the southwest corner of the Factory.

"We go across the roof and decide which means—a chimney, corner, or pipe—we'll use to climb up to the top floor of the building. We've planned for it to take fifteen minutes to get to the garage rooftop and across to the chimney area and a half-hour for the climb to the main roof.

"Once on the main roof, we'll make our way into the structure and check out any rooms or secure areas we find on the factory-floor areas. The primary target is the offices at the far eastern end of the building. We move fast and quiet. No contact. This is a sneak-and-peek and we'll pick up the hostages if and when we find them. We extract and climb down by 0430 at the latest. If we find hostages or have prisoners, we come down by the stairs at the southeastern corner or the fire escapes on the north face of the building, depending on the circumstances. We call for emergency extraction at point Alfa, Bravo, or Charlie—the stairs, fire escape east, or fire escape west—respectively. Drive-by extraction is at 0440."

Reaper could find no fault with his friend's rendition of the plan. Still he had a funny feeling about hearing his own family be referred to as hostages. That was exactly why they were called that, to make it a little easier to concentrate on the task at hand and not the people involved.

"The only part left to assign is call signs for everyone to use over the net," Reaper said. "Any suggestions about something we're not likely to forget?"

"Okay, our leader here has long been known as the Grim Reaper," Bear said.

"Only by you and a handful of guys in the Teams, Bear," Reaper said. "I always hated that nickname."

"Well, you're really going to hate this one then," Bear said with a wide grin. "Gentlemen, I give you the four horsemen of the apocalypse. Our marine sniper friend is War. This rather diminutive Air Force PJ is Famine. I shall be Pestilence, since I make such a pest of myself anyway. And the Grim Reaper shall of course be Death."

"That sucks, Bear," Reaper said.

"Yeah, but it fits," Bear said, "and there aren't enough of us to be the apostles."

Reaper sighed, "Okay, if there aren't any other ideas," he said, "we go with Bear's suggestion."

No one else made a sound.

"So I guess that's it, we're good to go," Reaper said as he stood up.

"Not quite," Bear said as he stood up and walked over to a cabinet. "We still have one more thing to do."

He pulled out a dark brown bottle of Canadian Club whiskey and five shot glasses. Setting them out in front of everyone, Bear set down the bottle and then picked up his paper bag. He pulled out five slim aluminum tubes, each less than an inch in diameter and about six inches long.

The tubes contained Romeo y Julieta, Romeo No. 1 cigars from Havana, Cuba.

"What can I say," Bear said. "It was illegal for me to run them across the river so we'd better burn the evidence. Besides, I had to get Max his Cubans."

"I'll get some of my own after this is over," Max said with a smile.

"Not bad, Bear," Reaper said as he lifted the bottle and filled everyone's glass, then he set the bottle down, picked up his glass, and held it out to his friends. A feeling of esprit de corps filled the room.

"A toast," Reaper said. "I've never had a mission mean more to me, or knew a group of people I would rather have with me on it. So here's to the start of it. Once we go, there's no turning back. So we go—and everyone comes back."

"Everyone comes back," they all said, Bear loudest one of all. Each man gathered the last of his gear and left the room. The cigars remained on the table, to be smoked after the mission had been completed and everyone returned home again—including Reaper's family.

Chapter Twenty-two

Heavy traffic still filled the main highways around Detroit as Reaper and his men headed into the northern downtown area. The next weekend would be the Memorial Day holiday so the streets would be more or less deserted by the same time on the next Friday. Reaper couldn't look that far ahead, in fact he made an effort not to anticipate anything at all.

Reaper, Bear, and Max sat in the back of the pickup truck, riding in the camper along with Max's shopping cart. The only member of the four horsemen who hadn't dressed to draw a second glance was Ben, who sat up front driving the vehicle. In the back, Bear got a chuckle out of the idea that Famine was driving around the streets of Detroit in a 4x4 GM pickup truck.

In spite of the traffic, the men made good time and arrived in the area of the target less than forty-five minutes from leaving the shop. They couldn't cruise the area around the target, the possibility of gathering any new intelligence was greatly outweighed by the chance anyone would notice the camper going by several times during the evening. Reaper made the decision to go ahead with the first insertion of the operation.

As Ben passed along the side road leading to the railroad bridge, the top floors of the Factory building rose less than half a mile away. Looking through the back window into the cab and the windshield beyond, Reaper watched the road and the area around them. He suddenly made a decision and told Ben to stop the truck.

"Go past this driveway and back into it," Reaper said, "back up close to those bushes in the rear there."

Reaper had seen a small industrial parking lot next to the bridge. The flat, dirt and gravel lot had scraggly grass, bushes, and scrub trees growing thickly along its borders. The squat masonry bridge itself blocked any view of the parking lot from the Factory, and at that time of day no vehicles were present in the area.

With the truck backed up to fair cover, Bear opened up the back door and took up a position behind the camper, where he could watch out for anyone who might be around them. Max and Reaper manhandled the shopping cart out of the back of the camper. Their practice sessions with this maneuver back at the farm now paid off. The cart originally hadn't fit easily though the rear door of the camper. Removing the inside screen door and the liberal application of a heavy hammer had adjusted the cart to more easily pass through the door.

Without a word spoken, Max slipped back up in the bushes as Reaper and Bear climbed back into the camper body. Reaper simply said "go," and Ben pulled out, leaving Max behind.

Inserting Max and his cart had taken well under a minute from the time that Ben started to back the truck into the parking lot to when they pulled out onto the road. Max saw no signs that the action had been noticed by anyone around the area, and only a few windows in any of the industrial buildings nearby allowed anyone to look out in the first place. The operation had now begun and there was no turning back.

The truck and the rest of the team had a long wait ahead of them before Reaper and Bear could insert for their penetration of the Factory. Their synchronized watches read twenty-hundred (2000) hours, eight o'clock on a Thursday night. From where the Horsemen watched, the crowd for the Factory club seemed light, but they soon started to build up in spite of the weekday night.

It would be dangerous for the pickup to remain in the area. Somebody could see it and connect it to another appearance later that night. One choice was to drive around—but that could expose them to a chance encounter with the locals or, even worse, a police cruiser. It could also put them out of radio range with Max in case War called for help or an emergency extraction.

Staying in the area while under some cover or blending in somewhere seemed the safest bet. The quiet area they had parked in before seemed good, and Reaper told Ben to drive over to where they had put the van during their observation-post vigil. The big open area still had a lot of industrial machinery parked about, as well as a number of vehicles. If the place had a guard that did the rounds, neither Bear nor Reaper had seen him. Among the other vehicles, the pickup camper rig didn't stand out at all. With the truck parked and hidden, and Ben remaining up on radio watch, Reaper and Bear did the only practical thing they had open to them—they settled in for some sleep.

Neither of the two SEALs would insert for six hours yet. Not only had Reaper and Bear been running on little sleep for the past several days, they had another reason to get some rest. Nerves can build up while waiting to launch an op, no matter how well trained an operative is.

That same nervous energy that can help keep you sharp and alert also saps your body's reserves. It can wear you down just as much as if you had been running a marathon, even though you were just sitting still. It was far better to try to relax and follow the soldier's rule—sleep wherever and whenever you could because it might be a long stretch before the chance for some sleep came around again.

So Reaper and Bear crashed. Ben remained in the front cab where he settled in comfortably and expected to make a night of it. With his police scanners running softly, Ben set his Motorola Talkabout on the dashboard, just behind the steering wheel. He could hear everything he had to and could function well enough as the sunset started to color the sky.

The bed pads still left in the camper didn't smell as springtime fresh as they could have been. Reaper and Bear considered them a hell of a lot more comfortable than some of the places they had slept during ops in the Teams. From where he lay in the bunk over the cab, of all things, Bear started singing softly.

"So we'll raise up our glasses against evil forces," the rough baritone voice growled out, "singing—whiskey for my men . . ."

". . . And beer for my horses," a surprisingly deep bass voice finished from up front in the cab.

"Great," Reaper sighed quietly, "two fruitcakes."

"Let me guess, Death, old friend," Bear said using Reaper's call sign, "you don't listen to the radio much either, do you? Country-western, Toby Keith, the *Unleashed* CD, any of those things sound familiar to you? Famine, old boy, our grim friend here simply has no culture."

Ben simply remained silent in the front and listened to his radios. They ran on power from the spare battery in the camper body, so he didn't worry about running the truck's battery down.

The noise from the scanners wasn't much to listen to, mostly static. But Ben made up plot lines to go along with the fragments of stories he heard over the scanners, something he had learned to do years ago. Soon, only deep, slow breathing came from the camper.

The evening went on and turned into the early morning hours without incident. Ben had occasionally called up Max to get a situation report, sitrep, on what was going on at the Factory. Outside of the ebb and flow of customers, the Marine sniper had seen nothing out of the ordinary. War was now well settled into a sniper's hide up on the billboard. He could look around the edge of the smaller billboard and see the entire front of the Factory building.

Using a Bushnell Yardage Pro Scout laser range finder he had accepted from Deckert before leaving on the op, Max had confirmed his ranges to the Factory—122 meters to the near corner, 164 meters to the far corner. He lay almost level with the fifth floor and still could have a good shot into the top floor if the blinds opened.

Then, at 0200 hours the time came to get ready to move out. As Ben prepared to wake Reaper, he turned and looked back into the camper. He could barely make out two eyes staring back at him. Either Reaper had been awake, or his internal alarm clock kept very good time. Reaper rose and moved to where Bear slept over the truck's cab. Bear remained sound asleep, but he came silently awake at Reaper's touch.

"Time to earn your whiskey and meet those evil forces," Reaper said quietly to Bear. Then he leaned forward and said through the window into the cab, "Move on out, Ben."

The night had turned chill, yet not too cold at about fifty degrees. So Reaper wouldn't have to worry about Max stiffening up. The sky had remained only partly cloudy, and a bright first-quarter moon still shone down on the area intermittently. The light could be a blessing to the climbers once they started on their way up the side of the building. But it would quickly become a curse if it revealed them to someone before they even got to the target.

The Factory had its last call at 0200, so the customers had mostly left by the time the camper truck eased its nose into the nearby neighborhood. A short radio call from War in his hide told the rest of the team that the coast was about as clear as it was going to get.

Patting themselves down one more time, Reaper and Bear made certain of the location of every piece of gear by touch. The balaclavas went over their heads and they pulled them down to bunch around their necks like a collar. Walking the streets wearing a ski mask was not the way to keep from drawing attention.

A large red clay brick three-story home had once been someone's pride. Now the abandoned building stood mute, almost all of its windows and doors covered with plywood. The attic windows of the old house looked down on the dirty silver and white camper truck as it stopped in front of the alley the house bordered. The mute eyes of the blank windows were the only witnesses to the two black-garbed men who quickly exited the back of the camper and darted into the alley.

The alley they ran through did not lead directly to the Factory, or the approach angle they wanted to make to the building itself. The alley did lead across the street and continue down the block. Only half a block from the street, the narrow passage crossed over a second alley that ran east and west. This second passageway ended directly across from the corner of the Factory where Reaper and Bear wanted to start their penetration.

The old Teammates recognized the danger in following the alleys. Some of the few occupied homes could have dogs standing watch in their backyards. That danger had to be weighed against the risks of two men walking the streets so early in the morning. Reaper had decided that he would rather take a chance on barking dogs that they could run away from than of being possibly caught in the open, away from cover, by someone in the street. In spite of his love of animals, Reaper would not have hesitated to use his suppressed weapon against someone's aggressive animal—he had far too much at stake to worry about the niceties of the situation.

Luckily, neither Reaper nor Bear ran into any dogs along their approach to the target. When they reached the passage leading to the Factory itself, their cover ran out. To their south sat a line of decaying homes. Directly in front of them stood the Factory, not much more than a hundred meters away. But to the north they had the open area of the abandoned parking lot.

No vehicles remained in the lot, nothing but the grass and broken blacktop they had noted earlier when the two SEALs did their original drive-by. Only now, they had to walk down the alley with no cover to their left, just the open spaces of the chain-link fence that surrounded the parking lot. But when an obstacle finally appeared, it didn't come from their open side, or even the Factory.

Jerome Slaneal had been given the brush-off by his girlfriend Lateasha. The fifteen-year-old now looked at a long summer ahead without a lady to help comfort him. Of course, if any of his friends suggested such a thing, Jerome would have had to introduce them to his blade. The young man considered himself an expert in knife fighting and close-quarter combat—even if he had never heard that particular term.

So Jerome had a mad on, and the two strangers he saw walking down the alley were just what he needed to take out his frustrations. There were two of them, but he had his favorite blade with him. Besides, the two strangers were white—he reasoned that they had to be lost or had parked in the wrong place. They might be headed toward the club, and Jerome knew well enough not to bother anyone who was a customer there.

The information on the streets was that anyone who caused trouble for the guys in the club soon turned up missing. But Jerome was high on the arrogance of youth, and the forty-ounce bottle of malt liquor he had finished just an hour earlier had given him the false bravery of alcohol. He could tell the two men walking by so silently weren't headed toward the club anyway, they weren't taking a direct route there. That made them fair game according to his rules.

The blade Jerome took so much pride in was a wicked-looking hook-nosed folding knife made of stainless steel, with a four-inch serrated blade. The young man had no idea that what he held was only a cheap knock-off of a Spyderco Civilian. He just knew that he could slice the clothes, or the skin, right off of somebody with that blade. And he could snap the knife open with a practiced flip of his wrist.

If the two outsiders gave up and surrendered to Jerome what he believed was his due, he would probably let them go with just a good scare—probably.

Both Reaper and Bear realized that someone lurked behind them at almost the same instant. Years of training and experience caused them to automatically spread farther apart so as to not get in each other's way. Both men had pulled up the bottom part of their balaclavas to cover the lower halves of their faces. It would have taken both hands to pull the back of the hoods over the tops of their heads. They wanted to keep their hands free, but not to have any trouble. Maybe they could just outwalk whoever was behind them. If he had intended to shoot, he would have done so already.

Then Jerome commanded, “Freeze, mufa.”

Damn, this is not what we need right now, Reaper thought as he recognized the youthful crack in the voice behind them. Both he and Bear looked at each other as they just kept walking. They remained out in the open and needed to get across the street and to the wall of the building only a few dozen meters away.

Then Jerome almost shouted, “I said freeze, motherfuckers!”

The sharp click they both heard behind them sounded like a knife locking open. They had no way around it now. This gate crasher was probably armed. Reaper stopped and looked at Bear, gave him an almost imperceptible nod. Then the two SEALs turned away from each other, rotating around smoothly until they faced their young opponent.

Even for a street tough, Jerome could get nervous when facing something he didn’t understand. These two didn’t move like normal sheep did when they saw his blade. And their eyes looked anything but scared as they bore into the younger man’s gaze. The black masks only covered the bottom half of the men’s faces, but that was enough to intimidate him. The fear only helped to make Jerome angry at himself.

“Give it up, you mothers,” Jerome said, brandishing his knife.

Reaper had had enough of the young punk and he was tempted to give him what he asked for—even if he didn't know it. Instead of raising a weapon, Reaper slipped his hands into the pockets of his overcoat—the same overcoat that Bear wore, a style that covered them to their ankles.

"I don't think you want any part of this," Reaper said, and he pulled the front of his coat open.

Jerome was suddenly looking at more hardware than he had ever seen even in the hands of SWAT cops. Then the other dude opened up his coat and he had an even bigger gun strapped to his chest than the first one did.

Even youthful enthusiasm loses ground when a young pup looks at the growling teeth of a pair of wolves. Standing his ground, but only because he was frozen with fear, Jerome completely forgot about the knife in his hand as it dropped from his nerveless fingers.

"Go your way," the big, bad dude in black said. Then the two of them turned back to the direction in which they had been moving and started to step away.

Jerome voiced one last burst of reckless bravado, in spite of feeling the results of his fear trickling down his leg in a warm flow.

"You say what, moth—" he started to shout.

Then the taller man in black, the one who had spoken, turned around sharply. His movement caused the long coat to fly open. His hands were no longer in his pockets, but were holding that horrible-looking gun strapped across his chest. Jerome knew that if he uttered one more word, that awful weapon would start talking to him—and it would be the last thing he would ever hear.

Jerome never looked back as he turned and ran

away. At any moment, he expected to feel slugs stitch across his back. It was something he would never mention to anyone. The two men he had just faced had to be stone-killers—the taller one looked and sounded likc Death himself. Jerome would never know just how right he had been.

Chapter Twenty-three

With a quiet sigh, Reaper turned back to the task at hand and both men moved quickly to cross the last few meters to their target. Along the way, the two SEALs fully pulled up the hoods of their balaclavas, completely covering their heads in black Nomex cloth, and shed their black overcoats. They stashed them nearby, where the coats could be picked up later during the extraction. If they had to be abandoned it wouldn't matter; they had been purchased from a thrift shop and were effectively untraceable anyway.

The western side of the Factory towered above the two SEALs as they ran up to the wall. The facade of the building was the last place they wanted to hang around. The red clay bricks had been painted years ago with a now-peeling coat of white paint. In spite of the gang graffiti along the first-floor wall, the two black-clad SEALs stood out in stark contrast against the white surface.

Reaper prepared to go up the corner of the chain-link fence when Bear grabbed him by the shoulder. Pointing, Bear indicated a corner of the building only fifteen feet away. The loading dock or garage building, had two fifteen-foot-high roll-up overhead steel doors, set about three feet back from the edge of the sidewalk. The main structure came right up to the edge of the sidewalk.

In the shadows of the corner caused by the setback, a four-inch-diameter steel pipe was strapped to the walls and extended up two stories to the upper roof, to the point where a number of the chimneys, stand pipes, and ventilation stacks started. Plans had to be fluid to meet a changing situation. Climbing up the fence and dealing with the barbed wire wasn't set in stone as being the only way up the side of the building.

The big steel pipe looked like a staircase to two men with Reaper and Bear's climbing skills. Grinning under his balaclava, Reaper went over to the pipe and started to climb. He placed a hand to either side of the pipe and pulled back hard on the steel to make sure it was still anchored solidly. When the pipe didn't move, Reaper set his feet on either side of it and, in a crouching stance, walked up the side of the building, pulling with his hands to maintain traction for his feet.

When Reaper gained the first roof, he unhooked the Hi-port weapons catch on his Chalker sling and swung the MP5K-PDW into position for use. Bear followed up the pipe. Even though the tube had been sturdy enough for one man to climb it, two men on it at the same time might have put too much stress on it. So while Bear ascended, Reaper held his position and maintained an overwatch.

Now the big climb loomed up in front of the two

SEALs. From their present position, they had to go up more than four stories to gain access to the roof of the factory building itself. The photos they had taken combined with their inspection during the drive-by only gave them so much information about the pipes and stacks. Seen up close they looked like a viable means of assaulting the building. But only a thorough inspection would tell Reaper and Bear which pipes were sound, and which stacks had walls thick enough to not echo like giant drums when they climbed them.

The first two stacks proved far too exposed for comfortable use by Reaper. And they turned out to be little more than sheet metal when examined. Putting your feet on the sides of these stacks would have caused the stacks to boom like dull cannons.

The rest of the stacks rose on the far side of the freight elevator housing. To cross around the structure, Reaper and Bear had to crawl out on a foot-wide ledge and make their way more than twenty feet to get to the far roof. The tar of the very short overhang roof had been cracked and pebbled from years of winter freezing and summer heat. The surface of the roof looked like wet alligator hide in the faint moonlight—and felt about as slippery, too.

But both men reached the other roof with little more than a fast heartbeat to show for their exertions. Reaper immediately went to a set of four large square stacks near the center of the building. The two middle piles had been shoved tightly together, while the outside stacks left a good two-foot space between themselves and the center ones. Best of all, the sheet-steel sides sounded solid, as though they were filled with insulating cement.

At the corners of the smoke stacks were steel shafts, pipes really, about an inch in diameter. The shafts were part of a support structure for the stacks that extended all the way up to the roof. By 0315 hours, the two SEALs had confirmed their means of reaching the roof and were still on schedule. Their alleyway incursion hadn't slowed them much, despite Reaper's sense that they had taken far too long just to reach the Factory.

Now they climbed up the side of the inner two stacks. Both men remained covered from almost any observation by the smoke stack on the outside of each of them. The shadows in between the sets of stacks concealed them from all but the closest inspection. No casual observer would be able to watch them make the climb.

The climbing technique to go up the stacks used both the sides of the structures and the pipes up along their outsides. Reaper and Bear would jam their toes into the space between the pipe and the stack. Performing a lay-back maneuver, they leaned back and pulled with their arms and practically walked up the side of the stacks.

Going up the stacks became a long and tedious climb. Only men in exceptionally good shape could even attempt such a feat. Reaper felt gratified that he had kept himself in top condition and Bear had always held up his end. The other SEAL may not have exercised to the point that Reaper did, but he had never, ever, let his partner down.

Both men had their loops of rope for prussic knots to rest with while on the way up. The climb went easily enough and no rest was needed by either man so the rope loops stayed in their pockets. Once they got to the top of the climb, the rope loop climbing aids came in handy for another purpose.

The tops of the smoke stacks were surrounded by a two-foot-wide steel grid catwalk. On top of the catwalks, guardrails made of steel pipe ran around them. Reaper saw no easy way up to the roof beyond the top of the stacks; the catwalks were in the way. They would have to use climbing techniques to get around the obstructions.

Taking one of his loops of rope, Reaper slipped it around the pipe and then put the end of the loop through the knot he had just made. Pulling the loose prussic knot up as high as it would go, Reaper snugged the knot down. Now he had a loop of line that he could place a foot into and it wouldn't slip down the pipe.

Reaper lifted one leg up and stuck his foot into the loop. He stepped on the loop and leaned far out into the air. He didn't look down, and he didn't think about the hundred-foot fall to the ground. Instead, Reaper worked to place his second prussic knot loop around the pipe stanchion at the corner of the catwalk that held up the guardrail. Once that knot was secured, it was a simple matter, though still a physical strain, to put his other foot into the loop. Now he could stand up and climb onto the catwalk, passing underneath the guardrail.

Being the faster and more experienced climber, Reaper made the top of the catwalk well before Bear did. But his partner followed almost exactly the same steps to reach the top of the catwalk. No more than a minute later Reaper bent over and helped Bear up to the grid. Now the two SEALs stood on the roof of the Factory, and their real mission could begin.

Like all of the other industrial roofs the two SEALs had seen, the top of the Factory roof consisted of a poured tar surface covered in rough gravel. The gravel looked old and thin in spots. The same thing could be said for the hundreds of pounds of bird droppings that covered the roof, the only difference being that the layer of guano wasn't thin in spots.

It had only taken the two men about twenty minutes to make the climb, putting them on the roof at 0342 hours. They had forty-five minutes to make their search of the interior and begin their exfiltration. If they had to climb down the outside of the building, it would be a lot easier and faster than coming up had been. If they found Reaper's family and got pinned down, as a last resort, they would call in the police and just hunker down until they arrived. But all of this depended on their getting inside the building, and doing it fast.

There was a central structure that ran the length of the Factory roof. It looked like a long, low building raising up from the gravel and tar. There were doors, windows, and vents in the structure, that was a skylight and ventilation system for the sixth floor paint shop.

One of the doors stood ajar and Reaper could feel a draft moving through it. The door had been tied off to a guardrail on a set of steps leading down into the building. It must have been propped open for ventilation when someone didn't want to run the big blowers. Peering around the frame of the open door, Reaper could make out a dim light inside, just enough to see by. He wouldn't need the red-lensed pilot's penlight he had clipped to his shirt pocket.

It looked like the best way in. Reaper could not see any alarms or trips around the door, so he signaled Bear and set up to enter. Bear snugged up behind Reaper, who was kneeling low to the ground in preparation to going in as the point man on the entry. With his Beretta up and pointed forward Bear squeezed Reaper's shoulder in the go-ahead signal. Both men rapidly went through the door and down the stairs, breaking to the right and left as they came to the floor.

It was pucker time: that moment when they first entered the building and were the most vulnerable. They raised their suppressed weapons ready for use, but found no one there to use them on. The floor spread empty before them, the lights they had seen came from a few bare lightbulbs standing up on floor fixtures. The lights were too few and too dim to really illuminate the football field-sized floor area. But they were enough to allow Reaper and Bear to see details of the interior.

The far eastern end of the building comprised the office area. That was Reaper's primary target. The two SEALs moved out across the floor to get up to the southern wall. Once near the wall, Reaper maintained a watch forward while Bear covered the way they had come. Both men trusted the other completely. This was their element, the darkness and danger made them feel at their most alert, their most alive. Reaper considered the reason for being here the worst he had ever known. Now that he had gone into action, the feeling of helplessness that had dogged him for days was gone.

Tracked areas on the floor and overhead showed where the car bodies had been moved along for work. Dominating the middle of the floor, several long sheds had tracks going in one end and out the other, had the look of paint booths or drying ovens to Reaper—something that they could come back and examine after they had covered the primary search area: the offices.

One of the booths had its big doors closed and plastic chemical drums were stacked up around most of it. If the light had been better, Reaper would have seen that those drums appeared much cleaner and brighter than anything else in the huge room. The drums were new and held the solvents used in the drug lab, the lab hidden behind the closed doors of the booth. The black booth walls and doors combined with the bad lighting to make it look as if the doors didn't even exist—no light leaked out from the drug operation inside.

The floors felt weird to walk across. Then Reaper remembered that the whole factory had been paved with wooden blocks to cut down on vibration. The concrete support pillars that had been noted by Bear during his visit to the first floor were up on the sixth floor as well.

The pillars blocked a clear view of the whole production floor. Piles of machinery, mostly abandoned flexible belts for the assembly lines and mounds of steel matting, grids, and wires, lay scattered around haphazardly. Yet, pathways appeared in places around the floor. Reaper and Bear used these paths to skirt along the edges of abandoned factory parts as they crossed the big room.

At the far end of the room a cinder block wall separated the production floor from the hallway beyond and the offices beyond that. Big doorways penetrated the wall at three points that Reaper could see. The biggest one was a double-wide opening near the southern side of the building. Lights remained on in the hallway, more than in the main floor area. The lights were not bright enough to make the area well illuminated, but they did show that no shadows could be cast across the floor. That became the deciding factor for Reaper to choose the right-side entrance as his way into the office area.

Normally, Reaper would have acted as the point man for a stack of at least four SEALs to go through the doorway and take control of the hall beyond. But since Bear was his only Teammate, they didn't have the manpower to work the doors and halls as securely as their training demanded. Reaper adapted their tactics to fit the situation. He and Bear crossed over to the far (north) side of the big door area and set up their short stack of two men to go through the doorway. The need for additional manpower became immediately evident as Reaper took his squeeze signal from Bear and swung around the end of the wall, straight into Musclehead who sat there on a chair.

The two men ended up right on top of one another, too close for Reaper to even bring his MP5K-PDW into play. In spite of his surprise, and the big bandage on his left forearm, the man in the chair responded amazingly quickly. The powerful man stood and grabbed the Raptor suppressor of the

MP5K-PDW in a single motion. He wrenched the weapon around, forcing the muzzle away from him. Reaper responded with the only action that made sense to him—he let go of the submachine gun.

In spite of his trying to wrench the weapon from Reaper's control, Amman was surprised when his opponent suddenly gave it up. As he pulled the weapon back and away from Reaper, Amman saw that it was attached to the other man by some kind of strap and buckle. Unable to free the weapon from its strap, he pulled even harder to yank the other man off balance.

As the strong man tried to pull Reaper over by yanking on the MP5K-PDW attached to the Chalker sling around his chest, the SEAL snapped his left hand up and yanked on the release. That feature of the sling was intended for exactly the situation Reaper was in.

When Reaper pulled the release, the shackle instantly let go of the submachine gun. With no resistance to his pull, Amman fell backward with the weapon in his hands. Normally, the action following an operator's release of his primary weapon from a Chalker sling was to immediately draw his secondary weapon. But since no real noise had been made yet, Reaper wanted to keep the penetration from being compromised.

Stepping forward into Amman before he could turn the submachine gun around, Reaper snapped up his right hand in a hard palm smash to the muscleman's face. As the big man's head snapped back, the upper and lower lateral cartilage in his nose was driven deep into his face. The shock drove the air out from Amman's lungs, spraying blood from his shattered nose out over his face.

Reaper had to quickly follow through on the big man and put him down for the count. He stepped forward, lifting his right leg in a hard knee butt into Amman's groin, barely missing smashing the testicles up into the pubic arch of the pelvis. The pain of the knee smash brought the musclebound Amman almost to his knees, bending him forward at the waist and exposing the back of his neck.

Seeing the target, Reaper brought down his right arm in an elbow smash, knocking Amman down and putting his lights out with a hard blow to the sixth and seventh cervical and first thoracic vertebra of his spine. The shock of the blow traveled almost directly into Amman's nervous system, causing immediate unconsciousness. If Reaper had struck his blow with a pointed elbow on a single vertebra, Amman would have died instantly from a severed spinal cord.

The fight had only lasted a few seconds, an eternity for Bear who hadn't been able to get a clear shot around Reaper. As Reaper recovered his MP5K, the doorway on the south wall, the one they had missed in the darkness and confusion of the sudden assault by Amman, slowly eased open. The muzzle of an M4 carbine slipped forward just an inch past the door frame and moved to center on Reaper's back.

Out of the corner of his eye, Bear saw the movement and recognized the threat. Snapping up his Beretta, Bear fired two quick rounds into the door. The heavy steel door stopped the subsonic EBR Hush Puppy rounds, but the impact of the bullets startled Nicholas. As he tried to dodge the bullets he thought were coming through the lavatory door, Nicholas pulled the trigger on his M4.

The stuttering burst of fire impacted next to Reaper who dove away from the stream of 5.56mm projectiles. Lying on the ground unconscious, Amman wasn't able to roll away and he took the impact of half a dozen rounds. He never felt himself die.

Missing his target and shattering the noise discipline of the op, Bear dropped his suppressed Beretta, allowing it to dangle at the end of the Pistol Leash lanyard connecting the butt of the weapon to his belt.

As the Beretta hung at the end of its stretched coiled lanyard line, Bear released the Hi-port velcro strip with the thumb of his left hand. His right hand solidly held the pistol grip of the Jackhammer as he lowered the weapon down and into firing position.

Nicholas recovered from his surprise at the impact of Bear's bullets. Swinging the muzzle of his M4 around, Nicholas knew that he had only fired a handful of rounds from the M4. He had loaded his carbine with a 100-round double drum Beta C-mag. Inside the magazine were more than eighty rounds of green-tipped M855 ball, the slugs having enhanced penetration from their steel-cored design. He knew it was more than enough ammunition to easily take out the interlopers.

Nicholas opened the steel door to the men's lavatory only enough to see a good target. His sense of time seemed to slow down, causing the whole action to seem as if it was in slow motion as he aimed his M4. Through the barely four-inch-wide open slit of the doorway, Nicholas saw that the black-clad man in front of him had a Jackhammer! Where the hell did he get that from?

That became the last conscious thought Nicholas

ever had as he watched a bright orange-red flame belch out of the end of the gun in front of him.

Bear knew that he would only have a small chance of hitting his target with any of the fifteen 0.33-caliber hardened-lead pellets in a shotgun load. But a burst of fire from the Jackhammer would make up for that by saturating a small target area with shot. As he saw the barrel of the weapon in the doorway swing toward him, Bear lined up his shot. As soon as he saw the silhouette of the man holding the gun, he squeezed the trigger.

The Jackhammer roared out a solid wall of noise, echoing in the huge room. The pellets smashed into Nicholas, penetrating his body up and down his torso and into his skull. Reaction to the shock caused his hand to clench on the trigger to his M4. Set on full automatic, the carbine ripped out a long burst of spinning death.

The unaimed bullets stitched across the room as Nicholas fell backward. The stream of slugs ripped open several of the plastic solvent drums on the other side of the room. The stench of ether and alcohol now started to fill the area as volatile liquids gushed from their pierced containers.

Inside the paint booth where he had been keeping a sleepy watch over his bubbling glassware, the young drug chemist Fazul Daoud was terrified by the sudden roar of gunfire. Diving under a lab table, Fazul heard the glassware above him shatter from the many steel-cored slugs tearing through the sides of the paint booth. Squealing and trying to cover his head while hiding under the table, Fazul never noticed the ether fumes thickening the air of the lab. The mewling sounds of fear in the small room faded and finally stopped as Fazul slipped into unconsciousness.

Fazul wasn't the only one to respond to the sounds of gunfire on the sixth floor. In his apartment just off his offices, Arzee sat up in bed. He had no idea what had happened, but the cracking roar of a 5.56mm weapon, possibly Nicholas's favored M4 carbine, had been followed by the deep booms of what might have been a shotgun fired unbelievably fast. Neither Amman nor Nicholas carried a shotgun. Aside from Fazul Daoud in his laboratory, they were supposed to be the only other people in the entire building at this hour.

Ishmael and his men had forced Arzee to send away the men who normally stood guard in the building. Only those men who were most trusted, Arzee's own family, had been allowed on the upper floors. Down in the club, where Ishmael and his men had refused to go, just the bouncers had been enough to keep watch. It had been a mistake not to put the guards back on duty as soon as possible.

Getting up, Arzee picked up the AKMS-47 folding stock assault rifle that he kept at the side of his bed. Now that the last of the Sons of Ishmael had been sent to the island, he had felt that he could finally get some sleep and recover from the beating he had received in the car crash. His left arm pained him at the thought, the twinge deep inside the cast on the broken limb. He still couldn't hear very well because of the ringing in his ears. He had even been forced to leave the office lights on, as a child might. His injured arm made him so clumsy that he now bumped into things if he got up during his restless nights.

Outside the offices, Reaper picked up his MP5K—

PDW and snapped out its stock. The time for the quiet approach had ended. Reaper and Bear would now have to go through the offices as quickly as they could. The first target would have to be the office in the center of the far wall, the only one with light streaming out underneath the door. He turned to see if Bear was back on his six and covering his back. Reaper saw his partner stop and pick up the smoking M4 carbine and sling it across his back. Then he grabbed something else from the body of the man inside the doorway and slipped it into his pocket.

A quick look at the pile of meat on the floor told Reaper that the musclebound thug he had fought would never bother anyone again. He spared the second it took to bend over and pull out the familiar folding Emerson CQC-7BW he saw sticking out of Amman's pocket. Bear came up to his side and silently squeezed his shoulder. The two SEALs moved forward to go through the door indicated by Reaper's pointing finger.

Panicking inside the office, Arzee opened the combination lock on the secure filing cabinet and was trying to pull out the large salesman's case in the bottom drawer. In his near terror, he twisted the case around and jammed it in the drawer. As he struggled to pick the case up, the door to his office shattered and two black-clad men stormed in, each of them heavily armed.

To pull at the drawer with his one good arm, Arzee had set his AKMS-47 down on the floor next to him. Now, while looking up at the cold, unblinking black eye of the suppressor pointing directly at his head, his own weapon seemed to be miles away instead of just inches. When he looked up past the muzzle of the unwavering gunbarrel, the eyes of the man holding it truly glowed more frighteningly than the muzzle of any gun. His gun simply promised a quick end to life. The smoldering orbs of the man holding it told of a long, lingering death for both Arzee's body and soul.

The eyes of the man holding the weapon darted around the room before settling back on Arzee—who had as much chance of looking away as a bird did when facing a king cobra.

"Clear," boomed a voice from across the room.

"Clear," shouted the voice of the man in black in front of him, his voice muffled by the black hood he wore.

Someone out of his field of vision passed by without getting near Arzee or the man in front of him. Whoever it might be completed searching the room and moved on.

"Clear," came the other voice, this time from behind where Arzee knelt. Whoever the owner of that other voice might be, he must have just gone through to his apartment. The only other door in the office, on the other side of the room, led to the barracks room where the Sons of Ishmael had rested.

"Wh-wh-whhoooo are you?" Arzee finally managed.

Without a word, the man in front of him did something strange. Instead of answering, he stepped over to the window, grabbed the line, and pulled open the blinds. He then reached out and flipped open the window. Finally, the black apparition spoke, and Arzee wished that he hadn't.

"War, this is Death," the man said. Then he seemed to listen and finally said, "Roger that."

After he returned to Arzee, the man in black reached up with his free hand, the muzzle of his weapon never wavering for an instant, and he pulled back the hood covering his face.

It was Reaper! In his entire life there had never been a man whom Arzee wanted to see less than the one standing in front of him.

"Where's my family?" asked a voice as cold as death.

Pushing the muzzle of his weapon underneath Arzee's chin, Reaper repeated, "Where's my family? I won't ask you nicely again."

"Th-they're not here," Arzee said with rising panic in his voice. "No one's here. But they're safe. I swear they're safe. No one has done anything with them. I can lead you to them. They're up at the . . ."

In the smashed laboratory, Fazul Daoud was breathing the heavy ether fumes that filled the small room. The ether was gradually depressing Fazul's breathing more and more. Ether fumes not only acted as an anesthetic, they were highly explosive.

Some of the smashed glassware had been filled with the ether solvent. Other parts were filled with water to cool and condense the solvent back into the extraction system. One of the smashed Freidricks condensers, a complex piece of expensive equipment that was now just glass shards, lay in a growing pool of water. The water crawled across the lab table, wetting down what it touched before dripping off onto the floor. Exposed wires torn from an electric heating mantle were touched by the pool of water and suddenly sparked.

The accumulation of volatile ether fumes were ignited by the spark. A huge roiling ball of flame exploded outward with a loud roar, engulfing the room and shattering the remaining glassware. The broken glass released even more ether to feed the explosion. The steel walls of the paint room tore away like cardboard from the force of the blast.

The office area was shielded from the bulk of the explosion by the cinderblock wall that separated it from the production floor. Tossed back by the explosion, Reaper escaped most of the blast. Glass shattered and sprayed from the door frame. Seeing what might be his only chance, Arzee snatched up his AKMS-47 and started to swing it one-handed over toward Reaper. Before Bear or Reaper could recover enough to fire, they heard a quiet thud.

Arzee dropped his weapon and staggered back against the filing cabinet. Before Arzee fell against the wall, a second thud was heard. From his sniper position, Max had fired as soon as he saw Reaper threatened with the weapon. There wasn't time to make the shot a wounding one and the open window provided a perfect line of fire.

"No!" shouted Reaper, as he watched the man who could tell him where his family was fall against the wall. Then a second blast thundered through the building as more solvent drums caught fire.

In spite of the damage from the two suppressed

shots, Arzee still had a single action left to him. He reached up with his uninjured hand and pulled down on what looked like a fire alarm switch on the side of the cabinet. Reaper dove forward to pull the man back from the wall, but his effort came too late. With a sudden pop and an acrid cloud of smoke, the M1A2 cryptographic document destroyer in the top of the filing cabinet ignited.

Reaper knew the device and the destruction its twenty-eight pounds of Thermate filler could do to the contents of a cabinet or a safe. The Thermate would burn for about a minute, producing a pound of molten iron and slag every two seconds. It would eat through the four drawers of the heavy steel cabinet—but with the top drawer closed, the papers in it would actually insulate the drawers below them for a few moments. The Thermate burned at four thousand degrees, but the paper still needed air to burn up completely.

Reaper thrust his hand in the open bottom drawer and tore out the heavy case jammed there, tossing it over to Bear. Bear threw a wastebasket at Reaper while he grabbed another one and turned to the big mahogany desk that dominated the center of the room. With no time to talk both SEALs collected every piece of paper they could and stuffed them into the plastic bags inside the trash cans. Reaper pulled open the drawers of the filing cabinet even as molten iron started to burn though the sides of its top. Files, papers, books, whatever he found got stuffed into the bags. They had lost their best source of information. Now they prayed they'd find some intelligence from around the room.

"Death," Bear shouted, "it's time to go!"

Bear twisted the top of his bag shut. Picking up Arzee's AKMS-47, he unsnapped the hook that held the front of the sling to the weapon. He stuck the rifle through the hand loops on the salesman's case that Reaper had tossed to him and snapped the sling back in place. Now able to hold it with a long cloth strap, Bear slung the case across his back and out of his way. The case must have weighed nearly fifty pounds but Bear handled it easily.

"Death, the fire," Bear shouted. "We have to go—now! You can't do Mary or Ricky any good if you burn to death!"

His partner's shouting finally got through to Reaper as he desperately gathered everything that he could. Crushing the neck closed on his stuffed garbage bag, he took one last look at Arzee's body lying on the floor then turned to Bear.

When they left the office, they could see the glow of the fire through the open doorway into the production area. They had no way to get back to their climbing site. The two SEALs turned to the stairs in front of them. As they ran down the dozen flights of stairs, Reaper shouted into his mike.

"Famine, Famine, Famine," he said, "Evac, evac, evac."

"Death," came back over the earpiece, "Famine, I'm with War. Evac, evac, evac."

What Reaper and Bear learned later was that Ben had seen the fire start to break out on the upper floor of the Factory and had decided to come up to the building. When he received Reaper's radio call, he was positioned next to the billboard and ready to pick up Max. When Reaper and Bear burst out of the front doors of the Factory, Ben moved to pick them up. They swung into the open door of the camper and Max grabbed their arms, pulling the two men in.

As the truck moved away from the Factory building, the upper floor exploded outward in a ball of flame. The entire top of the building became a huge conflagration as the remaining intact solvent containers burst apart from the fire. The ether and alcohol explosion engulfed the building. Fire truck sirens could be heard approaching from off in the distance.

There would be nothing that the fire department could do to save the building. By the next day, the old auto factory would have collapsed into a pile of smoking ashes and rubble. The wooden block floors, soaked for decades in oils and lubricants and augmented by drug solvents, burned with a fierce, hot flame. The strong factory building acted as a furnace before collapsing in on itself. The flesh of the bodies of Arzee and his men were consumed in the heat, burned more completely than if they had been professionally cremated. The final fragments of bones had been crushed to powder and mixed with the rubble when the walls collapsed.

Chapter Twenty-four

The four horsemen didn't hold a celebration or homecoming at the farm later that morning. The victory cigars still lay in their aluminum tubes—intact and unlit. The feelings of disappointment hung thick in the room as the men sat around the kitchen table. The group should have been rejoicing at the recovery of Reaper's family. Instead they sat in quiet silence while they decided on their next move.

A subdued Reaper got up from the table, went into the kitchen and started to get himself another cup of coffee. As he tried to pour the hot, black liquid into the mug, he sloshed some over the side and it spilled onto the counter. Only a little thing, nothing at all, really. But Reaper's nerves were frayed to say the least.

"Goddamnit all to hell!" Reaper cursed as he picked the mug up and smashed it down on the counter. The porcelain coffee cup was strong, but not indestructible. It cracked and shattered under the impact, splashing coffee over most of the countertop.

None of the people around the counter even

started at the outburst. It wasn't as though they didn't feel the same way. A major operation conducted with minimal support, too few personnel, and at lightning speed from conception to execution. They should have been proud, but they didn't have the hostages. And the one among them who had every right to feel the worst was Reaper.

"Did you get it?" Bear asked calmly.

"Get it?" Reaper almost snarled. "Get what? I didn't get anything."

"The spider," Bear continued in the same calm tone. "Did you get it?"

"What spider?" Reaper demanded. "What in the fuck are you talking about, Bear?"

"I figured you must have seen a spider there on the counter," Bear said. "I know you don't like them. And I would never think that you just wanted to smash up Deckert's crockery."

For a moment, Reaper stood there stunned at his friend's words. Then he looked down at the busted coffee mug and the mess he had made of the counter. As he smiled, Reaper shook his head at his own reactions. Taking a deep breath, he blew it out.

"Okay, Bear," Reaper said in a normal tone of voice. "I'm back."

"Never really thought you had left, Brother," Bear said.

"Okay," Reaper said, "we have to start up again. Only this time we might try not to burn the target down to the ground behind us."

"It really hasn't gotten all the way to the ground yet," Deckert said. "That building is a real inferno. I watched the news this morning and that fire is the big story. Apparently, the local water hydrants weren't working or somebody turned them off. Either way, the fire departments who responded couldn't do a damned thing about the blaze. They stood by, controlled traffic and made sure the fire didn't spread to the surrounding neighborhoods. Then they pretty much broke out the marshmallows and hotdogs for a barbecue.

"I'll tell you one thing," Deckert continued. "You guys would have a lot more to worry about if any of the locals knew you had a hand in that fire. The police can only arrest you, maybe shoot you. But most of the workers in downtown Detroit want to lynch you. That fire is right on the corner of two of the biggest highways in the city—and they shut them down a couple of hours ago because of the smoke and ash. You guys seriously fucked-up the Friday morning rush hour."

"Well, at least it'll be a while before they can pull out any bodies," Max said. He had already dumped his street-person clothing and taken the first hot shower. Now he sat at the table with his hair still wet and a towel draped over his shoulders.

"I don't think there's going to be any bodies to concern anyone with," Ben said knowingly. "I've picked up many a fire victim, and that furnace isn't going to leave much behind. Bodies, bones, bullets, brass, even teeth, they're all going to be part of a football field-sized pile of slag."

"The news said that the fire chief suspected that chemicals or paint had been stored on the upper floors," Deckert said. "They might consider the whole thing nothing more than an accident. No one has said arson out loud, or much of anything else really."

"Well," Reaper said, "what we have to do is go over every piece of material that we pulled out of that place before it went up. There's two stuffed garbage bags full of Intel that we need to digest. Bear stripped out the desk and I grabbed everything I could from the filing cabinet. That cabinet had a destruct charge on it—Arzee wanted it gone more than anything else. He was dying when he pulled the switch and that's pretty hard core for an asshole like that.

"So we'll start with that bag. Try and keep everything as separate as you can from the two bags. Anything from the desk or the filing cabinet may be significant. We'll go through the filing cabinet papers here. Keith, why don't you work on the counter and sort out the desk materials there."

"As soon as I clean up the mess somebody left behind here," Deckert said with a grin.

More than an hour later, the men were still sorting through the papers they had now separated into reasonably neat stacks. Before anyone had touched anything, Reaper had them all put on a pair of disposable plastic gloves from a box in the shop. The documents they had found still came from a crime scene and would be considered evidence by any police agency that got hands on them. It would be best if none of the men around the table left their fingerprints on any of the materials. Both Reaper and Bear had been wearing their FOG glove liners during the operation and had been the only people to handle the documents. They hadn't left any fingerprints anywhere so far.

After an hour of sorting and examination, they separated the papers into two sets of stacks. One set was from the desk, the other was from the cabinet.

Where the papers had come from might be important in figuring out what they were. Most of the documents didn't really mean anything. They were regular business items such as the utility bills, UPS shipper receipts, and bar supply lists. The desk had given up most of those items.

The next stack contained documents that the men couldn't read. These papers, maps, and booklets had been written in Arabic for the most part. Reaper now suspected that a hell of a lot more was going on than just what involved his family. The rest of the men also put two and two together and came up with the likely idea of terrorists operating on U.S. soil.

The situation could be a very serious one. Yet the primary mission was still locating Reaper's family. That was all that concerned Reaper for the time being. Once his people were safe, then the rest of the materials would be sent on to the right hands.

The undecipherable documents made the biggest pile from the filing cabinet. The last mound in both sets of papers turned out to be things whose use no one could figure out. Doodles, notes, phone numbers, everything that came from the drawers of the desk or filing cabinet had ended up in the bags of Reaper and Bear.

"There's something missing here," Reaper said.

"How can you tell?" Bear demanded as he looked up from a pamphlet he had been reading. The booklet had been extolling the virtues of a hunting lodge on a private island in Lake Michigan. It was an odd thing to find and had perked his interest.

"Because there's nothing on the Factory here,"

Reaper said. "By that I mean the company books, the records of their cash flow. Things like that."

"Maybe they kept them in that top drawer of the filing cabinet," Max suggested as he looked up from the table. "You said that you had to leave it shut to keep the papers from burning fast."

"True enough," Reaper said, "but that doesn't fit the rest of this stuff. These Arabic documents look important. I can't read the stuff, but the layout resembles some of the military materials we got hold of in Desert Storm and later in Bosnia. Why would they put the company books in the top drawer of a destruct-rigged cabinet?"

"They had a real and a cooked set?" Ben suggested.

"Then why can't we find the cooked set?" Reaper asked. "You keep those separate from the real set so that you can show the cooked ones to the tax people or whoever. If there's a crooked set, they should have been in the desk. We've even got a copy of their sales tax and liquor licenses from the desk. Bear, where's that big briefcase that you picked up?"

"The one from the bottom drawer of the filing cabinet?" Bear said. "It must still be out in the camper. I'll get it."

Bear headed out to get the errant case. While he was gone, they all continued their examination of the documents. In a few minutes, Bear came back into the house, lugging the heavy salesman's case with him. He had a very odd look on his face.

"I think these guys were running on a cash basis," Bear said. To the astonishment of everyone, he tossed a thick bundle of hundred dollar bills on the table. The paper strip wrapped around the bills was printed in bright red: $10,000.

"Jesus, Bear," Reaper said as he picked up the bundle. "Where in the hell did you get that? Hey! Be careful there!"

Bear spread out a towel over the carefully sorted papers on the kitchen table.

"It was with its friends," Bear said, and he dumped the contents of the case onto the towel. Bundles of hundred dollar bills cascaded out of the case—piling onto the towel and spilling onto the floor.

"I always wanted to do something like that," Bear looked up from the huge pile of cash with a big grin.

"Have I called you an asshole recently?" Reaper said.

As they went through the bundles and stacked them up, the men soon came up with 250 sets of $10,000 each.

"So that's what two and a half million dollars looks like," Max said.

"Funny," said Bear, "I always thought it looked bigger on TV."

"What the hell would someone have this much cash on hand for?" Reaper said. "And why in the hell would they try to burn it rather than let it be captured?"

"Maybe Arzee wanted it as mad money for his vacation," Bear said.

"Vacation?" came up from Ben at the table.

"Yeah," said Bear. "He had this brochure for a hunting lodge in his desk."

He picked up the document and handed it to Ben.

"Northern Lake Michigan?" said Ben. "Wait a minute, I saw something else like that."

Going through the regular business papers stack from the filing cabinet, Ben pulled out a faxed receipt on shiny thermal paper.

"Here it is," Ben said as he handed the fax to Reaper. "It's a receipt for a load of diesel fuel and groceries going to someplace called South Wolverine Island."

"I know that place," Deckert said. "It was in the papers a few years back. Some article about the whole damned island being sold to a private party. The environmental and native Indian groups raised a big stink about it."

"That anywhere near Leland?" Reaper asked.

"North of there, yeah," Deckert said. "Why?"

"Because that's where this receipt came from," Reaper said. "It was sent from a fax machine at the Leland Yacht Harbor, and it's dated only three days ago."

"This is a lot of food and fuel," Deckert said as he looked at the papers. "Enough for a large group of people."

"Enough for a big hunting lodge," said Bear.

"Not just that," Deckert said. "There's nothing in the way of fresh foods on this list. This is all canned and frozen stuff. Not what you'd expect a hunting lodge to feed paying customers."

"Arzee started to say something about my family being 'up' somewhere right before the explosion," Reaper said.

"Up North is what everyone down here calls that part of Michigan," said Bear. "It sounds good enough to me. I think we may have found them, Ted, or at least a real good place to start."

Reaper was excited by what they had found, and he agreed with Bear's assessment. As they went through more of the papers with an eye for anything regarding that part of Michigan, they came up with some more clues. Fuel receipts for stops on I-75, the main drag heading up north in Michigan. Restaurant receipts, even motel receipts. And most of them were dated within the last month.

Going back to his computer, Deckert looked for everything he could find about South Wolverine Island and the lodge there. All information stopped as of the year before. The stated reason had been for renovation of the facilities by the new owners. More searching through databases failed to come up with any listings of the permits needed for such renovations. Even the public hearings required by law weren't listed as ever having happened.

Satellite images were available on-line regarding the island. It lay twenty-five miles north of Leland, the closest port on the mainland. It was part of a pair of islands, the smaller, North Wolverine Island only being about five miles northeast of the much larger South Wolverine Island. Both islands boasted heavily wooded areas, large game populations, and airstrips big enough to handle small planes.

"Okay, we need a boat and some additional gear," Reaper said.

"Don't have a boat," Deckert said, "powered chairs don't swim for shit."

"Let me call a friend," Bear said as he left the room.

They spent the rest of the day and into the evening learning everything they could about South Wolverine Island and what might be happening there. When the other men finally went to sleep that night, Reaper remained awake until Bear reminded him that not getting any sleep wouldn't do Reaper any good. Finally, the big man agreed and went to get some rest himself.

At the lodge on South Wolverine Island, Paxtun had a bad situation he needed to discuss with Ishmael. Even as remote as the island was, the news of a major fire at the Factory in Detroit, and the incredible traffic jam it caused, had made the local broadcast media.

In addition to the loss of the building and the club, Paxtun had lost something he would have a very hard time replacing; a man he could trust. While he had trusted Arzee, his second in command, only because he could firmly control him, he still counted it a loss. The material and personal losses, the bulk of the liquid funds to finance Ishmael's operations in North America, the hawala bankroll, had gone up in smoke.

The terrorist leader's reaction was anything but what Paxtun had expected. Ishmael considered the loss of funds little more than *in'shallah*—Allah's will. Paxtun found his fatalism shocking.

"You feel that this very inconvenient fire resulted from some direct action by the authorities?" Ishmael said as he sat pensively in Paxtun's inner office. He accepted the will of Allah, but would listen to others' suspicions.

"I don't see how it could be," Paxtun said from where he sat behind his desk. "The Detroit police and federal agencies just don't work like that in this country, no matter what some conspiracy theorists might say. There is no profit in it for them, nothing for them to gain. Even if they were going after the drugs, and we never had any intelligence indicating any kind of active investigation, our police agencies are interested in confiscation and evidence, not destruction."

"You may be correct in this matter," Ishmael said. "Even if you are not, little can be done immediately. The blow to my further operations by the loss of the funds is not insignificant. We have been having difficulty moving finances around the world's banking system since your new president has seen fit to try and become something other than the adulterer, coward, and fornicating paper tiger that your last leader was. The best thing that I can do in reaction to the situation is move up my operational timetable."

"What," said Paxtun, "for Shaitan's Blessing?"

"Yes," Ishmael said. "I had originally planned for our most ambitious operation to be launched next week. That is the three-day holiday your corrupt people hold to celebrate their criminal military forces."

"You mean Memorial Day," Paxtun volunteered.

"A proper name," Ishmael said ominously. "It certainly will be a memorable day this year."

"Why this weekend?" said Paxtun. "There aren't that many major celebrations within range that would make a good target, a target with a great many people concentrated in a small area. Those gatherings that have large crowds of people usually do so because of celebrities or some of our leadership being there. This year, anything like that would be under very heavy security."

"But what also happens at that time," Ishmael said, "is that a large number of people and their boats are in this area all at once for the first time during the year. It is the beginning of the tourist season."

"Unofficially, yes," Paxtun said. "But the cold weather this year may put off a lot of the usual people from coming up here this early in the season."

"It doesn't matter," Ishmael said, "I shall not wait any longer. My people are here and we shall strike."

"Strike at what?" Paxtun asked. "Tourists? And aren't you limited for weapons?"

"Since no one will now leave this island or communicate with the rest of the world until after the action is underway and it is too late to interfere," Ishmael said magnanimously, "I will explain it to you."

Paxtun reasoned that Ishmael desperately wanted to brag about what he had planned to someone who didn't know the details. Despite all of Ishmael's talk about martyrdom and sacrifice, when it finally came down to it, he wanted someone to know about his personal dedication and sacrifice. Bragging was a weakness of megalomaniacs, and Paxtun was sure Ishmael was one. Besides, it wouldn't be any fun to be a martyr if no one knew you had been one.

"Our experts," Ishmael went on, "have been carefully examining the new security arrangements that have been put in place in this country since the Prince so successfully struck a blow at the heart of the Great Satan in 2001. The destruction of the World Trade Center and the damage to the heart of the Great Satan's war machine are things true believers look to with pride. And they shall be given even more to be proud of by my actions.

"The loss of Iraq to the Great Satan's invaders eliminated one source of weapons that could have struck a telling blow against this land's decadent population of unbelievers. A nuclear bomb would have been the greatest of tools, but Saddam was not able to deliver one before that country's holy Muslim soil was defiled by infidels. Even the diseases and poisons he had promised us had not been completed, though the materials were on hand.

"We searched out and located a potent weapon right here on the soil of the Great Satan itself. It is one the unbelievers created themselves in their foolish arrogance. And they barely recognize its existence."

"A weapon of mass destruction?" said Paxtun. "Here, in the United States? How? The nuclear storage sites always have tight security. Since the 9/11 attacks, that security has been beefed up a lot. Those sites are some of the most secure locations in the country. And there just aren't any stores of chemical or biological weapons that could even be approached."

"Allah, all blessings be upon Him, provides for the dedicated true believers," Ishmael said. "Not more than thirty miles from our location is the source for the mighty sword Allah has seen fit to put into my hands."

"Thirty miles!" Paxtun gulped. "But there's nothing within thirty miles, or even forty or fifty miles of here for that matter. Even the old Big Rock nuclear power plant is gone. They tore it down some time back."

"It is not quite gone," said Ishmael. "There are still some very useful materials on the site."

"What, reactor fuel rods?" Paxtun said. "Those are in a high-security bunker that's alarmed and guarded."

"The weapons and skills my men have can deal with the guards," Ishmael said. "They would not be expecting a boat full of fishermen to open fire on them as we will. It would have been better to have more firepower, but the shipment we received from our brother holy warriors will be enough, *in'shallah.*"

"But you can't move the fuel rods," Paxtun said. "They're in massive armored containers. The containers are designed to be too big to move without some special handling gear and that isn't kept on-site. The rods are too radioactive for anyone to remove from the containers without some very sophisticated equipment. If you even had some, what would you make with them, a dirty bomb? Spray radiation all over a target?"

"The fuel rods are as you say," Ishmael said. "They are highly radioactive and difficult to handle. The raid to obtain them would alert the authorities, and searching for such material can be done from aircraft and satellites. It would take too much time and be technically very difficult to grind the fuel rods into the fine powder needed for a radioactive bomb. And the faithful who did such work would die before they could complete the weapon. No, a radioactive dirty bomb would not be practical for us right now.

"But fuel rods are hardly the only useful materials on the site. When they disassembled the reactor, the sodium metal that they used as a coolant in that old model was also removed and stored for later disposal. That very radioactive sodium has been stored in fifty kilogram lots, each lot is in its own four-hundred-pound steel container. Those containers can be moved, given the strength of the faithful I have with me. And there is the special equipment that I had you install on the large fishing boat you acquired for us."

"What could you do with such a material?" Paxtun said as he sat stunned at his desk. "You can't make a bomb out of it. And it can't be made into an explosive."

"There are many more ways to apply such a poison than from a bomb," Ishmael said. "Just as you said, sodium metal is reactive, very reactive. It explodes violently on contact with water, and makes lye, in this case, radioactive caustic lye. All that has to be done is punch a hole in the steel containers and allow the water that is so abundant all around us, to react with the metal. My technician says that creating the holes will be easy when we use the shaped charges he has fabricated. The charges he made with the explosives you supplied.

"The fuses for the shaped charges will detonate when dropped in the water after a very short delay. A salt crystal is the only thing that will be keeping the detonator from initiating once the fuse is armed. The water will do all of the work for us."

"You're going to poison Lake Michigan with radioactive sodium?" Paxtun said incredulously.

"Perhaps not the whole lake," Ishmael said. "It will be enough to contaminate a great deal of the lake. The panic of this country's sheeplike people would be massive no matter where we dropped the containers. Imagine just how much greater that panic would be if we dropped the sodium overboard, say, on the fresh water intakes for the city of Chicago? The panic should be beautiful to watch. I have the GPS coordinates for those intakes programmed into the navigation equipment on both of my boats. And Chicago is well within the range of those boats given their additional fuel loads. We will poison Lake Michigan and, if Allah wills, Chicago itself.

"Even if our actions were discovered, it would be too late for the Great Satan's minions to do anything to stop us. My men are all dedicated mujahideen—they have waged the jihad, they are Islam's holy warriors. They would not balk at becoming martyrs. Becoming such guarantees their entrance into Paradise. I have confirmed it through my sources that the sodium is in place and we have what we need to seize it.

"There will be a major panic and destruction of a large part of the economies of a number of states and Canada. That would happen even if only a small part of the radioactive poison got into the water. The lakes would be destroyed. The water would be considered poison for years, if not decades. People are frightened by what they can't see or don't know. They could not see the poison, and they would be terrified of the radiation. Even a little bit of the sodium contamination would be enough to create a panic—and we shall have hundreds of kilos. An elegant plan, don't you think?"

Paxtun simply sat at his desk—too stunned to think of anything to say. The plan could work. Because of his involvement in something of such magnitude, he would be hunted forever and not be able to enjoy the wealth he had accumulated. He would have to disappear, and his mind was already considering how to do it as Ishmael continued to speak.

"Regarding practical matters," Ishmael said. "We

will launch the operation Sunday. My followers, my sons, will be forgiven by Allah, all blessings upon His name, if they continue their preparations for the operation over His Sabbath on Saturday."

Chapter Twenty-five

Dawn had been over hours earlier on Saturday morning, the day after the Factory raid. Friday afternoon had passed without the cell phone ringing to demand more weapons. It may have been that Bear had delivered the only extra Jackhammer in existence to Arzee's people the day before. But now Reaper and his men were running on borrowed time. Whoever had Reaper's family had to eventually learn about the fire at the Factory. Then they would probably decide to get rid of any excess baggage and Reaper would be too late to save his wife and child.

Reaper had been up since long before the sun had risen. He was studying all of the intelligence they had collected. Deckert had gone out and bought some Great Lakes navigation charts detailing the waters off Leland and North and South Wolverine Islands. The charts indicated extremely deep waters off the islands for the most part—except for some shallow reefs to the south of the main island.

The rest of the papers had been dealt with. The documents in Arabic had been collected and secured in boxes. Reaper knew that whatever those documents contained, their anonymous delivery to certain authorities would get the information they contained into the proper hands. He made certain that nothing on those documents, or the boxes that held them, could identify Reaper or any members of his team.

The men with him in the house that day were people that he felt closer to than blood kin. They were his brothers in arms who had offered all they had when he needed it. That meant a great deal to him and he swore to keep them as safe as he knew how. Part of this commitment came from the fact that Reaper knew he would have to ask them for their help once more. His family wasn't safe yet.

Reaper directed that the cash they had recovered from the factory be packed back into the salesman's case for the time being. He intended that his partners would all get to share in the proceeds, but for the time being, they had decided the bag was nothing more than a war chest. It would be used to pay for what they needed to get Reaper's family back.

As Reaper went over the papers that remained spread out on the kitchen table, counter, and just about every available surface in the room, he heard a heavy knock at the front door. The "Open" sign for the shop hadn't been lit in several days, and it was far too early for a weekend customer anyway. The police wouldn't have knocked like that and waited, and the men they hunted wouldn't have knocked at all.

Going to the front door, Reaper could see a

shadow through the optical peephole in the center of the door. Since no light illuminated the interior of the house, Reaper knew that his looking out the peep wouldn't make a shadow that someone else could see from the other side. That kind of shadow could show a gunman that a target was poised on the other side of the door. The huge man standing on the porch made Reaper very glad he had looked, and more than a little surprised at what he saw. He had to move quickly to unlock and open the door before many more of the heavy-handed knocks took it off its hinges.

"Enzo!" Reaper said as he pulled open the door. "God damn, it's good to see you."

The big man on the porch resembled a reincarnation of some pirate from centuries past. The huge muscular frame, square face framed off by a thatch of dark red hair, and a beard the same color, fit perfectly with the small gold earring in the man's left ear. The booming voice that sounded out of that barrel-chested individual also fit the pirate image.

"Reaper, you grim-looking bastard, good to see you, too," Enzo Caronti almost bellowed. "Now let me in before some woodland critter drags me off into this wilderness you live in."

"If it did, it would be too bad for the critter," Reaper said as he stood to the side and let his old friend and Teammate in. "How the hell did you know to show up? No, don't tell me—Bear called you, didn't he?"

"Well if I hadn't, it's not like you would have," Bear said with a big grin plastered on his face as he came down the stairs.

"Well, ho, ho, ho, yourself, Bearski," Enzo said as

the two men clasped in a strong hug. Stepping back, Enzo held open the door for Bear and Reaper to look out.

"It's time for Santa to bring all the bad little boys their presents," Enzo said as he indicated with his chin where the two SEALs should look. "I brought my sleigh."

In the driveway was a shining black Chevrolet Silverado Suburban with silver trim and dark-tinted windows. The big SUV was covered with road dust but still loomed impressively. What looked even more impressive to Reaper at the moment was what rode behind the Suburban.

Almost dwarfing the vehicle that towed it was a big, black boat on a multiaxle trailer. The boat looked a bit like an enlarged version of the inflatable vessels the two SEALs had long been used to, but its up-curved bow and other lines indicated it had a hard hull. Standing near the center of the craft they saw a glass-paneled "phone booth" coxswain's station. Surrounding the station was a canvas cover that secured the inner hull of the boat. At the stern of the vessel hung two large, powerful Evenrude Mercury 250-horsepower outboard motors. The black-painted covers on top of the outboards looked as if they could encase an average-size car engine.

"There you go," Enzo said. "Bear told me to bring a boat up from the Creek, and this is one of the newest available."

"This is from the base at Little Creek?" Reaper said.

"Not from the Navy, if that's what you mean," Enzo said. "This is the USIA Swift Attack Vessel II.

It's a low-profile attack vessel. Since I left the Special Boat Teams, I've set up my own marine security outfit. We're using these boats at my company for tactical waterborne training. This is the twenty-four footer, the biggest I could get on short notice that had a trailer available for it."

"She looks great," Bear said. "What's it like?"

"The design is based on the inflatable boats we used at the Teams," Enzo explained. "But the hull's made of welded aluminum for strength and durability. The boat's stable as all hell in almost any sea state and the aluminum tubes are individually sealed so sinking it is a real job. With those twin Mercs on the back, it'll hit fifty to fifty-four knots, so she's fast and agile as hell too. These boats practically dance across the water.

"Rangewise, the motors will draw a gallon a mile wide open. There's a 180-gallon fuel tank so that should take us as far as you want to go. If we need any more range, we can always pick up a couple of extra fuel tanks at any boat chandlers."

"Two outboards," Reaper said.

"You know the rule," Enzo said. "Two is one, one is none. If an engine folds, we still have the other to move us along. That top will protect the coxswain, and there's also a Global Positioning System, marine radios, marine radar, and a fishfinder sonar rig. Everything is a stand-alone system and there's a triple battery rig for power. The cooler is a little small, though."

"Damn," said Bear. "A small cooler, you say?"

"Yeah, we'll have to stock up on beer twice," Enzo laughed. "Speaking of beer, aren't you going to offer a Teammate one? I've been on the road for fifteen hours getting here, and that in[illegible] off for some more gear."

"More gear?" asked Bear as the trio headed back into the house.

"Yeah," said Enzo, "your message said to bring some heavy hardware if I could put my hands on some in a hurry. I couldn't get much, but I think you may like one particular item."

When Enzo entered the house, he met Ben and Max. He and Max stared at each other until Enzo recognized the ex-marine as the sniper he and Reaper had pulled out of a hot spot in Kafji shortly before Desert Storm kicked into high gear. That immediately made the two men fast friends. Meeting Ben MacKenzie and Keith Deckert resulted in the automatic mutual respect given among fellow warriors.

Seeing all of the documents spread out everywhere told Enzo that the mission Bear had spoken about was a very real one. It didn't take much of Reaper's explanation of the situation to convince Enzo to put his hat in the ring. These were his Teammates and one of them needed him—that's all it took.

After a few minutes of discussion, everyone went out to Enzo's Suburban to bring in the gear he had brought. The man had filled the back of the SUV, and there were more containers, packages, boxes, and tubes in the SAV II, secured under the canvas tarp.

What they found in the back of the Suburban intrigued Bear the most. He had asked Enzo to bring a heavy weapon in case they had to take on a small boat—in the paperwork they had gone through they had found a receipt for a forty-one-foot commercial fishing boat and a twenty-nine-foot Fountain

…er boat. They knew the group that had these boats were well financed.

What Enzo had brought was big; it filled two Army duffel bags locked together with a chain. It extended from the back door of the Suburban almost to the front seat, requiring the smaller side passenger seat in the rear to be folded down to let the bags fit. The package was heavy. One man could carry it, but it had to have weighed more than a hundred pounds.

Once back inside the house with everything, it became Christmas exactly as Enzo had suggested it would. Only this Santa had brought a bunch of really nasty presents. Enzo apologized for not being able to bring a .50-caliber Browning machine gun as Bear had suggested. What he had brought proved to be pretty fair-sized.

The twin barracks bags held a massive World War II 20mm L/39 Finnish antitank rifle. All the men in the house had a lifetime interest in weapons, but this blaster was something unusual even for them.

Enzo explained that the semiautomatic rifle measured eighty-eight inches long and weighed 109 pounds empty. One of the larger boxes held an unusual short wooden ski-folding bipod mount that attached to the bottom of the impressive weapon. And it was definitely impressive.

The stainless-steel harmonic-style flash hider on the muzzle of the weapon had five holes along the sides of the long, flat, rectangular device, each hole larger than an average man's finger. Two large triangular steel boxes with flat bottoms accompanied the gear, the boxes were outfitted with shoulder straps to make carrying them easier. Inside each of the boxes lay two huge black-metal magazines. A magazine held only ten rounds of ammunition—but what ammunition!

Each cartridge weighed three-quarters of a pound and launched a projectile the size of an entire 12-gauge shotgun shell. The foot-long rounds were mostly loaded with black-painted pointed steel projectiles. One magazine had been loaded with rounds with yellow-painted projectiles that had flat-nosed aluminum fuses screwed into their tips. The men all knew high-explosive ammunition when they saw it.

"Where in the hell did you get this rifle?" Reaper asked, "Steal it from a dinosaur hunter?"

"Naw, I didn't steal it," Enzo responded in a hurt tone of voice. "There are these older, what you might call 'southern Miami expatriates' who had it left over from their days of shooting up some island or other down south. They gave it to me some while back in partial payment for a debt. When Bear mentioned an island, I thought of this and brought it along. There's a ground mount for it, that bipod over there, and there's a specially machined pedestal mount that's in the front of the SAV. It's kind of a classy old cannon, isn't it?"

"I like it," Bear said from down on the floor where he played with the big gun.

"That hand crank on the side pulls the bolt back with a gear arrangement," Enzo said. "The big thing on the pistol grip under the trigger is a bolt release, you squeeze that in and the bolt slams shut—don't leave your fingers there. It's semiautomatic—they made a fully automatic version for shooting at planes, but this isn't it. If you want it to autoload each shot, you have to hold the bolt release in."

"Is that it?" Bear asked.

"Isn't that enough?" Enzo replied.

"What's in the other containers?" Reaper asked.

"More stuff," Enzo said. "Bear didn't give me a lot of time to grab shit, so this is what I could get. I have ballistic dry suits since Lake Michigan is going to be real cold this time of year."

"What are ballistic dry suits?" Reaper asked.

"Yeah, they're new," Enzo said. "They have pockets front and back to take a slip-in waterproof panel of Point Blank's Legacy I premier level 2A soft body armor. Give you a hell of a lot more protection than the old suits, and they keep you warm.

"The other boxes have the leg-inflator tanks for the suits in case you want to blow them up for more buoyancy. Also some Military Exotherm II jumpsuits for keeping you warm under the dry suit. Fins, masks, weight belts, waterproof bags for weapons. And that barracks bag over there has two M72A3 LAW rockets."

"LAW rockets?" Reaper gaped at him.

"Yeah, well, I could only come up with two of them. I got you two M26A1 frag grenades, too."

"Only two fragmentation grenades?" Reaper said with an eyebrow raised. "Enzo, you must be slipping."

Enzo just shrugged his shoulders.

"What's in the long tubes we left back in the boat?" Ben asked from where he stood near the door.

"Fishing poles," Enzo said.

"Of course," said Ben.

"I've also got an M14 rifle with a folding stock I use on the boat," Enzo said. "There are ten twenty-round magazines for that. And this thing's kinda cool," he said reaching for another box. "I couldn't come up with an M60 or a .30-caliber machine gun fast enough, but this should do for your guys."

Pulling up the box and opening it, Enzo lifted up what looked like half of a very strange machine gun.

"What's that?" Deckert said, looking on.

"It's a new weapon just on the market," Enzo said. "Really it's not a whole weapon. It's called a Shrike. It's an upper receiver assembly that lets you turn an M16-style weapon into a belt-fed 5.56mm light machine gun. The Teams are just starting to look at it and there are damned near none available. I talked the owner of Ares Inc., the company that's making this, into letting me have it."

"That must have been some talk," Deckert said as Enzo handed him the part.

"Well, that was the stop I had to make on the way here," Enzo said. "Bear told me on the phone that you guys had an M4. This can mount on that easily."

"Yeah, we can come up with something like that," Deckert said. "You got any belted ammo?"

"Four hundred rounds in two assault packs," Enzo said. "They clip on to an adapter that's in the box. The adapter goes up in the magazine well. If the belt runs out, you can drop the adapter and immediately load up a regular magazine."

"Or a hundred-round Beta C-mag," Bear said with a grin.

"Sure," Enzo said. "But when are you going to use all of this firepower? Bear just said get up here as fast as I could."

"Well, Enzo, I hope your ass isn't flat yet," Reaper said, "because we're leaving as soon as we can all pack our gear in your suburban and the pickup truck. It's about a five-hour drive to where we're going and I want to get on the road as soon as we can."

"Can we stop somewhere to grab a bite to eat?" Enzo said. "I'm hungry enough to eat a bear."

"You stay the hell away from me," Bear said.

"Not a problem," laughed Reaper. "I know a pretty good place for chow, Tony's at Birch Run. They can probably even fill a guy your size."

Chapter Twenty-six

The vehicles were packed and on their way within an hour of Enzo's arrival. Deckert volunteered to man the phone lines at the farm and maintain a communications base in case a call came in regarding Reaper's family or the demand for guns. Ted knew that his friend wanted more than anything to go with them on the operation, but Keith had long ago come to grips with his disability, and he considered going out in an assault boat something he shouldn't do.

The stop at Birch Run north of Flint proved to be a funny one. Enzo found Tony's to be a home-style Italian restaurant that seemed as if it had time-warped from the 1950s. The triple eggs, toast, hash browns, and one-pound of bacon were almost too much of a good thing even for him. The break refreshed them and lightened the atmosphere in the vehicles.

The men traded off driving at rest stops along the way. Reaper didn't want to use much time, but they all had to be as fresh as they could when they arrived in Leland. Ben and Max swapped off driving in Max's pickup truck while Reaper, Bear, and Enzo went tooling along in the Suburban towing the boat. They looked like either a part of a football team out on a jaunt, or the most dangerous fishermen the Great Lakes had seen in a long time.

The Suburban took the lead when the short caravan turned to the west off I-75 and headed out toward Traverse City along M72. About a quarter-hour west of Kalkaska, Bear suddenly told Reaper to turn up a short road they were rapidly approaching.

Bear had been in the back of the Suburban for much of the trip, complaining about a miserable headache. The demand to turn off seemed unusual for him, but Reaper didn't feel like arguing. The spot turned out to be a scenic turnoff that went partway up a hill to where the road spread out into a wide parking area. Picnic tables and a place to stand and look out over the inland lakes had been added. The view made it worth the stop, even Reaper admitted to that.

"Damn, look at that," Bear said as the rest of the guys piled out of both vehicles.

The sun had slid lower in the sky and stretched out in front of their eyes were three magnificent lakes, the blue water of one going on past the horizon. Far to the west they could see the barest sliver of blue that was Lake Michigan.

"That short lake in front of us is Skegemog," Bear said. "To the left there is Elk Lake, and that really long one is Torch."

"How do you know so much about the lakes up here?" Ben asked.

"I used to ride my bike all around up here," Bear said with a faraway look in his eye. "I used to camp in the state forest up off of Dockery Road just west of here. This used to be a town called Barker Creek. Or at least it was near here."

"Nothing of a town here but that little fenced-in graveyard over there," Max said as he looked off to the west of where they were standing.

"Yeah," Bear said, "that would be a real nice place to rest for a while. Nice view and all."

"A while?" Max said. "That's a graveyard, Bear, you'd have to want to rest for a long while there. And that nice view of yours doesn't include the trees around here, does it? That one across the road way down there looks like the top got stepped on and squashed."

"Damn," said Bear, "you are a city boy. That's an eagle's nest. I heard they were back up here in numbers—never seen one though."

"You okay, Bear?" Reaper asked. "You don't usually talk like this."

"I'm fine," Bear said shaking his head. "I must be a little dingie from the trip."

Ben leaned close to Bear and looked him square in the eyes.

"No, really," Bear insisted, "I'm fine. Just wanted to take a look is all. We'd better get moving."

Reaper agreed and they got back into their vehicles. In spite of the rush, Reaper didn't begrudge Bear a few minutes in an area he seemed to know so well and cared about.

The little caravan hit the road again, heading farther out past Traverse City and on to Leland on the shores of Lake Michigan. Leland was a small town on the Leelanau Peninsula, a large finger of land bordered by Lake Michigan on the west and Grand Traverse Bay on the east. The town itself rested on a thin strip of land that lay between Lake Michigan and Lake Leelanau on the peninsula.

When the men finally reached the Leland harbor, right at the mouth of the Leland River, it was already after six-thirty in the evening. Several hours of daylight remained, enough for them to launch and get to South Wolverine. Enzo had said that the SAV II would do more than fifty knots, close to sixty miles an hour, fast enough to get them over the twenty-five miles to the island before sunset. The team wanted to keep a low profile and launching a big boat that late in the day would draw some unwanted attention—attention they received in spite of their efforts.

At the large public boat ramp area were a number of fishing boats, most of them tied up to the docks. It was an active fishing area and the Michigan Department of Natural Resources, the DNR, kept a close watch on sports activities at the ramp.

Wearing a green uniform and looking like a police officer, down to his SIG P-226 sidearm and handcuffs, was a DNR man, a Michigan game warden. He came up to Reaper and Bear as they got out to check the boat ramp.

"How you boys doing today?" the man said. His name tag read BERINSKI.

"Not bad officer. How's yourself?" Bear said.

"Well enough," Berinski said. "You going out kind of late, aren't you?"

"Not really," Bear said. "We planned on maybe doing some night fishing."

"Oh, fishing for what?" Berinski asked.

"Brown trout," Enzo said as he walked up to the three others. "The news down south said they were running off the peninsula and farther out in the lake. We thought we might get an early start before the crowds came up next weekend."

"That's a good idea," Berinski said, "if you don't mind the cold."

"We aren't bothered a lot by cold," Reaper said with a smile.

"Good, a lot better than some of the people who have been coming up here recently," Berinski said. "To look at how they acted, you'd think they were freezing. You've got all of your approved flotation devices, signaling and emergency gear, radios?"

"Not a problem on all counts," Enzo said. "You need to check anything out?"

"No, by the looks of you, I'd say I can take your word for it," Berinski said easily. "I see that's an out of state plate on the SUV. Got your fishing licenses?"

"Damn, I knew there was something I was supposed to stop for," Enzo complained loudly. "Weren't you supposed to get one for me?" he said as he looked at Reaper.

"Shit, I'm sorry," Reaper said, "I was asleep in the car. Do you know where we can pick some up, Officer?"

"Sure," Berinski said. "There's a sporting goods store just up the docks. They'll still be open this time of night. You can get what you need there."

"Is there a good motel nearby?" Reaper said. "It looks like it may be getting late and we might just strike out in the morning."

"Sure," Berinski said. "The closest one is the Anchor Motel, that's just a block up the street there," he said, pointing the direction.

"Thanks," Reaper said, "we'll get our act together now."

"Not a problem," Berinski said. "Good luck tomorrow."

Back in the Suburban, Bear leaned over the front seat and looked at Reaper.

"Well, that was fun," he said. "I can see about the licenses, the devil is in the details. But just what the hell was all that crap about a motel? We're not going out tonight?"

"No, we may have something else to do," Reaper said cryptically. "Do you still have those notes from the OP?"

"Somewhere here," Bear said. "You've been going through all of that stuff since we left the farm. What do you need?"

"Remember the van we saw come and go that night?" Reaper said. "I need to know the license number."

"YXLC-493," Bear said. "Why?"

Then Bear caught the stare coming his way from Enzo in the driver's seat.

"Hey, it's something I do, okay?" Bear said.

Astounded by this display of recall, Enzo shook his head.

"Take a look at the parking area left of where that officer was when we got here," Reaper said. "Does that van look familiar?"

"Damn," Bear said. "YXLC-493. There can't be two of them. We found them."

"I think so, too," Reaper said. "Now let's go get the

others and shop for some fishing licenses. I don't think that officer is going to be leaving for a while. It's a Saturday night and he's checking boats as they come in. I'll bet he's going to issue one or two tickets this evening. And I don't want him to see us loading up the boat. That cannon looks like anything but fishing gear—even in the bags. By the time he's gone, it will be too late to head out. The sun will be down and the sign says the ramp will be closed."

"Looks like we need that motel," said Enzo.

An hour before sunrise the next morning the two vehicles returned to the boat ramp. They arrived twenty minutes before the ramp officially opened to avoid any traffic from other boaters. Enzo put the boat in the water with ease, rolling the trailer down the ramp. Years of practice had eliminated his need for a ground guide to help him back up a trailer. As Reaper tied the boat up to the dock, Enzo drove the Suburban over to the parking area and left it.

All of the men hustled to hump their equipment and gear into the boat. The weapons had been packed up in USAI waterproof bags delivered by Enzo. No one was around in the early Sunday morning hours, but Bear still paused for a minute while he surveyed the parking lot. Then he pulled the Lahti 20mm cannon from the back of the SUV and hoisted it up to his shoulder. Trotting, he hurried the huge gun in its duffel bag case over to the boat.

Enzo emerged from the SUV already dressed in his ballistic dry suit. He busied himself prepping the boat and checking over everything while the rest of the guys stowed the gear on board. He didn't have time to suit up, so he had worn the gear he wanted from the motel under loose-fitting street clothes.

The Exotherm III insulating fleece jumpsuit that Enzo had on under the dry suit would have kept him warm in a winter wind. The ballistic dry suit prevented any water from getting to the jumpsuit. The armor panels of the dry suit made it feel that much more assuring.

Since he wore one of the ballistic dry suits on a regular basis, Enzo had modified his for his own comfort by cutting off the integral boots. The mottled green-black-and-brown camouflage pattern of the outer suit didn't extend to the boots. He preferred different footwear for his movements on the boat. On top of his head, he had squashed down a badly worn boonie hat, a veteran of many missions over the water.

The suit was warm, but it could quickly become very hot if you weren't in the cold water or blowing wind. To add to his comfort level, Enzo wore a neck ring that held the soft black rubber neck seal away from his throat. The ring kept the suit from being watertight at the neck, but it made Enzo's working on the boat a lot easier.

The rest of the men dressed in their suits while Enzo checked the boat and warmed up the engines. They all had the same ballistic dry suits as Enzo wore, but none of them expected to keep them on during the land operation on the island. So instead of the extremely comfortable Exotherm II jumpsuits they had available, Ben and Max both wore a standard woodland camouflage battle dress uniform (BDU) under their dry suits. Reaper and Bear had put on the same black shirts and Royal Robbins range pants they had worn during the Factory raid.

To put the suits on, over the uniforms and clothes, was a two-man job if you wanted to get dressed fast. The entry to the suit came through a long zipper across the shoulders. Once one had pulled the boots up onto his feet, the person stood and pulled up the rest of the pants portion of the suit. Arms went through the sleeves and the tight, soft black rubber seals at the wrists. Ducking one's head, the wearer pulled the neck part over his head and settled the neck seal in place. Then a partner was needed to pull the zipper across the back of the shoulders and seal up the suit. No one had arms flexible enough to pull the zipper by himself.

The suits crackled as they moved. The rustle of the waterproof material would be lessened when it got wet, but the new suits remained stiff. Yet they would keep each of the men protected from the thirty-nine-degree water of Lake Michigan. It had been a long, cold winter, and the spring had not been a warm one. Unprotected exposure to the water could kill a man almost instantly from the shock—and within half an hour from hypothermia if the shock hadn't gotten him.

The men placed all the gear on board and secured it. The boat's outboards were warmed up and running smoothly and everyone was now aboard. Ben had a particularly hard time gearing up because his suit was too big for him. Enzo said it was the smallest size he had in stock. When Ben accidentally dipped his hand into the lake water, he fully appreciated the suit, too large or not.

A gleam of sunrise came up over the land as the boat sped across the waves. Enzo reveled in his element, and he handled the small, agile craft with the steady hand of a master. All the waves only swelled a few feet high at the most, but Ben MacKenzie was not used to the pounding. He crawled into the crowded but protected cockpit area and tried not to look as miserable as he felt.

Reaper, Bear, and Max, all having spent a lot of time on the water while in the service, found the trip cold and wet but nothing new. As they skimmed over the water, they checked out their gear as much as they were able to. When they lost sight of the mainland, Enzo reached into the huge pocket on the outside of his dry suit and pulled out an Eagle tactical thigh holster. The rig held his favored 9mm SIG P-226 which he strapped to his leg with practiced fingers.

The marine radar screen in the cockpit showed open water ahead of the speeding small boat. With one eye on the screen, another on the water, and occasional glances at the GPS locator, Enzo knew the boat's position, where it was headed, and that no other craft moved on the water around them. They traveled swiftly across a steel-blue lake, the water spewing white as the wave tops broke in the wind. As the sun came up, so did the view of an island on the horizon.

A dark mound arose from the water, the darker covering of trees and brush became more distinct as they approached. Now Reaper stood behind Enzo, focusing on the island on the radar screen. He also checked for any signals that radar from the island might be painting them electronically, but was pleased that the screen remained clear of interference.

As they approached to within five miles of the island, Enzo cut back on the power and the SAV II settled in the water a bit. At Reaper's questioning glance, Enzo pointed to the fish finder. The simple sonar showed that the lake bottom rose rapidly ahead. From more than a hundred feet down, it quickly came to thirty, twenty, ten feet. Off to the right a buoy marked the top of the rocky reef only a few feet under the surface.

They were unknown waters to everyone on the boat, and Enzo wanted to play the situation as safely as he could. Only danger awaited them on that chunk of land in front of the boat. With the sunrise, the colors of the trees and brush could be made out against the tan and browns of the sand and earth. Reaper pointed and Enzo nodded as he swung the boat to the west.

They would land on the western shore of the island, close to the southern tip. Deckert's research had shown that the only major structures on the island were the mansion that made up the hunting lodge and a scattering of smaller support buildings at the airstrip and boat dock. On the southern point of the island stood an old lighthouse, which had been abandoned and dark for years. They would put in on the shore just to the north of that lighthouse, above the sandbar that separated it from the main body of the island.

A tree-covered rise above the sand concealed a small valley with a stream or a ravine that cut through its center from west to east. That rise would be where the men could look down on the lodge facilities only a few hundred meters away. Everything should be visible to them in the one panoramic view. From the base of the ridge to the eastern shore of the island, all the aerial and satellite images had shown a gentle grass-covered slope. The time had come to see if that intelligence was true.

Chapter Twenty-seven

With the arrival of the boat at the island, Reaper and Bear once again slipped into a comfortable, familiar mode of operating. They had performed the actions they would be doing countless times before during training and real-world operations, two combat-experienced SEALs about to slip onto an enemy-held beach as a pair of swimmer-scouts. Before the rest of the team could land, the swimmer-scouts would check the shoreline for unfriendlies, select the specific beach landing site, and provide security for the landing.

Reaper and Bear prepared to enter the water. They kept the weapons and equipment to a bare minimum: Their dry suits for protection, a nine-pound lead weight belt, a set of 3XL Turtle fins over the suit's boots, and a black U.S. Divers Maui model face mask made up the bulk of the two SEALs' swimming gear.

With a look to his partner, Reaper gave a ready signal and saw it returned. Then the two men slipped silently over the side of the boat and into the dark waters. The frigid water closed over their heads with barely a splash as they sank out of sight.

The USIA ballistic dry suits now proved their value. The hands of both men were red from the compression of the soft rubber wrist seals that kept out the water. But their hands still had their feeling and flexibility. Now those hands told them exactly how cold the water all around them was as they went numb within a minute of leaving the boat.

Discomfort in the water means little to a SEAL; it can't mean much because they spend more than half of their operational lives in the water all over the world and Reaper and Bear were no different in this respect. They quickly sorted out their locations in relation to each other and the island ahead. Bubbles gushed out of the two and one-half-inch-diameter round black plastic valve on their upper left arms. The pressure of the water pushed at the suits, squeezing out the excess air. If they had lost too much buoyancy, a quick squirt of air from the gas bottle in a pocket on their upper left thigh would reinflate the suit.

The arms and legs of the dry suits clamped around their limbs as the water squeezed down. The armor panels on their chest and backs kept the suits stiff across the chest and back and they barely felt the effects of the water there. Slowly and carefully returning to the surface, the two swimmer-scouts headed toward the beach.

The strong legs of Reaper and Bear pushed the black Turtle power-fins toward the beach, the big neoprene blades of the flippers driving the SEALs effortlessly through the water. SEALs regularly swam for miles, and ran for even more miles, in order to build up their leg strength for just such an operation. The driving force of the fins allowed the two SEALs to keep their hands free to move them over the lake bottom as they approached the softly pounding surf on the beach.

Reaper and Bear crawled up to the edge of the surf zone and lay there as the cold waves swirled around them. Raising his AKMS-47, the same weapon that Bear had picked up at the Factory, Reaper prepared it for action.

During the years Reaper had been in the Teams, the SEALs had not found another weapon that worked as well in the surf zone as an AK-47. The sand, mud, and water just didn't jam up the rugged Russian design. It wasn't as accurate, long-ranged, or comfortable to shoot as one of the weapons from the M16 family, but it always worked. And it was the weapon of choice for scout-swimmers passing through the surf zone. But Reaper and Bear only had one of the rugged Soviet designs. As the primary point man, Reaper carried their AK.

Over his shoulder, Reaper wore a yellow canvas pouch holding four thirty-round magazines for the AK. From somewhere in the boxes and from the shelves of their shop, Deckert had come up with the Iraqi ammo pouch and magazines along with fresh ammo for the weapon itself. The experienced gunsmith had gone over every inch of the weapon, making sure that even its rugged design didn't have any flaws. Reaper now held a weapon as dependable as anything mechanical ever could be.

The only thing Reaper had done to prepare his weapon for the swim in was to stretch a latex condom over the muzzle. The thin rubber could have been fired through if necessary without any damage to Reaper or the weapon. And the latex helped keep the water from entering the AK's barrel.

Now Reaper stripped the latex condom from the muzzle of the AK, as he pulled the bolt back partway. While he prepped his weapon, Reaper also kept watch along the beach and the tree line just beyond. Even though the condom would have kept the bore of the weapon relatively clear of water, cracking open the breech would release the seal of the cartridge in the chamber insuring that any water in the barrel drained away.

For his weapon, Bear didn't have to worry about water exposure. He was carrying Reaper's preferred MP5K-PDW. With the Gemtech Raptor suppressor secured on the barrel, the compact submachine gun had been secured in a special small waterproof weapons container Enzo had brought. The MP5K-PDW fit snugly in the bag. The flexible weapon container even had an inflator tube that allowed air to be blown into the bag to make it buoyant. The feature of the bag that Bear liked best was the built-in glove. The glove allowed the shooter to fire his weapon if necessary without taking it from the bag, the reason Bear had carried it out in front of him during the insertion.

After waiting a few minutes in the surf zone to be sure they hadn't been spotted, or that anyone else might be around, Reaper and Bear quickly moved inland to conduct a recon of the area. The aerial views of the island they had all studied had shown a small valley along the side of the ridge line where Reaper wanted to establish their observation post.

What the views hadn't shown was a wide inlet of water extending into the tree line along the floor of that valley. This would be their beach landing site and would be a safe place to cache their gear and secure the boat.

Going back to the shore, Reaper pulled a flashlight from a pocket of his ammunition pouch. The operators had devised a system to ensure that the operation hadn't been compromised on insertion. The man on shore would use a series of flashes to signal the men in the boat. The returned countersign had to add up to seven flashes. Any other result would mean that the men had to break off contact. Holding out his flashlight, Reaper squeezed off four slow flashes.

Three flashes returned from the boat. As Reaper watched, the SAV II emerged from the mist that had come up from the water. As it approached the shore, Reaper could see Ben and Max on either side of the bow, their weapons at the ready. Following his arm signals, Enzo spotted the opening in the beach that led into the valley. Slowly guiding the boat along, Enzo entered the crevasse with just one outboard engaged, cutting off the other motor in case he ran aground in the unknown waters and lost his propeller. The water in the gorge ran deep enough that he managed to scrape by and come in under the cover of the trees.

Not a word had been spoken since they left the boat.

Every member of the team had studied the maps and photos of the island. The routes they would take had been committed to memory. The whole operation had been originally planned to take place under the cover of darkness. Circumstances now denied them that option.

The men would only have to patrol about four hundred meters to reach the top of the ridge line at the point Reaper had selected. While travelling only a short distance, their patrol needed to go through an unknown area with the possibility of discovery a very real one. They would stay off any paths they might find along the route and proceed as silently as ghosts through the woods and brush.

Returning to the water, Ben and Max helped Enzo turn the boat around so that its bow pointed toward open water only fifty meters away, preparing the group for a fast extraction. Then all except Enzo stripped off their ballistic dry suits. He would stay and secure the boat, their only sure means of extraction from the island.

If the men got separated or forced apart by heavy combat, the emergency rally point was at the tree line overlooking the old lighthouse. If everything went completely to hell, Enzo would call in the Coast Guard and the men would have to trust that they could hold off any forces until help arrived. The Motorola Talkabout radios they each had in their uniform pockets had a two-mile range. These would have to do as a final backup in case the boat's radio became unavailable.

It might be a loose plan, but that also made it flexible. Though they preferred stacking the deck in their favor at every opportunity, all of the men had long operated right out on the edge. One took chances only when he had to and prepared for as many contingencies as possible, and saved his luck for when he really needed it by training constantly.

Taking the lead as the point man in the patrol, Reaper moved out with his favored MP5K-PDW back in his hands. Now that he was on dry land, the suppressed MP5K-PDW would be the best choice in case he had to fire a shot. So Reaper had taken the MP5K from Bear and given the AK and ammo pouch to Ben.

Reaper's Chalker sling again spanned his chest and shoulders. Too bad that he would never be able to tell the retired command master chief just how well the sling had worked for him. Somehow, Reaper figured that this operation wouldn't be a story that got a lot of public release.

The gear Reaper had strapped on was almost a mirror of what he had carried at the Factory only the day before. That thought gave him pause. Had it only been a day?

This time, Reaper had loaded the Serbu Super-Shorty shotgun in the holster on his thigh with Winchester 00 buckshot. Every person on the island could be considered an armed enemy except for the hostages—Reaper's family. There would be little need for less lethal ammunition. Also, the nasty little shotgun would be useful for blasting locks or hinges if they had to open secured doors. In case he encountered a larger group of hostiles, Reaper had one of Enzo's M26A1 fragmentation grenades in the flash-crash pocket of his ammunition pouch. The deadly little green ovoid would spray out hundreds of steel fragments when detonated—enough to wreck anyone's day.

Immediately behind Reaper in the patrol came Max, who filled the position of automatic weapons man. He carried the Shrike belt-fed conversion unit mounted on the receiver of the M4. Slung across his back was the TTR-700 sniper rifle in its compact case. Max could place a single round exactly where he wanted with the bolt-action rifle. But he could also practically write his name with an automatic weapon when he wanted to—Bear had been right in nicknaming the young man "War."

Coming next in the patrol line was Bear. The stout SEAL now had the Jackhammer shotgun he liked so much hanging from a sling. Across his shoulders, Bear held the massive 20mm Lahti rifle. Ahead of them lay a long downhill, potential field of fire they would have to cross before they reached the lodge. Bear had accepted the responsibility of dragging the big gun along in order to give them the best base of fire they could have to cover that crossing.

The brochure for the lodge had pictures that showed the castlelike walls to be made of light brown stone. The 20mm cannon could make large, precise holes through that stone. The weight of the gun had become Bear's burden. The bipod and heavy ammunition magazines had been spread out among the rest of the patrol.

Bringing up rear security came Ben, armed with the AKMS-47. He watched their backs, "covering their six," in militaryspeak. While he made sure that no one came up from behind them, Ben also tried to wipe out the marks of the patrol's passage as much as he could. He walked backward much of the time, scanning behind them as well as to either side.

Reaper led the patrol along the sides of the ridge to the north of the valley. The group climbed higher as they continued to move generally eastward. Coming up to a saddle, a depression in the middle of the ridge, Reaper silently called a halt by raising his clenched fist. As the men settled down into a diamond formation, their weapons pointing outward into the brush, Bear breathed heavily, even his great stamina sapped by carrying the huge 20mm weapon.

Getting down low on his hands and knees, Reaper crawled forward to approach the edge of the saddle. As the ground started to open up and fall away to the east, he dropped down even flatter. Finally, he slithered on his belly. Reaper pulled up to a huge fallen tree and slowly peered over it, his head partly blocked and hidden by a big branch forking out from the fallen trunk.

The lodge was standing only a few hundred meters away. It stood in the open surrounded only by flower gardens. Though the gardens hadn't been kept up, they seemed almost out of place in what Reaper perceived as a hostile environment.

No one moved down at the lodge. The huge mansion had the appearance of an old castle with its rock walls and crenelated roof line. Bear had the right idea in struggling up here with the big Lahti.

A further hundred meters along the ridge, as it slanted down to the east, the tree line came to within a hundred meters of the lodge. That would be the most secure approach Reaper and Bear could take to reach the big house and penetrate inside. Withdrawing from the log, Reaper spoke into his radio headset.

"Come up, stay low," he said.

Going back up to peer down at the lodge, Reaper maintained a watch as the balance of his small patrol moved up to where he lay. Max came up and placed his Shrike down after looking over the fallen tree. Snuggling down next to the log, Max pulled up his case, opened it, and pulled out the parts to his sniper rifle. His skilled fingers almost assembled the rifle solely by touch as Max leaned his head against the log and looked over at Reaper.

As the sniper prepared his hardware, Bear crawled up, pulling the Lahti along by its barrel. Placing the big antitank rifle alongside the log, Bear then pulled up the rest of the components—taking a magazine box from Max as he handed it over. Finally, Ben came up and lay next to Max, lifting up the Shrike from where it lay.

Max and Ben would provide cover fire as needed. Ben could handle his gun well enough to allow Max to concentrate on precision shooting to cut down opposing numbers. When he saw everything was in hand and his two men set up and in position, Reaper signaled for Bear to come with him. The red-faced, shorter SEAL looked up and gave an okay signal by circling his thumb and forefinger. Bear was a little short of breath, but anyone would have been after dragging that big gun through the woods.

"Did you hear that?" Hadeed said in a loud whisper.

"Hear what?" Joseph replied. "I didn't hear anything. You've been jumpy about everything ever since you got here. You hear shit that no one else does."

"Hey, I didn't join up with this mob to wander in the woods," Hadeed said. "I grew up in Dearborn, not the forest, just like you did. Arzee told me that I would have to drive the van, and I've been driving that thing up and down from here to Detroit for weeks now. It's not like you or I are one of those Afghan chosen ones."

"Yeah, well now you've been told to walk the property line," Joseph said as he hitched the sling of the AK-47 rifle on his shoulder up to a more comfortable position. Turning to his partner in misery, he continued. "Or do you want to tell one of the chosen brethren that you are too good to watch trees? You do that and Paxtun will let them eat you when they get back from the other island."

"I don't give a shit about those better-than-us sand-soldiers. All they do is think they're better than we are and run around on the other island firing their guns. Put them in the street and I'll do just fine keeping up with them," Hadeed said. "It's only these damned woods. There are critters all over around here—and none of them are people. It's cold and windy, there's nothing to guard against but some trees and birds—I'm going back inside."

As the street tough turned, his eyes grew large as a shadow from the trees suddenly stood up in front of him. He saw no face on the black apparition, only a pair of piercing eyes that looked out from a blank, black-painted face. The AK-47 in his hands went unremembered as Hadeed never even noticed the slight cough and flash on the muzzle of the weapon in the spirit's hands.

Joseph had even less time to react to Reaper's appearance. As he turned, Bear simply said "War," into his radio's headset. A solid "thunk" rang out a moment later as a subsonic 220-grain 7.62mm EBR Thumper put the other thug's lights out.

Though he would never know it, the initial kills of the island assault had been the two men who had actually kidnapped Reaper's family. He and Bear then ran to the lodge not quite a football field away. They had been watching to see if any other guards appeared. The lodge remained silent as they approached. The two SEALs knew they were exposed and at risk during the rush across the open field—but the eyes and muzzles of their teammates up on the ridge covered them.

With a swift dart across the terrace at the south end of the main building, Reaper and Bear immediately went through the big doors in front of them. If they had been spotted from inside the house, the faster they could get to cover the better.

No one responded to their rapid entry.

The two SEALs didn't know they had entered the old music room, only that they didn't find any threats immediately visible. Instead of their normal shout of "clear," the two partners remained silent as they moved through the richly paneled room. Dark woods and paintings looked down on the two black-clad and heavily armed SEALs as they penetrated deeper into the lodge.

They passed through what had been the billiard room, the muzzles of their weapons sweeping across the stone fireplace and wall like lethal extensions of their arms. The living room was next, and another sweep turned up nothing. Only after they moved into the next hallway did they find a target—an unexpected one.

Hassan Akrit had been a kitchen helper at the Factory. Arzee had given him a bonus to come to the island and cook for a large group of men. The cook didn't know what Paxtun did with the extra food tray he had Hassan bring him twice a day. He only knew that the boss ate in his office upstairs. And Paxtun didn't look like someone who ate double meals, yet that's the amount of food he packed away. Sometime after being served, the second tray always came back, brought to the kitchen for Hassan to clean.

The young man froze in place as a tall, black-clothed ninja suddenly jumped out in front of him, waving a big, black gun under his nose. The trays he had stacked on top of one another shook in his hands, but they didn't fall—which boded well for him, Hassan reasoned, because the noise might have caused that awful gun to make some horrible noise itself.

"Where are they?" the tall ninja growled.

Hassan stared blankly, uncomprehending. The shorter ninja went past with an even bigger gun and did something behind Hassan. The terrified young cook did not even think to turn and see what the other was doing, but remained hypnotized by the black spot in the center of the weapon he was staring at.

"Don't you understand English?" the tall ninja snarled in a low voice. "Where are they!"

Being poked at with the big gun finally broke Hassan's concentration on the hole in the muzzle.

"Who they?" he said, totally confused. "They what?"

"Where are the hostages?" Tall ninja said.

"Hostages? What hostages?" Hassan asked in a quavering voice. "All of the others left in the boats this morning. Only the boss and four of the guys are around. There are no hostages."

Once Hassan's vocal logjam had been broken, the SEALs found it hard to shut him up.

"Enough," the tall ninja said. "Six tangos on site," he said, apparently to no one. "Six tangos. No hotels as yet."

"Who are you talking to?" Hassan asked.

Now that his initial shock seemed to have fled, the cook became positively talkative. Maybe he could tell Reaper something useful besides who else was on the island.

"Where's the boss you mentioned?" Reaper said.

"Upstairs in his office waiting for breakfast," Hassan said lightheadedly, the shock beginning to make him sway. "At the head of the stairs, to the left, last door on the right . . ." He was anxious to please the deadly strangers. Then Bear tapped the panicking man in the back of his head and the world went black. The cook had just enough time to hope this wasn't a permanent change.

Reaper barely managed to catch the young man as he wilted and sank to the floor. Grabbing the trays, Reaper noticed that there was a hell of a lot of food for one person. This boss would be the next person he would talk to.

"Bear, take him," Reaper said as he placed the trays on the floor. They hadn't made any real noise yet and it would be worthwhile to keep it that way.

"Secure him," Reaper ordered seconds later as he looked up the huge stairway.

Bear pulled the unconscious cook to the side and stuffed him into a small cloak room under the stairs. Before leaving his unconscious acquaintance, Bear secured his hands and feet with nylon tie-ties brought for the purpose. The very strong nylon ties were intended to hold bundles of heavy cables and wires together. They would have to be cut to get them off the cook's arms and legs. The white apron the cook had been wearing was made into a quick gag and the door to the big closet shut tight.

Reaper already had a foot on the first step, set to head up the stairs. Bear hustled over to catch up with him and they both went up to the landing in three short flights. The upstairs of the lodge was huge—and there were still at least four people around based on what the cook had said. But the boss was supposed to be down the hall on the left. So they would clear that room first.

Stacking up outside the last door on the right, Reaper gave Bear the squeeze signal since this time he would go first through the door. Reaper reached over and checked the knob, and saw that the door was unlocked. Instead of barging in, he decided to try another tack to see if they couldn't maintain the advantage of surprise. He squeezed Bear's shoulder again and raised one finger. Bear looked up and nodded—then Reaper knocked on the door.

"It's about goddamned time," a strangely familiar voice said inside. "Get in here with my breakfast."

Now the two SEALs flashed into the room, Reaper breaking high and right, Bear low and left. It was hard to say who had the greater surprise; the man standing inside the room, or the two SEALs as they recognized Cary Paxtun.

In spite of his astonishment, Paxtun was quick as

he jerked back and slammed the door to his private office. Bear covered the rest of the room and the door they had come in through while Reaper darted to the door Paxtun had slammed and forced it open.

Paxtun was behind a big desk, scrabbling through a drawer. He froze with his hand in the drawer as Reaper pointed the suppressed submachine gun at him.

"Both hands on the desk, now," Reaper said.

Paxtun wasn't about to argue with those eyes peering at him through the sights of a weapon. He slowly sat down with both of his hands on the desk in plain sight. He sweated heavily and could feel his heart beating its way out of his chest. It was the look in those eyes. All he wanted to do right then was to just keep his heart beating.

"Where are they, you son of a bitch?" Reaper asked slowly and distinctly.

"Who?" Paxtun tried to bluff as a cold chill came over him. "Where are who? Who are you, anyway?"

Reaper reached up with his left hand and pulled back the black balaclava he had over his head. As his features came into view, Paxtun blanched as recognition flooded his face. Then he started to panic.

"Where are who? There's no one here. I don't know what you're talking about," Paxtun's tongue started to trip up as the words poured from him. Then Reaper glanced over to his right.

A wooden box lay open on a set of drawers, a box that looked very familiar. And what looked even more familiar was the shining bright broadsword that lay inside of it. Reaper walked over to the case, never taking his eyes off Paxtun. Reaper switched hands on his weapon and reached down to grasp the hilt of the big sword.

"My family, now," the Grim Reaper said to Paxtun. "Give them to me and I'll let you live."

Paxtun collapsed. To the SEAL it seemed like watching a wax dummy melt in the sun.

"They're in the basement," Paxtun said in a cold whisper. "A storeroom under the south wing. They're fine, nothing has happened to them. No one has harmed them at all."

For a moment, rage swept through Reaper like a white-hot flame. He looked at Paxtun and his hand clenched on the grip of the sword.

"Why?" Reaper said through gritted teeth. "Why me? Why the fuck did you screw with me and my family?"

Paxtun looked up with a blank, hopeless look on his face. He was lost and knew it.

"You were just available," Paxtun said in a neutral voice. "It wasn't anything special. We needed something you could supply. Besides, you had fucked me over once. It was a chance for payback. That's all, just payback."

Paxtun dropped his face into his hands. His shoulders shook and his knees bent slightly. From the sound of it the former spook was having trouble breathing.

"So, it was all just something personal," Reaper said. "Well, payback's a bitch, or didn't you know that?"

Reaper looked at the suddenly broken man who had caused him so much grief. He didn't even seem worth wasting a bullet on. Reaper looked down at the sword in his hand and sighed. Then he turned his back and looked at the glass-fronted case on the wall over the chest of drawers.

Paxtun wasn't completely done yet. Seeing Reaper's back turned, he slipped his hand back into the drawer. His fingers finally closed over the cool plastic grips of the SIG 228 pistol he kept there. There would be more men between him and safety, but he could kill Reaper and still get away.

"Now that I know where my family is, I'll let the cops deal with you," Reaper said. "Now it's your turn to face a court."

"I don't think so," Paxtun said as he started to lift the pistol.

From his position in the other room, Bear glanced in to where Reaper was standing. He could see Paxtun slip his hand into the drawer. Before Bear shouted a warning or aimed his weapon, he saw Reaper's hand lift the sword. Then he saw his Teammate's eyes looking intently at the wall in front of him. The whole of Paxtun's movements had been clear to Reaper in the reflection in the glass of the case. As Paxtun stood, Reaper spoke.

"I thought you might see it that way," he said as he spun around with the sword extended out from his right hand. The reverse grip swung the razor-sharp blade out, and it barely slowed as it sliced through Paxtun's neck. The head fell from the shoulders of the body as blood fountained out and sprayed the wall nearby. Like a child's abandoned ball, Paxtun's head rolled across the floor and bumped up against the wall, his unseeing eyes staring in shock.

Chapter Twenty-eight

"Downstairs now," Reaper said as he left the room where Paxtun's body lay cooling. Reaper had stopped and picked up the leather scabbard that had been in the top of the case.

Nodding at the bloody sword in Reaper's hand, Bear said, "Better wipe that off or it'll rust."

Reaper stood and looked at his friend for a moment, then bent down and wiped the blade off on what looked to be a priceless Persian rug. Then he slipped it into its scabbard and stuck it diagonally down across his back, underneath his Chalker sling. It had been made for his son and he would give it to the boy personally.

"Better?" Reaper said.

"Oh, much," Bear agreed almost smiling, and led the way out the door.

As the two SEALs reached the head of the stairs, below them Paxtun's remaining two men, Kerah and Pali finally came in for some breakfast. The two men had been on guard at the front of the lodge, covered from Ben or Max's view from the hillside.

As they saw the two black-clad SEALs appearing on the stairs, Pali bellowed a strangled cry and pulled up his AK-47, squeezing off a long burst. The 7.62mm steel-jacketed slugs did nothing more than tear up a lot of expensive paneling as Reaper dropped backward out of sight.

Bear pulled up his Jackhammer and fired off a burst as Pali tried to swing his AK-47 around. The thunder of the Jackhammer roared out as Pali jerked and danced from the impact of the buckshot. It was something barely recognizable as human that dropped its AK-47 and slid down the far wall.

Now the problem was that Kerah controlled the downstairs landing. And Reaper wanted down those steps and into the basement. Having seen what happened to Pali, Kerah had pulled back under the stairs and was firing wildy in all directions.

With no desire to expose either himself or Bear to fire, Reaper reached into his pouch and pulled up an M26A1 fragmentation grenade. Holding the grenade up so that Bear could see it, Reaper pulled the pin. He popped off the safety spoon, and counted a long "one" before tossing the grenade over the landing they crouched upon. As the deadly green bomb bounced on the floor, Reaper and Bear scuttled back off the landing.

Kerah had few choices of where to go and no time to decide. The concussive blast of the 156 grams of Composition B explosive inside the grenade, boosted by eight grams of tetryl pellets, shattered the sheet metal body and broke up the notched square steel-wire fragmentation coil. The tiny steel fragments flew out at thousands of feet per second, shredding anything they hit, wood, plaster, cloth, or human flesh.

As they rolled to their feet, Bear and Reaper darted down the stairs, following the rolling thunder of the explosion. It was most definitely no longer a silent operation. Neither of the two men could hear very well right then, but that seemed of little concern.

At the bottom of the stairs, a quick shotgun blast from Bear made certain that the horrible mess inside the front door didn't suffer, or cause the SEALs any more trouble. The gruesome pile against the wall obviously didn't need a finishing shot. Moving quickly down the hall, Bear led the way to the stairs he had seen while Reaper had been questioning Hassan.

Both SEALs quickly moved down the stairs into the basement of the lodge. The basement consisted of an area as big as the rest of the building, with a lot of storage rooms.

"Mary, Ricky," Reaper bellowed, "Mary, Ricky!"

"Here," Reaper heard a muffled voice. "We're in here."

"Keep talking," Reaper shouted as he followed the sound to a padlocked door. While Bear kept cover on the stairs and passages they had just crossed through, Reaper reached behind his back and swept the padlock and hasp from the door with one stroke of the sword, then yanked the door open. Inside the bleak room he saw two mattresses, a bucket, and a blanket that had been pinned up to give anyone using the bucket a fraction of privacy.

And standing at the far corner of the room he saw his wife Mary and their son Ricky.

Mary ran into her husband's arms, ignoring the blood and stink of powder smoke on him. Ricky wrapped himself around his father's leg, hugging him as if he were a dream that had suddenly come true. If the boy let go, the dream might disappear.

Then Ricky noticed the blood on his father's leg.

"Daddy, you're hurt," he said in sudden fear.

"It's all right, I'm fine," Reaper said to his son.

"Ted . . ." Mary started to say.

"It's not mine," Reaper said quietly. "Come on, we have to go."

"But . . . Ted," Mary said, suddenly afraid to leave her prison, "those men."

"They aren't going to bother anyone ever again," Reaper said.

Mary shrank back for a moment from the man she had married years before. She knew what Ted had done while in the military. He had been a SEAL and she knew that he had been a good one. Yet the tone in his voice and the look of him remained alien to her. Swallowing her fear, she followed Reaper out the door.

"Think you can carry this for me, Ricky?" Reaper said as he handed his son the big broadsword.

The feel of the large weapon reassured the boy. It contained the power of his father, something he needed right then. For Reaper, he felt it gave the boy something to do that would distract him from the escape they had to make.

With Bear leading the way, the four ran through the passages and back up the stairs. As they passed through the hallway, and headed back to the music room and the doors there, Bear suddenly stopped and dove back toward Reaper and his family.

"Down!" he bellowed as a shattering burst of AK-47 fire roared out. The bullets slammed into the house from outside, moving across the room toward Reaper. One of the steel-jacketed Russian slugs smashed into the receiver of Reaper's MP5K, almost tearing the weapon out of his hands. Only the shackle of his Chalker sling kept the weapon from hitting the floor.

Reaper could see his assailant. One lone figure crouched on the porch at the front of the house, trying to reload the smoking AK-47 in his hands. Without conscious thought, Reaper reached down with his right hand and pulled the Serbu Super-Shorty shotgun from the thigh holster—his thumb pushing free the safety strap.

The SEAL grabbed the folding operating lever with his left hand, pulling the shotgun up and into line with the man on the porch. A single shot boomed from the weapon's short barrel, tearing into the man and knocking him back. Reaper then pulled back and down on the folding handle on the operating slide, rotating it away from the gun. As it locked into place, he pumped the gun's action, ejecting the spent case and putting a fresh round into the chamber. Another rolling boom sounded out as he made certain that the man who crawled on the porch couldn't get to his weapon—empty or not.

But the four escapees didn't emerge unscathed from the attack. Bear lay on the ground, not moaning, but struggling to push himself up, his legs refusing to support him.

"Bear, are you hit?" Reaper asked.

"No, but I think I'm screwed," Bear said in a weak voice.

They were interrupted by a call coming in over their radio headsets.

"Death, Pestilence, this is War," Max said over the radio, "you had better get out of there fast."

"We have the hotels," Reaper said, "repeat, we have the hotels, but Pestilence is down. Do you have tangos?"

"Two boatloads of them," Max said, abandoning procedure for expediency. "Get up here now. Do you need assistance?"

"Negative," Bear said as he struggled to a sitting position. "Okay, Boss," he said through gritted teeth. "You have what you came for. Now let's get out of here."

Giving an arm up to his partner, Reaper helped Bear to his feet. The man's legs were barely able to support him, and he struggled to make a step. Finally, Reaper picked Bear up and slung him across his back.

"Let's go, Mary, Ricky," Reaper said. Taking two rounds from the three on the outside of the holster, he reloaded the Super-Shorty with his free hand as he went along. With one hand still hanging on to his partner, the SEAL walked with the shotgun held out in front of him like a big pistol.

Once they got outside, Reaper could see across to the east and what had been bothering Max. Two boats headed in toward the island, one long one and a short, broad one. They looked like the sports boat and fishing boat that they had found the receipts for. The sudden zip . . . zip . . . above their heads told

Reaper that someone was shooting at them from the boats.

With Reaper in the lead and Bear across his back, Mary and Ricky followed him to the cover of the trees. They ran, stumbled, and ran some more to get back to the ridge where Ben and Max lay. Reaper hit the ground next to Ben, then rolled Bear to the ground.

"He's hurt," Reaper said quickly. "His legs don't work and he can't walk."

While Ben turned to his patient, Reaper moved to where Max lay with his rifle up to his shoulder.

"Who's out there?" Reaper asked.

"I have no idea," Max said as he looked through the Leupold scope on his rifle. "But there's a bunch of them in two boats, and they're waving weapons over their heads."

"Coast Guard?" Reaper said.

"Not unless the Coasties have taken to carrying AKs," Max said. "Those curved magazines are kind of distinctive. And they have a bunch of them."

"Time to go, Boss," Bear said from where he leaned against a log.

"Fine, get up." Reaper turned to Ben. "What can you do for him?"

"Nothing," Ben said quietly.

"Nothing he can do," Bear said with a ghost of his old grin across his face. "The cancer's finally winning."

"Cancer?" Reaper said. "What the hell are you talking about, Bear?"

"What they call a high-grade brain stem glioma," Bear said simply, "I don't have time to explain it and you don't have time to listen, but it's inoperable. It's why I've been so weak. Not that old yet, guess I never will be. Ask Ben when you get back on the boat."

Reaper looked at Ben who sadly nodded.

"You knew?" Reaper said.

"Don't blame him," Bear said. "He couldn't tell you. I met up with him back when he drove an ambulance for the VA hospital where I got my treatments. He couldn't tell you, I wouldn't let him."

Just looking into the pain showing in Ben's eyes told Reaper that he had heard the truth.

"So get the hell out of here," Bear said. "My arms still work and I have a machine gun, bullets, and a really big rifle. I carried it, I get to shoot it. I'll give those suckers out there in the boats something to work with while you get everyone away."

"No," the word seemed to tear from Reaper's chest. "We all came, we all go home."

Bear pulled an orange plastic pill bottle from his shirt pocket.

"These are painkillers," Bear said, "really powerful ones. You know those headaches I've been having? Well, these are the only things that have been able to make that hurt go away, and then only for a while. You think I can keep living like this? My legs don't seem to think so. It's check-out time for me, Ted. There's nothing anyone can do to change that. My only choice left is when and how. Let me do this."

Almost in a panic, Reaper looked to Ben for help. All the smaller man could do was look back at him.

"No," Reaper snarled through clenched teeth. "I carried you out here, I can carry you to the boat. No one gets left behind—ever!"

"Fuck you," Bear said. "One stays or we all stay. Think your boy would like that? Ted," Bear said in a quiet voice, "let me do this, please. It's a pretty good way to go."

Reaper looked to his son, and then to his wife. Tears streamed down both of their silent faces as they watched the man who had come to get them, pull them out of hell, struggle with a fight he didn't know how to win, or accept.

"Company's just about here," Max said from where he watched the approach of the terrorists. "It's time to go."

Reaper looked at his son, who took a tighter grip on his father's sword. Then he looked down at his friend, his Teammate, his brother.

"Are you sure, mate?" Reaper said softly.

"Yes," Bear said with a lopsided smile. "Now go."

Without another word, Reaper turned away. He signaled to the others, who melted into the tree line as more bullets started snapping around them.

Max came over and moved the Shrike closer to Bear.

"Have fun, you crazy squid," Max said.

"Go puke in the lake you cross-eyed Jarhead," Bear said with a wide smile now on his face.

Max turned and went into the woods.

It had taken an argument, but now Reaper quickly got the heck out of Dodge with his family. His family's safety depended on Bear to buy them the time they needed to get clear.

Lying by his weapons, Bear looked around for a

second. It really hadn't turned out a bad day at all, the sun shone brightly now and only a few clouds floated in the sky. It was not a bad day at all.

Bear pulled the Shrike up and quickly checked out the belt. There were two feed boxes and one was clipped to the weapon with the belt fed into the feed way. As he snugged himself down into the prone position, Bear felt something sticking into his chest from inside his left shirt pocket. Realizing what it was, Bear paused for a moment and then reached into his pocket. It was his bottle of OxyContin, the pain killers that he had been taking for weeks now. He had put them back where he could reach them easily without thinking about it after showing them to Reaper.

Bear held the bottle in his hand for a moment, looking at the orange plastic container with all of its warning labels. Slowly, he closed his hand in a crushing grip, first cracking and finally collapsing the bottle. He threw the smashed plastic and pills from him, knowing that he wouldn't be having any of his headaches any more. Yup, he thought as he snugged the light machine gun into his shoulder, it was going to be a good day.

The fishing boat had pulled up to the dock and a bunch of shouting men charged toward the house and the hillside beyond. Bear let them exit the boat. Then he opened fire.

Normally, a machine gun is fired in short, controlled bursts. But Bear had no interest in keeping to regulation fire right then. He hadn't anywhere to go, and had plenty of ammunition. The time had come to burn some up. The belt zipped from the ammunition box, feeding the voracious appetite of the machine gun as Bear watched his bullets rip gouts of dirt and grass from the lawn. A lot of those bullets also tore into terrorists. When the first ammunition box emptied, Bear pulled it from the weapon and tossed it away. Quickly reloading with another box, he laid the Shrike back down on his targets.

The long bursts of 5.56mm fired from the Shrike up on the hill ripped across the walls of the mansion. The thick limestone rock that faced the walls of the structure chipped a bit as they easily resisted the onslaught. Windows, doorways, and other openings proved another matter. The high-speed, steel-cored bullets whizzed through the open doorways and tore through the house, ripped and smashed furniture as cushions, dishes, books, and artwork burst and exploded off the shelves and walls.

Three of the terrorists took the weapons they had brought from the boat and ran up to the second floor of the mansion. Quickly diving through several of the rear bedroom's windows, the terrorists made it to the roof above the rear porch without being hit from the machine gun on the point of the ridge only a few hundred meters away. Shooting at that range would be nothing for the men of the Sons of Ishmael; they had trained to fire accurately at much longer ranges.

Bear knew that he would see some real trouble from the roof if he didn't do something about it. He fired the last of his belt through the Shrike in one long burst of fire, raking the lower floors and making sure that anyone who was there would be keeping their heads down for a while. Then he rolled over to the big Lahti antitank rifle. The limestone walls of that big castle might keep the bullets from the Shrike from penetrating into the house, but the builders had never envisioned a rifle this big when they were putting that place up. And the terrorists who took cover behind those upper walls probably thought themselves safe for the moment.

Crawling up to the weapon, Bear picked up the butt end of the big cannon and loaded it. Bright shiny brass shone through each of the three holes in the back of the magazine, indicating that the box was fully loaded. That meant that ten of the foot-long 20mm shells sat in the mag, ready to be fired. Each hardened-steel projectile had been designed to penetrate more than half an inch of armor plate at five hundred meters. They wouldn't have a lot of trouble with the rock walls of the mansion.

Snugging the curved, padded shoulder rest into place, Bear grabbed the silver knob of the rack-and-pinion cocking mechanism on the right side of the gun, right above the pistol grip. Pushing in on the knob unlocked the mechanism. One and a half rotations of the knob pulled the massive bolt back against its springs until it locked in place in the fully rearward position.

A squeeze on the switch on the pistol grip, underneath the trigger guard, released the bolt and it surged forward, stripping a round from the magazine and ramming it into place in the breech of the barrel. Just the sound of the big bolt slamming forward startled Bear a little bit and he jerked his head up. Dirt and wood chips flew from the log he lay behind as a powerful rifle slug slammed right next to where Bear's head had been a moment before.

Somebody in the house had a good idea of where Bear was, but the SEAL had managed to catch a glimpse of the muzzle flash of the rifle that shot at him from behind cover on the roof of the mansion. With the big weapon pulled in hard against his shoulder, Bear tracked the cannon across the house and settled in on the roof area where he had seen the shot come from. He started to squeeze the trigger.

The thundering concussion of the big antitank weapon smashed into Bear's face and the muzzle blast kicked up dirt and leaves in front of his position. Whoever had fired at him absolutely knew where the SEAL hid now. There was no use saving it, he wouldn't be moving this massive gun from his present position. So Bear gritted his teeth, and kept pulling the trigger and the Finnish war machine he controlled started to pump out over 2,200 grain (148 gram) slugs, pushing them through its fifty-one-inch barrel until they left the muzzle at more that 2,600 feet per second (800 meters per second).

Kedar had been a sniper during the jihad against the Soviet invaders of Afghanistan. Many troopers fell to his marksmanship with the long SVD Dragunov rifle. His first shot had been rushed and aimed at nothing more than movement up on the ridge. He had missed but the machine gun fire had stopped for the moment and he had the patience of all who had fought the infidels in Afghanistan.

All Kedar had to do was get a single glimpse of whoever fired at them from the woods and he knew that he could bring him down easily. Distances on the island were nothing to someone who had shot across the crags and valleys of Afghanistan. Hidden as he was behind one of the rock crenelations decorating this decadent infidel house, he knew it was only a matter of time before his prey fell to him. Then there came a brilliant flash up on the hillside.

Before the sound of the shot even reached the house, the first of the huge, hardened-steel projectiles fired from the 20mm rifle smashed its way through twelve inches of limestone. The round had been intended to kill the smaller and lighter tanks of World War II and the soft limestone of Ohio was no match for its power. Shards and chips exploded from the inner face of the rock, spraying the terrorists crouching on the roof with the razor-edged fragments. In spite of passing through several layers of rock, the shotgun shell sized projectile still had more than enough energy to kill.

Before Kedar could think "Allah is great" and long before he could react to seeing the dust and debris kicked up by the muzzle blast on the crest of the ridge, he fell dead. The Finnish-made tank killer entered his left shoulder, at the base of his neck. The thundering bullet bisected the terrorist's body completely—exiting at his upper right thigh after making a hash of almost every one of his internal organs.

Bear's second and third rounds struck little more than limestone as they smashed through what proved nothing more than a decorative parapet. The mansion may have looked like a castle, but it couldn't stand up to a siege with modern weapons—not even those sixty years old.

The blue-painted steel projectiles and whizzing rock fragments caused three of the terrorists—Mibsam, Dumah, and Adbeel—on the roof to duck down and cover their heads. They had all been under fire in the mountains of Afghanistan, and 7.62mm steel-cored slugs from Soviet PKM machine guns had tossed rock splinters at them before. Even the finger-sized 12.7mm slugs from the powerful DShK "Dashaka" machine guns on the Soviet tanks had smashed up rocks and caused injuries from the chips and shards. But nowhere had they faced bullets that passed right through the rock, causing the stone itself to explode.

Some of the projectiles from the 20mm cannon may not have struck anything more than stone, but the stone itself did more than a little damage. Adbeel had faced Soviet fire in Afghanistan, military weapons in the Sudan, and Serbian steel in Bosnia. In his combat experience, he had never felt pain such as that coursing through his body at that moment. Screaming, he looked at the shattered remnants of his right hand, and the red-stained six-inch splinter of stone that stuck through it, severing the median nerve as it eliminated any future use of the now paralyzed lump of bleeding flesh.

Adbeel's suffering was short-lived, as was the terrorist, when Bear's 20mm cannon finished the job.

As Adbeel screamed and reacted to his wound, his left hand lifted the PG-7 rocket grenade it held. He had prepared the missile for Mibsam's launcher; his fellow warrior was kneeling right next to him. The blast of the powerful RPG-7v launcher was capable of killing a main battle tank, it would have made short work of a simple machine-gun position. But before the round had been loaded, it had been pushed into the path of Bear's fourth shot.

The 20mm projectile smashed through the fluted-metal cone that made up the nose of the RPG-7 rocket warhead. The 380-gram (over half a pound) loading of A-IX-1 high explosive in the shaped-charge RPG-7 warhead did not react to being violated by the 20mm steel slug passing through it. The smaller, but much more sensitive, base detonating element of the fuse was not so forgiving. When the 20mm slug smashed into the 21.8 grams of PETN that made up the detonating booster, it reacted and the fuse element initiated the detonation of the 95 percent RDX explosive filler of the warhead. The resulting blast also detonated the other two RPG-7 rocket rounds that were in a pouch lying on the rooftop. All three high-explosive warheads went up in a sympathetic detonation.

The multiple explosions turned the area behind the parapets into a maelstrom of thundering concussions, flying steel splinters, and ripping shards of rock. The blasts cleared the parapets of functioning terrorists. The body of Miasma, the most experienced RPG gunner of the Sons of Ishmael, flew from the roof, over the crenelations, and down to the flagstones below. Even in death, Miasmaa held on to the weapon he had used so much in life. The loaded RPG-7v launcher lay across the terrorist's body and it sprawled across the stones like an ugly, abandoned puppet.

The size and ferocity of the explosion surprised Bear as he lay next to the Lahti antitank rifle. The SEAL didn't know what he had hit, only that the results were spectacular. The orange-white ball of flame from the exploding Soviet munitions put on a good show in addition to the bad guys on the other side of the wall.

Five more rounds from the big antitank rifle fired across the parapets, the big slugs smashing stone, wood, and anything else that got in their way with equal contempt. Even a man as big as Bear got slammed around by the recoil of the Lahti as it rocked back against the springs in its bipod mount. If it hadn't been for the efficiency of the multiholed harmonica muzzle break mounted to the barrel of the gun, the recoil would have been uncontrollable. As it was, the recoil, though fierce, seemed not as bad as the thundering concussion of each shot as it fired.

It took a lot of powder to push that big slug down the long barrel of the Lahti. And that much powder also made a really big bang. His ears now rang painfully, so Bear could no longer hear anything around him, but he could still see quite well.

From the far side of the house, initially out of his sight, the remaining terrorists made a break for the boats that they had left only short minutes before. The docks lay almost four hundred meters away from the house, but the remaining terrorists made a good attempt at imitating Olympic sprinters. They had no idea of the nature of the big gun that had started to tear through the house around them, but they did know they wanted no part of it. Besides, the bulk of their remaining weapons and ammunition remained aboard the two boats.

As the terrorists ran, Bear yanked the now-empty magazine from the top of the Lahti. By his count, there was still a round in the chamber. But he would need something with a little more power, though maybe not as much penetration, as the armor-piercing rounds had given him. One magazine had a broad red stripe around its body. That bright red tape identified the only magazine out of the four they brought that held high-explosive (HE) rounds.

Pulling the big magazine over to him, Bear struggled to lift the heavy ammunition device up and into the Lahti. The massive muscles of his strong body started to fail him at last, his shoulder being badly bruised from the 20mm's recoil not helping any. But he still had the energy and determination to lift the HE magazine up and snap it down and back into place.

Bear knew that his end had finally come. He didn't fear it—death was not only something he had worked with during his SEAL career, but something that he had learned to live with over the past six months. Everybody died, no one got off the planet alive, at least not permanently. But he still had this job to do. His Teammates, his friends, his brothers, all depended on him. It was not in his makeup to let them down and it somehow made his dying have more meaning.

For a few seconds the world seemed to darken, the raging tumor announcing itself in a new way.

The terrorists split up into two groups, the larger band of four men piled aboard the broad-hulled fishing boat and fired up its still-warm engine. The smaller group of three men, including the retreating leader, Ishmael himself, clambered aboard the Fountain Fever speedboat. The big, twin 320-horsepower Mercury engines of the speedboat rumbled and then roared as they started and quickly came up to full throttle. The big, heavy diesel of the fishing boat made much less noise as black smoke belched out of its exhaust stacks.

The speedboat pulled away and accelerated swiftly as Bear finally brought the big 20mm gun into play against the vessels. He slid the rear sight adjustment forward to account for the range he had to use to get to the boats. The speedboat moved too fast for Bear to expect to get a clean shot into it. The fishing boat was another matter.

Steeling himself against the recoil and punishing noise of the shots, Bear opened fire on the fishing boat. From the muzzle of the cannon, 20mm high-explosive shells, intended to destroy light-skinned vehicles or rip apart World War II fighter planes, slashed into the boat hull, passed through the fiberglass and exploded on the other side.

Tearing open the fuel tanks of the fishing boat, the HE rounds soon had even the hard-to-burn diesel fuel merrily ablaze. As the small vessel started to list to one side and founder, survivors of Bear's high-explosive fusillade tried to jump overboard. When the flames and explosions of the 20mm shells reached the ammunition and explosive stores aboard the terrorist boat only a few seconds later, the thunderous blast left little more than a hole in the water, which immediately closed over the heads of the terrorists' bodies to form a watery grave.

The youngest, but most enthusiastic and driven member of the Sons of Ishmael, had chosen to remain behind and fight the infidel to cover the withdrawal of his brothers and their leader. Hadad's youth limited his experience, yet his fanaticism burned with a white-hot heat, and he fully believed in the cause of Ishmael and his followers. He wasn't only courageous, he had made himself completely unafraid of death. Dying in battle against the infidels simply insured his arrival in Paradise that much sooner.

The booms of the infidel's monster weapon up on the hillside still sounded out, but the deadly shells had stopped crashing through the building. Hadad lifted his head up as he crawled across the floor and looked through the open door out across the porch and to the woods beyond. The flash and spray of materials kicked up by the muzzle blast of the infidel marked his position clearly. He was sure that the AK-47 in his hands would do little to the emplacement.

On the path a short way past the porch walls the body of Mibsam lay sprawled where it had landed after being thrown from the roof. Hadad could plainly see that his brother was dead. No one could survive having his head so flat from hitting the rock walkway. But lying across Mibsam's body was his favored RPG-7v—and the round loaded into the launcher had survived the explosion on the roof. Allah was great and He would see to it that the weapon remained intact and functional, the young terrorist believed with surety. Why else would Allah, all blessing be upon Him, leave such a tool in his path?

Darting forward, Hadad grabbed the RPG-7v and continued to move away from the house. He took cover behind one of the many decorative flower bushes in the huge garden that spread along the rear of the mansion. The fanatic looked over his weapon. Allah be praised! The weapon looked unbroken and functional.

Pulling the pin from the nose of the grenade, Hadad stripped away the safety cap, completing the final preparation of the round for firing. Lifting the almost-twenty-pound launcher and rocket grenade to his shoulder, Hadad pushed the safety button behind the trigger in from the right, taking the firing mechanism off safe. As he brought the weapon to his shoulder, he thumbed back the hammer on the rear of the trigger group.

Knowing he would have only one real chance to make his shot, the terrorist offered a short prayer to Allah, all blessings be upon Him, and then he stood up. Swinging the nose-heavy weapon around to the left, Hadad stuck his right eye firmly to the rubber cup on the back of the 2.5-power PGO-7 prismatic telescopic sight. Setting the two-hundred-meter stadia lines on the top of the grid of the sight reticule on the hillside where the muzzle flashes came from, he pulled the trigger on the firing mechanism.

The huge blast of the propelling charge roared out the back of the launcher, canceling the recoil of the projectile ejected out of the muzzle. Four thin metal fins unfolded from the PG-7 rocket as it flew forward, the sustainer rocket motor firing up with a roar ten meters in front of the launcher. Hadad felt only a puff of warm air from the igniting of the sustainer motor. But the initial blast of launching had deafened him, and shattered several windows in the house behind him.

Unfortunately for Hadad the big antitank rocket

whooshed forward and impacted ten feet below and to the left of Bear's position. The blast of the explosion rocked the big SEAL as he lay behind the Lahti. Steel shards from the rocket's warhead and splinters from the log cover sprayed across his left side. Bleeding badly from a number of wounds, Bear was slammed against the Lahti from the force of the explosion and slumped down onto his weapon.

A warm sensation spread along Bear's left side as he tried to clear the spinning in his head. He knew that there was something very important that he had to do, something that couldn't wait. But he just didn't have the energy to act on it. Then he remembered his Teammates. The same force of will that pushed him through Basic Underwater Demolition/SEAL training, that kept him from quitting during that awful cold and strained exhaustion, that will pushed at him now.

He lifted his head and tried to wipe away whatever had run into his eyes. To his shock Bear's left arm wouldn't obey him anymore. Letting go of the pistol grip, Bear wiped away enough of the blood that had sprayed across his face to see again. Blinking at his blurred vision, Bear could see through what looked like a tunnel. At the end of that tunnel somebody stood and waved something over his head. Bear didn't know the identity of the person, but he knew he had to do something to him.

Blood gushed from his wounds, the worst being at the left side of his neck. Bear didn't know what had happened to him. And if he did, he wouldn't have cared. As the tunnel vision got worse, Bear tried to swing the big cannon around and force the muzzle down and in line with the target. Blurred vision focused on the front sight blade as something in the back of Bear's mind kept saying. "Shoot him in the ass."

The sights of the Lahti remained set for a much longer range than Bear would shoot at now. Only his subconscious mind maintained function well enough to tell him to aim low on his target.

As he started to feel warm all over and the buzzing lessened in his ears, Bear pulled the trigger of the big cannon for the last time. He never even felt the recoil slam him back, or his head fall to the ground. He just lay there and let the warmth and softness finally sweep over him. Satisfied that he had done his job, that his mission was over, he gave up the fight. His last conscious thought was a pleasant one—that it had been a really good day.

The young terrorist didn't have any real thoughts after firing the RPG-7v. As his youthful exuberance caused him to jump up in joy at hitting the infidel's weapon, he waved his arms, yelled, and never thought of the consequences. Turning back to the house, he started to walk back past the body of his brother. He stopped and looked down at the man and realized that he had been better than Mibsam. He could be better than any of them. What they hadn't been able to do, he had done. Yes, him. Hadad. He was the best of them all.

Hadad never felt the big 20mm slug smash into his upper back. As the high-explosive-filled steel projectile crushed into the young terrorist's spine, the old Nazi German-made nose fuse initiated and detonated the filler. The PETN blast went off inside the chest of the terrorist—literally blowing him apart as the shock wave of the explosive combined with the kinetic energy of the projectile.

The combined energies of Bear's last shot blew Hadad's chest open and shattered his torso—it tore him apart as if he had been drawn and quartered by four charging stallions. It was a suitably barbaric end for a barbarian.

Chapter Twenty-nine

Once the decision to move had been made, the team moved fast. Slipping quickly down the side of the small valley, Reaper, his family, and the rest of his men made their way back to the boat much faster than they had left it. With no need for silence, and very little for concealment, speed was what mattered most. As they approached the boat, a voice sounded from within the trees.

"Four," Enzo said.

"Shit," Reaper cursed, having forgotten the countersign for just a moment, "three, I mean three."

Stepping from the brush where he had concealed himself, Enzo held his M14 at high port as he looked at the group.

"Where's Bear?" he asked.

"He had something to do," Reaper said gruffly. Just then, they heard the first burst of machine-gun fire from the far side of the ridge.

"Sounds like he's doing it, too," the SEAL said as he glanced back at the hillside.

The look in everyone's eyes told Enzo that this wouldn't be the best time to ask what had happened. The bursts of fire in the distance were long ones. Whoever was shooting didn't care a whole lot about what they were doing to his gun's barrel. Enzo noticed that along with Bear, the Lahti and the Shrike weren't in sight either. Bear's Jackhammer shotgun was slung across Reaper's back, but that was the only sign of the other SEAL.

The thoughts took only an instant as Enzo started moving and within seconds they had the boat in the water and he was pulling Mary and Ricky on board. Then he moved into the coxswain's position to operate the boat. The rest of the men moved through the water, pushing the SAV II back out into the lake. The little bay's water was cold, but not nearly as bad as that out in the deeper lake. With the weight of the rest of the men off the boat it made the SAV II ride a little higher in the water and helped insure that the props didn't drag on the bottom as Enzo fired up the outboards.

In the background came the thundering booms of the 20mm rifle. After a few rounds had sounded out from the big gun, a much louder blast reached them as something exploded. Reaper was climbing aboard as the roar thundered out. He almost turned and headed back to shore when nothing but silence followed the explosion. Then the thunder of the 20mm opened up again and Reaper knew his friend still played in the game. He climbed aboard the boat and joined his family.

With everyone on board who was coming, Enzo pushed the throttles wide open. The agile boat leaped like a racehorse leaving the starting gates as the outboards roared, the boat dancing across the waves as it picked up speed. Now was not the time for niceties, Enzo thought. They had the precious cargo on board and they had better get a move on.

Another large explosion boomed out from the island, the sound mostly drowned out by the roar of the outboards as the distance between the boat and the island increased. They did not slow down to see what had exploded. One of their own had just given his all so that they had a chance to get away—they were not going to squander that sacrifice.

Off the eastern coast of the island, Ishmael did more than think about the attack; he screamed and cursed about it. Even Bear would have been impressed by the terrorist's command of invective as he swore in Arabic and five other languages. His mission, Shaitan's Blessing, had been destroyed before it was even launched. He cared little for the men he had lost, but the glory he would have reaped and the blow to the Americans was impossible now.

They had been training out on their range at the smaller island, the same place where they practiced with their boats, and had come back to heavy fire—fire that came from near their own headquarters! It had been less than twenty-four hours before they would have launched the greatest operation of Ishmael's career, his life's crowning glory, and it was a shambles! What had happened? How had he brought down this retribution on himself and his men?

As he took a breath and assessed the situation, Ishmael told Naphish at the helm to immediately head south and get them to the mainland as quickly as possible. Maybe whoever had raided the island, probably one of those accursed special operations groups of the American police or military, had missed the transportation that waited in the parking lot back at the harbor. If not, they still had enough arms and ammunition on board the speedboat to come close to wiping out that lakeshore city.

As the 29 Fever sports boat passed the southernmost point of the island, Jetur shouted and pointed. Off to the southwest, skimming across the low waves not more than a few miles ahead, was some black watercraft. It had to be the boat that had been involved with the raid on the island. No helicopters or planes had been heard approaching and no parachutes had been seen dropping in. The only way the raiders could have come in was by boat.

If the people on this boat off in the distance had nothing to do with the shattering of Ishmael's plans, then that was too bad for them. The letting of their blood would help slake his thirst for vengeance for the destroyed Sons of Ishmael.

Aboard the SAV II, a signal started beeping from the console of the marine radar. Looking at the panel and then studying the water to starboard, Enzo saw the approaching sports boat.

"We've got company!" Enzo shouted to Reaper.

Staring out to where Enzo was pointing, Reaper saw the long, pointed shape of the 29 Fever sports boat. It moved fast and headed in their direction. It looked like one of the boats from the island.

"Can you outrun them?" Reaper asked.

"Not if that's the boat you had listed back at the farm," Enzo said. "That craft can put on a third more speed than we can. And with the seas having gone down since this morning, we can't outmaneuver them here in the open."

As the sports boat gradually drew closer, Enzo performed a dazzling display of seamanship as he put the SAV II through her paces. No matter how he twisted or turned, the other boat followed his every move. All he accomplished was to give the other boat some time to come a little closer. Finally, Enzo decided on a desperate trick.

"What are you doing?" Reaper said as the boat turned hard to the east and remained on that heading.

"I'm heading for the Wolverine Shoals," Enzo shouted. "Maybe we can sucker these guys in a little too close. The lake's gone down over the last couple of years and the charts don't show the real water over those rocks. We only draw about a foot of water, but that long bastard needs three feet under her keel. With any luck, we can gut them on the rocks."

The idea sounded like something from an old pirate movie, and Enzo was as close to a pirate as they had right now. He had thought it a desperate action, and it was. As the 29 Fever drew closer to the SAV II, the crew aboard it started shooting at the smaller boat.

Behind his beard, Enzo gritted his teeth as he headed for the buoys marking the shoals. Two buoys were anchored on the shallow shoals. Much deeper water lay between them. Enzo wanted to tease the bigger, faster boat around the buoys, draw them in as he made a pass through safe water. Cutting across the shoal would put the bigger boat in real danger.

As he swept through the channel, Enzo wished the buoys indicating the underwater threat weren't so obvious. It became plain to him that whoever drove the sports boat knew just where the dangerous waters were, and would not be suckered in by his risky stunt.

Bullets snapped by overhead as Ishmael and his men fired their AKM-47s wildly at the SAV II. Pointed steel slugs cracked past, and bounced off the water all around the smaller boat. Inside the tiny booth, Mary and Ricky crouched down at Enzo's feet. The rest of the men had covered them with the ballistic dry suits so that the armor panels gave them some small degree of protection. With the AKs puncturing the air around the SAV II, the inevitable finally happened.

An AK slug fired by Jetur skipped off the water, went between the two laboring outboards, and passed through the frame of the seat supporting Enzo. The pointed spitzer slug smacked the big man square in the back, missing his spine by less than an inch. Enzo grunted and staggered, but stayed upright at his station.

The armor panel in the back of his ballistic dry suit had never been intended to stop such a round. But the bounce off the water had taken much of the energy from the 123-grain bullet. The resistance of the armor panel slowed the steel-jacketed projectile and almost stopped it. Enzo wouldn't die from that round, but he would have an incredibly sore back for a while with a spectacular bruise.

Moving quickly up to the big man when he heard him get hit, Ben MacKenzie quickly checked his wound as best he could. When Ben saw that the slug stuck out from the armor in Enzo's suit, he knew the big man was not in any danger from that wound.

Max then opened fire at the sports boat with Enzo's M14. The powerful rifle had the range to hit the other craft, but the bouncing and swerving on the SAV II made any kind of accuracy nearly impossible. The best Max hoped for was to keep the other crew's heads down and reduce their fire. But his shooting had no apparent effect on the 29 Fever.

When Reaper caught a nod from Ben that Enzo was all right, he realized that they had about reached the end of their run. They were being outrun, were outgunned and his family had to be protected. A very dangerous plan formed in his mind. When they had heeled over as Enzo made a turn across the shoal, he could see the rocks speed past no more than a foot or two beneath the surface. That formed the seed of an idea in Reaper's mind. There would be a danger to the SAV II, which would be nothing compared to what the risk would be to him. But Reaper had never been one to consider the risks when the need was great.

"Enzo," Reaper said, "I want you to cut back and make another turn near that buoy. I want you to cut across the shallows back there and then turn her hard to starboard."

"But that will put us even closer to that boat, and they aren't suckering in," Enzo said.

"They might if they think they could grab someone who had fallen overboard," Reaper replied.

"Overboard?" Enzo said. "Who in the hell would go overboard while . . ."

As he asked the question, Enzo looked over at Reaper and saw the M72A3 LAW antitank rocket he had in his hand. His eyes lit up as Reaper's plan became clear to him.

"You got it, Chief," Enzo said as he leaned the boat hard over in a tight turn back along the way they had come.

The M72A3 LAW was a light antitank weapon contained in a green Fiberglas tube. The tube was sealed at both ends and only had to have the covers removed and the tube pulled open to be ready to fire. The 66mm high-explosive rocket in the tube burned all of its propellant while still inside the launcher, making a horrendous boom of a launch signature. But that launch put out a high-explosive warhead that held 304 grams, over half a pound, of the 60-40 HMX/TNT explosive known as Octal. The rocket packed a wallop. The shaped-charge warhead could put a hole in a foot of armor plate once the rocket had traveled past its arming point nine meters from the point of launch.

The buoy flashed past and Enzo put the wheel over hard. Pushing off with his strong legs, Reaper sprang away and catapulted from the side of the boat. He landed and skipped out across the water like a flat, flung rock. Mary screamed and Ricky cried out as they both saw Reaper ejected from the boat as if shot from a cannon. Ishmael also saw the "accident," and he indeed relished the idea of a prisoner. They had been firing back so these were the heathens responsible for his failure. This one could tell him how the Americans had known of Shaitan's Blessing, and he would relish taking a long time finding this out.

Directing Naphish to turn toward where the man had fallen in, Ishmael searched the waters to find a body, but he saw nothing. He hoped the American was just wounded. Having studied the charts of the area carefully as part of his preparations for Shaitan's Blessing, Naphish was careful not to approach the shallows too closely.

The almost freezing water crushed into Reaper with much more impact than his slam across the waves had done. He could hold his breath for several minutes if necessary, and this was the most necessary time for that in his life. Yet he found it hard not to gasp as the frigid waters closed over his head.

The weight of the gear he had on helped pull him down. Only a couple of feet of water washed over the rocky floor of the lake. He stayed down and swam away from where he had hit to try to give him a better shot at the sports boat. He held the M72A3 LAW cradled protectively in his arms, but the sealed rocket couldn't take a long submersion. Reaper listened to the sound of the sport boat's engines as it drew closer to where he held fast. The noise of the engines slowed and almost stopped. Reaper crouched and braced his legs against the bottom.

As Ishmael watched astounded, the water burst upward as a figure suddenly rose not fifty meters from where they floated. Even as he overcame his surprise and brought his AKM up to fire, the terrorist leader could see the figure struggle with something in his arms, tossing a line away and pulling something apart in his hands. Suddenly, Ishmael understood that was preparing to fire a weapon.

As Ishmael opened his mouth to scream an order at Naphish, the tube on the figure's shoulder exploded with noise, smoke, and flame. The rocket streaked across the waves only a few feet above the water as it passed the nine-meter point where the M412 fuze fully armed. The rocket smashed into the Fiberglas hull of the boat and detonated. The explosive jet formed by the shaped-charge warhead tore through thc hull and ruptured the fuel tank. The fury of the rocket's explosion became magnified by thc gasoline spray, the boat consumed by a billowing cloud of flame.

EPILOGUE

It was a long four days later that Reaper once again traveled down into Detroit from the farm. Mary hadn't been able to handle what had happened to her and Ricky, and Reaper couldn't blame her. She had decided to move away and take up her maiden name again. That seemed a polite way of telling Reaper that the divorce would go through—and he wouldn't fight it. He had become a danger to Mary and his son, and that wasn't something he could accept.

The divorce might not matter much after the meeting he was headed for. The summons was an official one and he rode his bike to the Federal Building in downtown Detroit. At least they hadn't sent a car full of federal marshals for him.

Moving through downtown on his Harley, Reaper passed the ruins of what had once been a six-story factory and successful nightclub. Construction equipment already worked to clear the mess. The SEAL couldn't see the young black man who had gotten his first real job working with the construction people. A meeting with the devil a week before had changed at least one person's life for the better.

Arriving at the Federal Building, Reaper had a hard time finding a parking space anywhere close to the structure, and an even harder time waited for him as he tried to enter the building. The intense security check included a detailed pass with a magnetometer after going through the normal metal detector. Identification was carefully checked and matched up against the appointments list.

The nation had gone to Orange Alert status only a few days earlier. The heightened state of alert against a terrorist attack was caused by a credible threat to the country. Reaper wondered if he might not have met someone more closely involved with that terrorist threat. If he had, they weren't much of a threat anymore.

The office he finally arrived at had the nondescript look of bureaucracy. The only thing missing was the one-way mirror in the wall. Then the spartan room would have looked just like a police interrogation office—which Reaper suspected it most likely was.

He had no choice in the matter He had fought as part of the system for too long to now fight against it. He hadn't even brought a lawyer to the meeting, over the protests of the rest of the guys at the farm. They had pointed out that they could afford the best defense available for Reaper. But he hadn't wanted to take advantage of the money they had.

Not that Reaper had a fatalistic streak, he simply accepted what he had done. And he would take the blame for everything that had happened on his own shoulders. None of the men who had helped him would even come into the equation. And he wouldn't cost them any more than what they already had given to save his family.

So Reaper sat in one of the available steel-framed, gray upholstered chairs. He placed his hands on the brown-plastic top of the steel-framed table that dominated the center of the room. When a person finally came through the door, Reaper's eyes went wide with the shock of recognition, his reflexes bringing him immediately to his feet.

"At least you still know how to show respect," said Admiral Alan Straker gruffly. "Although you exhibit little for the law. Now, sit down, Reaper, I'm retired now."

Sitting again, Reaper looked over at the man who had once tried to save his career. The admiral, Reaper would always think of him as that, wore a spotless blue suit, snowy white shirt, and a black tie. On his lapel was an American flag pin, and below it a miniature gold SEAL Trident. At least Reaper would be taken down by one of his own.

As Straker sat at the table, he began shuffling through some papers in a file he had brought with him. Long moments stretched out as he read the reports—moments that seemed an eternity for Reaper. Finally, the admiral closed the file and pushed it away.

"It appears that someone thought to ship the feds a box full of illegally obtained intelligence documents," Straker said. "I'm with the Office of Homeland Security now and those documents quickly ended up in my hands. Whoever came up with them knew their value and where to send them so they could do the most good.

"Just to be plain with you, Reaper, you and your partners have broken enough federal, state, and local laws to be put away for roughly forever. Even the Fish and Game people want a piece of your ass. And, pardon the image, but that ass is squarely in my hands right now, Chief.

"You fought your own undeclared war against terrorism, Reaper. I know what drove you to it. It seems that when a Coast Guard team investigated the explosions they found a cook, someone named Hassan Akrit, had survived what I've been informed had to be a serious firestorm on an island resort up in Lake Michigan. He mentioned someone in black, and evidence we found there suggested that there had been two prisoners held against their will—a female and young male. That this evidence resided in the same house as a headless corpse, the corpse of an officer you have had a serious history with, will go unmentioned.

"Chief, the United States is at war now, a declared war against international terrorism. That war has to follow precise rules, and it has to follow international law. And some of those laws prevent certain actions from being officially taken.

"Reaper, I have a choice for you. You can pick what's outside that door or what I'm going to put on the table right here. And what's outside the door are federal marshals waiting to see if I hand them a prisoner."

"And what's on the table?" asked Reaper.

"Not quite a free pass," Straker said, "but as close to one as you're ever going to see. I'll make all of the legal problems go away—but the only way that can happen is if you admit that you've been working for my office as a special consultant over the last several weeks. And that offer extends to those four who are waiting for you out at that farm north of here. Yes, we know about them. And you will remain as my special consultant for an undetermined length of time, receiving support and assignments as my office issues them . . . and only as we do."

Reaper just looked at the man who was one of the leaders he had followed for years. He had been willing to do so then, and he would be willing to do so again. But he had some questions that had to be addressed first.

"All I can do is speak for me, Admiral," Reaper said, "and I will agree to work for you as you see fit. But I have two conditions first—and they aren't really negotiable."

"Conditions!" Straker exploded. "I offer you a part of your life back and you want to list conditions? Exactly what are they?"

It was only a few days later when Ted Reaper, Keith Deckert, Max Warrick, Ben MacKenzie, and now Enzo Caronti found themselves back in northern Michigan. This time, they had come to pay their final respects to a fallen comrade. They found it fitting that it was Memorial Day, a holiday when America pays homage to its fallen heroes, because it was a hero who the men came to bury that day. Though had someone called him that while he was alive, he probably would have punched that guy's lights out. There are no heroes in the Teams, only operators.

"How the hell did he get this place opened on a holiday?" Max said as they looked at the closed grave.

"He's an admiral," Enzo said. "They can do things we mere mortals can't. Besides, he said he really liked this place."

"I'm just glad they got his body back for us," Ben said.

"Amen to that," said Deckert. Looking around he added, "It is a nice place, though."

Reaper just looked at the ground where they had placed his Teammate. Bear was in his casket in his motorcycle leathers. A Cuban cigar, its aluminum tube never having been opened, resided in his jacket pocket. On the front of that pocket, polished and gleaming now for all eternity, was the gold Trident of Naval Special Warfare. It had been the last Trident that Reaper had worn while on active duty. He wanted his Teammate to have it.

A glass rested in the casket as well, a twin to the glasses in the hands of the men around the grave. The premium Canadian Club whiskey in the coffin remained in a bottle, the bottle that had already filled the glasses that the men now drained to their friend.

As Reaper stood, smoking a really good Cuban cigar, the sound of a screeching cry in the sky caused him to look up.

Max pulled his own cigar from his mouth as he said in astonishment, "Son of a bitch, is that an eagle?"

Soaring overhead was a bald eagle. It had come back with its mate to the nest that they built up every year. The nest would grow larger, and the eagles would be flying over the area for a long time to come.

"Oh, that's way too corny," Enzo said with a big smile. "Bear would have loved this. Think he set it up?"

"I wouldn't put it past him," Reaper laughed as he watched the magnificent bird fly overhead.